From the readers' reviews on Amazon:

"My favorite book ever. I will never part with my copy. The only, and I stress, the 'only' convincing book about fall from grace." ---A reader from Israel

"This is one of the best books I have ever read. It happens to be the ONLY book I have ever sought across the world when my copy was tattered and destroyed. The author held nothing back in his portrayal of an evil society. It is so candid and brutal that you will likely be amazed that someone had the nerve to write it." ---Deva Winblood, Lake City, CO

"Zorachus is one of the finest novels I have ever read (and believe me I have read a lot). The imagination and excitement in this book are amazing. The story is fast paced, the characters well thought out, and the settings are absorbing. If you like a thought provoking, original story, this one is for you." ---Dwayne Worley, Gatlinburg, TN

"There should be a sixth star for books like this. This is the one that started it all...virtually created its own fantasy genre. As different from Terry Brooks as Beethoven is from Ace of Base. I read this book 40 or so times and it always delivered a different kind of punch to a different part of my being. Anyone who can read this and not come away genuinely affected is a) lying or b)an alien." ---Nicholas Prata, DE

"I read Zorachus 16 years ago. I just reread it. Zorachus is still leading the pack of imaginative fiction and no contenders are anywhere in sight...The writing is well paced, the atrocities gruesome, the pervasive erotic assault stimulating, all of it showing the temptations Zorachus faces daily, while the constant cruelty of Khymir stokes his downfall. The book poses moral questions and offers a great ride through Mark Rogers' twisted world. I am so glad I found him. If you want a fresh persepctive on fiction and aren't afraid to open your mind, then Zorachus is a book I highly recommend." ---Brian L. Smith, Howell, NJ

"The essential dark fantasy. Tired of Lord of the Rings rip-offs? Weary of characters who lack believable motivations and interesting philosophies? Falling asleep reading fantasy that seems like bedtime stories written for children? Well, wake up with Zorachus. This book is fresh and exciting. You'll see things you've never seen before in a fantasy novel. The story manages to stay shocking, amusing, and intriguing throughout, never resorting to the boring, page-filling style of too much of today's fantasy. The book is a rushing river of bloody action carrying you on a journey of spiritual despair through a valley of lust and depravity." ---Rich Marcozzi, Newark, DE

"You'll never be the same. The chilling details of Zorachus's fall from grace and descent into madness are well thought out. The magic system is very fresh and original. The depiction of darkness and depravity is unlike anything I've encountered before...Read the first five pages and see if you can put it down." ---Robert Locke, Sunnyvale, CA

"Buy a seat on the rollercoaster to Hell. I dare ya! This book takes you on an extraordinary ride as good and evil fight to take control of Zorachus's soul. It makes Lord of the Rings look like a walk in the park. A must read for dark fantasy fanatics." ---John Rocksvold, Gilroy CA

"Highly original, mind-boggling fantasy. This thing gets right in your face and doesn't quit. It's sharp, smart, and very vicious heroic fantasy, quite unlike anything else out there. If you're sick of elves and dragons, take a look at this!" ---A reader from Phoenix, AZ

"Creepy as Hell. Damn this book is good, but it made my skin crawl. It's not for the kiddies, as other people have pointed out. But it isn't simply sex and violence for their own sake, since it shows the reason for Zorachus's descent into madness. The scene with the High Priest's mushroom garden is, ah, worth a million." ---Jay Verkuilen, Urbana, IL

Zorachus

Author/Illustrator
Mark E. Rogers

Infinity Publishing
October 2002

ISBN 0-7414-1375-2

Published by:

INFI∞ITY
PUBLISHING.COM
519 West Lancaster Avenue
Haverford, PA 19041-1413
Info@buybooksontheweb.com
www.buybooksontheweb.com
Toll-free (877) BUY BOOK
Local Phone (610) 520-2500
Fax (610) 519-0261

Printed in the United States of America

Printed on Recycled Paper

Published December 2002

Many thanks to Lena and Chantal,
my lovely proofreaders

Dedication:

To Kate, who lived through it all.

"That evil is deadliest which contains most share of good"
----Sibi Gayaan Bayazid,
City of the Damned,
Book IV, Chapter 4

Prologue

GRIPPING THE WOUND in his side, bright scarlet blood leaking through his scorched fingers, the wizard Mancdaman Zancharthus paused beside the great stone seat at the head of the banquet table. His long red hair was lank with sweat, his skin frost-pale; his breath came in gasps. But as he turned to face his foes, he bared his teeth in a fierce grin, and his eyes glinted defiance.

Twenty men in horned helms and red-lacquered scale-mail, soldiers of the Cohort Ravener, were coming towards him, holding their long curved swords two-handed. Their unhurried advance bespoke their confidence; they were certain he could not withstand their numbers, had used up too much power.

"We're going to give Ordog your head, High Priest!" one cried.

Zancharthus coughed out a gout of blood and laughed. "Maybe," he answered. "But haven't you wondered ... why he didn't come for it himself?"

Halting and ragged as his voice was, it still carried enough menace to stop them in their tracks. More than one sword trembled.

His grin widened.

"At him!" a redclad shouted, and they charged, some rushing along the sides of the table, others leaping onto the top, scale-mail rattling, booted feet clattering on marble and wood.

Zancharthus laughed again, bounded up on the table and, like a black dragon unfolding its pinions, swept his cloak open. In a blaze of burnished metal, a swarm of tiny knives hissed from the cape's lining, each seeking a different target, some shooting straight at the foremost redclads, the rest swerving to strike the ones behind, all driving home with tremendous force, punching through armor. Screams rang out; dead and dying men collapsed on the tabletop, dropping on either side of the long trestle.

Not a single redclad remained on his feet.

Coughing, the wizard crumpled to his knees. He knew more would be coming; he would have to use the demon-rings again. He looked at his soot-crusted fingers. The rings had already burned them cruelly. Thinking he might shift the circlets to other digits, he tried to remove one, but the pain worsened hideously...the metal was stuck to his burns. Relenting, he rose slowly.

A hail of footbeats echoed through the door. He spat, blew sweat and blood from his mustache. Tightening his concentration, he readied himself to meet the next onslaught.

The footbeats grew louder and a second group of redclads poured into the hall, a scale-mailed wave rushing toward the table.

He extended his fists. The rings, each set with a single white gem, glittered wickedly.

A redclad sprang for the tabletop. Two bolts of blue-white lightning, crackling from the jewels, converged in him while he was still in midair; as if struck by a giant hammer, he hurtled backwards head over heels, trailing steam and flying mail-scales, a huge hole gaping in his chest.

The others rushed along the table to left and right; Zancharthus dealt bolts one at a time, jolting them off their feet with fists of white-hot energy, vapor mushrooming from their riven bodies.

But with each discharge the rings grew hotter. The stench of charred flesh assailed the wizard's nostrils. He struggled ferociously to hold the pain at bay, to maintain his concentration ...

Through bleared eyes he saw the remaining redclads waver. A few ran. For a moment it looked as though they all would.

But the moment passed; most of them rallied. He took a grim satisfaction in their courage----he had recruited well.

Firebolts took the brave ones. None got within five yards of him. And as the last struck the floor, the wizard's ring fingers dropped away, bones burned through. The rings rolled from the table.

Zancharthus looked at the stumps of his fingers. The sight was so strange he found it hard to believe he was looking at himself. The pain seemed much less vicious now, distant, as though he had gotten beyond it---he did not know what to make of this.

He climbed down to retrieve the rings, paused as a door opened on his left. A huge man was running towards him, the chief of his Kragehul "Hounds," Hoskuld the Unkillable; behind came the giant's massive consort, Torgunna, who was cradling a small squirming bundle. Another Hound, Gudmund, tiny compared to his companions, brought up the rear.

Zancharthus flung himself up and staggered over to them. Torgunna handed him the baby.

Drawing back the covers, Zancharthus saw it was his son, Zorachus.

"Thank you," he said, to Torgunna. "Oh, thank you."

Head bowed, he held the baby to his breast.

"My Lord," Hoskuld said, looking with horror at the wound in Zancharthus's side.

"Take him and go," Zancharthus said, kissed the baby on the forehead with bloody lips, and handed him back to Torgunna.

"We can't leave you---" Gudmund began.

"You can and you will," Zancharthus said, and coughed. "I'm dying. Save my son. Get him out of the house. Out of the city. Take him south, to the Sharajnaghim..." He pointed to the rings. "He'll need them when he reaches manhood...he alone can use them..."

Gudmund had no difficulty picking them up; only the inner surfaces had been heated by the blasts. He put them into a pouch at his belt, then looked at Zancharthus once more.

"My Lord," he said. "Come with us please..."

Zancharthus shook his head. "Stay clear of the redclads. Let them all come to me."

Eyes streaming tears, they stared at each other; Zancharthus took Gudmund's hand. Then he clapped Hoskuld on the shoulder, asking:

"How's your back?"

"Fine."

"Good. Now go."

Hoskuld wiped his nose. "Come on," the giant told Gudmund and Torgunna. As they went back through the door they had come out of, Torgunna turned, giving Zancharthus a last glimpse of Zorachus. Then she vanished in the shadows.

"Good bye, my son," Zancharthus said.

A horn sounded; he could hear more redclads on the way. Determined to occupy them as long as possible, he faced the arch through which they would come, considering his choices.

The rings were gone. The Influences had shifted against him, denying him many spells, and he had exhausted most of his native power---but not all.

Assuming a sorcerous stance, he muttered a formula. Half the redclads killed by the cloak-knives began to stir, jerking as the blades within worked their way outward. Emerging swiftly, the knives rose into the air, drawing into a cluster and hanging suspended, pointing toward the door, awaiting a mental command.

The third group of redclads appeared in the doorway. Wiser than the others, they had brought crossbows.

Zancharthus sent five blades streaking forward. Men clutched at faces or chests, crossbows dropping to the floor; the front rank crumpled.

The other redclads retreated shouting, several loosing quarrels even as they disappeared. Steel points rammed into Zancharthus's left arm and right thigh. He howled and staggered, and as he fought for balance two redclads leaped back into view and took aim. He resumed his stance an instant before they loosed; knives pierced them, but their quarrels were already humming towards him. One sliced his cheek, whipping his head to one side. The second caught him full in the stomach, a numbing impact, and he felt his tunic and cloak tug at his shoulders as the bolt, passing clean through his body, ripped out of his back; he heard it rattle loudly over the floor behind him. Deadening coldness spread from his midsection down into his thighs, and his legs began to buckle; his whole body cried out for surrender.

But that was inconceivable. He forced himself to think of his murdered wife, and what would be done to Zorachus if the redclads caught him...

"Come on!" he cried, straightening to his full height. "I'm not done yet!"

Six redclads rose to the challenge, fanning out as they rushed in. His last knives felled three before the survivors sent their quarrels thumping home.

He toppled.

The redclads watched him quiver, then go still. "It's over!" they bayed triumphantly.

Whooping, those outside rushed into the hall, congratulatingthem and slapping them on the back. Their company would be fabulously rewarded; Mother Khymir, the richest city in the world, would be at their feet. They had slain the mighty Mancdaman Zancharthus.

Or so they thought.

With a screech of protruding quarrel points against marble, he twisted, then raised himself from the floor; the redclads watched awestruck as he yanked two bolts from his body,

"What's the matter?" he asked hoarsely. "Bite off more than you can chew?"

With that they recovered their wits, and the arbalests still loaded came up; bowstring after bowstring twanged. With each impact, Zancharthus hurtled backwards, finally crashing against the wall, nailed to the wooden panels, head sagging forward on his chest.

The redclads moved nearer, watching him warily, ready to re-prime their crossbows at the least sign of life. But there was not even a hint of breath. At length, they heaved laughter and grinned at each other, relaxing.

"Now," one said, "that present for Ordog."

Handing his arbalest to another man, he drew out his shortsword and strode forward. Cocking the blade back, he jerked Zancharthus's head up by the hair, and---

Loosed a tremendous shriek. Zancharthus's eyes were wide open, furiously alive, and he was even then rocking forward from the wall, wrenching out the quarrels that pinned him, hands still gripping the bolts he had pulled from his own flesh; the wizard's arms flailed round and the quarrels punched through the redclad's helmet on either side. Grimacing, the man dropped the shortsword and reached up at the shafts, just touching them; then his hands fell limply to his sides, and a final breath hissed through his clenched teeth.

Zancharthus knocked him over with a contemptuous kick.

The rest gaped at the bolt-riddled figure rearing up over their comrade's body; muttering curses and prayers, they backed away in dread. Zancharthus shambled after them, tugging with both hands at a bolt embedded in his chest.

"Hold your ground!" the redclad commander bawled to his men, barely mastering himself. "Prime your bows!"

They continued to retreat.

"Hold, damn you! Prime and shoot!"

They swore and shook their heads. Hurling his bow aside, drawing his sword, the commander had to slash one down before they obeyed.

Zancharthus drew closer, still tugging on the bolt. It came free with a splash of blood; he brandished it like a dagger.

Quarrels slid into grooves and the redclads took aim. Zancharthus kept coming, straight towards the gleaming points, blood-shiny free hand clawing the air.

"Kill him!" the commander cried.

The bows twanged again. Three whistling flights pounded into Zancharthus, knocked him right, then left, then stretched him out beside the table, dead.

But the redclads took no chances this time. Keeping their distance, they shot every quarrel they had into his body. Only then did they dare take his head.

Chapter 1

AS WAS HIS privilege, the greyrobe rose from the carved granite seat known as the Chopping Block, scratched his head, stretched, and began to pace, speaking all the while. Behind their great stone table, the white-robed Masters listened closely, struggling to remind themselves that they were his judges, not his students.

Back and forth he strode, moving with a grace that belied his size. Well over six feet tall, he was powerfully built, wide-shouldered and broad-chested. His face was broad, with blue-grey eyes under heavy brows, and there was a small scar on his left cheek where an arrow, nearly spent, had struck him and lodged in bone. His hair was long, of a slightly browner red than his beard; it gleamed richly in the clear desert sunlight pouring in through the window.

Thirty-three years old and already an Adept of the Sixth Level, he was in the process of trying for the Seventh. The first test, the Trial of the Intellect, was going well; he had shown a deep knowledge of Sharajnaghi doctrine, and for his original contribution had given a proof of the dependence of free will on God's existence. Now he was defending that proof. The Masters pressed him hard, but he demolished their counterarguments one after another.

Finally, there came a lull in the debate. White-bearded Ghaznavi looked round at the other Masters.

"Here we are," he said, "the assembled Seventh-Level Adepts of the *Comahi Irakhoum,* and young Zorachus here---this *infant*---has stopped us cold. Shall we simply admit defeat?"

"Let's have the proof again," said *Sibi* Faschim. He had asked the aspirant to repeat it twice before, and had led the attack with great ferocity and skill. Unlike his colleagues, who were brown-skinned Kadjafim, he was a black from the southern kingdom of Numalia, the so-called "Land of Philosophers." Numalians were known for their hard-nosed rationalism, and he was no exception, widely thought to be the sharpest logician in the order.

Zorachus nodded. He did not mind Faschim's request; in spite of the onslaughts he had endured, he felt quite fresh.

"Free will," he began, still pacing, "is the power to act and think in accordance with the truth, or to ignore it. It is therefore dependent on the ability of the mind to perceive truth---in short, upon reason.

"Now, reason is not a reflex. A rational conclusion is not a spasm triggered by irrational causes, for rationality cannot be an extension of irrationality. Hence, the source from which human minds come must be rational, a mind itself; we must accept the notion that minds have their origin, directly or indirectly, in God. Since reason is dependent on God, and free will is dependent on reason, free will is dependent on God."

Faschim pondered this awhile; then he leaned forward, stabbed the air with his hand (a gesture that always preceded his arguments) and said: "Another problem has occurred to me. I'm not sure the dependence of free will on reason has been shown. Consider this: a man from a heathen land believes he has a moral responsibility to sacrifice his firstborn child to a certain god. Now as we would all agree, he is mistaken in this. However, if he chooses to ignore what he considers to be the truth, and not sacrifice his child, he is demonstrating free will. But he never had the opportunity to act freely in accordance with the truth, for he had no knowledge of it; the action of his will was not dependent on rationality."

Zorachus shook his head. "I disagree," he replied. "For rationality is not limited to the perception of *moral* truth. A heathen who thinks he has an obligation to sacrifice his firstborn is certainly mistaken. But if, because he believes that proposition, he then sacrifices his child, he is being rational; and he is ignoring what he sees as the truth if he doesn't. It takes a certain amount of understanding for a man to realize that a moral precept applies in each individual case; he has reached his conclusion through a valid syllogism, if not a sound one. It also takes reason for the heathen to realize that the physical action of sacrificing his firstborn constitutes the desired moral action; and conversely, that by not taking the child to the altar and not plunging the knife in, he is not doing sacrifice, and is therefore acting, as he would think, immorally. Thus any action of the will is to some extent dependent on rationality ----though it may indeed be rationality of a very elementary sort."

Faschim opened his mouth to speak, began the stabbing gesture---and stopped.

"You're quite right of course," he said.

For the first time during the trial, Zorachus showed his wide foolish grin. Even though he had all his teeth, there were large spaces between them, and the grin always dispelled his characteristic air of sagacity. Stopping in front of the chopping block, he folded his arms on his chest.

"Are there any more questions?" Ghaznavi asked again. There were none.

He eyed Zorachus. "Well then. The Council finds no objection to your proof; it appears both sound and orthodox, worthy to be entered into the body of Sharajnaghi doctrine, to be taught and defended. You've passed the First Trial, Zorachus. The Second awaits you."

The Masters rose from the table. But as they began to leave the chamber, their long white robes rustling, Ghaznavi paused, looked back, and said: "That was an extraordinary performance just now."

"Thank you, *sibi*, " Zorachus replied, no longer grinning, showing his appreciation of the compliment with a slight quick bow of the head. Already he was banishing the distracting joy of victory, putting all thought of the First Trial from his mind. Complete concentration would be needed in the Second---the Trial of Will.

Ghaznavi turned once more and left. After a time, Zorachus followed, keeping well behind the Masters as they passed down the long stone corridor that led to the gymnasium.

Shouts and laughter echoed up ahead. The voices hushed respectfully moments after the Masters entered the gymnasium, but then the din resumed, louder than before.

Zorachus went in. The great chamber was well lit; a huge crystalline oculis in the ceiling admitted the sun, and the walls were painted a bright reflective white. Dozens of greyclad lower-level Adepts were gathered around the sparring-pit, some standing, others sitting on benches. The Masters were off to one side, conferring; they too were shouting, trying to hear each other in the overall racket. Zorachus caught Ghaznavi's leathery old bellow quite clearly.

Some of the greyrobes spotted Zorachus as he headed for his armoring-chamber, and a cheer of encouragement went up from the group. Feeling a mixture of embarrassment and elation, as well as a slight annoyance that his concentration was being disturbed, he entered the chamber and shut the door.

A small devotional bar lay to the right, beneath a plaque blazoned with the white flame that was the chief Sharajnaghi symbol of God. Zorachus knelt at the bar, bowed his head, and prayed awhile; then he removed his oxhide sandals and rose, stripping down to his breechclout. After donning a leather jerkin and trews, he slipped into a knee-length quilted gambeson with elbow-length sleeves. A steel byrny went over the padding, mail of the finest riveted mesh, the strongest that the best Sharajnaghi smiths could contrive. He put on heelless knee-high boots studded with iron and

3

plates of boiled leather, then girt his swordbelt about him and drew the shortsword from its sharkskin scabbard to inspect the blade. Its edges and point had been completely ground off. He turned the weapon hilt-floorward and sprang its pommel-catch. The hilt was long and hollow and contained three feet of chain, fine-linked but strong. One end of the chain was attached to the sword's crescent guard, the other to the pommel. In a typical Sharajnaghi shortsword the pommel would have been made of studded iron, but this was leather-covered cork. When he sprang the catch, the pommel dropped floorward, swinging pendulumlike at the end of its clinking tether. Zorachus smiled. He had never lost his keen appreciation of the Sharajnaghi hidden mace.

Satisfied that the weapon was ready, he carefully put the chain back in the hilt, fixed the pommel once more, and resheathed the blade. From a table he took up his helmet. It was spired, but otherwise without ornament; a camail fringed it, and a wire cage long enough to protect both face and throat was attached to the rim in front. The cage would have been little use in real combat; Zorachus usually fought without it, finding it a distraction, but it was adequate against blunted edges and points, and its use was mandatory in trials. He donned the helm, fastened the chin straps, and put steel vambraces on his forearms. Slipping his hands into heavy padded gloves, he made one last genuflection before the white flame and went back out into the gymnasium.

Another cheer, this time thunderous, greeted him as he made for the pit. Perhaps a hundred more greyrobes had joined the crowd, most of whom had no chance of getting close enough to the pit to see the trial. But this was a major event; no one under the age of forty had ever before tried for the Seventh Level, and it was considered a tremendous privilege merely to be close to history in the making.

The crowd parted to let Zorachus through; even so, he took many friendly buffets before descending the steps.

Reaching the bottom, he went to the center of the pit. The sparring mats were gone now. The hard-packed earth floor was bare. A black doorway yawned in each of the pit's four walls.

He looked up at the tier on which the Masters were assembled. Before it, at the edge of the pit, was a small platform on which stood *Sibi* Dauud, a tall, thin Master with close-cropped white hair and a wispy grey beard. His eyes met Zorachus's, and he raised his hands. The spectators quieted, and in a great voice he cried:

"'The body is a rebellious machine, the most persistent opponent of the will. Yet over it the will must have sovereignty, and the means by which this is achieved shall be the martial arts; a strict regimen shall reduce the flesh to the slavery which is its proper place. And only those who can prove their supremacy in these arts shall be admitted to the seventh level.' So wrote *Sibi* Washallah Irakhoum. Are you prepared to prove, Mancdaman Zorachus, that your body is a mere extension of your mind?"

"I am," Zorachus replied.

"God grant you show your true mettle," Dauud said, lowering his hands. He stepped down from the platform; the greyrobes opened a path for him and he strode to the stairs, descending into the pit. It was his task to oversee the trial, to judge the 'deadliness' of the blows dealt, and to stop the combat at the first sign of serious injury. He halted several yards from zorachus. Ten long seconds passed.

"Begin!" he shouted.

Zorachus heard the door behind him open and a roll of footbeats. He wheeled and drew. His opponent, bearing a long padded club, was clad, like him, in full Sharajnaghi armor; he was also much taller than Zorachus, though less massive.

He closed, club arcing down at Zorachus's helmet, a blur of speed. Zorachus dodged and jabbed his sword into the man's mailed side. The armor withstood the blunted point, but the sheer force of the thrust hurled the fellow clean off his feet and he landed with a grunt. There was no need for a ruling from Dauud. The victim crawled away on hands and knees.

He had almost reached the door he was making for when a second attacker, carrying a shield and a padded axe, leaped out, bounding over him. The newcomer was on Zorachus in an instant, feinting with his shield, then hacking at Zorachus's neck. Zorachus ducked and the axe looped down at his legs. He jumped over the blow and launched, in midair, a thrust at his opponent's face. The shield shot upwards to block the stab---too late. Face-cage deeply dented, the man rocked backwards to the ground.

Immediately, a third man rushed in from the right brandishing a two-handed oaken sword. Zorachus disarmed him with a lightning kick, and lunged. The other man leaped back and lashed out with a kick of his own, and Zorachus's sword flew from his hand. The combatants stared at each other for a breathless moment, then dashed for the longsword. Zorachus's opponent reached it first, but Zorachus tackled him in the next instant and once again the sword flew through the air. Scrambling free, Zorachus charged after it, his opponent hard behind; but when they were almost to the sword, Zorachus spun and dealt him a savage kick to the head. The man cartwheeled to the ground. Zorachus had the sword a second later, but heard the man gasp "quarter," and paid him no further heed. Retrieving his shortsword, he dropped the two-handed weapon. The rules of the trial forbade him to use two weapons at once, and he preferred stabbing to slashing.

His opponents were under no such constraint, however; the longsword had barely struck the ground when a fourth attacker entered the pit armed with a small padded axe and a corkheaded mace-and-chain. Zorachus stood his ground as the man pelted toward him. The mace-head came lashing; Zorachus blocked with an armored forearm. The chain wrapped around his vambrace, and he yanked his arm back, wrenching the mace's truncheon from the man's hand. The axe whirled down; Zorachus parried with his sword and jabbed his steel into the wires warding the fellow's throat. The man staggered, gasped, and wobbled off.

As Zorachus untangled the mace chain from his arm, the last attacker appeared, carrying a shortsword. This one did not rush to the encounter--- he moved slowly, cautiously. He was short, and even with the armor it could be seen that he was spare of build. But there was whipcorded sinew in every step he took, and he moved with crisp precision. His face was unrecognizable behind his helmet-cage, but Zorachus knew that stride well: this was Raschid Kestrel, his greatest friend, and reputedly the deadliest fighter among the non-masters.

The two circled each other warily. Raschid feinted at Zorachus's chest. Zorachus lifted his left arm to block; Raschid jerked his sword back and snapped a kick into Zorachus's shin. Zorachus grunted with pain but did not retreat, and parried a lunge with a powerful sweep of his blade. The block seemed to throw Raschid off balance, and Zorachus succeeded in stabbing his sword arm. Raschid howled and leaped back, switched sword hands, and put his "wounded" arm behind him. Zorachus charged and Raschid, who was equally good with either hand, landed a slash across Zorachus's left bicep. Zorachus did not think it a crippling stroke, but Dauud disagreed; Zorachus put his left arm back.

The fight continued. Zorachus and Raschid leaped over singing strokes, blocked thrusts with scissor kicks, slashed and parried and lunged. Sword clashed on sword, and the pit resounded with the ring of struck metal, with cries and the stamping of feet. Second by second, the fight's fury intensified; swifter and swifter went the pace, and Zorachus felt the blood running like joyous fire in his veins. Dauud dodged and circled the opponents, displaying hardly less agility than they, eyes gleaming in admiration of their prowess.

Zorachus parried a swipe at his throat; his blade chipped. He lashed out at Raschid and their swords met with a terrific clang, and Zorachus's broke off at the hilt; out of the corner of his eye, he saw the blade flash as it hurtled through the air. Backpedaling, he reversed his grip on the hilt, tried to spring the latch on the pommel-mace, found it jammed---Raschid had struck the pommel a glancing blow earlier in the fight. And Zorachus had only one hand to work the latch....

Raschid charged after him. Zorachus twisted aside from a glinting thrust, blocked another with his vambrace. Raschid landed a solid kick in Zorachus's midriff, almost doubling him over; coughing, nearly retching, he felt Raschid's sword connect with his leg and went down on one knee. Raschid lunged; Zorachus hurled himself onto his back, avoiding the stab. Raschid tried to hack at Zorachus's good leg, but Zorachus managed to kick the blade aside. In desperation, he hooked the pommel latch behind the edge of his helmet-cage and pulled; the latch opened, even as he rolled aside from another of Raschid's strokes.

He got up on one knee. Raschid bounded at him, shrieking, swordpoint speeding straight at Zorachus's face. Zorachus deflected it with his vambrace at the last instant. The sword rang as it glanced upward, screeched and skidded over the top of Zorachus's helmet. Zorachus flailed the mace, striking Raschid square in the helmet-cage. It bounced off harmlessly, but was a killing blow nonetheless.

Dauud signaled that the trial was over. The spectators, who had remained silent up until that point, erupted into cheers and applause. Realizing he was beaten, Raschid spun several times, "dying" as spectacularly as possible, collapsing at last in a grotesque heap.

Zorachus went over to him. Raschid leaped up and took off his helmet, grinning at his conqueror. Sweat trickled down his swarthy face, dripped from his dark mustache and beard.

"You're mighty proud of yourself, aren't you?" he panted. The words were drowned out by the thunder from the audience, but Zorachus lipread. He nodded jokingly, removed his helm and wiped his brow. His lungs burned, his stomach ached, his heart hammered against his ribs, but his mind floated on the verge of euphoria.

7

Dauud climbed back up the stairs and went to the platform. He raised his hands once more. The spectators were slower in quieting this time.

"You've passed the second trial, Mancdaman Zorachus," he cried. "God grant you fare as well in the third and last." Turning, he left with his white-robed peers.

Zorachus went up from the pit and strode towards his armoring chamber through a churning sea of greyrobes, each pouring out congratulations. He laughed and smiled, but his thoughts were distant; once again he had thrust the joy of victory from his mind, his triumph in the pit already irrelevant. Entering the chamber, he closed the door and, as the noise outside died, stripped back down to his breechclout, transfixed by the knowledge that the last and ultimate trial was before him. Terror and agony would engulf him, perhaps even death; intellect and will would both be pushed to their utmost limits.

He rested for a time, then prayed beneath the sign of the flame. Finally, he slipped back into his regular garb and left the chamber. Out of the gymnasium and through twisting corridors he went, then down a flight of well-worn, torchlit steps.

At the bottom, he entered the crypt where generations of Sharajnaghi Masters were buried. The air was cool, but not damp; it seemed oddly fresh, and there was even a hint of some sweet fragrance.

The Masters had been laid in sealed niches, and beside each vault stood a statue of the buried man, life-sized, wrought with tremendous skill. All held burning tapers; stone faces flickered in the golden light, some grim and ascetic, others well-fed and robust. There were warrior faces, saintly faces, countenances that proclaimed "I am a scholar," others that seemed to say "I am a jester." It was a gloriously varied company and one that was hard to ignore; Zorachus found his concentration slipping as he passed through, but somehow that did not disturb him. He felt presences watching over him, reassuring him; even as his concentration wavered, his confidence grew.

He came to a second torchlit stair and descended a long way. Deep beneath the earth, he reached a small door marked with the sign of the flame.

"Open, please," he said.

An unseen warden swung the door back.

8

"Thank you, Antascar," Zorachus said, and went through, striding into darkness.

"Good luck," a voice whispered behind him.

Far in the sunken distance, Zorachus saw a blot of green luminosity and made toward it down a gentle slope. After what seemed an eternity, he drew near. The emerald glow played over a great flat circle surrounded by stone pillars. The light came from above, but did not appear to radiate from any definable point; it was almost as though the air itself were glowing.

The pillars were thirty feet tall and spaced five feet apart. In each gap stood a hooded figure, a Seventh Level Adept. No others were present. The Third Trial was no mere athletic contest to be gaped at by spectators, but a dark and terrible business. Things often got out of hand....

Zorachus arrived at the ring. The Master before him, *Sibi* Nawaf, stepped aside to let him pass and sang out a few words in Amoritic, the ancient language from which the Kadjafi tongue derived.

Zorachus went a short distance into the circle and halted; the Masters turned, facing inwards, and two advanced from the side opposite Zorachus, planting themselves fifty feet away from him, slipping their hoods back. He recognized Ghaznavi and Khuroum. The latter cried:

"'The intellect and will of each candidate for the Seventh Level must be great; but they will not avail if they are not in perfect harmony. Indeed, such harmony is the single most important characteristic of a Master.' so wrote *Sibi* Washallah Irakhoum. Are you prepared to prove, Mancdaman Zorachus, that your will and intellect are so united that one is the completion of the other?"

"I am," Zorachus replied.

"*Then let the wizardry begin!*"

Echoes ran and fled.

Khuroum and Ghaznavi entered Dragon Stances.

Zorachus did likewise---and immediately attacked.

Twin cataracts of bloody light poured from his fists. Snaking and crackling, they sought his opponents.

Just in time, Ghaznavi and Khuroum raised their defensive shields, force-screens that emanated from their palms; the cataract-bolts rebounded into the stone. Viewed through the overlapping barriers, the two Masters writhed like phantoms in a mirage.

Zorachus conjured his own bucklers, waiting. Ghaznavi and Khuroum stood rock-still for an agonizingly long time. Were they hoping he would attack again? Or were they simply force-letting, draining off repellent energy through their shields? If they drained enough, they could start in with binding magic, spells and conjurings. But he could play that game too....

Suddenly dropping their righthand shields, the two launched a keening barrage of yellow flame-needles, which shattered on Zorachus's defenses with small scintillant flashes. The attack intensified swiftly. Shocks began to penetrate, lancing up through his arms. One of his shields dissipated; he poured more power into the other.

Khuroum's strikes stopped. At first, Zorachus thought he had been unable to maintain that mode of attack.

He realized his mistake when the blue cloud gushed from Khuroum's mouth. Crossing the ring in a heartbeat's space, it hurdled Zorachus's shield and engulfed him.

He kept enough wits to hold his breath, but his concentration broke; his shield blinked from existence and Ghaznavi's flame-needles shrieked in through the cloud. A storm of yellow-green light broke about Zorachus's brow, and his head snapped back as if he had been clubbed.

But the needles had a more terrifying effect. The smoke thickened as they passed through, grew cold, then wet; in seconds he was immersed in a great bubble of water. It conformed to his every move, denying him escape, and through it sang the current of Ghaznavi's strikes, excruciatingly magnified. Zorachus's mind reeled.

But he did not accept defeat.

With a tremendous effort of will, he shut out all distractions, plucking a freezing spell from his memory. Between maintaining his shields and his first strikes, he had spent enough repellent force; slipping a trembling hand over his mouth, he articulated the words of the formula.

Just as Ghaznavi launched a new sheaf of flame-needles, the water hardened into a man-shaped azure statue. There was a terrific blast of splintered ice as the needles struck, and Zorachus's prison shattered. Drawing breath once more, he laughed.

After a stunned pause, Ghaznavi resumed his attacks.

Zorachus raised a shield against him and turned his attention to Khuroum. The latter had spent much energy maintaining the bubble and was shifting into a Chimera Stance, one shield up.

Zorachus uttered a spell.

Beneath Khuroum, a circle of floor spun halfway round, and he wobbled but spun with it, his shield swinging away from Zorachus; the instant his back was exposed, Zorachus struck him between the shoulders with a cataract bolt, and Khuroum sailed forward, landing in a heap.

Zorachus turned to Ghaznavi. His new shield was giving way under the old man's onslaught; a countermeasure was necessary. He sent power surging into his left hand and immediately his flesh was lit from within. He closed his eyes, and from his palm leaped a burst of fierce light, showing near-white even through his eyelids.

The flame-needles stopped. Looking at Ghaznavi once more, he saw the old man pawing at his eyes, momentarily blinded. Zorachus prepared to finish him.

Ghaznavi cried out in Black Malgronese. At the shout, a creature like a gigantic squid materialized, hovering in the air between the combatants. Its curtain of tentacles lifted and, where its squid's beak should have been, there was a miserific parody of a human face, eyes glistening with lunacy, mouth wide open, filled with chisel-like teeth.

Tentacles darting, the monster drifted towards Zorachus, and from between the distended jaws came a long pink chancred tongue, whipping and questing. Zorachus conjured a second shield and held both at arm's length; swinging them side to side, he managed to bat tongue and tentacles away.

The creature came closer. Arms circled past the shields, snaring Zorachus, binding him with rubbery flesh at knee and hip and chest, pinning one arm. His shields vanished; he felt a tingling charge dispelling his repelling energies. The tongue slathered his face with slime and the tentacles reeled him towards the mouth, which gaped ever wider; the tongue withdrew behind the fences of vermin-clotted teeth and foul breath spewed over him, an exhalation like the gust from a bloated rotten stomach ripped by a hook.

Shouting a formula, he swept his free hand in a sorcerous pass. Fierce spasms wracked the tentacles gripping him; his ribs were squeezed almost to cracking. Then the coils loosened, and he slipped out and dropped to the floor.

11

Looking up, he saw the monster's lunatic expression had not changed, betrayed no agony; but the squid-like body drifted back, tentacles dragging over stone, the ones that had held him twitching and jerking.

Zorachus assumed a Griffin Stance and sped through a binding spell. As he did so, the monster, guessing perhaps that the pain-rune could only be worked once, swept back in, tentacles slithering to seize him again. But Zorachus took control of one and sent it coiling with tremendous force around the creature's conelike upper body.

The monster stopped short. Its other tentacles whipped upwards to pull the crushing arm away, but the effort was useless. Normally, Zorachus could not have exerted such control, but the Influences were with him today, greatly strengthening his binding powers; his proxy grip grew tighter and tighter.

At last the creature's expression changed, becoming more mindless, more lunatic; the eyes popped wider and wider, bulging out bloodshot between distended lids. Tormented veins began to burst, spewing out little jets of inky filth.

The crushing tentacle pressed ever deeper into yielding flesh. In one last desperate effort, the creature let fall the other arms and went for Zorachus again. But by now it was near death and he eluded its clumsy sweeps with ease.

Bit by bit, the squid-like body drifted floorwards. Its arms went slack. Some great bag of fluids ruptured inside the cone; black slush poured from the hideous mouth. And, as abruptly as it had appeared, the monster vanished.

Zorachus and Ghaznavi faced each other once more.

Ghaznavi was visibly weakened, swaying on his feet; the shield he raised now was but a dim convection. It had cost him dearly to bring the monster from its own dimension and maintain it, second after second, in this world.

Zorachus never trifled with a shield of his own. Striking power seethed in his arms; his repelling energies had been restored the instant the creature released him. He was stronger than he had been at the beginning of the trial; the trial itself had freed his goetic genius to an extent he had never known before. He was a human thunderhead, the power within him building, building.

Ghaznavi struck out at him. An orange nimbus looped around Zorachus's shoulders, seeped into him. His flesh and eyes glowed, and thread-thin lightning crackled in his hair; his bones hummed with pain. But the attack was not enough.

As the glow faded, he entered a Basilisk Stance. Two white bolts sprang from his fists, shattered Ghaznavi's shield in a spray of sparks, and knocked the old man to his knees.

Zorachus debated whether he should blast him again, just to make sure. Ghaznavi answered the question for him by rising and trying to reenter his stance.

Zorachus loosed two more strikes. Ghaznavi toppled, stunned.

The trial was over. All around the circle, the watchers dropped the shields they had conjured against the possibility of stray bolts.

Zorachus walked forward to his stricken opponents, helped Khuroum up, then the swiftly reviving Ghaznavi. As the other Masters gathered round, Ghaznavi stared at him in stark amazement.

"You beat us both," he said slowly. "The most we expected was that you'd hold your own."

"I tried to give my all, *Sibi,* " Zorachus replied.

"For my part," Khuroum gasped, "I wish you'd been more lax. My back's one huge ache. And my pride's hurt beyond cure, I think. The very idea we could be so manhandled by a mere Sixth Leveler..."

"Take comfort," Ghaznavi said. "Zorachus can hardly be considered a Sixth Leveler anymore, can he?" He looked at Zorachus and smiled. "go to your chamber, Young Master. I'll send word when all is ready."

Zorachus nodded, beaming, and strode out from among his white-robed mentors. Leaving the dueling circle, he went back up toward the door, which put out a faint white light like a far-off beacon.

Young Master: the words echoed in his mind. Now at last he allowed himself to savor the joy of victory, bask in his own elation.

After what seemed a surprisingly short walk, he arrived at the door. He did not realize he had run much of the distance.

"You won, eh?" whispered a disembodied voice.

"How did you know, Antascar?" Zorachus asked, breathing hard. "Could you see the trial from here?"

"No. It's your aura. Pity you can't see it. Such colors ......"

"Well, we've all got our talents. And being human can be very pleasant."

Antascar gave a reedy laugh. "I know."

Zorachus was taken slightly aback. "You were human once?"

"For a while. Just after I was a rhinoceros---or was it a water buffalo? Anyway, I cut quite a swath among the young ladies in Fyrkaz. But that's a long story. I suppose I should let you out, shouldn't I?"

"Please."

The door opened.

"Thank you," Zorachus said, going out.

"Congratulations," Antascar said after him.

Zorachus waved over his shoulder. Taking the steps three at a time, he soon reached the crypt.

"As you probably know, I did it," he told the statues there as he half-marched, half-jogged along. "And if any of you helped, thanks. I'll try not to disappoint you."

He came to the second stairway and started up. At the top he began to sing "The battle of Ghoramzaar," a stirring ballad about the exploits of the first Sharajnaghim. As he neared his room, his voice got louder and louder, becoming a thundering bellow. He paused in his song only to shout greetings to comrades, who collected behind him shouting questions. Blissfully unresponsive, he continued singing. They did not mind, especially since it was obvious how the trial had come out, and they had a fine time using their semantic training to phrase their questions as many ways as possible.

Coming to his door he turned to face them at last, still singing. But shortly Raschid shouldered his way out of the crowd, carrying a naked (and very sharp) shortsword; thrusting it at Zorachus's throat, he halted the point a fraction of an inch from his flesh.

Zorachus's song died. The crowd became deathly silent. Raschid's harsh drill master's voice broke the stillness:

"Civil questions demand civil answers. Speak, jackal!"

Zorachus replied with a swift forearm block, brushing the point aside; resuming the song where he had left off, he punctuated a particularly

14

heroic phrase by planting a kiss on Raschid's forehead. The crowd whooped, and Zorachus dashed into his room and bolted his door.

He offered up an exultant prayer of thanksgiving, then undressed and washed at a wallside basin. For a time he strode back and forth, humming, afterwards stretching himself out on the bed, reliving the trials in his mind, finally falling into contented sleep.

There was a knock at the door. He woke instantly.

"It's time," called a voice from outside.

"Coming," Zorachus cried. He leaped from the bed, threw on fresh garments, combed his hair, and bustled from the room. Trailed by Ghaznavi's messenger, he managed to compose himself on the way to the mighty dome that formed the heart of Qanar-Sharaj, the order's home.

A lush green smell filled his nostrils as he passed under the arch. All along the pillars and pendentives of the dome's interior, as high and higher than the huge round windows, grew thick vines of ivy and flowering plants, an encircling sea of emerald leaves shuddering in the cross-breezes, dotted with color, sending green skeins out across the mouths of the smaller domes. Shafts of light slanted down from the western windows, one falling on a huge dais-borne altar in the center of the chamber. Upon the altar, plants had also been encouraged to grow, and while the green had been cleared away in spots for the placing of relics and vessels, the stone was covered with leaves, tendrils, and shoots. Mounted on a tall pedestal, a white-silver flame symbol reared up from the midst of the greenery, and it seemed as though the plants strove to touch it, curling up the pedestal in mysterious devotion.

A great assembly, most of the inhabitants of Qanar-Sharaj, stood before the dais. Three Masters were mounted on the stone platform: Ghaznavi, Faschim, and Dauud. They wore no vestments other than their robes, but nothing could have added to the splendor of those garments, which were worn only on days of ordination. Their stabbing whiteness made the trappings of the other masters seem dingy by comparison.

As Zorachus approached, Ghaznavi lifted his right hand in benediction of the order as a whole, then lifted his left to bless the initiate. At the second gesture, a lane opened in the throng and Zorachus passed through, stepping up onto the dais, halting between Faschim and Dauud. They laid hands on his shoulders and he knelt, head bowed. Presently, Ghaznavi, Grand Master of the order, began to speak:

"In ancient times there was a wizard, Washallah Irakhoum; and he dwelt in a black castle in the Mountains of Shahm, and practiced deadly arts of intellect and will; and in supplication of Athtar *Saathranu*, the Great Tyrant, he shed the blood of children on an altar darkly stained.

"But one day his acolytes brought him a captive boy, and as the victim was sacrificed a vision came to Washallah Irakhoum. He saw the majesty of God almighty, Maker of Heaven and Earth, who so loved all things that he brought them into being; and the boy's blood sang, and the wizard heard, in words sweet yet terrible, the doom that the Maker had put upon him. And when the vision left him and the voice ceased, he looked upon the altar once more and saw the boy was gone, and that the sacrificial knife was clean, as though it had never tasted blood.

"From that day on he was a chastened man, accepting the Maker's decree. He burned his grimoires bound in human skin and destroyed the altar darkly stained; and the spirit went out of him and into his followers, and he led them from darkness. Thus was founded an order which did much to heal the wounds of this fallen world, and prevent new wounds from being dealt; soon outsiders began to call its adherents the Sharajnaghim, the Bringers of Light. The Seventh Level of this order was made up of Great Masters; and the Masters ruled the Sharajnaghim through the grace of the Maker.

"Today, in this holy place, a new Master joins the old. In the Trials of Intellect and Will, and both combined, he has been found worthy. All honor under God, and the Grand Master, is his. Lift your eyes, Zorachus."

Zorachus looked up at Ghaznavi. The old man's face was solemn but his eyes gleamed with sacramental joy. Ghaznavi continued: "Do you swear to uphold the high office of a Sharajnaghi Master, to lead the order and preserve its sanctity, to use your great powers in the service of life, to obey the will of God in all things, to follow His Great Dance?"

Listening to the words, Zorachus sensed a great weight pressing on him, as if the hand of God had sought out his shoulders. Yet he felt neither suffocated nor enslaved, but as a woman might, accepting the body of her true lover, pressed down with his weight, but rejoicing in his unsurpassable nearness.

"I do so swear," he replied.

Ghaznavi smiled and placed a palm across Zorachus's forehead. A pulse of gentle energy passed into the initiate, bathing his soul with warmth.

16

Ghazinavi bade him rise. Faschim and Dauud went to the altar and removed from the reliquary the robe that had served initiate Masters for a thousand years. It was brighter even than the robes the three celebrants wore, and there were instants when one could see in it not only the fabulous unity of whiteness, but also the colors of which its whiteness was composed, a sight maddening but for its beauty.

They put the robe on Zorachus and, with them, he turned to face the congregation.

"His place is now upon the Seventh Level," Ghaznavi said. "He is *Sibi* Mancdaman Zorachus, and to him is due the obedience of all Sharajnaghim who are not Masters."

Zorachus looked out over the faces before him, rejoicing in each one, and the smell of leaves and flowers delighted his senses.

Chapter 2

THE NEXT DAY, Ghaznavi summoned Zorachus to his study. The room was small and comfortable, equipped with a formidable if compact library; the walls were lined, floor to ceiling, with huge leatherbound tomes, iron-hasped, filled with doctrine and arcane lore. Ghaznavi's desk was by the window, and whenever he grew tired of work he could look out from his third-floor vantage over a half-mile of greenery bordered by red dunes, the western ocean rolling beyond. Sea breezes wafted in through the window, stirring the edge of weighted papers on his desk, making the potted flowers nod and sway.

Scattered amid the flowerpots and papers and paperweights were a dozen or so figurines. Several of them, strange reptilian shapes with horns and spikes and frills, had been cast in iron by the order's chief smith at Ghaznavi's direction; Ghaznavi had wanted them for a lecture in which he expounded the theory that Thorgon Karrelssa had once been populated by such creatures. Among his evidence was a collection of petrified bones, which he said had belonged to these beasts. Needless to say, nobody believed him; that episode had been one of the great disasters of his life. And though he still kept the reptilian figures at his desk (the bones were gathering dust in a storage room), he was no longer interested in them. Out of his whole menagerie, his present favorites were a crystal centaur and a manticore carved in amber, poised to strike with its scorpion tail. As Zorachus settled himself, Ghaznavi reached around, took up the manticore and toyed with it.

"I think this one helps my arthritis," the old man said. "The dealer said it would."

Zorachus smiled. "How much silver did he squeeze out of you?" He asked, with a familiarity he and Ghaznavi had long shared. Ever since his mid-twenties, he had been treated as a near-equal by several of the Masters--- in private.

"None of your business," Ghaznavi answered. "Sceptic."

Zorachus shrugged. "It would be simple enough to test it for healing properties---" He checked himself. "Excuse me. It's amber, isn't it?" For some undiscovered reason, amber was not susceptible to the name-magic that underlay Sharajnaghi experimental technique.

"Do you remember the orphans who visited us?" Ghaznavi asked.

"From Karradesh?"

Ghaznavi nodded. "The one who claimed to be a wizard natural said he saw an aura around the beast."

"He also said he could read minds, and we caught him cheating," Zorachus countered.

"True. But naturals often cheat when the faculty isn't running."

"Why don't you show the figure to Antascar?" Zorachus asked. "He can see auras."

Ghaznavi harrumphed. "Too much of a bother."

"Well," Zorachus said after a short pause, deciding to humor him, "Maybe it does help. Your hands must have been limber enough yesterday. The flame-needles were very nasty."

Ghaznavi smiled quietly. "Not bad for an old man, eh?" He pursed his lips and shook his head slightly. "But it didn't make much difference."

"You don't know how sorely you tried me."

Ghaznavi shook his head again. "I saw what was happening," he answered. "Do you have any idea of your real strength?"

"I'm not sure," zorachus said. "There was a moment towards the end. . . ."

Ghaznavi said: "You may be the greatest sorcerer who ever lived."

There was silence for the next few moments. Zorachus was both unnerved and embarrassed. He knew he was powerful, but he had never dreamed of such language being applied to him. He flushed, the arrow scar on his cheek going white.

"Other men have beaten two Masters at once," he said. "Moujiz of the Black Anarites…"

"Defeated two of his own lieutenants. You, on the other hand, defeated a Master *and* a Grand Master. Amazing performance. You didn't even try to counter my demon with one of your own. I thought perhaps you wouldn't have remembered."

"You taught me too well. I recognized that dribbling cuttlefish even before it showed its face."

Ghaznavi laughed. "See what I mean? I marvel to think what you'll be like twenty years from now."

"Burnt out," Zorachus replied. He did not say it to get assurances to the contrary; it was a thing that often happened to sorcerous prodigies.

"Perhaps," Ghaznavi said. "But in the meantime we'll put your gifts to the best advantage. That's why I summoned you." He put the manticore back on the table. "An envoy from the High Priest of Tchernobog has arrived."

After a pause, Zorachus asked: "Arrived? *Here?*"

Ghaznavi nodded.

"We let him in the gates?"

"Kept him waiting in Thangura for a week...he wants to speak with you. Very badly."

"And you want *me* to speak with *him?*"

"He isn't an assassin."

"You're sure?" Zorachus asked. Early on, Khymirian spies had learned that he had been brought to Qanar-Sharaj; a number of attempts had been made on his life.

"Reasonably," Ghaznavi said, then added: "Your uncle's of the same opinion." He was referring to Jagutai Jen Shian, who had been educated by the Sharajnaghim and had risen to become the Urguz Khan's Grand Vizier.

"Does *he* think I should meet with him?" Zorachus asked.

Ghaznavi ignored the question, saying: "There's been a change of regime in Khymir. A man named Ghorchalanchor Kletus is now High Priest."

"And?"

"He wants you to return to Khymir. To claim your inheritance."

"Inheritance?"

"Your father was a fantastically wealthy man."

"Before he was overthrown and killed...why would Kletus want to give me such wealth? Surely he could find good enough uses for it himself."

"If so, why did he make the offer? It would seem he wants to link himself to the Mancdaman name. Your father was extremely popular and you're the sole heir."

"But you still haven't told me why you brought up this whole matter. Do you think I'd have the slightest interest in my 'inheritance'?" At the last word, Zorachus's voice thickened with disgust. He was closely acquainted with his father's history; while Zancharthus had conceived a burning hatred for the deity he ostensibly worshipped, and had set

20

himself in mortal opposition to his own sect, Zorachus wanted nothing whatsoever from the cesspool of a city that his sire had fought so ferociously to redeem.

"You do have a duty to the Order," Ghaznavi said.

"We need gold from devil worshippers?"

"To thwart certain of their plans, yes. Though the Mancdaman name will be even more useful, I think. I want you to return with the envoy."

"To Khymir?"

"Yes. How's your Old Malochian?" Khymir had been founded by exiles from Malochan, and an archaic form of Malochian was still spoken there, though it was used elsewhere only by scholars and wizards.

"Fluent," Zorachus replied. "But what do you want me to do? Convert everyone there?" He laughed.

Ghaznavi laughed too, but sadly. "That would thwart the Black Priests neatly enough. I wish to God there was some chance of it."

"If Uncle Jagutai's to be believed, my father would've settled for rational government..."

Ghaznavi nodded. "And even that was far too ambitious."

"What do you have in mind then?"

"Containment. Forcing the Priests to make do with what they've got."

"I don't follow you."

"As you know," Ghaznavi said, "Tchernobog has a terrible hunger. And the Priests, by offering up Khymirian criminals and paupers, and preying off the Kragehul barbarians surrounding Khymir, have been able to keep it satisfied---so far. But it's been growing since Khymir was founded; indeed, since Tchernobog and his followers fell from heaven. And soon the Priests will no longer be able to spill enough blood, at least with their present hunting grounds. That leaves them two options. They could choose not to satisfy Tchernobog, but that would be the end of them. If they lost the sorcerous aid he grants, they'd be finished by their enemies in the city. On the other hand, they could try to feed him, but they'd need a much wider hunting ground than they now have. It seems Thagranichus Ordog, the man who overthrew your father, was deposed for failing to make the second choice. From what I could gather from the Khanate's intelligence reports, he was losing confidence, growing afraid of overextending himself. His successor, Kletus, is a much tougher sort. I've reason to think he's planning a campaign of conquest the like of which the world has never seen---the Influences will be magnifying black sorceries for the next two decades, and the Priesthood could take awesome advantage. Who could stand against such an onslaught? Not the Kragehul. They're brave fighters, but it would be hopeless."

"And you don't think it would stop with them?" Zorachus asked.

Ghaznavi shook his head. "The lands south of the Utgards are full of potential victims, most of whom are far less able than the barbarians to defend themselves. The Khymirians will need them after they've exhausted their supply of Kragehul. Tchernobog's hunger grows by leaps, and like any pampered hunger, the more it gets, the more it craves."

"But how exactly am I going to stop all this?" Zorachus asked.

Ghaznavi's face wrinkled in a cunning smile. "I was surprised by the envoy's proposal, needless to say; but also delighted. With your uncle's aid, I've long been keeping track of events in Khymir, hoping the Priests would give us an opening. Now they've come right to our doorstep to do so.

"As I said before, Kletus wants to ally himself with the Mancdaman name. He'll almost certainly take you into his confidence. If he is indeed planning an invasion, you must expose and publicly repudiate the scheme. That would throw him off balance, maybe even topple the Priesthood. The Khymirian Merchant's Guild has long opposed the Priests, though there's an uneasy truce in effect; the Guildsmen are very powerful themselves, and keep magicians of their own. They don't need sacrifices, and the sources of their wealth are so great and secure that they wouldn't want any part of the invasion. You could point out how Kletus would have to recruit thousands of mercenaries for his great campaign---victories won by sorcery still have to be consolidated by troops. But those troops would also give Kletus the strength to crush the Guild once and for all. Needless to say, the Guildsmen would be mightily aroused; and with you on their side, their chances of overthrowing the priests would be good. Your name---not to mention your magic---would bolster them enormously. Your father tried to destroy the Priesthood from within. Kletus probably wants your support to reassure his foes, keep them off guard; but the son of Mancdaman Zancharthus would be, if anything, an even more obvious asset to the Guild."

"Your plan sounds very clever," Zorachus said. "But has it occurred to you that I might not live long enough to achieve anything at all? Kletus's offer might be bait. After all, he probably sees me as a potential rival. Perhaps he simply wants to dead."

"Maybe," Ghaznavi said. "But I think it's more likely that he'd try to wring every last ounce of benefit from you before moving in for the kill."

Zorachus shifted in his seat. "That's supposed to comfort me? Surely he'll turn the moment I turn on him."

"In which case you'll defend yourself. And after those exhibitions yesterday, I think you'll manage. Especially with the Guild on your side. Of course, you'll be in the gravest danger. . . . "

"And not just physically," Zorachus broke in. "The real threat's against my soul, isn't it? Tchernobog fosters Khymir as an argument against organic life. Its whole purpose is to make converts for him---"

"That's why I'm not going to command you to go," Ghaznavi answered. "I wouldn't blame you if you didn't touch the mission."

"You did, however, make a point of mentioning my duty to the Order."

"A man also has a duty to himself. If you think the threat's too great, stay here. If not...."

"But *you* think I'm up to it, don't you?"

"The *Comahi Irakhoum's* the greatest of the White Orders, and you're its greatest son, the strongest human soul I've ever met."

Again Zorachus was deeply embarrassed. "I wish I had as much faith in Mancdaman Zorachus as you do."

"I know you're not perfect."

Zorachus leaned forward. "*Angels* have fallen with less provocation than i'll get in Khymir. "

"Yes, and one of them is behind the Khymirian threat," Ghaznavi answered, unfazed. "Which renders the mission all the more urgent."

Zorachus leaned back, folding his arms on his chest. "I know. But I can't help feeling uneasy about Kletus's assumption that I'd even consider allying myself with him. Maybe he knows something about me that you don't."

Ghaznavi smiled. "I doubt his spies could be *that* good. But undoubtedly he thinks he knows all about you. Indeed, he probably thinks he knows all about everyone. Khymirians, particularly the Black Priests, believe all men are motivated by the same drives they are. When they look at us, they see we're powerful, able to defeat other orders again and again; they see we have influence on the Khanate. *Therefore,* the Priests think, *the Sharajnaghim are sane--- they are the same as us.* They can't understand an order like ours. The fact that they think they could enlist your aid proves it."

"But given that," Zorachus said, "won't they think I'll be trying to subvert them? Trying to extend Sharajnaghi influence?"

"The envoy seems to take it for granted. He didn't mind speaking with me, for example...seemed quite content to have a Grand Master passing on his message. However much the Priests fear us, they think the benefits of having you outweigh the risks."

"Does that mean I could bring someone with me? Raschid perhaps, just for companionship? Seeing as how they already suspect---"

"No. It would be better to reduce the suspicions they already have. We want them to take you into their confidence as soon as possible. The farther Kletus's plan is from fruition, the better. And so you should pretend you're making a clean break from the Order. Having Raschid with you would make that much more difficult."

"They wouldn't have to know he's a Sharajnaghi. He could pose as a servant, or--"

"They probably know we don't keep servants or slaves, though God knows what they think our motives must be. And it's not as if you could simply pick Raschid up on your way to the harbor. Believe me, the less complicated we make things seem, the better. And the best way to do that is to send you alone." Ghaznavi paused. "Will you accept the mission?"

Zorachus sighed. "Seems I'm the only man for the job, doesn't it?" He stared blankly through the window. "My vows seemed so beautiful yesterday."

Ghaznavi laughed sympathetically. "And now, suddenly, you have to take them seriously and they appear a lot less seductive. I know the feeling."

"Do the other Masters know about your plan yet?" Zorachus asked, shifting his gaze back to the old man.

"No. I'll summon the council shortly."

"You've discussed all this with Jagutai, I take it?"

"Yes," Ghaznavi answered.

"Even though you haven't spoken to the Council yet?"

"He's practically a Sharajnaghi as it is...might as well be a member of the council. And he knows Khymir. Advised your father, fought alongside him..."

"And what was his opinion of your plan?"

Ghaznavi hesitated before answering: "He was not enthusiastic."

"What were his objections?"

"He doesn't want you subjected to 'that place,' as he put it."

"He thinks I'll fail?"

"No. He said he had too much affection for you."

Zorachus smiled, pleased to hear this. He had the greatest love and respect for his 'uncle.'

"What about the envoy?" he asked. "Is it wise to keep him waiting?"

"I told him you'd be indisposed, for a while at least. He said he'd be back in three days."

"If he only knew what we have in mind...." Zorachus's voice trailed off.

"I don't imagine he'd approve. But considering what his master seems to be planning, I don't think we have an alternative."

"You know," Zorachus said, "the Guildsmen will want my help when the fighting starts. They'll want me to kill for them."

"If the fighting starts," Ghaznavi said. "My information might be wrong."

Zorachus hardly heard him. "I won't be able to conceal how powerful I am. Not when Kletus attacks."

Ghaznavi shrugged. "You know when killing's lawful. The Guildsmen will just have to go along with you. You'll be too valuable to them in other ways. Of course, before Kletus confides in you, you'll have to be more careful about revealing your scruples. A certain amount of lip service to our ideals would be allowable, I suppose; you were, after all, brought up as a Sharajnaghi, and I expect the Priests will take that into account. But anything more than lip service would be dangerous---especially if you didn't conceal your motives. "

"Why? Don't the Priests regard our scruples as mere subterfuge?"

"I'm sure. But if you act consistently in accordance with our moral teachings, and Kletus can't detect any other kind of behavior, he'll likely conclude you're insane. Or worse yet, that you're plotting in some way he can't fathom. Either way, he might keep his distance. Luckily, though, unless your temporary alliance with him provokes some kind of hostilities from the Guild, the question of killing for him---rather than for the Guild--shouldn't arise." Ghaznavi paused, as though he had just thought of something. "And while we're on the subject of bloodshed. . . ." Producing a brass key, he unlocked a drawer in his desk, took out a small leather bag, and tossed it to Zorachus. "Another part of your inheritance."

Zorachus untied the pouch and upended it. Two rings fell out into his palm. The circlets were of some unfamiliar grey metal with a single dazzling blue-white gem set in each; the jewels' glare made his eyes hurt. He winced and looked at Ghaznavi.

"They're gorgeous," he said. "Bit hard on the eyes, though."

"They're not for looking. They contain demons. Flame demons."

"So these are---?"

Ghaznavi nodded. "The Mancdaman rings."

"Are they truly as powerful---?"

"Truly. Which is why we decided to withhold them---"

"Until I reached the Seventh Level?"

"Yes. Put them on and stand up."

They both rose.

"Look out the window," the old man said. "See the outcropping off to the left?"

Zorachus nodded. A lone chimney of stone rose above the vegetation.

"Extend your fists, concentrate on it briefly and will the demons to destroy it."

"Simple as that?"

"Simple as that."

Zorachus obeyed. Lightning leaped from the rings, striking the outcropping, shattering it, sending stone fragments hurtling through the air.

"My fingers are cooking!" Zorachus gasped, slipping the circlets from his hands and dropping them on his chair. "Is there a spell I can put on the rings so they won't heat up?"

But Ghaznavi was distracted. Bending over the desk, he eyed some of his potted flowers. Two blossoms were smoking.

"Damn," he said. "You've singed my nasturtiums." He straightened and turned. "What did you say?"

Zorachus repeated himself.

"There's already a spell on the outside of the circlets," Ghaznavi said. "Protects your other fingers, even as it allows the heat to dissipate. But the inside has to be in perfect contact with your skin. A spell would interfere. Don't worry, though. The demons won't generate so much heat when you're dealing with people."

"How are the bolts against force-shields?"

"Not very good."

"What's their range?"

"Not much better than the distance to the outcropping. Something else you should know: you can use the rings when you're traveling over water. The demons aren't affected."

"Not even by the ocean?"

"No."

"Who gave you the rings?"

"One of your father's northmen. The little one, Gudmund. Do you remember him at all? He used to come and visit you with the giant..."

"Hoskuld," Zorachus said. "I remember *him.*"

"He was memorable."

"I used to wonder how my father could've been beaten if he had a giant like that working for him..." Zorachus picked up the rings. "Even these didn't save him..." He paused, then asked: "How did you learn how to use them, by the way? I thought they'd only serve---"

"A sorcerer of the Mancdaman line?" Ghaznavi asked. "There are inscriptions to that effect on the inner surfaces. But it's not exactly true. Faschim found a spell to bind the demons for short periods. We learned much about them. Fascinating creatures, but incredibly deadly."

"The demons can be lawfully used?" Zorachus asked.

"Would I give you the rings if they couldn't?" Ghaznavi asked, irritated.

"Pardon me. I was only trying to make sure. You and Faschim have been known to get so wrapped up in experiments that certain key facts slip by you. . . ."

"The demons are almost completely malevolent," Ghaznavi said. "It's as legitimate for a Sharajnaghi to enslave them as to perform an exorcism."

"I'm familiar with the First Justification," Zorachus said. "It was one of the first things you taught me, remember?"

Ghaznavi's expression softened. "You were so young...." He laughed. "You're so young now!"

"It won't last." Zorachus picked up the rings, found they had cooled considerably, and started to put them on again.

"Don't wear them," Ghaznavi said. "Not unless it's necessary. Keep them in the pouch. The circlets begin to eat through flesh after a quarter of an hour or so. Some property of the metal."

Zorachus put the rings back in the pouch, tightened the drawstring, and slipped the thong around his neck. "Will there be time for me to get something to eat before the council?"

"I expect so. But if you meet any of your lower-level cronies, don't mention my plan. There's always the chance we've been infiltrated. It would be better if we passed you off as a renegade, for reasons I've already mentioned."

Zorachus's face twisted with dismay. "You mean it'll be necessary for most of the Order to think i'm a traitor?"

"I'm afraid so. But the news doesn't have to get out till you've already left- -we can spare you that much discomfort, at least."

"How can you possibly hope to pull it off? After all, I've just been ordained, and. . . . "

"There are precedents. Nadim Shawarra abandoned the Order one week after being ordained a Master. For a slave girl. I remember it clearly. She wasn't even that pretty."

"But---"

"If there's any doubt, certain secret writings of yours might be found. I could conjure up a diary in your handwriting, in which you express all kinds of doubts."

"I see," Zorachus said dejectedly.

"It must be done," Ghaznavi told him.

Zorachus looked pleadingly at him. "Could I at least tell Raschid? He's my best friend. I don't want him thinking i'm an apostate."

"The council would have to vote on it," Ghaznavi answered, his face very hard. "I for one would vote against it."

"He'd never tell anyone."

Ghaznavi was silent.

"I trust him completely," Zorachus went on.

"So do I," Ghaznavi said. "But---"

"If you agree he's trustworthy, you've got no case."

Ghaznavi eyed him for a few moments. "Does it mean that much to you?"

Zorachus nodded.

"All right," Ghaznavi said, and wagged a finger at him. "But I can't guarantee what the other Masters will think."

Zorachus smiled.

Chapter 3

THREE DAYS LATER Zorachus went to one of Qanar-Sharaj's many gardens. Awaiting him were three men.

Two were broad shouldered, similar to Zorachus in build, wearing black leather scale-mail and carrying triangular crimson-lacquered shields blazoned with the sign of a black hand; on their heads were round steel helms with cheekguards and nasals, and long straight swords in shagreen scabbards hung at their belts. Their eyes were shadowed under their helmet rims and their lips were thin.

The third man was short and sagged with middle age, though Zorachus guessed he had once been well proportioned. His face was still handsome by most standards, framed by long brown hair and a well-trimmed beard. Yet, to Zorachus's mind, it was quite unpleasant-a satyr's face, almost mindlessly sensual. The frank lewdness of the milky blue eyes was startling. The man wore a black silk blouse embroidered with coiling ruby-red firedrakes, and his black brocade cloak, traced about the borders by swirls of platinum thread, was clasped at his right shoulder by a brooch in the shape of a black hand. His trews were scarlet, stuffed into knee-high boots crafted of some dark blue reptilian hide, and at his hip was a sword much like those of his armored companions but much more ornate, its pommel and crosspiece of damascened iron, grip tightly wound with electrum wires. He smelled heavily of perfume, so much so that the scent of the nearby flowers was utterly smothered. The perfume was unpleasantly familiar, but Zorachus could not quite place it.

"Mancdaman Zorachus?" The man asked.

Zorachus nodded.

"I'm Brachus Lir Tchernaar," the other said bowing, "Emissary of His Anointed Steward Ghorchalanchor Kletus, the High Priest of Tchernobog and Lord of Khymir. Have you heard my Lord's proposal?"

"Yes," Zorachus replied. "I accept."

Suddenly he realized what Tchernaar's perfume was: a blend of aloes and myrrh.

Burial spices.

"My master will be delighted," Tchernaar said. "And Mother Khymir will be at your feet."

Zorachus forced a smile. He hoped it looked genuine. "That should take the sting out of losing my friends here."

"Losing them? Not just leaving them?"

"Let's just say that my decision will not be understood."

"Unfortunate," Tchernaar said. "But you'll make new friends. There are many handsome men and boys in Khymir. You'll have your pick." He spoke without the slightest trace of unctuousness; there was nothing of the procurer in his voice. He could have been talking about food.

There was a long pause.

"When do we leave?" Zorachus asked at last.

"As soon as you're ready," Tchernaar answered. "I've three ships at Thangura."

"Three?"

"Two for escort. You're valuable cargo, my Lord, and the voyage north is dangerous. We have to pass along the Muspel coast, and Muspellheim's populated by barbarians called the Kragehul; they hate Khymirians and prey on our shipping---those who won't accept tribute, that is. And even the ones that do attack from time to time. To make matters worse, the coast itself is a pirate's paradise---thousands of fjords and offshore islands. We might need some of your magic---you Sharajnaghim are formidible wizards, I've heard."

"I'm no longer a Sharajnaghi, I'm afraid," Zorachus answered. "And even Sharajnaghim can't do much magic at sea." He wanted to keep his possession of the demon-rings secret as long as possible. The less Kletus found out about his capabilities, the better.

"Pity," Tchernaar said.

There was another pause. Zorachus noticed one of the envoy's men playing with a beetle that had apparently lighted on him. The guard overturned his hand and righted it again, allowing the insect to scuttle all the way round. Then he brushed it off and stamped on it, grinding his foot powerfully, pointlessly, against the stone walk.

"Well," Zorachus said, looking back at Tchernaar, "I've something to attend to now, but I could be ready shortly."

"In an hour, perhaps? We could catch the afternoon tide."

Zorachus nodded. "That's the hottest part of the day."

"We don't mind if you don't. We khymirians aren't much bothered by heat...do you have any baggage you need help with?"

"No."

"Do you have a horse?"

Zorachus shook his head.

"No matter," Tchernaar said. "I've brought one for you."

"Very good."

"All right then, we'll wait for you at the south gate."

"One last thing," Zorachus said. "If anyone asks you why you're waiting, say you're merely expecting a message from me. It might spare some unpleasantness."

"Certainly."

31

"In an hour, then."

Leaving the garden, Zorachus went to his chamber. Closing the door, he leaned against it for a time, looking fondly at the room and its contents. Then he crossed wearily to his bed and sank down on it, one arm behind his head. Already low, his spirits sank steadily.

He knew he must leave Qanar-Sharaj. It was his duty to the Order. But that did not comfort him. And everything in the chamber seemed to be conspiring to make leaving harder. The mattress, which had always been hard and lumpy, had somehow become preternaturally comfortable; the paint on the walls had turned a shade of white hardly less wondrous than that of the robe he had donned at his ordination. He began to treasure even the cracks in the ceiling, and that cobweb dangling in the corner seemed like a gift from God....

He thought about Tchernaar and Khymir. The city's evil was legendary, but no legend, he was sure. *Impossible to exaggerate,* Faschim had said during the council. The words still rang in Zorachus's mind. He wondered: what depravities would he be confronted with? What atrocities? Utterly isolated, could he keep his sanity? Ghaznavi had perfect faith in him. So did the other Masters. But was it justified? Despite everything they had said, Zorachus's doubts remained, and ultimately his faith in Ghaznavi's judgement had weighed more heavily than his own estimate of himself. Ghaznavi was a wise man, full of experience; he had often placed full confidence in Zorachus when Zorachus himself had recommended against it, and every time that confidence had been vindicated. Yet Zorachus kept coming back and back to the question: could anyone truly know his heart of hearts better than he did?

Dejection became apprehension. He knelt beside the bed and prayed. But he had hardly begun when there was a knock at the door.

"Come in," he called, rising.

Raschid entered. Eyeing Zorachus's face, he asked:

"When do you leave?"

"Less than an hour," Zorachus answered.

Raschid laughed. "Don't take it so hard."

Zorachus's eyes widened with amazement. "How can you say that?"

Raschid laughed again, as if it were perfectly obvious. "You get to visit Khymir, wonder of the northern world. Think of its history--""

"I am," Zorachus broke in.

Raschid went on as if he had not heard him, striding about the room: "You'll travel the very streets where so many colorful characters have walked. You'll see Banipal Khezach, the famous Black Tower, exchange points of view with people of different religious backgrounds ... Think of how stimulating it'll be!"

"It's a shame the envoy's seen me already," Zorachus answered. "We could send *you* with him."

"There aren't many of us who'll get a chance like yours," Raschid answered flippantly, leaning against a wall.

"What do you mean?" Zorachus demanded. "I could very well find myself with half the wizards and soldiers in Khymir after my blood."

Raschid shrugged.

"And I'm not too pleased about having to plunge myself nose-deep into a tarpit of vice."

Raschid grinned and folded his arms on his chest. "You'll appreciate Qanar-Sharaj that much more when you return."

"What in God's name is the matter with you?" Zorachus exploded. "You didn't seem to think this was all so funny the other day."

"You weren't wallowing in your own sweet misery then."

"No? I would've had cause enough. How would you like to be surrounded by Khymirians? By hateful men when hate's forbidden?"

At that a squint of annoyance replaced the patient good humor in Raschid's eyes. "I don't suppose I'd like it very much. But there's something that seems even worse to me right now. How would you like it if your best friend decided to spend his last hour with you---rather, his last less-than-an-hour---chewing your ear off with self-pity?" He headed for the door.

"Wait!" Zorachus cried. Raschid knew how to communicate scorn in absolutely withering fashion, a skill acquired in several years of drilling cringing recruits. And, while Zorachus had not cringed, much of the whining mood had been cleansed from his mind.

Raschid turned and sneered: "The tragedy queen commands." He curtsied.

"You know," Zorachus laughed, "You have a gaping void where your sympathy should be."

Raschid grinned once more. "You noticed, eh? Perhaps you should stop snivelling. It makes you seem...unsympathetic."

"Watch your tongue. I'm a Master now. And I might point out that I wasn't snivelling at you very long."

"It seemed like hours, *Sibi,* " Raschid answered, delivering the last word with a great dose of sarcasm.

"As a matter of fact,," Zorachus said, "it seemed like *you* were chewing *my* ear off most of the way. All that nonsense about Khymir..."

"I thought it was funny."

"I suppose it was. But that only made it more infuriating."

"Sorry. I was only trying to take you out of yourself."

Zorachus continued: "And I really wonder how you'd like it if you had this mission."

Raschid sat on a stool. "You know, ever since you told me about it, I've been wondering about exactly that."

"And?"

"I think I'd be pleased."

Shaking his head in disbelief, Zorachus sat on the edge of his bed. "Why?"

"Any number of reasons. Because I'd been judged worthy of such a task. Because I had a chance to do something really important. Because I'd be confronted by such evil that I'd have no doubt of goodness. Or God."

"The last seems pretty dubious to me," Zorachus said sourly. "I don't need that kind of bolstering---especially if it means exposing myself to such temptation."

Raschid looked at him sidelong. "You really meant that nonsense about hating the Khymirians? You, the man who nurses Black Anarites back to health and then has the patience to convert them? I don't think you're capable of hating anyone."

"If what I've heard about the Khymirians is true," Zorachus said, "The Black Anarites are saints in comparison. The Khymirians have been under the enemy's shadow for a far longer time. I can easily imagine them provoking me."

"To do what?"

"Abuse my powers."

Raschid shook his head smugly, unwilling to entertain the possibility. "I'll tell you this, dear friend. That won't be your problem at all. It'll be making sure you use enough power when the time comes. If there's anything that really hinders a Sharajnaghi, it's all that sweet reasonableness."

"You're dead wrong," Zorachus replied.

"Well, maybe. But here's another thing for you to consider. The very fact that you're so worried means you've got nothing to worry about. I know perfectly well you'll be your usual even-tempered self during the troubles ahead. And you know it too. Otherwise you wouldn't have agreed to go."

Zorachus was silent for a few moments. "I have agreed, haven't I?"

Raschid nodded cheerfully. "You know," he said, "Once you leave, everyone's going to be trying to figure you out. Except the Masters and me." He chuckled. "Now, Jaffar of course will think he's got you pegged. And he'll be wrong as always...."

Zorachus laughed grimly. "But he'll get more of an audience than usual. After all, what better evidence for him than an apostate Sharajnaghi?"

"Sharajnaghi *Master*," Raschid said.

"I can hear him even now," Zorachus went on, "preaching about the infinite corruptibility of all men, demonstrating that the commandment against judging others stems not from imperfect human knowledge, but from the fact that everyone's a swine, and swine can't judge other swine. . .

"And so on till nausea sets in."

"I wish the council had declared Total Depravity heterodox a long time ago," Zorachus said with a sigh. "After all, I don't want to score points for Jaffar---even if they're only temporary." He paused. "Let's talk about something else."

"Such as?"

"How are you coming with that new kick?"

"Not so well. Can't get my leg up fast enough---"

"If anyone can manage it, it's going to be you."

"I don't know...."

"It's just a matter of time...."

In the end, Raschid was compelled to agree, and they passed on to a highly technical discussion of the moves they had used in the second trial.

Presently, Zorachus eyed his water clock. It ran on the flow that filled his basin; the design was his invention, and the whole order had adopted it.

"I'd better be going," he said.

They rose and went to embrace each other, but Raschid stopped dead, staring at something on the floor. Zorachus looked too. A large centipede was crawling slowly along. Raschid lifted his foot to crush it.

"Don't," Zorachus said, recalling the Khymirian and the beetle. "That kind's not dangerous."

"Yes, but you know how I hate the sight of them. One bit my mother..."

"I know. But that fellow's not hurting anyone."

"And you're going to massacre all those Khymirians?" Raschid asked. "Mercy incarnate, that's what you are."

"Right."

They hugged. And all at once Raschid was weeping bitterly.

"Now look who's feeling sorry for himself," he said, and stormed out cursing.

Zorachus wept too, but quickly brought himself under control. Taking off his sandals and white robe, he folded the latter and laid it reverently on the bed. Then he donned trousers and a tunic, both grey, and girt on a swordbelt. After putting on a pair of brown boots, he got his sack and slung it over his shoulder. In it were his mailshirt and padding, helmet (with the cage removed), vambraces, armored gloves and boots, and two changes of clothes identical to those he now wore. There was also a set of woolen cold weather garments, for while Khymir was known to be unnaturally hot all year round, the the climate of the region surrounding it was brisk at the best of times.

He gave his room one last, lingering look. Then he went out and made his way to the gate. The lower-level Adepts he met seemed surprised to see him without his Master's robes, and some spoke to him, but he answered them with silence. The gatewardens, both of whom he knew quite well, asked him where he was going; he passed them by without so much as a glance.

Tchernaar and his men were outside, waiting in the shadow of the gatehouse. The envoy was mounted on splendid black horse, one of the guards on another. But the guard got down as Zorachus approached---the Sharajnaghi guessed he had climbed up only to keep the gatewards from wondering who the horse was for. Zorachus allowed the man to take his bag and fasten it to the saddle; having been raised without servants of any kind, it irked him to accept such aid, but it was a minor enough matter for him to let it pass. He mounted up.

"Zorachus!" one of the gatewards cried. "*Sibi* Zorachus!"

Ignoring him, Zorachus put up the sunhood attached to his tunic; Tchernaar donned a Kadjafi headdress, and his men did likewise, wearing theirs over their helmets.

"Where are you going, *Sibi*?" the gateward called.

Zorachus and the others set off.

"*Sibi* Zorachus!"

Zorachus did not look back.

It was breathtakingly hot on the road. Convections rose shimmering from the baking red clay surface. Tall date palms lined either side, but they gave little shade. A few birds sang in the palm fronds, but their chirping came only in short gasps, as if they were all but choked by the heat.

As his horse clopped along, Zorachus spied something writhing in the road's red dust---a large scorpion with sunstroke was stinging itself to death.

Suddenly dread seized the Sharajnaghi; somehow he knew the scorpion was an evil omen. He felt a powerful urge to leap off the horse and tear back to the safety of Qanar-Sharaj....

Yet he remained in the saddle. He could practically hear Ghaznavi: *You saw a scorpion stinging itself! That's why you came back!*

He steadied himself. He had no reason to trust his own premonitions. He had never gotten anything but false alarms. Bit by bit, the dread left him.

They rode on.

Thangura was a mighty fortified city with tall red sandstone walls;
Zorachus and his companions reached it just as the heat eased and people
were beginning to venture from their houses. Welcome breezes swept
through the narrow streets, which soon grew crowded.

Zorachus's party threaded a path to the harbor. Hemmed on the west by
castellated breakwaters, it was wide and horseshoe shaped. Two towers
flanked its mouth, a giant chain stretching between them.

Striding through the newly revived bustle of the port, Tchernaar's men led
the way, making for a narrow pier set off from the others, which lunged far
out into the harbor. Three long black ships were moored to it, moderate of
draft, their bows tall and curved, bearing hands carved in black wood
instead of figureheads. Each vessel had a single tall black mast, and their
poopdecks were ringed with loopholed castles.

"Our fleet," Tchemaar said. "We'll be on the ship at the end, the
Zancharthus."

Zorachus noticed a man fishing on the nearest of the three. Making a
catch, the angler took it from his hook, sliced its tail off, and tossed the
maimed, flopping creature back into the water. He started to rebait his
hook, looked up and stopped.

"Lord Tchernaar's coming!" he cried in Khymirian. Word spread to the
other ships as Zorachus and his companions went out along the pier; men
flocked to the rails. Most were Khymirians, large and red-haired, bearing
a strong resemblance to Zorachus. The rest were swarthy Kadjafim and
sandy-haired Tarchans.

"Lord Tchernaar!" one fellow called. "Is that him? Lord Mancdaman?"

"Yes!" Tchernaar replied. Cheers broke out. Men started to pour down the
gangways, but their officers called them back.

Zorachus's party reached the *Zancharthus's* plank. He and Tchernaar
dismounted and went aboard, the guards bringing up the rear with the
horses. A noisy crowd of sailors and men-at-arms hemmed in Zorachus .
and the envoy near the rail. "Make way for the Captain!" came a bull-
throated bellow. "Make way!"

The throng quieted and a lane opened. A short fat man approached
Zorachus. He wore a white linen shirt and an embroidered blue vest,
baggy trousers, and boots with upturned toes; his skin was brown, his
pate bald and shiny, his huge hooked nose archetypically Kadjafi.

Tchernaar nodded towards Zorachus. 'This is Lord Mancdaman," he said. "Lord Mancdaman, Captain Klazmouran."

The captain bowed. "Welcome aboard, my Lord."

"I want to leave as soon as possible," Tchernaar said.

Klazmouran nodded, and collared a sailor. "Tell the other captains to make ready." As the man made off, the captain shouted: "The rest of you dogs know what to do! Don't stand around gaping. Bogra!"

The crowd began to disperse, but a barefoot Kadjafi youth ran up beside Klazmouran. The Captain pointed to Zorachus, saying:

"Bogra, show our honored guest to my---rather *his*---quarters. Here's the key. And take his bag."

Zorachus was even then swinging it down from his horse. He doubted the slim adolescent would be able to handle the weight of the armor, but let him have it anyway, only to take it back after a few paces as Bogra buckled under the load. The youth led him under the poop to a richly carved hardwood door, which he unlocked; taking the key, Zorachus dismissed him and entered.

The cabin was spacious and luxuriously furnished. Beside one bulkhead was a large bed, with many silken pillows strewn across its wine-purple cover; opposite were an ornate table and bench. An empty chart rack stood on one side of the table, a massive ivory-inlaid wardrobe on the other. All the furniture was bolted to the floor. From the panelled ceiling hung several fine gold lamps; two portholes stood open in the stern bulkhead.

Zorachus opened the wardrobe, minded to stow his bag. Inside, he found a full rack of clothes. At first he thought Klazmouran had forgotten his garments, then he realized they were for him. They were packed very close together, but even so he could make out at least ten different designs. There were a half-dozen garments of varying lengths cut in each style--- lacking his measurements, whoever made them had compensated in the only way possible.

Zorachus took out a silk robe in which serpentine motifs of purple, crimson, and deep blue were fantastically intertwined. The workmanship was astonishing, and he considered putting the robe on; it was the longest of the six in that pattern and he guessed it would fit. But his sterner self prevailed; he was not about to acquire a taste for such decadent fineries. He hung the garment back up, shut the wardrobe, and shoved his bag under the bed.

Footsteps approached, and he turned as Tchernaar came in looking very upset. The funeral smell of his perfume filled the cabin; he had just given himself a fresh sprinkling.

"Is something wrong?" Zorachus asked.

Tchernaar tossed his hands up. "Indeed there is, my Lord. We brought some slaves for you from Khymir, two women and a boy. We were going to surprise you. But they escaped last night, Klazmouran doesn't know how, and. . ."

"Don't worry about it."

Tchernaar looked amazed. "You're not angry?"

"It's not as if I was expecting them. And I've been celibate all my life. I think I can hold out."

"Well, that's nice for you, my Lord," Tchernaar said. "But those whores took my bedmate with them."

"Did you come here just to tell me all this?"

Tchernaar shook his head. "I thought I'd see how you liked your quarters."

"Very much, thank you."

Tchernaar's face seemed to brighten a bit. "Finest cabin on the ship. I slept here myself on the voyage down."

"I thought this was Klazmouran's cabin."

"I persuaded him to give it up, and now I'm surrendering it to you. Have you looked in the wardrobe?"

Zorachus nodded.

"What do you think?"

"The workmanship's magnificent."

"We had a team of Malochians on the job. Our Khymirian clothiers have been falling off lately and we wanted you to have the best."

"Very kind of you," Zorachus said, smiling. "But I'll wear my own clothes."

Tchernaar nodded towards the wardrobe. "Those *are* yours. "

Zorachus caught himself. "Of course. But fine silks don't make very practical shipwear."

"It doesn't matter if you ruin them. We've got more for you down in the hold."

"I don't want to make a habit of wastefulness," Zorachus answered firmly. "Especially with my own property."

"But---"

"Is it wise to use things not in accordance with their purposes? To destroy them without good reason? Does an intelligent man chop wood with a sword when he has an axe?"

Tchemaar shrugged. "I suppose not. Still---"

"Would you excuse me for a while?" Zorachus broke in. "I'd like to sleep a bit. It's been a trying day for me, leaving home and all---"

"I understand, my Lord," Tchemaar said, and left, closing the door behind him. But the funeral smell lingered, sweet and cloying.

Zorachus sat on the bed. He did not need sleep, but Tchernaar made him acutely uncomfortable.

Trying to take his mind off his situation, he thought about the proof he had presented in the First Trial. He suddenly realized there was a hole in it, or something like a hole---perhaps. He set about trying to devise a way around the problem. In the end, he succeeded to his satisfaction. And by then, the voyage had begun.

Chapter 4

FOR THE FIRST few days, he considered spending the trip locked in his cabin. It was a grim prospect, but perhaps less so than spending much time outside.

First, there was Tchernaar.

Whenever Zorachus went on deck, the envoy was always around, even in the dark hours of the morning; the Sharajnaghi wondered if he ever slept. Finding Zorachus, Tchernaar would attempt conversation. Sometimes Zorachus humored him, trying to ignore the Khymirian's advances. Sometimes Zorachus would say he wanted to be alone and Tchernaar would leave, but come back shortly on some pretext. Sometimes Zorachus said nothing at all and Tchemaar would go on with a monologue, and if that died out, he would still stand there, lingering silently. And when Zorachus went back to his cabin, Tchernaar would follow all the way to his door.

Yet Tchernaar did not disturb him nearly as much as the men kissing or fondling or even buggering each other. Zorachus would avert his eyes, or keep them fixed on sea or shoreline, but even then he would still hear obscene commands, simperings, moans, passionate slobberings. Some of this behavior was plainly for his benefit, and Tchernaar had hinted several times that Zorachus and he should join in.

But despite all this, Zorachus found he could not keep entirely to his cabin. Spacious as it was, he still felt too confined--- and the long voyage had just begun. Finally, he decided he could force himself to ignore the others whenever necessary, and practiced spending more and more time on deck. He came to feel comfortable enough.

Up the coast the convoy pressed, day after day. Hundreds of miles of desert slipped by to starboard.

The ships hugged the coast tightly---even when much time could have been saved by cutting across the larger bays. Zorachus asked Klazmouran why.

"There are things in the deeper water, my Lord," the captain replied. "Surely you've heard of sea serpents--- or worse."

"Yes," Zorachus answered. "But I've seen ships that weren't keeping so close to the shoreline. Are their captains reckless?"

Klazmouran shook his head. "Those weren't Khymirian ships."

"The monsters single out Khymirians?"

"Strange, isn't it? But true. If we ventured out much farther than we are now, we'd be gobbled down. Luckily, the beasts don't like the shallows. They come in once in a while though, and that's more than enough."

"Why are they so particular about their victims?"

"I've no idea," Klazmouran said. "Why is anything the way it is, my Lord? It's just the way things are, and we have to live with it."

"You don't have to," Zorachus replied. "Couldn't you get a command on a Kadjafi or Tarchan vessel?"

"Wouldn't consider it," Klazmouran said. "There are too many benefits to serving the Black Priesthood. Particularly to a man of my tastes."

"I see," Zorachus said. He did not carry the exchange further.

The convoy pushed ever northward, passing the Achaean isles to the west and the seaward end of the Andohar Mountains to the east. Beyond the Andohars, the coast was very flat; the weather began to get chilly, at least to Zorachus's mind. He was used to the perpetual heat of the Kadjafi lands, and warm days by northern standards seemed almost raw to him; even on the brightest days, the sun looked positively watery.

About halfway up the Tarchan coast, the towns began to be surrounded by earthworks and stockades; timber watchtowers loomed. The Kragehul sometimes raided this far south.

The convoy's men at arms, Khymirian marines, started wearing their helmets and black scale-mail, and kept their triangular shields close at hand. Zorachus took likewise to his armor, and thought often of the demon-rings. Tchernaar went about in a spired helm and ring-mail; Klazmouran spurned armor, but most of the sailors wore whatever protection they could.

The country to starboard continued flat for a long distance, then rose in arid ridges, running east to west, which sometimes thrust out into the ocean. Before long, the ridges piled together to form the buttressed fastness of the Utgard Mountains. The Utgards were high and grim indeed; serrate snowpeaks stabbed up through layers of cloud, their spires bitter sharp. Thick forest darkened the lower slopes.

The cold worsened drastically, though Zorachus was told this was a balmy spring for that northern clime; he broke out his cold-weather clothes, wearing them under his armor.

The convoy wove in and out between dozens of small islands. There were many places where it could have been ambushed, but the chief danger was a meeting with pirates heading south; the waters west of the Utgards were the territory of Kragehul who accepted Khymirian tribute, but who made no attempt to stop attacks on Khymirians by northern corsairs simply passing through.

The convoy's luck held. It encountered only single Kragehul ships and there was no challenge from them---save a single arrow from a long galley speeding by under oar. The shot amazed Zorachus; it had been against a strong, sleet-filled wind, and the distance between the ships was not small. Even so, the shaft took a sailor on the *Zancharthus* through the ear and pinned his head to the mast.

But the man was not killed outright. Screaming, he snapped the arrow and ran a few paces before a marine tripped him, grinning. He got up again; another man tripped him. This time he stayed on the deck, moaning, trying to pull the rest of the shaft from his head.

"Finish him!" Klazmouran ordered.

Marines gathered round, drew their swords, and happily obliged, laughing and joking as they hacked at him. A severed finger landed near Zorachus.

"Throw him overboard!" Klazmouran cried.

Grumbling, annoyed at their amusement being cut short, they gathered the dead man up and complied. Zorachus nudged the finger over the side with his foot, hardly believing what he had seen.

Tchernaar came up to him. "That Klazmouran," he said. "Just can't stand the men having any real fun."

One grey afternoon, three Kragehul ships were seen approaching from the southwest. Their bright yellow sails indicated they were pirate craft from Dreykjar, an island a hundred miles off the coast. The Dreykjar Kragehul attacked Khymirians without hesitation.

The Khymirian vessels were traveling in file, the *Zancharthus* in the middle; with horn blasts, Klazmouran signaled the escorts to close in. The basic Khymirian naval tactic was to grapple vessels together, forming a floating fortress.

Both escorts sprouted oars. The one behind sped to catch up, but the other only drew farther ahead of the *Zancharthus,* its captain obviously hoping the other two ships would satisfy the Kragehul.

He had not reckoned on the reef, however.

Hardly had he embarked on that treacherous course when his ship ran aground, mast snapping off, black sail fluttering forward.

Sizing up the situation, Klazmouran decided not to link up with the escort behind; better far to sacrifice it. He guessed at least one of the Kragehul would fasten on it, and that another would go after the grounded ship. The third might keep coming, but he thought it more likely it would join one of the others for easier pickings. He ordered his sweeps unshipped; as the *Zancharthus* picked up speed, he gave a wide berth to the stranded escort, avoiding the reef, smirking as he eyed the men scurrying in panicked confusion on her deck.

After a time the other escort was attacked, grappled from either side. The remaining Kragehul vessel continued forward, making for the stranded ship. The reef proved no obstacle to her shallow hull as she glided toward her prey, archers loosing swarms of arrows.

Locked in his cabin during all this, Zorachus lay serenely on his bed, deep in a trance. Suffering from a splitting headache, he had lowered himself into that state some time before the Kragehul were sighted.

Rousing himself several hours after the *Zancharthus* made good its escape, he was dumbfounded to learn what had happened.

Leaving the Utgards behind, skirting the Muspellheim Peninsula, the ship passed the vast swamp called Fengarth; northward, the country grew mountainous again, and great fjords extended inland between treeclad slopes ridged with white.

As the distance to Khymir narrowed, the *Zancharthus* traveled more and more by night, sheltering by day in small bays on uninhabited outer islands. Most of the northern Kragehul refused to deal with Khymirians; living closer to the city, they knew them too well.

One morning, as Klazmouran steered towards a hiding place, a hulk was sighted, floating bows-up. A closer look showed the prow bore a carven black hand.

Suddenly a cloud of dark smoke boiled up from the western side of the island Klazmouran was making for. Was another Khymirian ship burning there? Klazmouran changed course, rounding the island on the eastern side.

It was a dangerous predicament. There was no real shelter for twenty or more leagues, but there was no help for it; they had to risk running north under the sun, by sail and sweep.

Zorachus, who had been awake most of the night, decided not to go back to his cabin, too apprehensive to want sleep. Leaning on the port rail, he watched the island slipping by, half-listening to Tchernaar, who stood next to him complaining that their present plight was somehow Klazmouran's fault. At last Zorachus suggested he should take his complaints to the captain; Tchernaar hustled off to do precisely that.

Not long after, a swarm of gulls circling over a patch of water drew Zorachus's attention. Presently, to his astonishment, a whale surfaced beneath them and lay blowing among the whitecaps for a while. The birds skimmed down, and seemed to be picking things off the vast beast---little clinging animals, or so Zorachus guessed. Astonishment had become sheer delight; he had never seen a whale before, and stared at it wide-eyed and open-mouthed, childlike in his wonder.

The leviathan submerged. The birds circled for a moment longer, then flew over the ship. Zorachus hurried to the starboard rail hoping they would show him where the whale would breach again.

They did. The whale rose spouting under them--- but quickly went down once more. Zorachus muttered a curse in disappointment.

Then he noticed the water boiling not far from where the beast had disappeared. Huge bubbles rose and burst, domes of trapped air yards across; spray and foam leaped thirty feet above the churning sea. A tremendous rumbling swelled beneath the surface, and as it reached its crescendo a titanic scaly arch lifted from the seething deep like a portent of doomsday, the head and neck of a colossal serpent, the serpent of serpents; the rear half of the whale's body dangled from the fang-studded jaws, flukes trailing foam. The serpent flipped its head back and the whale was *gone;* there was not even a bulge in the reptile's neck as its victim went down. Awestruck, Zorachus felt as though he was contemplating the very idea of *monster* in the mind of God, revealed in all its fearsome glory.

The serpent turned. Loop after loop of scaly body appeared in the foam. Leisurely the creature swam toward the *Zancharthus.*

The marines and sailors, who were already frightened half out of their wits, now went mad; many rushed below deck, while others cowered against the starboard rail, Tchernaar and Klazmouran among them. The ship veered, no one at the wheel.

Slowly, Zorachus took out the demon-rings and put them on. He doubted he could kill the serpent or drive it off, even with such terrible weapons, but they were the best he had. He prayed.

The monster came closer and closer, but its pace remained unhurried. It did not seem to be moving to the attack. Zorachus resolved not to strike until it made a hostile move.

It came in range of the demon-rings, swimming for a while parallel to the ship. Its gaze remained fixed; Zorachus had the uncanny feeling that the huge green eyes were staring directly at him.

The serpent moved slowly inward once more. Zorachus readied himself. He let the monster get very close. It occurred to him that it might go into ship-swamping throes of agony if he managed to wound it, but he knew he would have to take the risk.

He heard Tchernaar shouting, then pounding footbeats. The envoy came up beside him, voice raw with desperation: "Isn't there anything you can do? Are you *sure* there's no spell?"

"Get away!" Zorachus snapped.

"We'll die if you don't do something! This is no time for keeping secrets! You Sharajnaghim must have worked something out. . . ." He began to sob. "Please do something, anything. . . . "

"Get away!" Zorachus cried.

Tchernaar plucked at him. "You have to--"

Zorachus struck him. Tchernaar toppled to the deck, stunned.

Some fifty feet away, the serpent was once again swimming alongside the ship. Its dripping underside was hung with long strands of kelp; bright red crabs the size of dogs clambered in the hanging gardens, and pink shrimp a yard long squirmed among the dangling leaves.

47

Zorachus studied the serpent's face. The eyes still seemed to be fixed on him, deep and calm and very wise. He wondered if their wisdom was only an illusion, if the serpent was really nothing but an unreasoning brute.

I reason, said a voice in his mind.

With a shock, Zorachus realized the voice was the serpent's.

"Are you going to attack?" he asked aloud.

No, the serpent replied. *I will spare the ship for your sake. I merely wanted to see you.*

"Why?"

Because you are the one. And now is the best time.

Zorachus did not know what the serpent meant, but an exquisite thrill of fear ran down his spine.

"Who are you, my Lord?" He asked.

I am Zathlan, the serpent answered, and disappeared gently beneath the waves.

Groaning, shaking his head, Tchernaar got to his feet. "You know, Lord Mancdaman," he said, "I thought I heard you *talking* to that thing."

"I didn't realize I was speaking aloud," Zorachus replied. "I heard him in my mind."

"Has he gone?"

"Yes. " The envoy leaned over the rail, looking down into the water. "He's not lurking under the ship somewhere?"

"I don't think so," Zorachus replied.

"What did he say to you? Why didn't he attack?"

"I didn't understand him. I don't know why he spared the ship." Zorachus paused. "I'm sorry I struck you, but you were distracting me."

"From what?" Tchernaar asked, leaning back, a suspicious glint in his eye. "Could it be you know some spell after all?"

Zorachus shook his head, ready with an answer: "He was already speaking to me."

"I see."

They turned. The sailors and marines abovedeck were still cowering against the far rail, apparently expecting the serpent to rise any second and destroy them. Klazmouran had not budged. Tchernaar went across the deck, crying, "The danger's past!"

Ill at ease, Zorachus stared westward, pondering the things Zathlan had said. He took the demon-rings off and returned them to their pouch.

The *Zancharthus* reached the second hiding place without further incident. Zorachus went to his cabin and fell asleep.

When he woke, it was night, and the ship was moving again. He had had some kind of evil dream, but could remember little of it, save that Zathlan was in it, suffering from wounds that Zorachus knew he had somehow caused....

After having some of the food and drink that he kept in his cabin, the Sharajnaghi went back on deck. Tchernaar found him almost immediately and began to regale him, as he had several times before, with descriptions of the Mancdaman inheritance. Trying to take his mind off the encounter with Zathlan and the dream, Zorachus paid closer attention than usual.

After a while, Tchemaar paused. Then he said: "You know, my Lord, Providence has been very good to you."

"You believe in Providence?" Zorachus asked, surprised.

Tchernaar laughed, teeth gleaming in the light of a nearby lamp. "Not really. You know how you find yourself mouthing old sayings and worn-out words when you don't have anything to say?"

"I suppose."

"We Khymirians used to believe in it," Tchernaar went on. "But we've put such nonsense behind us. We believe in the Powers, of course. They've been kind to you. But not out of some kind of benevolent forethought. They make chaos, not order. They're nothing but chaos themselves, and we're their handiwork---little bits of squawking confusion."

Zorachus's curiosity was piqued. He had never heard philosophy from Tchernaar before. He asked:

"Are you a Priest?"

"No. I'm Lord Kletus's man. A family retainer."

"Do you believe your Master's god is nothing but chaos?"

"I suppose."

"Lord Kletus doesn't care?"

"About my opinion? He wouldn't even if he knew it. He's very...self-absorbed. Not that I'd dare to criticize him, mind you. But I'm inclined to think that most Khymirians incline towards my views, for what it's worth. The Powers give us life, then kill us, but don't even know why."

"And we know even less?"

"I suppose," Tchernaar replied.

"If I live in Khymir long enough," Zorachus said, "Will I come to share your views?"

"About the powers?"

"And myself?"

Tchernaar laughed again. "As if you don't already."

Zorachus had expected such an answer. "Well, what if I didn't?"

"Then Mother Khymir would certainly convince you. The truth about things is very clear there. Clearer than anywhere else."

"You know," Zorachus said, "It's hard for me to imagine that I'd be able to enjoy my wealth, or anything else, if I thought I was nothing more than a little bit of squawking confusion."

"Come now, my Lord," Tchernaar said. "What do you think enjoyment is? Distraction."

"Would you believe me if I told you I was taught to think differently?" Zorachus asked. "To think that true pleasures *deepen* one's knowledge of reality?"

"I would *not* believe it," Tchernaar answered. "But if I decided to take such an idea seriously, I'd ask first what you meant by 'true pleasures.'"

"Ones that don't destroy---that aren't only pain disguised."

"But everything's a disguise," Tchernaar countered. "And if one's tastes run to pain, what of that? Pleasure's simply a matter of preference."

"What if some preferences rob the mind of reason? Without reason, man's only a beast."

"Man is only a beast," Tchernaar said. "The one that lays human dung."

There was a pause.

"Tell me," the envoy said presently, "about the arguments you were just making. . . "

"What of them?"

"I've heard that members of your order regularly trot out such nonsense as if they believed it. Why the pretense? Anyone could see through it, you know."

"I'm not a Sharajnaghi anymore."

"Of course not, my Lord. But that doesn't answer my question."

Zorachus said, "Perhaps the answer lies in the fact that not everyone sees through that 'nonsense.' As long as that's true, it has its uses."

Tchernaar shrugged. "If indeed people can be taken in by it.... But they'd have to be very stupid."

"You can't leave stupid people out of your calculations," Zorachus answered. "It's also good to learn who *is* stupid."

Tchernaar laughed. "Is that why you were arguing with me?"

"To be honest, I *did* want to see how you'd react. I've had few Khymirians to study until recently. But you only confirmed my expectations."

"I see," Tchernaar said. He was silent for a few moments, then laughed again. "You know, my Lord, I just had an amusing thought. Can you imagine a man in your position going to Khymir, someone who really believed in that Sharajnaghi sham doctrine? How frustrated he'd be! It would probably drive him right out of his mind."

"If he really believed it," Zorachus said casually, "Why would he go to Khymir?"

"He wouldn't, of course. But it's just splendid to think of him biting his lips when some delectable piece of meat wiggled by, just begging to be buggered or sliced. Can you imagine it?"

"I think so."

"Aren't you glad you're the sensible sort? There's nothing to keep you from appreciating Khymir. To a man with enough power and will, she offers total freedom."

"So I've heard," Zorachus said. "However...."

"What, my Lord?"

"You must forgive me, but sometimes I wonder if any freedom could be so complete. Nothing's forbidden?"

Tchernaar shook his head. "Not to a man of your rank."

"I could rape?"

"Yes..."

"Kill?"

"Provided you made sufficient reparations. And you'll have the money. When I spoke of slicing, I meant precisely that. "

"I could do anything to anyone I took a fancy to?"

"If they weren't of your rank. And if they were, you could always ask. Some will submit to anything."

"*Anything?*"

"Yes."

"They'd eat dung if I told them to?"

"Yours? Some would, I think." Tchernaar smiled.

"They wouldn't be looked down upon?"

"Certainly not. Most of us have tried it. Experimentation is essential in Khymir. There are so many diversions---take some of the creatures our wizards have bred. Remember me mentioning my bedmate?"

"The one the prostitutes escaped with?"

Tchernaar nodded. "She was a hybrid. Just the right combination of human and beast. I imagine she fetched those whores a good price. I miss her very badly. She struggled *deliciously.* I had to keep her chained *so* tight." He sighed. "Domination's such a thrill. I hope you experience it soon." He giggled. "Of course, you could come to my cabin and try it right now."

"Tchernaar," Zorachus said, struggling to restrain his disgust, "When are you going to realize that I want nothing to do with your body?"

"I realized a long time ago," Tchernaar said cheerfully. "But there's always the chance you'll come round."

"I think not."

"Even if that's true, my Lord, I don't mind. Humiliation can be very stimulating."

"God in Heaven," Zorachus said under his breath, almost unconsciously.

"What was that, my Lord?"

"Never mind," Zorachus replied, deciding to return to his cabin.

But at that moment there came a cry from up near the bow, and he and Tchemaar went to see what was going on, as did many others.

One of the cooks had been fishing with a large pole and had snagged something very heavy; two sailors had had to help him haul his catch up onto the deck---a dead man wearing the quilted leather gambeson of a Khymirian marine, the fishhook lodged in his belt. The corpse's face and throat were badly slashed, and one hand still clutched a tuft of blond hair.

"Kragehul hair, I'll warrant," said the cook. The corpse had not been in the water long; the crabs had just started in on the pale flesh.

"His ship must've been taken somewhere near," said another man.

Klazmouran came up, having left the wheel to Karim, the first mate. "Get rid of the damn thing," he said. "There's no point gaping at it." He stalked off. The corpse went back over the side.

"How many of us will join him before this voyage ends?" a marine wondered aloud.

"We all will, if the wind doesn't pick up," a sailor said---it had been falling off for some time. But just as if to realize his worst fears, it chose that moment to die out completely. The sail flapped, going slack. His comrades burned glares at him.

"Had to open your mouth, eh?" one snarled.

"Maybe it'll start up again," Zorachus said.

"Not for a good long while, my Lord," a veteran sailor answered grimly. "When the wind stops off Muspellheim, it stops for hours."

Men cursed and prayed. Klazmouran ordered the oars unshipped, and the _Zancharthus_ crawled northward. Zorachus remained on deck. Tchemaar kept close by, alternating between horror stories about the Kragehul and knuckle chewing silence.

The wind returned at first light. Canvas billowed and the ship plowed the waves with renewed speed. But it continued under oar; the nearest refuge was still three hours away.

53

The sun rose in an oyster-colored sky, painting the clouds with fire. The *Zancharthus* swept on.

And two red sails appeared astern.

Tchernaar vanished belowdeck. Klazmouran ordered more speed from his sweepsmen, but there was no hope of losing the Kragehul. They were gaining too swiftly. Nor was there a way to beach the ship and flee on foot; the coast was too rugged.

Zorachus pondered the situation. Using the rings, he guessed he could cripple or even sink both Kragehul vessels. But bolts powerful enough to do it would heat the rings fearfully. Finding a bucket, he filled it with drinking water from a cask and went onto the castle. Klazmouran was up there, bellowing orders at the bowmen who crouched at the loopholes.

The Kragehul ships drew nearer, oars beating, sails taut. Their topstrakes were painted bright red; black dragons coiled on the long yellow flags fluttering from the masts, and gold-decked dragonheads were carved on the prows. Bright-helmed warriors strained at the oars; others sent arrows whistling once the *Zancharthus* came in range. Aimed at the Khymirian castle, most of the shafts stuck in the bulkhead, but a few streaked in through the loopholes and black-clad bowmen slumped. The other Khymirian archers tried to return fire against the wind; their shots fell short, striking the water in spurts of foam. But as the distance narrowed, they began to pick off some of the Kragehul. Several pirates toppled into the brine.

Pulling a dead man away from a loophole, Zorachus eyed the Kragehul ships; they were now in range of the rings. He took the rings out and put them on, extending his arms through the loophole.

Lightning blazed forth, striking the mast of the starboard dragonhead. Oaken fragments flew, peppering holes in the square red sail. Kragehul clutched at splinter-riddled bodies and two fell overboard; the mast toppled backwards, draping the canvas over oar-stand, sweepsmen, and stern-post. The galley began to fall back.

Scorched fingers trembling, Zorachus turned to the waterbucket just as Klazmouran, an arrow in his throat, crumpled and knocked it over. Water splashed across the boards. Zorachus tried to cool the rings as it ran out the scuppers, but in vain. Blowing on the rings, he turned back to the loophole.

The other Kragehul ship was still closing; even after what had happened to the first dragonhead, its oarsmen had not stinted. And before Zorachus could loose more bolts, one of its archers put an arrow into the Sharajnaghi's left shoulder.

Gasping, Zorachus snapped the shaft and twisted away from the loophole, battling a tide of blackness welling up in his brain. Gritting his teeth, he fought to remain conscious, calling on deep reserves of will and training.

The blackness subsided. His shoulder throbbed, but he knew he could ignore the pain.

He crouched before the loophole once more, extended his hands and concentrated. Firebolts crackled from the rings, struck the second ship's mast and shivered it to kindling. The upper part of the tree toppled over the side, sail and rigging fouling the long sweeps to starboard. The dragonhead fell back.

Zorachus smiled. The *Zancharthus* was out of danger. Exaltation drowned the pain in his fingers and shoulder.

Then he saw the burning streaks hurtle across the widening but still too-narrow gap between the ships. Fire arrows.

He watched them pass overhead, turned to see them strike the sail. In half a minute the canvas was consumed.

Still blowing on the rings, he looked back at the Kragehul ships. The men on the first dragonhead had managed to hurl the sail and broken mast overboard, and those on the second were disentangling their oars. On both vessels, the unmanned sweeps had acted as brakes, and the pirate vessels were now well behind the *Zancharthus,* which was still coasting forward. But soon the dragonheads were pressing north again, slower than before, yet fast enough. Zorachus was amazed by the pirates' bravery. He guessed they had never seen, and had probably never heard of, such magic as he had used against them. Yet they were not dismayed. He was deeply saddened that he would have to send most of them, perhaps all of them, to their deaths.

"Blast them again, Lord Mancdaman!" a marine cried.

"Not till they're back in range," Zorachus answered. Pain flared in his shoulder; he could feel blood spreading warmly through his gambeson.

"You'll send 'em under?"

Zorachus nodded.

"Praise the Powers!" The marine shouted. "War magic at sea!"

The dragonheads closed in once more. Arrow after arrow thudded into the *Zancharthus's* castle, killing or wounding many of the remaining Khymirian archers. A shaft narrowly missed Zorachus's head.

The dragonheads came in range. Zorachus extended his hands, but an instant before he willed the demon-rings to strike, there was a burst of pain from the arrow-wound, and his concentration wavered; the dragon-prow of the starboard ship exploded, but nowhere near the waterline.

The twinge in his shoulder subsided, but pain shrieked marrow-deep in his fingers at the heat from the rings. His concentration was even worse when he struck again, the bolts falling far short of the mangled Kragehul bow.

He paused for a few moments, focused his mind as powerfully as he could, and launched two more strikes. The pirate's bow disintegrated; a wave poured down the hull, and the ship sank in seconds. Cased in mail, most of the crew went with it, but a few managed to save themselves by clinging to rowing benches.

The other dragonhead neared the *Zancharthus*. Zorachus knew he must cool the rings if he was to use them again; the pain was simply too great. He rushed to the front of the castle and bounded down the steps. Dashing to the water cask, he tossed the lid aside and plunged his hands in; steam rose in wisps. He whipped his hands back and forth through the water. The pain in his fingers lessened and he pulled his dripping hands out.

It was then that he saw the dragon prow slide up along the port side, its grinning jaws set with interlocking rakes of killer whale teeth; oars shipped, the Kragehul vessel skimmed forward on momentum, crunching through Khymirian sweeps. Arrows and casting axes decimated the sailors and marines along the Zancharthus's rail. Grappling hooks followed. The two hulls clashed with a terrific jolt and the Kragehul leaped aboard, byrnied blond giants hacking furiously at their foes, warding off Khymirian strokes with huge wooden roundshields.

Zorachus saw the melee was too wild for him to use the rings and drew his sword. Despite the burns on his hands, he could grip it well enough.

"Oh my God," he said, summoning his strength, "deliver me." Then he roared and charged.

Churning confusion engulfed him; the din of combat assaulted his ears, mad shouts and shrieks of agony, the crunch of triangular shields splitting under axe blows, the clang and slither of steel on steel. The air was full of flying blood, metal fragments, wood-splinters. A thrown knife clanged off zorachus's helmet. A spear passed under his arm, its wielder taking Zorachus's swordpoint just below the jaw. As the Kragehul sagged, eyes bulging, another pirate rushed up, sword gleaming. Zorachus ducked a powerful slash and cut off the man's swordhand. The Kragehul turned rime-white and stumbled backward. A third charged in from the left; Zorachus wheeled to meet him, stepped forward, and opened the pirate's throat before he could launch a stroke. Face registering awful surprise, the man staggered, then lashed out with his sword in a final desperate bid for vengeance. Zorachus dodged the blow with ease. Sword and roundshield dropped from the Kragehul's hands and he fell onto all fours. A dead Kadjafi sailor flopped down across his back, and the Kragehul collapsed. Howling in triumph, the Kadjafi's slayer, a huge yellowbearded pirate, turned to look for new prey; his eyes locked with Zorachus's and he grinned fiercely, apparently not even seeing Zorachus's point shooting toward his face. The thrust screeched in and out between the Kragehul's teeth before the grin could drop from his lips.

Having cleared his left, for the moment at least, Zorachus pivotted in time to see four Khymirians fall, almost at once; three Kragehul stormed over the gushing bodies. Zorachus got under the foremost's two-handed axe and stabbed him, leaped back, sidestepped the second man's mighty downward stroke, and bounded over the blow the third man aimed at his legs. But no sooner had his feet touched the deck when he sprang back up, and the third man took his shortsword through the cheek. Zorachus atop him, the pirate rocked backward dead, the Sharajnaghi struggling to pull his sword free. Roaring, the second man whirled and bounded forward, axe singing down; releasing his sword hilt, Zorachus threw himself out of the axe's way, and the weapon sank deep into the dead man's ribcage, sticking tight. Zorachus slammed his vambrace against the axe-wielder's kneecap, shattering bone. The Kragehul howled, loosed the axe-helve and clutched his knee. Zorachus punched him in the side of the throat and the Kragehul fell in a heap, helmet rolling free, blond locks spilling forward over his head.

Zorachus rose, breathing hard. He craved rest---a few moments at least. He was growing dizzy from blood loss, and the arrow-wound and the burns were sheer torment. But he could see that his allies were being slaughtered; with a powerful tug he freed his sword and goaded himself towards the nearest knot of carnage.

Kragehul after Kragehul went down before him. Seeing a group of sailors pinned against the starboard rail, he rallied a handful of marines and charged to the rescue…wherever the fray was sharpest, he went. All over the ship Khymirians took heart.

The tide turned. The Kragehul had been outnumbered from the start, but now, thanks to the Sharajnaghi, they were being overwhelmed. Point sinking into flesh again and again, he strewed the deck with bodies, his allies following eagerly in his wake, hacking, slicing. One group of Kragehul after another was annihilated.

The fight hastened towards its close. Stubbornly courageous, most of the remaining pirates went down fighting on the *Zancharthus*, but the rest slipped back onto the dragonhead and tried to cut the grapnel lines, only to abandon their efforts as marines swarmed aboard. The Kragehul formed a small, doomed shield-wall up near the bow.

Zorachus did not join in that final butchery. He had done all that was necessary. He wiped and sheathed his sword, barely able to slide the blade back into the scabbard. His head spun; he had lost much blood. His gambeson was soaked. Eyes half closed, ears ringing, he leaned on the port rail. Pain gnawed at his fingers. It occurred to him that he should take the rings off before they ate further into his burns, but all he did was stare stupidly at them through slitted lids.

He half noticed that the din of combat had stopped. The Khymirians were laughing and shouting. But above their racket he heard a voice bellowing in what he guessed was the Kragehul tongue; almost unconsciously he snapped his eyes wide open and looked toward the bow of the Kragehul ship. A large crowd of marines milled there.

All at once, a giant Kragehul rushed naked out of the throng, crisscrossed wounds dripping blood. Several marines bolted in pursuit, seized him, and forced him down over a rowing bench. One took off his armor, unbuckled his belt, and let his trousers drop.

Zorachus gripped the rail with both hands, nails digging into the oak, mind echoing with a single maddening thought: *you saved these vermin!*

His fury mounted till he could contain it no longer. Trembling in every member, eyes distended, arrow scar flaming red on his cheek, he screamed, seeing the other deck as through a fever dream, the details impossibly distinct. Every bead of sweat stood out clearly on the rapist's forehead as he looked up, and every strand of his hair glistened with its own greasy sheen. The men holding the Kragehul looked up too, as well as those who had come up behind the rapist waiting for their turn, and the moist whiteness of their eyes, the redness of their dripping tongues, and the

58

fulsome pink of their sweaty faces were so vivid that they seemed to vibrate; the whole world reverberated with Zorachus's cry.

He thought of turning the rings on them, blasting them to rags for the sheer pleasure of it---and recoiled instantly from the idea, shocked by the murderousness of his own emotions. Never before had he experienced such hatred. Nothing had prepared him for the sheer terror of it. It was like coming face to face with a demon ...

A tremendous spasm of pain swept out from his shoulder-wound. His hand shot up towards the arrow-stump. Then the quivering world exploded in sparks.

Chapter 5

HE WOKE IN his bed, feverish, bathed in perspiration, his blanket
damp with it: an evil taste was in his mouth. Vicious aches badgered him,
running from his fingers to his elbows, and down from his wounded
shoulder along the left side of his chest. He stank of infected, seared, and
sweaty flesh.

He looked at a porthole. It was dark outside.

He sat up, the bed creaking beneath him. There came a sharp breath from
outside his cabin, and a marine entered.

"I see you're awake, my Lord," he said.

"I see you are too," Zorachus said groggily, and pulled the blanket aside.
His armor and padding had been removed: he was clad in a finely
embroidered knee-length, white linen shirt.

He looked at his hands. His burned fingers were rudely bandaged, the
dressings stained with dark ointment.

"Where are my rings?" he asked, wondering if they were still on him.

"In the table, my Lord," the marine replied. "Righthand drawer...we put
them there after you pulled them off."

"I woke up?"

"You did, my Lord. Don't you remember? Karim was trying to pull them
off himself, and..."

Zorachus sniffed his fingers. The smell was grievous, but not as bad as
what was coming from his shoulder. Above the arrow wound his shirt was
blotted with glistening umber. He yanked the garment open, popping
buttons. The arrow stump had been removed, the wound dressed even
more greasily than his fingers. Karim apparently swore by unguents;
wondering if there might be some perverse unguent cult in Khymir, the
Sharajnaghi ripped the bandage off. The revealed skin was black where a
cauterizing torch had been applied far too long.

"My Lord," the marine groaned, "now look what you've done. Karim'll
have to put another dressing on...."

Zorachus spat a laugh and started taking the bandages off his fingers.
The marine grabbed him.

"It's for your own good, my Lord."

60

"Let me go," Zorachus said.

"No."

"Let me go," Zorachus repeated, simmering.

"Not till you agree to stop tampering with your bandages. Karim and master Tchernaar'll have my hide."

"Well then, I'll give you an excuse." Racked with pain and fever though he was, Zorachus was still several times stronger than the marine, and freed himself with ease.

But the marine would not give up, trying to lay hands on him once more. Zorachus struck him in the face. The marine shot back across the room and tumbled out into the passageway.

"Tell Karim and Tchernaar I can heal myself," Zorachus called after him, grimacing. The hand he had used launched a horrendous protest; its burned digits seemed to be threatening secession.

The marine rose, pawed at his mouth, and vanished from sight. Moments later Zorachus heard him speaking to someone in the passage; the word "delirious" was all the Sharajnaghi caught. Tchernaar and Karim came in shortly, the marine in tow. Zorachus had his fingers uncovered by then.

"What's all this, Lord Mancdaman?" Tchernaar asked.

"I'm *not* delirious, if that's what you're wondering," Zorachus answered. "I *am* running a fever, but my head's clear. I smell my wounds very distinctly."

"I did my best," Karim said. "But I'm no doctor."

"I'll treat myself from now on," Zorachus said.

"How?" Tchernaar asked.

"A healing spell," Zorachus replied. "It's one of the few Sharajnaghi magics that can be worked at sea."

"That, and sinking ships," Tchernaar said. "I understand you blew one of those dragonheads clean out of the water."

"Not quite."

"I wish I'd been abovedeck to see it. But tell me, my Lord: why did you keep such powers secret?"

"A wise man never displays his strongest weapons---unless he has to." Feeling dizzy, the Sharajnaghi lay back down. He guessed he would not

61

be clear-witted for long, and knew he should begin the healing spell as soon as possible. "I'd like to be left alone now. Would you see I'm not disturbed for the next twenty-four hours?"

Tchernaar turned to the marine. "You heard him. Tell the next man on duty."

The marine nodded. Still fingering his split lip, he shot a peeved glance at Zorachus.

"Well then," Tchernaar said, "we'll be off."

"Would you close the door on the way out?" Zorachus asked.

Tchernaar nodded, leaving with the others.

Zorachus took one last look at his seared fingers, folded his arms on his chest, and closed his eyes. Concentration was difficult, but he attained the necessary level, then uttered a spell that had been revealed to Washallah Irakhoum by the Angel Shuriel himself. Finishing, Zorachus dropped off into a deep trance.

Twenty-four hours later, alert and refreshed, his pains and fever gone, he reassumed physical perceptions. He still reeked of sweat, but the other stenches had vanished.

Sitting on the edge of the bed, he took a deep breath, rose, and stripped off his shirt. His once-wounded shoulder was coated with a dark gelatinous substance, the residue of dead flesh. His fingers were likewise gummed. He wiped them and his shoulder off with the shirt, then washed as well as he could, using strong soap and seawater from a barrel.

While he was drying himself, he realized how hungry he was; wrapping himself in a blanket, he got out bread and cheese and made short work of them, washing them down with wine from a skin bottle.

His gear had been laid out on the bench, the cloth goods cleaned, the arrow hole in the byrny repaired; the new links, browned iron, stood out clearly against the grey steel.

Chain mail, he thought. *Ugh.* He felt too good to want to bother with the weight; the trance had left him in a slightly euphoric state. His better judgement protested, but he decided to dispense with his armor for the first time in several weeks.

Once he had his clothes on, he took the demon-rings from the table drawer, put them in their pouch, and went on deck.

The moon was up, bright and full. He looked at the mast. A new sail had been set.

He went up to the poopdeck where Karim was at the wheel.

"Good evening, Lord Mancdaman," the new captain said.

"Good evening," Zorachus answered, striding over to the port rail. He looked at the silverlit coast, watching the mouth of a fjord slide past. The air was cool but pleasant, the sea calm. The only sounds were an occasional flap of the sail and the gentle rush of the water. He was perfectly content to remain at the rail for a long while, gazing at the coast and the mild waves. He knew the ship must be very close to Khymir, and he wanted to enjoy as much tranquility as possible before his true ordeal began. He prayed that Tchernaar would not appear, at least for a few hours.

God obliged.

The moon set. The night grew old, and the breeze stiffened. A fringe of yellow light appeared behind the eastern peaks. The glow grew steadily, and finally the sun lifted over the mountains.

Karim did not run the ship toward cover; there were no good hiding places nearby and the distance to Khymir was short. He steered northwestward around a jagged cape, the northern tip of the great island the *Zancharthus* had been skirting for two hundred miles. The ship pushed out across a broad expanse of open water. The walls of Muspellheim were blue in the distance, but a long stretch of coast was obscured by a towering line of thunderheads. The ship made straight towards those titanic clouds.

"Aren't there monsters in these waters?" Zorachus asked Karim. "We're so far from the coast. . . ." Zathlan had spared the ship, but the Sharajnaghi had no reason to think other leviathans would do likewise.

Karim shook his head. "Too many reefs. The beasts can manage in narrows and shallows, but they prefer not to."

The ship skimmed onward, the black hand on its prow still pointing toward the clouds. Zorachus gazed at them. They seethed visibly, full of movement. But they did not, as far as he could tell, drift on the wind.

Midway through the morning, Tchernaar appeared on the castle and came up to him.

"You're looking fit, my Lord," the envoy said appreciatively. I see your hands are healed."

Zorachus nodded.

"We should reach Khymir sometime early this afternoon, I think," Tchernaar said. "The Great Mother lies beyond those thunderheads up ahead---or rather, inside them. They hem her in, a perpetual barrier. And in the center it's always warm, even by Kadjafi standards, I think."

"The clouds keep the cold out?"

Tchernaar shook his head. "The spell does it. It was laid down a thousand years ago, by the men who brought the cult of Tchernobog to Khymir, Black Priests from Malochan.... Five weeks of constant blood offerings were required."

"Then why the thunderheads?" Zorachus asked. "Such angry-looking clouds."

"Aren't they? Always roiling and threatening. They're the reaction to the spell. And to Khymir. There are powerful presences in Muspellheim, you see, spirits of stone, sea, and air. They hate Khymir, jealous of all her comfortable, incongruous heat. You'll feel it when we pass under the clouds; it'll be all around you, boiling, probing rage."

"Do these presences ever gobble up ships?"

"They've been known to," Tchernaar replied. "Sometimes the seas are mountainous beneath the clouds, and ships are struck by lightning and vanish without a trace. But when the situation gets too unruly, our wizards massacre some of the neighboring Kragehul with sendings. That usually quiets things."

"You take reprisals against the weather?"

"It works," Tchernaar said. He scanned Zorachus's face. "If you're worried about our passage, relax. There was a fine slaughter of the barbarians shortly before we left Khymir. Things should be reasonably calm. Respectful, I might say."

The ship sailed ever nearer the clouds. For all their menace, Zorachus thought them gorgeous: tremendous billows of thick vapor, huger than the hugest mountains, shimmering white above, darkening to blue, then deep purple beneath. The water below was steeped in shadow, but every few seconds the darkness was torn by forked lightning.

The sea grew choppier with each passing mile, lashed by swelling crosswinds. The *Zancharthus's* progress became more difficult, and the hull heaved violently. At Karim's order, sailors strung heavy-weather lines on both decks. Tchemaar got nauseous and went below, but Zorachus remained on the poop; going to the castle's forward bulkhead, he gripped it with one hand and a heavy-weather line with the other. The ship's motion did not bother him; he rather enjoyed the jouncing ride.

After much tacking, the *Zancharthus* eventually reached the thunder-racked western fringe of the clouds, and there Zorachus saw a vista which surpassed his wildest notions of grandeur. The clouds rose like a wall above him, layer after purple-shadowed layer, and as the ship entered the darkness beneath, he looked skyward along that vapory expanse like a man standing at the base of a cliff. For all he knew, it might have risen ten miles, and he could see all the way to the mushrooming heights, which rolled out mightily against the blue vault of heaven.

Then the vision was gone; the ship sailed on into lightning-fraught gloom. When the bolts streaked down, everything on deck stood out in vivid relief, and stark shadows fled across the boards. Zorachus's ears were nearly split by the blasting thunder. A hundred yards in, torrential rain pelted the vessel, and he was soaked to the skin as he eyed the brief flashing vistas of cloud and tormented sea.

He waited to feel the hostility Tchernaar had described, and after a while his mind began to hum with sensation; the hatred *was* there, a seething field of it playing about the ship. The farther in the *Zancharthus* went, the more intense the field grew.

Suddenly, somehow, he knew the lightning itself was becoming charged with hate; the Presences were not so respectful after all. Damp as they were, the Sharajnaghi's shorthairs began to lift, and his scalp crawled as with the pricks of tiny needles. Noticing a crimson glow playing weirdly about the masthead, he knelt, still clutching bulkhead and rope, and looked out through the castle gate.

Seconds later the black sky split open in a bloody flash; a red bolt slashed down, struck the masthead and forked to the deck beneath, blasting two sailors to bits.

Most of the men on deck scrambled below, leaving too few to tack the sail. The crosswinds changed; the ship was driven back.

But the Presences had taken some satisfaction in the killings, enough for the moment---feeling the anger in the clouds recede, Zorachus stood back up. The men below deck felt it too and soon returned to resume tacking.

The ship continued on its tortuous course. The storm's violence lessened. The *Zancharthus* began to make better progress.

Zorachus looked past the plunging prow. A bar of light gleamed through the rain, between the churning cloud-ceiling and the waves. The ship closed on it gradually, emerging at last from the dark and rain and wind.

Steamy warmth settled over Zorachus's wet flesh, a cloying hothouse exhalation. He suddenly felt as if he were entombed in the womb of a gigantic dead animal rotting and cooking in the sun.

The ship heaved no longer. Sail slack, it coasted out into a wide, glassy, greenish expanse. The sea was impossibly, unnaturally calm; it almost seemed as though the heavy air were pressing it flat, smothering it with a damp, warm pillow. The horrible tranquility was storm-bounded to north, west, and south; thunderclaps reached Zorachus's ears, but there was an odd dampened quality to them, as though they were being muffled by the thick enchantment hovering over the water.

To the east great mountains rose dark and sheer; though they were easily the tallest Zorachus had ever seen, there was no snow on them, even on the topmost peaks. Three thousand feet above the stifled sea, on a shelf that looked as though a giant blade had planed it from the stone, lay Mother Khymir, extending for miles along the clifftop.

Nothing had prepared him for the sight of her; Khymir's opulence was proverbial, but the reality was beyond his wildest imaginings. Thangura, city of the Great Khan, was small and rude by comparison. Behind the Great Mother's massive walls of blue-black stone rose hundreds of purple, silver, and golden domes, needle-like turquoise minarets, and adamantine arches, all of breathtaking size. Titanic equestrian statues and figures of monstrous creatures reared up on the peaks of black pyramids. Immense aqueducts spanned the city from the encircling mountains. A vast blank-eyed stone face stared seaward, smiling cruelly, flanked by two black hands set on pillars. Ziggurat-like structures, with what appeared to be ruined temples on their crowns, thrust skyward.

But mightiest of all was the sky-raking black tower lunging up out of the city's heart; Zorachus hardly believed his eyes. It loomed incredibly stark against the slopes behind---the other buildings could not counterbalance its awesome severity. The surrounding precincts seemed a mere sprawl in comparison.

Zorachus felt a strong pang of foreboding. The tower had the look of a weapon, of a sword or spear poised to disembowel the heavens; it was a colossal blasphemy, rendered still more terrible by its domination of the city at its feet. Khymir might well have been the Great Mother, a vast supine pillow of flesh. But at her center rose a mocking masculine power, a mad force battening on a multitude of human lives. The Sharajnaghi did not need to be told that the tower was Banipal Khezach, the temple of Tchernobog, the Black God, the archangel who fell because he opposed the creation of organic life. Zorachus wondered if the Khymirians knew what they had in their midst, if they realized that their every wallow in flesh and cruelty was but a vindication of the Tchernobog's ultimate purpose---to cure creation of the Organic Plague.

Karim called to a sailor on the main deck, sending him down with orders for the sweepsmen. Shortly, the long oars were clacking in their ports.

The captain steered directly for a chasm in the cliff face, which cut off the southern approach to Khymir. The *Zancharthus* drew slowly near the cleft.

Two Khymirian warships waited ahead on either side of the opening, a barrier-chain strung between them. As the *Zancharthus* approached, the chain was lowered and she passed through.

It was low tide and huge runnels stood revealed in the stone to left and right; in the ages before the waters were magically stilled, powerful waves had undercut the chasm's sides. Mast shipped, a large vessel could have passed easily beneath the curving overhangs. The grooves were matted with seaweed; dark strands dangled down.

Strange sea birds, gorgeously varicolored, soared and swooped between the chasm's frowning walls, their cries echoing and reechoing a perpetual chorale. A marine shot one that dipped too close to the ship; the dart went clear through the creature, which jerked in midair but somehow continued flying. Flapping towards the northern wall, it smashed into it and hung there, head caught in a crevice. The other birds flocked round; one by one, they swept down on their still-twitching fellow, pecked and tore, and flew off with gaudy feathers clenched in their beaks.

The ship pressed deeper into the channel. Looking up, Zorachus saw a long bridge spanning the gap. It was a brilliant feat of engineering; he had no idea of how it had been accomplished, and he knew a good deal about bridge building. But he was not surprised. Not after seeing Banipal Khezach.

Presently, Karim ordered the ship's lamps lit and steered to port. A gigantic cave mouth yawned in the northern wall; the *Zancharthus* passed inside.

After some distance, the ship rounded a bend. A broad disc of green twilight slipped into view and the *Zancharthus* entered an immense domed cavern a mile or more across. Five hundred feet high at the peak, the ceiling was an unearthly star chart of green-glowing lights.

The cavern's far wall was girt with an enormous semicircular ledge, upon which warehouses had been built and from which led many stone quays. Moored to the quays were hundreds of ships of all classes, and a smaller number were anchored in the harbor. Thousands of lamps and torches burned upon their decks, prows, and rigging, so that the vessels looked like luminous fish in the depths of a dimly green-lit sea.

The *Zancharthus* crossed the harbor slowly. Karim ordered the oars withdrawn and steered for a quay on the right, where space was reserved for the Priesthood's warships. The vessel coasted alongside and was soon moored.

Tchernaar came up on the castle.

"When do we leave?" Zorachus asked.

"We could go now," Tchernaar said. "Wouldn't be able to ride, however." Because the tide was so low, the *Zancharthus* was too far down for the horses to be unloaded even with the ship's winches. Iron-runged ladders set in the side of the quay were the only way up.

"I don't mind," Zorachus said.

"Shall I have your clothes sent to your house?"

"I can carry my own bag."

"One of my men can manage that. I was referring to the clothes in your wardrobe."

"Oh, of course. By all means, send them."

"I suppose you can't wait to start wearing them. But I expect they'll seem rather tawdry compared to what you'll be wearing tomorrow night."

"Tomorrow night?" Zorachus asked.

"Lord Kletus will almost certainly be holding a banquet to celebrate your arrival. You'll be presented to the lords and ladies of Khymir, and it's important that you come clothed in special gifts from Kletus, to show your respect for him. He'll send tailors beforehand, and they'll make sure you're dressed as spectacularly as possible."

"Fine."

They went down from the castle, Zorachus going to his cabin to get his bag and change out of his cold-weather garb. When he came back out, Tchernaar was shouting to someone in the hold, giving instructions regarding his horse and possessions. When he was finished, the envoy summoned up a half-dozen marines.

"Ready, Lord Mancdaman?" he asked.

Zorachus nodded. The group climbed one of the quayside ladders and made their way to the crowded waterfront. Passing between two torch-flanked warehouses, they came out close to the cave's curving wall. Cut through the stone was a wide ramp-tunnel; traffic to and from the ships traveled that path.

But there was another way up. A shaft had been bored in the cave's ceiling, and from it hung two huge hawsers, one attached to the top of a great steel cage, the other running via pulleys into a gigantic pit nearby. The pit was guarded by marines with bows and spears, and a strong reek of excrement and sweat rose from it. As Zorachus's party made for the cage, the Sharajnaghi got close enough to the pit's edge to glimpse a battalion of filthy slaves chained naked to the spokes of a hoisting machine; most were Kragehul, or so he guessed from their looks. Armored overseers with whips and swords stood about them.

Zorachus and his escort reached the cage. The keeper opened the gate and they filed in. Zorachus winced to think of the labor they were going to cause the slaves in the pit.

The keeper entered the cage, shut the door, and whistled to the pit guards. They signaled the overseers and the crack of whips split the air, followed by brutish grunts of pain. The cage began to rise.

Talking and joking with the keeper, the marines clustered toward the back. Zorachus and Tchernaar remained near the gate.

"This lift is reserved for servants of Tchernobog," Tchemaar explained, face red in the light of a hanging taper. "And their friends, of course. It's quite handy."

"Must be horrible taking cargo up that ramp," Zorachus said.

"People and animals are always dropping dead. Fouls the traffic something awful. It's good we don't have to depend on foreign food. The traffic would be five times as heavy and perfectly impossible."

Zorachus's eyebrows arched with surprise. "I would've thought most of your food was imported. Do you have farms? The land looked so rugged around the city. . . ."

"Far too rugged for farming," Tchernaar agreed. "But even if it weren't, all that dirt-grubbing's such a bother. So's fishing, for that matter. Luckily, the Founding Fathers gave us food as well as warmth---plants conjured from another dimension. They need little sunlight and only a bit of soil. Large numbers can be raised indoors, in the smallest rooms, and the fruit can be prepared many ways."

"Sounds like the ideal crop," Zorachus said.

"No, there are drawbacks. Three, to be exact. To start with, the fruit's versatile, but bland by itself. Nourishing, but unfit for the discriminating palate. We need spices. That's why we trade so heavily with the southern countries."

"Isn't it possible to find alien spices?" Zorachus had a broad knowledge of military magic and many scientific forms, but he had never studied the agricultural sort.

"In theory, yes," Tchernaar answered. "But most alien plants don't flourish on our plane. The right types, if indeed they exist, have eluded us. Some of the Guild wizards are still looking, I believe. If they ever succeed, we won't have to deal with those southern pirates. We'll be completely self-sufficient---like a maid with a mirror, as the saying goes."

"How do you pay for the spices?"

"With gold. There are rich lodes in the mountains. Apparently inexhaustible. But we have other riches too. Booty from our wars with the Kragehul, slaves, amber, resins. Our wizards also supply wealthy southerners with bedmates. The Emir of Fyrkaz got one recently. Part cuttlefish. Charming beast."

"Do you ever trade those fruit-plants?" Zorachus asked. "There'd be quite a market. Famine would become a thing of the past. . . ."

"And then the market would dry up, wouldn't it?" Tchernaar laughed. "But the plants won't grow outside Khymir. There's something about the atmosphere here. The ambience of the place, if you will. That's their second drawback."

70

"You mentioned a third. "

Tchernaar nodded. "They need human blood," he said matter-of-factly. Casual discussion of the most loathsome things seemed to be a typical Khymirian trait, as far as Zorachus could tell.

"Why is that a problem?" the Sharajnaghi asked after a while, having raised silent thanks that the *Zancharthus* had reprovisioned in Thangura. "Do you think there's something sacred about human blood?"

Tchernaar harrumphed. "It's costly stuff, that's all. The blood- slaves in the upper-class households could be put to other use. And among the poor, parents have to give their firstborn to the plants. Can you imagine sacrificing something so delicious?"

"No," Zorachus said. After a pause, he asked: "Why do the plants need *human* blood? Won't some other sort do?"

"Yes, but only if it's from rational animals, creatures that can think. And there's no point in chasing through alien dimensions after them, not when we've got a healthy supply of people. And it's not as though we go through a lot of slaves; they aren't killed. We just graft shoots into two of their major veins. Blood flows through the plants and their sap flows through the slave. Plants and victim become parts of each other, and the bodies begin to produce extraordinary amounts of blood. One human can serve a roomful of growths. The plants are all connected."

"And what happens to the slave's mind?" Zorachus asked.

"It *vegetates*, as you might expect," Tchernaar laughed. "After the first few weeks, the slaves lose the power of speech, and soon they don't react to anything at all. They just hang on the stakes, staring off into space. Some don't even blink and their eyes get frightfully thick with dust, like grey cataracts." He paused and seemed to slip into a reverie; Zorachus guessed he had nothing more to say.

Just as well, the Sharajnaghi thought.

But Tchemaar was not finished.

"When I was young," he went on, "I used to go into the garden and look at the slaves. We had a large garden, so we needed more than usual.

"I was sixteen when a young girl was installed. She was Kragehul, golden-haired, about my age. She already had very nice breasts---we hang the victims up nude, of course.

71

"I visited her often. She was wide awake for a long while, longer than most garden slaves. Unfortunately, she was too far up on the pole for me to enter her, and that was a genuine torment to me---I was still fond of plain womanflesh back then. She excited me greatly, trussed up there the way she was. But I had a fine time with her feet and legs---that is, until her nerves went dead and she didn't react anymore. I used to burn her. My parents didn't want me to waste a drop of that precious blood, so I just raised a lovely crop of blisters. And each morning when I came back, they were gone; the plant sap healed them from within, very quickly, so I could start all over again each time, playing with fresh new skin..."

By now Zorachus had heard far more than enough, but knew from experience that whatever he did---short of violence---Tchernaar would find some pretext to finish his story sometime during the next hour. There was no stifling the envoy when he waxed autobiographical.

"I often think of her," Tchernaar said. "My first love, as the southrons would say." He sighed. "I tried to find out how she felt about me. I begged her to tell me. But I never got anything but curses and shrieks out of her. She refused to admit the truth to me or herself. Never accepted the fact that she was just playing a game."

"Game?" Zorachus asked. "Do you think she liked being burned?"

Tchernaar never blinked. "Of course she liked it," he answered, as if it were the most obvious thing in the world. "I've already told you how she cursed me. That was one of the best indications."

"I would've taken the curses for curses. Simply because *you* enjoy pain. . . ." Zorachus's voice trailed off.

Tchernaar smiled patiently. "In some ways you're very naive, my Lord. There are two kinds of people in the world: honest and dishonest, those who acknowledge their desires and those who deny them. And the dishonest ones are always most aroused by the very things they pretend to find most repulsive. I've seen this in many countries---particularly in your Kadjafi lands, if I might be so bold. Most Kadjafim, the hypocritical majority, are always condemning us Khymirians, calling us degenerates because we roger our mothers and fathers and sons. But they burn to do the same. Moralizing about our pleasures gives them an excuse to dwell on them at length. And then they scuttle into their rooms and stroke themselves behind locked doors, or pretend that their wives are their daughters or their sons."

"You sound so sure," Zorachus said. "How many Kadjafi minds have you read?"

"Khymirians see through things." Tchernaar said. "We live authentically, so we recognize sham when we see it. Except for that, all human beings are like us. There isn't a virgin that ever lived who didn't dream of being raped by a horse, or having another girl's mouth between her legs. Our virgins differ from the others only in that they're more honest, and so they don't remain virgins long. Believe me, that girl in the garden enjoyed it. She would've enjoyed anything I might have done to her, even if she thought she didn't. Deep down, the pleasure must've been there."

"Once again, are you a mind reader?"

"I know myself. Self-knowledge is the key. From that you can learn everything about human beings. We're all made of the same stuff. How often must I repeat it? I knew what she felt because I'd felt it myself. I'd seen that the most dominant people, the proudest, most dominant men enjoyed humiliation and pain, just as I did."

The envoy began running a palm up and down a steel bar in front of him. "We had a retainer. His name was Drathazcar. He said I was the prettiest thing he'd ever seen, but I spurned his advances. My father was very old and hadn't instructed me in the arts of manhood; I was still uninitiated. And uninterested, even though Drathazcar was very handsome.

"One night he got tired of my rejections and came into my chamber. He held a knife to my throat and told me he'd kill me if I cried out. I submitted. At first, I hated the pain. But then I came to enjoy it. *Intensely.* And, as he lay atop me panting, I told him so. He said he'd known I'd enjoy it all along.

"He came to my room every night after that. Once he let me see how I'd like mounting him and holding the knife to *his* throat. I was amazed; he seemed so dominant. But my amazement didn't keep me from taking him. He asked me to cut him slightly. I did so, several times---and then, on a whim, sliced deep into his throat. Opened him ear to ear. He bucked beneath me most satisfactorily, and as the red streams gushed over the pillows and covers I thought I'd never surpass the pleasure I felt that night.

"But even as I rolled free, he turned his head weakly towards me. There was nothing on his face but fulfillment. Not emotion, not intelligence, nothing but gratification. His whole being was drowned in pleasure. His eyes were glazed, completely mindless. They might have been the eyes of an idiot.

"I realized then how feeble my pleasure had been; what's more, I saw how basic his desire for pain must have been. I'd long known, of course, that my parents and older brothers and friends had such needs; I'd learned I was like them. But now I'd seen how strong the desire was, even in a powerful man like Drathazcar. I realized how truly, universally human it must be. The appetite for feeling pain was every bit as basic as the need to inflict it. I had both in equal measure, as far as I could tell; so did everyone else. Everyone was like me.

"I sat up late into the night with Drathazcar's corpse, paddling my fingers in his blood, licking them clean, thinking about life more deeply than I ever thought before. I analyzed what I knew, saw that all human motives derived from the twin desires. I was delighted. For the first time I had a real sense of community with the rest of the human race.

"My discoveries were still fresh in my mind when the girl was strung up. I felt a matchless sense of adventure as I courted her. I never let her seeming lack of enthusiasm discourage me. I knew that all the cursing and writhing and spitting was only a front. She needed to feel sweet helplessness, to embrace mindless pain. I served her until she couldn't accept my aid any longer. But never a word of gratitude did I get from her."

Zorachus saw a tear well up in the envoy's eye and spill down his cheek. Tchernaar no longer looked satyrlike, but more like a sad infant, aged horribly beyond its years. Despite his revulsion, Zorachus was filled with pity.

Even he was a child once, he told himself, then shuddered at the possibility that some remnants of that innocent might still exist in Tchernaar, near-strangulated and ineffectual, the only regions where the sinner had not yet become his sins. Was there any way that they might be reached?

"It depresses me to think of her," Tchernaar continued after a time. "She reminds me of my youth, and I'm getting old. I don't enjoy things as much anymore, and I'm beginning to sag. I've got arthritis now, and wrinkles. I don't think my life will be very nice if it lasts much longer. I think it will be horrible. To be tormented by memories of desire and have nothing to wake up to but increasing debilitation.... I'm forty-three, Zorachus, forty-three! I used to be as potent as a stallion, but now...."

"When you were younger," Zorachus said slowly, "did it never occur to you that decay would begin long before your death? That the pattern you imposed on your life would only make the end that much more hideous?" He guessed what Tchernaar's answer would be like, but simple charity had forced him to speak, to try and raise such questions, perhaps for the first time, in Tchernaar's mind. He doubted Tchernaar would fathom his true intentions; more than likely the envoy would think he was simply trying to mock him.

Tchernaar gave a fleshless, cackling laugh. "What are you saying, my Lord? That I should've made my life wretched and pleasureless from the first, so that I'd feel less discomfort when the blood dried in my veins?"

"I've nothing against pleasure," Zorachus replied. "But perhaps there are kinds, very deep kinds, that don't fade with age, that you never bothered to investigate."

Tchernaar shook his head adamantly. "Nothing worthwhile could've escaped me."

"You're sure?"

Tchernaar nodded. "It would be splendid if I were wrong, of course. Certainly I want more than I can get from life. But there simply isn't any more."

Zorachus laughed. "Have you experienced everything in the world? Have you studied philosophy? Prayed to any of those Powers, as you call them? Is it inconceivable to you that there are joys that surpass the giving and receiving of pain and humiliation?"

Tchernaar smiled bitterly. "I know perfectly well what's available in the realm of metaphysics. It's very much the same sort of thing we have here. How could one realm be so totally different from another? Friction may be supplied by an alien slit, but it's still friction. The blood may be a different color, the screams of pain perfectly uncanny; but one tires of such things just the same. There's nothing more than what we have. The universe is meaningless chaos. It signifies nothing more than the gurgle of vomit in a drunken beggar's throat. Our only refuge is pleasure, and that can't last. But it becomes that much more vital for us to hurl ourselves into our senses, to escape the truth. We must let our senses enslave our minds. We must be devoured, just as Drathazcar was. We must sample all distractions, drink from every cesspool, leave no sanctuary undefiled. And when we reach the limits of our capacity to delude ourselves, there's only one alternative. . . . "

The envoy gulped, nodded to himself, and went on. "You know, Drathazcar's face still haunts me. Even more than the girl's. There could be few things more exquisite than what he felt." He laughed. "Pardon me, my Lord. There *is* a pleasure I haven't sampled yet. But I will soon. I *must* do it soon. The old grow insensitive. They slide too gradually to their deaths..." His eyes took on a shimmering delirium. "I'll seize my chance while I can still savor it. It'll be even better than a slit throat. I'll surpass Drathazcar.... Lord Kletus gave me a present. A jar full of worms. I'll use them at the banquet." He giggled.

"What do you mean?"

"You'll see. You'll be there to watch my face. You'll see." Tchernaar glanced up through the latticed ceiling. "Why, we're almost to the top." He began to hum a little tune.

Zorachus looked away from him, wondering if God Himself could touch such a soul. The Sharajnaghi's mind boggled at the miracle it would take.

Chapter 6

Shortly the cage came up in a broad stone hall. Narrow windows admitted knifelike shafts of sunlight, and racks of mailshirts and polished weapons lined the walls. A marine stood guard at each door.

The cagekeeper went to the gate and threw it open. Zorachus and Tchernaar strode through, followed by their troops. The envoy drew the Sharajnaghi aside by a table where a clerk was working. The clerk looked up, but before he could speak a great commotion began. The doorwards had guessed who Zorachus was and were calling other men to come and see; perhaps a score of blackclads came rushing toward Zorachus's party. Tchernaar was nonplussed to learn that word of his mission had filtered down to the lower ranks, but he recovered sufficiently to say that Zorachus was not Zorachus at all; Lord Mancdaman, it seemed, had decided to remain on the ship.

"This is merely his retainer," the envoy explained.

Disappointed, the crowd receded. Tchernaar was pleased; word of Zorachus's arrival would have spread swiftly and he did not like the idea of a mob dogging the party through the streets of Khymir.

The envoy turned back to the clerk, pointing to Zorachus. "Lord Mancdaman's retainer is of Khymirian blood, but was raised in the south."

Looking at the, Sharajnaghi, the clerk said: "Within two weeks you must attend a demonstration in New Execution Square." He droned on in a bored voice, which clearly indicated he had recited the words many times. "There you'll see what becomes of those who plot against the Black Priesthood..."

"It's an exhibition by swordsmen of the Cohort Ravener," Tchernaar broke in. "The Cohort is the Priesthood's elite guard."

"All newcomers are required to attend," the clerk went on, "under penalty of death. Give me your hand."

Zorachus extended it and the clerk pressed it with a stamplike device. The Sharajnaghi examined his hand, but could see no mark.

"You're now the proud bearer of an invisible---and permanent---brand," Tchernaar said. "Only specially trained agents of the Priesthood can see it. It tells when you were stamped. When you go to the demonstration, you'll be given another. If you went more than two weeks without the second, you'd be assassinated by the first agent that noticed."

"There's an exhibition every third day," the clerk said. "One should be starting within the hour."

Tchernaar nodded. The group passed from the hall. On the way to the street, the envoy had to explain to various guards three times that Zorachus was not Zorachus. Finally, Tchernaar put his hood up; if people did not recognize him, they would not guess who Zorachus was, either.

Leaving the armory, the group pressed northward. Zorachus was amazed by the number of stone buildings he saw; everything seemed to be masonwork. Minor gods were supplicated in temples every bit as huge as the great shrine of El-Sharaj in Thangura.

The streets were thronged with people, churning floods of them, gaudily dressed Khymirians, turbaned Kadjafi sailors, Tarchan merchants in austere homespun, Urguz and Mirkut wanderers in handsome tooled-leather vests and trews. This was Khymir's Foreign Quarter; a hundred tongues merged in a steady yapping babble, interwoven with shouts and laughter. Musical instruments twanged and rattled from streetside inns. Animals bleated and lowed in mangers and butcher shops. The smells were thick and cloying; the Khymirian burial-spice perfume would have been nauseating if unalloyed, but luckily it had to compete with the perfumes favored by the various nationalities, as well as raw sewage running in the gutters, animal manure, decaying offal, and rank human sweat.

Amid all that, Zorachus caught the pungent scent of Kadjafi goat's-milk cheese, and instantly was acutely aware that he eaten only once since rising from his trance. Finding the stall where the cheese was being sold, he had Tchernaar buy him a hunk of it, some bread and a bottle of wine. The company proceeded. Zorachus polished the meal off in minutes as he walked along.

While he was eating he had paid virtually no attention to his surroundings; hunger always made him single-minded. But now he began to feel a deepening claustrophobia, as if he were crawling through a narrowing tunnel. Indeed, the streets were narrowing, and growing more heavily packed; the frowning stone piles on either side developed ledges and balconies that leaned out against the sky and blotted the way in shadow. The facades grew more and more ornate, and precarious-looking, some kissing above the passersby; catwalks and bridges arched between opposing windows and roofs. Sticky fluids dripped down, and stalactites of unknown substances depended from the overhangs. Stinking, bloated insects hovered in the thick air.

Zorachus noticed that the myrrh-aloes scent had grown considerably. They were now well out of the Foreign Quarter, and while there were still many foreigners on the streets, they were far outnumbered by the Khymirians. There was less racket; indeed, there were often short lulls in the street pandemonium, like pauses between breaths, and then the shuffle and squelch of feet in offal-choked alleyways could be heard, and low moanings from the leaning windows; the very houses seemed to be whispering to each other, and the stinking insects droned. Squalid images assaulted the Sharajnaghi's eyes: old women roasting skinned rats over a small fire, consumptive children with painted faces peering out of dark doorways and licking their lips at passersby, squinting cripples with festering, fly-ridden bodies, leering up from dollies or stumping along on crutches. Realizing he was still holding the empty wine bottle, Zorachus tossed it onto a mass of offal bulging out of a hole in a crumbling, mold-splotched wall. The bottle started a small avalanche of garbage; among other things, a bare, blackened rotting human foot was revealed.

The company entered an area with many shops. Pornographic statues writhed along window ledges, flanked by wooden phalli. Mummified crocodiles and cockatrices could be seen hanging from the ceilings of apothecaries' nooks. In one such shop, Zorachus saw a huge pot belching plumes of yellow smoke, and a wizened little man pulling some sort of pale hide out of it with a pair of tongs. Part of the skin drooped over the tongs, swaying and dripping; empty eye holes stared blankly, and a mouth sagged open in a silent steaming howl. The wizened man looked critically at the sacklike human face and lowered the hide back into the cauldron.

The company turned onto an unusually crowded street. It was lined with brothels, and though the group had already passed a dozen or so whorehouses, none had been as large or ornate as these. Each house catered to a different clientele, and before them were stages squirming with live demonstrations. Every permutation of the sex act was on display, and most of the stages revolved so that no one might be deprived a glimpse of pumping genitals.

After the apothecary's cauldron, Zorachus thought the demonstrations a relative improvement, but there was stronger fare up ahead. Hot brands sizzled pinioned flesh, and wheels popped arms from sockets; one lavish house, its facade painted to look as if it were splattered with fresh blood, even sported a gruesome echo of Tchernaar's tale: a swarthy, hook-nosed man atop a black woman, both driving small knives slowly and repeatedly into each other's flesh, their faces idiotically slack.

"That's it!" Tchernaar exclaimed. "That's the way Drathazcar looked! Have you ever seen anything so pure? So empty?"

"Never," Zorachus said, in all honesty.

"Genuinely inspiring," Tchernaar said. "Strengthens my resolve. Must use the worms. Simply must." His chest swelled; he nodded.

Shortly, passing through a line of marines after Zorachus's hand was stamped a second time, they entered New Execution Square. Once inside, Non-Khymirians were not allowed to leave; all the exits were blocked with troops.

The square was two hundred yards on a side. To the north, it was bordered by a crumbling stone wall some forty feet tall, part of an abandoned, partially collapsed temple. A platform bulged out from the wall's center, and before it a crowd of perhaps a thousand had gathered, and more were arriving all the time. Zorachus's group headed for the throng.

"Do you see those fellows tied to the stakes on the platform?" Tchernaar asked.

After the gloom of the streets, Zorachus's eyes were not used to the hazy sunshine. He squinted, making out ten men.

"What's going to happen to them?" Zorachus asked.

Tchernaar smiled knowingly. "Something drastic."

"If this exhibition's for newcomers," Zorachus said, "Why's it held so far from the Foreign Quarter?"

"My masters have more on their minds than making life easy for foreigners."

"What do you mean?"

"The Merchant's Guild controls the southern part of the city. But the Guildsmen publicly acknowledge the authority of the Priesthood---as long as they're granted certain favors, and a good deal of autonomy. They were disturbed when foreign patronage of the brothels in this area dropped off recently; they wanted more traffic flowing through. The demonstrations used to be held near the armory, but the Priests agreed to move them to this square, as a favor to the Guild."

The group reached the outskirts of the crowd and pressed in, the blackclads shouldering a path to the front, where a semi-circle of marines hemmed the throng, keeping it well back from the platform.

Zorachus looked at the men tied to the stakes. All were naked and had received cruel and recent beatings. Six were blond Kragehul giants; the remaining four were redhaired, with brandmarks shaped like black hands on their foreheads.

Now and then children in the crowd would pry up cobblestones and hurl them at the captives; fully one-third of the throng was made up of noisy Khymirian youngsters. The others were mostly adult foreigners.

"All these children," Zorachus said, "and so few Khymirian adults. Why?"

Tchernaar laughed. "No matter how wonderful a spectacle is, it gets tiresome if you see it too many times. When these cubs reach their teens, they'll be bored with this, on to something else…"

Soon after, Zorachus noticed the children quieting, the adults following suit. Once the crowd was silent, he heard a sound like the rush of a sword slashing the air. It seemed there was only one blade, but the sound seemed distant, too far off to be the rush of a single edge. It came from the east, growing louder all the time, and presently the crowd drew back from the wall on the eastern side; Zorachus saw something glittering over their heads. The rushing grew still louder, and shortly a file of tall men in red lacquered scales appeared, marching between the crowd and the wall, the marines letting them pass. The redclads wore crimson helms with cheekguards and neck-plates, and short curving horns on the sides; their scale-shirts had elbow-length shoulder guards and reached to their knees. The redclads moved with fluidity and practiced assurance, their only sound that fearsome whooshing as they performed a five-stroke drill again and again, holding their blades with both hands, slashing vertically right, then left, then right-left-right in three descending horizontal strokes, swords blazing like metallic fire.

Never faltering in their intimidating rhythm, they reached the platform steps, marched to the top, and lined up before the prisoners.

One of the Kragehul grinned with smashed lips and shouted a few lines that sounded like verse. The other Kragehul laughed. The men with the branded foreheads began to scream, offering bribes, begging mercy.

As if in answer, the redclads tripled their gleaming strokes.

The Kragehul who had shouted spat at the swordsman before him. Zorachus could not see if he hit his mark.

Abruptly, the redclads went motionless, swords stopping short in midair.

The Kragehul prisoners eyed the blades calmly, smiling; the others continued to scream, faces writhing under the shadows of the swords, the foam of terror bursting from their lips. For ten long seconds the blades hung motionless.

Then the redclads loosed a thunderous cry and stepped forward, slashing; in a moment the drill was done. The victims simply seemed to burst apart in tremendous splashes of blood, arms severed at the shoulders, heads flying, torsos sliced through below the shortribs, legs at mid-thigh.

The redclads stepped back, swords motionless once more.

The crowd gasped, finally reacting. There was scattered applause, mostly from the younger children.

Dripping, the redclads resumed their drill; turning, they went down the steps, rounding the stage to the west. The crowd quickly opened a path along the wall.

Zorachus pondered what he had seen. Much as he had been revolted by the slaughter, he was extremely impressed by the way it had been carried out. He had never seen anyone but Sharajnaghim use horizontal strokes so devastatingly.

"Now don't tell me you didn't appreciate that, Lord Mancdaman," Tchernaar said. "You being such a fine swordsman and all."

"Is the whole cohort that good?" Zorachus asked.

"That was a special squad. Still, I've heard it said---by people who would know---that the redclads are the finest swordsmen in Thorgon Karrelssa. But after hearing about your deeds on the ship, I wonder if you Sharajnaghim…"

"If I were you," Zorachus broke in, "I'd try to avoid hasty generalizations."

Tchernaar smiled, thinking it a joke.

The crowd was dispersing. "Let's be off," the envoy said, and the company headed east.

"Could've used some of those men during the sea-fight," Zorachus said.

"True," Tchernaar answered. "But they don't leave the city---part of a tithe agreement. The Guildsmen pay half their upkeep---"

"Do they?"

"---in exchange for a promise that the redclads won't be used in 'foreign adventures.' The Merchants would've been particularly insistent if they'd known what Lord Kletus was up to..."

"So you didn't inform them."

Tchernaar said: "The thought of you under his wing would've been most alarming to them. But once I was dispatched, Kletus must've let the word slip, to create a sense of anticipation...in any case, it was thought the convoy would be enough to bring you back safely."

"Should've sent some redclads anyway." Zorachus wiped sweat from his brow. "Are there many Khymirians in the Cohort?"

"Why do you ask?"

"Just wondering."

"They're mostly foreigners," Tchernaar said. "Nine out of ten. The Great Mother bears few real warriors these days."

Zorachus had suspected as much.

They left the square and eventually turned north on a wide boulevard flanked by palatial homes. A quarter-mile or so ahead, the mansions gave way to colossal black columns, and at the end of the pillared stretch rose Banipal Khezach, a mountain unto itself, bastion upon bastion, culminating in the titanic, sky-raking black spike.

"You're taking me to the tower?" Zorachus asked.

Tchernaar shook his head. "Your palace. That house on the right. The big one." A monstrous mass of black stone, it stood head and shoulders over the buildings nearby.

"I'm surprised it's not closer to the tower," Zorachus said.

"Why? Because your father was High Priest?"

Zorachus nodded

Tchernaar said: "He was the scion of a noble family, and the palace predated Banipal Khezach...it *was* strange that he chose to spend so much time there, but eccentric behavior was positively expected of him after a while. Things *were* a good deal slacker then, but even so it was unheard-of for a man in his position to take a wife, let alone one who was the High Priestess of a rival cult. The fact that he made no secret of you was also most unusual, although the mob loved it...anyway, the palace was given to one of his lieutenants once your father was killed."

After a time the company reached the palace's outer gate. The gatewards crossed their halberds, but they recognized Tchernaar when he pulled his hood back and they raised the weapons. Looking at Zorachus, they guessed his identity but said nothing, dumbstruck. Zorachus entered, went only a few yards before he halted, staring at the palace.

For all its height, it seemed squat and oppressive. The first story was marked by a line of heavy, bulging columns, the upper stories by fluted pilasters; there were many balconies and tall windows, and scrollwork abounded. Carven nudes entwined next to rearing monsters, all of them wrapped in stone tendrils and about to be buried under avalanches of black fruit.

"Quite a sight, eh?" Tchernaar asked.

Zorachus nodded blankly and looked back down, feeling a bit of a headache. They started forward again.

The walkway bisected a garden of gaudy, waxen-looking flowers. The blossoms gave off a thick scent similar to myrrh and aloes; Tchernaar's perfume was utterly lost in it. Attracted by the smell, bloated, buzzing insects lit on the flowers and crawled inside, vanishing under heavy petals. Zorachus never saw any of them come back out.

He and the others reached the massive stone steps and went up to the doors. The brazen valves were taller than three tall men, the knockers so heavy that Tchernaar needed both hands to lift one. He banged once. A postern opened.

"Lord Tchernaar," said a guard, "is that *him*?"

Tchernaar laughed. "What do you think?" he said. The guards let them through. The envoy leaned close to the man who had spoken, and said: "Fetch Louchan."

The guard, wide-eyed, looked Zorachus over one last time and dashed off shouting. His cries roused a racket that quickly spread through the house, and servants and men-at-arms began to pour from the doorways, emptying into the chamber whispering and pointing. Finally, a tall bald man appeared with the guard Tchernaar had sent off.

"Lord Mancdaman," Tchernaar said, "Kirmar Louchan, head steward of your household."

Louchan bowed, the guards and servants all following suit.

"And so," Tchernaar told Zorachus, "my mission's done. I must report to the tower. But I'll see you tomorrow night, I think---for the last time, if my Master permits." He bowed. "Your Lordship." Then he left, the marines with him.

Zorachus eyed Louchan. The Steward was clad in purple robes and seemed to be a young man, but his skin was jaundiced, as if from age. His eyes were pale green, almost yellow; the left seemed to be a trifle crossed and had a catlike slit-pupil. Zorachus realized it must be made of glass, and noticed a thread-thin scar running from forehead to chin, bisecting the eyesocket.

"How might I serve you, my Lord?" Louchan asked unctuously.

Zorachus thought a bit. "Tell me how you feed this household."

"We have certain plants---"

"Take me to them," Zorachus broke in.

"Right now?"

"Right now."

Louchan shrugged and turned, signaled two guards forward. "The rest of you, back to work!" The crowd scattered. "Follow me, my Lord."

Flanked by the guards, the Sharajnaghi walked behind him. At first the hallways were wide and lavishly decorated; there were statues in marble and bronze, vivid murals, and medallions on the ceilings, all of it wonderfully wrought and extremely pornographic. But presently the lewd opulence vanished, and the corridors narrowed; the group had entered an area of workshops and storerooms. Louchan stopped before an iron-braced door.

"We have to keep the garden closed up tight," he said, fishing out the proper key. "Otherwise, there's a good deal of pilfering. You'd think we never fed the help..."

The lock snicked and he opened the door. He and Zorachus went in, the guards remaining outside.

The garden chamber was high-ceilinged and very large, dimly lit by several murkily tinted crystal skylights. The air was humid, even for

85

Khymir, and curiously odor-free, although it did have a strange, rusty *taste.*

Like blood, Zorachus thought.

The floor was dirt; arranged at regular intervals were nestlike whorls of pale intertwined finger-thick creepers, the vines leafless but covered with small nodules that twitched and shimmered. Cradled like eggs in each whorl were a dozen or more bulbous fruit, glowing faintly, bloodily; from the center of each clutch rose several transparent, yellow-glowing tubular growths filled with pulsing fluid, and these snaked up poles set in the earth nearby, into the naked human bodies pinioned near the tops, entering the major veins of forearms and thighs.

Sickened, Zorachus squinted through the twilight at the slaves. Most of their faces were vacuous, but the eyes of a blond man and woman near the front burned down at him. The man was huge, muscled like a war horse, handsome but for a broken nose. The woman was long-limbed and broadhipped, with large breasts; her face was round, pretty, and snub-nosed, her tangled yellow mane hanging down over her shoulders.

Zorachus said: "That blond pair in front---"

"My Lord?" Louchan asked.

"What did they do?"

"To get themselves hung up there? The man was a gladiator---killed the best fighter from the stable that eventually bought his master out. When his new owner heard we needed blood-slaves---"

"What about the woman?"

"Came with the man. His original master wanted to pacify him, decided he'd better not break them up---saw he was dealing with a couple of *genuine* barbarians. They simply refused to get used to Khymirian ways. But the second owner---well, he kept them together to twist the knife. You should've seen him when we strung them up. He was so happy that he just started jigging….heart gave out. He collapsed right where you're standing. Then it was their turn to laugh."

"They're Kragehul?"

"Yes."

"Do they understand Khymirian?"

"Very well."

86

"If they were separated from the plants, would they live?"

"If their wounds were tended."

"What about the other slaves?"

"They're too far gone."

"I see," Zorachus replied.

Must put a stop to this, he thought. A Sharajnaghi was not duty-bound to oppose every evil he encountered; he could use discretion, particularly if some larger matter were involved. But complicity was strictly forbidden, and Zorachus was the master of the house, the slaves his chattel.

"I want every plant in this chamber rooted up and burned," he said.

At the words, Louchan's mouth dropped open.

Zorachus went on: "The slaves will be allowed to die unmolested. The ones who are 'too far gone,' that is."

Louchan seemed, if anything, more puzzled by this command than he was by the first. "And after they're dead?"

"They'll *remain* unmolested. And receive decent burial."

"What about those Kragehul?"

"See to it they get the finest care. When would they be ready to walk?"

"Tomorrow morning, perhaps. But---"

"Bring them to my chamber then."

Louchan nodded, but he was plainly very agitated.

"What's wrong?" Zorachus asked.

"Why destroy the garden, my Lord?"

"It's dangerous."

Louchan cocked his head forward, squinting with his real eye. "Dangerous, my lord?"

Zorachus spun out a story: "About five years ago, a member of my erstwhile order conducted a series of experiments…"

"Experiments---?"

"On plants that had fed on human blood or flesh. He concluded that such growths absorb spiritual residues from the corpses. On battlefields, or in other places where there's been much killing, the plants are imbued with rage, and they're quite capable of inflicting considerable harm. Fatal and near-fatal accidents happen with distressing frequency to people living near such plants....am I correct in assuming that all the slaves in this room were hung up without their consent?"

"All but two, as far as I know. But---"

"Surely you realize the implications. The plants must be absolutely *humming* with hatred."

"I've never heard any humming---"

Zorachus declared: "I will *not* allow myself or my servants to be jeopardized by malign residues!"

Louchan rubbed his bald pate. "We Khymirians have been using these plants since time immemorial, Lord Mancdaman, and we've never had any trouble."

"What about that fellow whose heart gave out?"

"He had a bad heart."

"Hmm." Zorachus said. "Perhaps I should investigate for myself. But until the matter's settled, I want to be on the safe side."

Louchan sighed. "And you don't want anyone to play with the bodies?"

Zorachus nodded.

"Why? Some of the guards could have a splendid time with them. It would keep their morale up."

"When the plants are destroyed," Zorachus answered, "those residues will rejoin the spirits of the victims. Surely you realize the implications..."

"No, my Lord."

"If the bodies are abused, the spirits will be much more inclined to linger. To seek revenge."

"I see," Louchan said heavily.

Zorachus smiled, pleased with his inventions. They were actually quite plausible, conflicting with nothing he knew about the spiritual realm; he had, in fact, heard similar notions seriously proposed.

"You know, Lord Mancdaman," Louchan said, "There are a great many mouths in your household. Once the garden's gone, we'll have to use imported food, and it's not cheap---"

"I'm a vastly wealthy man, am I not?" Zorachus asked.

"Your strongroom overflows."

"Then there's no problem," Zorachus said cheerfully. "Buy as much imported food as you need. Dispose of whatever blood-fruit you have around the house---anything made from it as well. Get rid of it today. And I don't mean by feeding it to the staff."

"What about dinner?" Louchan demanded.

"I won't be having any tonight, I think. As for everyone else, use whatever foreign food you have around. If there isn't enough, go out and get more."

Louchan nodded, muttering under his breath, sweat dripping from his nose.

Zorachus's eyes drifted to the Kragehul. He smiled at them; the fury of their glares doubled in reply. Undoubtedly they were imputing all sorts of horrible motives to him, but he could only appreciate their anger.

Not Khymirians! he thought. After weeks of going cheek by jowl with degenerates who seemed barely human, he couldn't *wait* to speak with the slaves. It troubled him---somewhat---that the man had been a gladiator, but that was kill or be killed, and Zorachus was no stranger to bloodshed himself....the fellow might even prove useful. Even before learning about the Kragehul's past, Zorachus had noted that he had the look of a formidible fighter---bodyguard material.

Louchan saw Zorachus studying them. "How do you want them dressed tomorrow?" he asked. "Any whim can be accomodated."

"Just dress them. Nothing fancy or strange."

"Very well, my Lord."

"Now show me to my room."

They turned and made for the door, but before they reached it, Louchan tripped and fell violently. His glass eye rolled out. Snatching it up, he wiped it off, and Zorachus helped him to his feet.

"What did I tell you?" Zorachus asked. "Bad residues."

Louchan said nothing, replacing his eye.

They went back out into the hall and the guards flanked Zorachus once more. Louchan closed up the room, then led the way to the second floor.

When they came to the door of Zorachus's chamber, Louchan unlocked it, swung it wide, and gave the key to the Sharajnaghi.

"Bring my breakfast at the Ninth Hour," Zorachus told him. "Bread, cheese, and butter. Also some strong wine. Bring the Kragehul at the same time. See there's enough for the three of us." He went inside. "Make sure I'm not disturbed tonight," he said over his shoulder, and shut the door.

Paying no attention to the room's sumptuously obscene decorations, he went to the bed, took off his swordbelt, and lay down. He was completely exhausted, drained by what he had seen that day; yet his insides still seethed with frustration. He had put a halt to the horror in the garden, but there had been so much else he had been powerless to stop ... For the thousandth time he wondered if he could fulfill his mission without snapping. His mind returned to that delirious instant back on the ship, when he had thought of blasting his allies with the demon-rings. How much greater would the temptation be when allies became mortal enemies? Confronted by one atrocity after another, would he find it irresistibly easy to respond with atrocities of his own?

Worn out as he was, he was a long time falling asleep.

Chapter 7

UPON WAKING THE following morning, Zorachus changed into fresh clothes and went out onto the balcony, which overlooked a great enclosure crowded with short, waxen-leaved trees. Flesh-colored blossoms nodded on the boughs, even though there was no breeze; here and there a fountain gushed, sending up ponderous foamless surges that looked more like clear oil than water. Facing each other, two gigantic bronze statues towered above the treetops, one a grimacing male nude poised to hurl a spear, the other a woman in flowing robes, baring her breast to receive the impact.

Thunder rolled off westward, muffled but menacing. Zorachus watched the clouds, noticing a purple-shadowed cavern yawning in one of them, flickering with red lightning. Four smaller holes widened slowly above, like eyes and nostrils over a gaping mouth. Zorachus knew the resemblance to a face was not accidental; the Presences were at work, he was sure of it, threatening the city they hated. For a time, the face stared hungrily towards Khymir, then shifted shape, becoming a huge menacing fist. Gradually the fist sprouted spikes, changing into a gauntlet, which melted in turn into a dragon-headed ship. Many of the other clouds had taken on the appearance of weapons, hammers and axes and bladed mauls, tinted red as though the vapors themselves were dyed with blood; a greenish serpent- shape reared up, reminding Zorachus briefly, ominously, of Zathlan, before it became a charging warrior. An opening appeared, very dark, shaped like the black-hand figureheads of Khymirian ships; it was soon smothered by a billowing avalanche of white.

Eyeing the thunderheads, Zorachus felt like a soldier on the battlement of a besieged fortress. A wall of magic held the spirits of earth and sky and water at bay for now. But he read the warning in the clouds, heard it in the thunder: *Our day will come.*

Eventually, the strange shapes vanished from the clouds. Yet even then the thunderheads lost little of their threatening look.

He went back into his room and was about to lie down again when he heard a knock; girding on his swordbelt, he went and opened the door.

Louchan entered, followed by a black slave with a folding table, and another with a tray of bread, cheese and butter. A tall red wine bottle reared up in the midst of the food. The slaves retired after setting the tray up, and Louchan signaled. Looking surly, the Kragehul slaves marched in, household guards at their backs with drawn swords.

"Everything satisfactory, Lord Mancdaman?" Louchan asked.

Zorachus nodded. "You can go. The guards too."

Louchan's face lengthened with dismay. "I think it would be better if they stayed, my Lord. The doorwards might not be enough. These slaves are dangerous."

"I don't think I'll have any trouble," Zorachus replied.

Louchan gestured helplessly. "But..."

"Obey me."

The Steward nodded and headed out with the guards. Zorachus went to the table and tore a chunk out of one of the thick round loaves.

"Are you hungry?" he asked the Kragehul.

They said nothing, eyes full of suspicion.

"More than enough here for the three of us," he said.

Their silence continued. Using a small spoon, he smeared cheese on the bread, then took a bite.

"It's very good," he said.

Still no response. He shrugged. Bread in one hand, wine bottle in the other, he backed over to a chair and sat down.

The Kragehul man looked at the table and said something to the woman in their tongue. They stepped up to the table, grabbed a loaf apiece, and started slowly towards Zorachus.

He eyed them calmly. They came closer and closer.

"Are you going to eat that bread or throw it at me?" he asked.

They glanced at each other as if he had discovered their hidden intention; then the man shouted and they hurled the loaves. It was a foolish-looking attack, but the bread was heavy and hard; Zorachus leaped sideways from the chair, and the missiles struck the chair's back with substantial thumps.

The Kragehul charged, the man holding a small knife that Zorachus had not noticed on the tray. The Sharajnaghi put the wine bottle on the chair and, still holding his cheese-smeared bread, drew his sword with his free hand.

The man reached him before the woman and lunged with the knife. Zorachus slapped it out of his hand with the flat of his sword and dodged the woman's flying tackle. Arms flailing, fingers outstretched, golden mane streaming, she sailed past him shrieking. Her mate went for the knife, but a kick from Zorachus bowled him across the floor.

A doorward poked his head in.

"Everything's under control!" Zorachus told him.

A moment later he heard a snarl and footbeats. Taking a bite of bread, he dropped to one knee, bending forward. The woman hurtled over him, landing hard.

The guard shouted and rushed in, sword drawn. Zorachus bounded up and sped past the woman, tossing the bread aside, sheathing his blade. Grabbing the guard's hauberk, he hurled him mightily at the second doorward, who was hard behind. Dropping their swords, the two rolled backwards in a tangle of arms and legs. The Sharajnaghi ran after them, and hardly had they regained their feet when he flung one through the door, then the other.

"Damn it all!" he cried, "I told you, everything's under control! Don't come in here again unless I call for you! That's an order!" He shut the door.

Turning, he saw that both Kragehul had recovered and were charging once more. He drew his blade again. The man, hardly pausing in his headlong rush, grabbed up one of the fallen swords, and with a roar, brought it down at Zorachus's head. The Sharajnaghi dodged, then dodged again as the woman dashed in, jabbing with the second sword. Knocking her senseless with a blow to the jaw, he pivoted to meet her companion blade for blade. The man was a splendid fighter. Before, Zorachus had disarmed him easily because of the unequal length of their weapons, but now, with the shorter blade, he was hard put to it. Back and forth they swept, feet clattering over the marble floor, steel clanging.

Finally, Zorachus knocked one of the Kragehul's legs out from under with a kick. The man fell heavily on his back. Leaping forward, Zorachus stamped the sword from the Kragehul's fist, kicked it aside, and placed his point at the fellow's throat.

"No more tricks," he growled. "I'll spare you if you let me."

Wind knocked out, the Kragehul could not speak for a time, but presently he gasped: "What do you want with us?"

"First off," Zorachus said, "swear on your honor that neither you--- nor your woman--- will try to escape, or attack me or my servants." He did not know if the man took his own honor seriously, but he was fairly sure that any reluctance to swear or attempt at trick wording would show that the Kragehul would consider himself bound.

"I won't attack you or your servants," the man said. "And I won't try to escape."

"Not good enough," Zorachus said. "You didn't mention your woman, and ..."

"She's my wife, you pig!" the Kragehul broke in.

Pleased the man thought the distinction important, Zorachus went on: "You didn't swear on your honor, either."

"I swear on my honor."

"Don't try to fool me," Zorachus snapped. "Give me the *whole* oath. All at once."

The Kragehul's face was purplish with rage. He looked as though he would spit venom. Zorachus pricked his neck, almost drawing blood, and said:

"Come on."

The Kragehul's face grew darker and darker, and he closed his eyes.

"Kill me," he said.

Zorachus saw his mistake. Obviously, the Kragehul thought all manner of horrors were in store for him and his wife--- and that the oath would leave them unable to resist.

"Please believe me," Zorachus said. "I mean you no harm."

"Tell me another," the Kragehul answered.

"How can you know what's on my mind?"

"I wouldn't put anything past you."

"I don't blame you. But why assume that you two are my idea of fun? My tastes might run to old men. Sheep. Carp. Those bread-loaves, perhaps..."

The Kragehul opened his eyes; he stared hard at Zorachus.

"Why force me to kill you if you just don't know?" Zorachus pressed.

The barbarian hesitated a few seconds more---

Then swore the oath.

Satisfied with the wording, Zorachus was aware that he might still be trying to fool him; he had thought all along that the barbarian's reluctance might be pure sham. But he took the chance, withdrawing his sword. The Kragehul rubbed his throat.

Zorachus got the man's blade and pulled the woman's from her unconscious grip. Returning to the door, he opened it and handed the weapons back to the guards, who looked at him sheepishly.

"Quarrel's over," he announced, and closed the door again, going to the table. Sheathing his sword, he tore off another chunk of bread and smeared cheese on it.

The Kragehul man was over by his wife now, kneeling beside her. She was coming to. He took one of her hands and stroked it.

"She'll be wide awake soon," Zorachus said after a swallow of bread. "I only tapped her." Taking another bite, he asked between chews: "How are your wounds holding up? The ones where the plants were attached?"

The man examined his bandages and looked at the ones on his wife, pushing her shift up to look at the dressing on her thigh.

"Any blood?" Zorachus asked.

The man shook his head. "Catgut works wonders."

"Even so," Zorachus said, "You're lucky you didn't spring a leak while we were fighting. A thigh wound's bad business---though I expect you know that from your gladiator days."

The Kragehul eyed him narrowly. "Why are you so interested in our health, you Khymirian dog?"

The epithet stung. "I wasn't raised in Khymir," Zorachus replied. "I'm only Khymirian by blood. Do you know anything about me?"

"I heard one of the gardeners talking about you. Your father was High Priest of the Black God."

"Well, to begin with," Zorachus said, "I'm not my father. Though I'd think that would be obvious." He finished his last two bites of bread.

The woman was fully conscious by then, and sat up. Her husband spoke to her in Kragehul, and her face pinched with shock and amazement; Zorachus guessed she had been told about the oath.

The man continued talking---explaining the mitigating circumstances, no doubt. Presently, his wife looked fiercely at Zorachus.

"What are you going to do with us?" she demanded.

The Sharajnaghi laughed. "What do you think?"

"That you want to fuck us. Why have us brought to your chamber?"

"You couldn't be more..." Zorachus stopped suddenly, realizing the room might be penetrated with listening holes, and that even now some spy of Kletus's might be eavesdropping; the High Priest had, after all, provided the household staff. Aching to reveal himself, to speak without having to conceal his detestation of everything Khymirian, Zorachus decided to shift the scene .

"Come out onto the balcony," he said, and picked up the tray. "We'll talk there." He went outside and put the tray down. It was some time before the Kragehul joined him. As they came up, he snapped his fingers and said, "The wine." Going back, he returned with the bottle.

"What are your names?" He asked.

"Halfdan Skarp-Hedinsson," the man replied. "My wife's name is Asa."

"Mine's Mancdaman Zorachus, as you already know; but I prefer proper introductions. When were you strung up in the garden?"

"A week ago," Asa said.

"Louchan said you two were very loyal to each other," Zorachus said. "That you wouldn't give in to Khymirian ways."

Asa nodded. "And we won't give in to you."

"How exactly would you go about resisting me?"

"We could kill ourselves," Asa said. "Halfdan swore nothing about that."

"But he did swear that you wouldn't try to escape. And suicide would be escape---of a sort."

"I don't know about that," Halfdan said.

"Moreover," Zorachus went on, "it wouldn't be easy. True, it's a good drop from this balcony, but I could probably keep you from jumping---one of you at least...you *will* wait until you're sure of my intentions, won't you?"

"We *are* sure of your intentions," Halfdan snapped.

"No you're not. You wouldn't have let me spare you. Believe me, I don't want to rape either of you. Or seduce you, for that matter."

"Why else would you have us taken down?"

"It made me sick to see those plants feeding on you."

Halfdan spat a laugh. "You expect us to believe that?"

"Just hear me out," Zorachus said. "How much do you know about the Kadjafim?"

"I've been to Fyrkaz."

"Do the people there grow crops with human blood?"

"Not as far as I know."

"Do you think they'd want such plants?"

"Probably not," the Kragehul admitted.

"They'd regard them as abominations, wouldn't they?"

"What's an abomination?"

"A very bad thing."

"Oh," Halfdan said.

"I was brought up by Kadjafim," Zorachus continued. "Their customs are my customs. When I say those plants horrify me, I speak the truth."

Halfdan rumbled deep in his throat.

"If I were lying," Zorachus said, "why would I order all the bodies taken down?"

"For the reason you gave Louchan," Asa said.

It was a good point. Zorachus paused. He thought for a while, but could come up with no better response than the truth. "That was nonsense I made up to hide my real reasons."

"Why did you have to hide your real reasons?" Halfdan inquired sarcastically.

"Yes, why?" Asa asked.

Zorachus blinked, scratched his head. He had been so anxious for their company that he had not anticipated any of this.

"Well?" Halfdan demanded.

97

Zorachus uncorked the wine and took a pull, then sat down beside the tray.

"What do you want with us, you bastard?" Halfdan growled down at him.

"Would you believe me if I said I simply wanted to talk to you?" Zorachus asked.

"Do you think we're idiots?" Asa snarled.

Zorachus looked up at them. In spite of his frustration, and the hatred in their eyes, he ached more than ever to prolong the conversation. He greatly admired their fierce loyalty to each other and their resistance to Khymir; he suddenly wished he could have not only their company but their friendship. He would need friends in the days ahead, people who would remind him that there was a world of sanity outside Khymir...

Having received no answer from the Sharajnaghi, Asa had started haranguing Halfdan in Kragehul. Zorachus waited till she was done, then asked:

"Would you agree to become my bodyguard, Halfdan?"

"Why would you want a Kragehul bodyguard?" Halfdan demanded.

"I don't trust Khymirians. Also, they seem to be poor fighters. They're too bent on preserving their own hides. That's a fault you don't have. And you're an expert with a sword."

"You beat me," Halfdan sulked.

"That doesn't mean I've no use for you. There's just so much one man can handle."

"But why should I agree to serve you?" Halfdan gritted, fists knotting at his sides. "I hate Khymirians."

Zorachus said: "I understand. I've seen so many loathsome things since I've been among them ... I'm a Sharajnaghi, Halfdan, and i've faced evil before, but..."

"Sharajnaghi?" Asa asked.

"It means *Bringer of Light*," Zorachus explained. "Sharajnaghim are members of the *Comahi Irakhoum*, a holy order of wizards."

"You're a holy man?" Halfdan asked incredulously.

"Well, I'm a member of the order."

"Why'd you come to Khymir?"

"I can't tell you."

"Then why should we believe you about anything?" Asa asked. "A holy man wouldn't come here. Not unless this city had something he wanted. In which case he wouldn't be too holy, would he?"

"He came to get his inheritance," Halfdan put in. "Louchan said he would." He grinned down at Zorachus. "You like gold too much, holy man."

"Do you like gold?" Zorachus asked.

"Of course. But I don't pretend not to. I don't try to seem better than I am."

"I don't imagine you do," Zorachus answered. "But that's beside the point. Will you become my bodyguard?"

"Do I have any choice?"

Zorachus nodded. "If you refuse, I'll free you both and you can leave Khymir."

"I'll refuse," Halfdan assured him.

"However," Zorachus continued, "If you stay, you'll be freed just the same. And when I no longer need your swordarm, you'll leave this city an extremely rich man. I'll pay you fantastically well. Money means nothing to me."

Halfdan jeered. "If that were true, you wouldn't have come here in the first place."

"If it weren't true, would I have ordered the garden ripped up? That was a very expensive command."

Halfdan grumbled something under his breath.

Zorachus asked: "If I'm so greedy, why am I offering you so much? Just think. If you go now, you'll go as a penniless freeman. If you help me, you'll leave with more gold than you could carry in a wagon."

"You're insane," Halfdan said with great conviction.

"I'm nothing of the sort. I think you'll discover that for yourself---if you give me a chance."

"You're trying to trick me."

Zorachus shook his head. "I don't have to trick you. I don't even have to bribe you, though I've tried my best. You owe me much. You and Asa both. I saved you from the plants, and I could have killed you when you attacked me. I won't force you to repay those debts; if you insist on leaving, I'll let you go. But I don't think you will." He did not know if the Kragehul would feel themselves obligated, but the gamble paid off. Halfdan's face darkened once more, and he and Asa launched into a furious conversation in Kragehul. Finally, he looked back down at Zorachus and said:

"I'll be your bodyguard."

"Very good," Zorachus replied.

"Can Asa stay with me?"

"Of course. You two can have the room next to mine. Whenever I don't need your services, you can keep each other company." He took another pull of wine, and offered the bottle to Halfdan. "Have a drink---to seal our agreement."

Looking sullen, Halfdan hesitated before taking the bottle---then downed several gulps.

"Good stuff," he said sourly, wiping his lips.

Zorachus nodded. He knew the vintage. "Thanguran, thirty years old. We Sharajnaghim use it on feast days."

Halfdan handed the bottle to Asa. She sipped it delicately, her drinking style coming as a surprise to Zorachus; dressed in a shapeless grey shift of coarse fabric, hair unbound, she looked too barbaric to be capable of anything so ladylike.

"It's no good drinking on an empty stomach," Zorachus said. "Have some food. There's plenty, and one shouldn't let things go to waste."

"You sound like my mother," Asa said.

"She sounds like a very intelligent woman," Zorachus replied. He patted the tessellated pave. "Take the weight off your feet."

They sat down across from him. Halfdan was the first to start eating. Asa watched him for a few moments, almost as if she expected him to spit the food back out; then she followed his example. Both ate with tremendous vigor, Halfdan almost savagely, Asa with a quiet grace that utterly belied the amount of food she was packing away. Zorachus also did his share. The wine bottle went round and round, and the food pile shrank. Finally, tray and bottle were empty, and the trio reclined on the checkered stone. Resting on one elbow, Zorachus eyed his new confederates.

"How did you like that?" he asked.

"Well enough," Halfdan said. "But don't think we're off guard because we're stuffed."

"I wouldn't think anything of the sort," Zorachus replied. "But---" there was a knock at the door inside. "What now?" he wondered aloud as he rose.

"Do you want me to come with you?" Halfdan asked.

"You're my bodyguard," Zorachus replied, and went to answer the door--- Halfdan got there first and opened it. Louchan entered, arms tucked inside his hanging sleeves, yellow forehead beaded with sweat.

"Well?" Zorachus asked.

The steward said: "News of your arrival has spread, my Lord---"

"And?"

"A crowd of beggars has gathered outside."

"What, to catch a glimpse of me?" Zorachus laughed, then realized the idea was not so absurd--- hadn't Kletus brought him back precisely to play to the mob?

Louchan said: "A handout would satisfy them, I think---"

"Are these beggars organized?"

"There are several gangs---no one would give them anything otherwise."

"And just how big *is* this crowd?"

"I don't know. Five, six thousand maybe...they've been gathering since dawn."

"Why didn't you inform me earlier?"

"It wasn't so bad at first, and afterward I feared to intrude. You did want to be alone with your guests. I thought of sending a messenger to the tower, to fetch enough troops to drive the scum off, but then I thought you might want to make some kind of gesture. The Priests must think so too, otherwise they would've acted on their own. Word must've reached them...."

"Is the crowd very quiet? I was just out on the balcony and I heard nothing."

"It's almost as if they want to make a good impression. Your father was so well respected. But I expect they'll get ugly if they don't get a response soon. What are you going to do, my Lord?"

"I certainly don't want to offend anyone unnecessarily," Zorachus answered. "I'll go and speak to them."

"If I were you, my lord..."

Zorachus shook his head. "I'd better go out." He nodded towards Halfdan. "This is my new bodyguard, by the way. Give him the room next to mine. See to it that he's armored to his satisfaction before the afternoon's out. He'll be coming with me tonight."

"Where?" Halfdan asked.

"A banquet. At Banipal Zhezach."

The Kragehul grunted.

"Another thing about Halfdan here," Zorachus told Louchan. "He's to be freed."

"Me too," Asa broke in, having just come up.

"Her too," Zorachus said. "And while you're procuring their papers, get enough for the rest of my chattel."

"You want to free *all* your slaves, my Lord?" Louchan asked, incredulous.

"Yes. Slaves hate their masters. They're untrustworthy. But once they're freed, they're grateful."

"Grateful, my Lord? Most of them will just up and leave immediately."

"So? Hire replacements. I will not tolerate an unhappy household...but in the meantime, we'd best see to the beggars."

In the hall they were joined by several guards Louchan had brought; going downstairs, they passed outside, entered one of the small towers flanking the gate, and went to the top, where Zorachus looked out over the throng of mendicants. He could not help but pity them; squatting or sitting on the cobbles, some were nearly naked, while others seemed little more than shapeless bundles of rags, scratching at themselves under their tatters. Many were horrendously deformed, and all were sewer-filthy; flies swarmed over the crowd. Thirty feet above the paupers, Zorachus could smell nothing but the stench of unwashed and diseased bodies.

He looked north and south along the street. Groups of mounted redclads waited on the outskirts of the crowd.

A murmur went up from the back of the throng: he had been noticed. Outstretching his arms, he cried in a great voice:

"Hear me! I am Mancdaman Zorachus!"

Scabby, grime-crusted faces lifted. Ragged figures leaped up; cripples scrabbled for crutches, prying themselves from the cobbles. A storm of voices rose. Zorachus made no attempt to stifle the uproar; it was a long time before the mob quieted.

"I'm a stranger in this ... *Remarkable* place, the city of my birth," he continued. "As yet, I have few friends here. But I'd like to change that; and to secure the goodwill of Khymir's less fortunate, I'll buy the largest granary in the city, and there will be a daily dole of Tarchan wheat."

The beggars thundered approval. He turned to see Louchan's reaction. The Steward was clearly appalled, rubbing his pate frantically with both hands, eyes closed in disbelief. Zorachus could not help but laugh. Nor could he help noticing how well his maneuvers were keeping Kletus's hireling off balance.

He looked at Halfdan and Asa. They too were thunderstruck; evidently he had proven his contempt for money.

He returned his gaze to the beggars. They were ecstatic, flailing their bandaged paws, blessing and thanking him. He was pleased--a few more such gestures, and he guessed he would have the allegiance of much of the Khymirian mob. But he was also glad he could feed so many people.

He waited once more for the racket to die down. "Furthermore, I'll contract with foreign dealers to keep the grain coming; no one will go hungry in Khymir if I can help it." There was another wild demonstration. But some in the crowd were not satisfied.

"Food's all right, my Lord," one cried. "But man doesn't live on bread alone!"

"What else do you want?" Zorachus asked. "Medicine, lodging. . . "

"Entertainment!" the beggar answered. "Open the whorehouses! Give us children with pretty backsides and fresh faces to slice! Let the arenas swim with blood!"

The others roared enthusiasm.

Zorachus's pity deserted him.

103

Your father gave his life for creatures like this? Truly he was a madman...

Where once the Sharajnaghi had seen victims, human beings trapped in the great mother's rotting womb, now he saw twisted monstrosities, filth-caked demons, things delighting in evil, their outer hideousness a mere reflection of the hideousness within. As he stared at them from on high, he told himself: *this is what it's like to be God, to see men as they really are...*

But instantly, this blasphemy brought him up short.

But you're not God, are you? So how would you know?

Wiping sweat from his face, trembling slightly, he silently begged God's forgiveness. Then, remembering his audience, he raised his hands, wondering how to satisfy the beggars without promising anything. Once they quieted, he said:

"Please bear with me---I just arrived yesterday. Once I'm better acquainted with what this city has to offer, I'll see to it that you share the diversions that I myself enjoy. Fair enough?"

The crowd clamored the affirmative. In the lull that followed, he cried:

"And so I take my leave of you, truly hoping I've won your affection. You're the people of my blood, and I pray my return to Khymir will usher in a new era of improvements!"

The crowd roared a final time. He and his escort went down from the tower. As they headed towards the front steps, Louchan pushed up beside him.

"A whole granary, my lord?" he demanded..

Zorachus paused at the foot of the steps. "The biggest in the city. I can afford it, can't I?"

"Yes, but..."

"Meet any price."

"Yes, my Lord."

"Have you seen to the garden?"

"It's being torn up as we---"

"Have you made new arrangements? To feed the household?"

"I'm well along---"

Zorachus broke in: "Make sure to take care of those manumission papers, too."

"Yes, my Lord."

"When you have the time, of course," Zorachus said, and headed up the stairs with the Kragehul and the guards. Louchan remained below; sitting on the lowest step, he buried his face in his hands.

Chapter 8

KLETUS'S TAILORS came just before the Twelfth Hour, accompanied by a train of slaves bearing bales of fabric and large pattern books. Lacking any ideas on how he should be attired, Zorachus told them to do as they thought best, which proved a mistake---he was deeply embarrassed by the results.

Their work took the better part of the afternoon; once they were done, he dismissed them, sent for Louchan and the Kragehul, then took a look in the mirror. He had tried to avoid looking at it while he was being fitted, thinking he had to rely on the tailors' judgement no matter what; what he had seen out of the corner of his eye had not been comforting. But now, confronting his reflection straight on, he realized that he should have rejected the tailors' ministrations altogether. They had him in a red-lined, emerald-dotted cloth-of-gold mantle, a heavily embroidered purple and crimson silk tunic, a broad python-skin belt, miserably hot black leather pants embossed with floral designs, and low boots crafted from the scaly blue hide of some unearthly reptile; dismayed as he was, he could only stand and stare, transfixed by the spectacle.

Louchan's arrival snapped him out of it; looking exhausted, the Steward had a sheaf of manumission papers.

"Thirty slaves in this house," he declared. "Had to hire five scribes to draw up the documents."

Seated at his desk, the Sharajnaghi signed each paper with a quill pen, asking Louchan about his errands all the while.

He signed Halfdan's and Asa's as they came in; Asa was hanging on her husband's arm, golden hair shining. The sight of her filled Zorachus with pure pleasure---for the first time, he saw she was not merely pretty; her beauty was so fresh and unrefined that it had fooled him. But that only made it more exhilarating to recognize.

She was still clad in the simple shift she had worn that morning, but her husband was now sumptuously outfitted. He had on a knee-length shirt of silvered chain-mail, and his conical helm was of brightly burnished steel; from his neck depended a large silver medallion, and a gold-hilted sword hung from his belt. As he neared Zorachus, he smiled.

"What?" Zorachus asked.

"Oh, nothing."

"What?"

"You're quite a sight, my Lord." Halfdan laughed again.

Louchan looked at Zorachus, clearing expecting him to rebuke the Kragehul. But Zorachus, redfaced, only handed Halfdan and Asa their freedom.

"What do these scribblings say?" Halfdan asked, squinting at the paper.

"That you're no longer my property," Zorachus replied.

Asa laughed for joy and beamed at him, then ran her eyes repeatedly over her document, feasting on the words, even though she was holding the paper upside down. Halfdan was more reserved; he looked Zorachus straight in the eye and thanked him earnestly.

Zorachus signed the last document in the stack and rose. "You can go now, Louchan," he said. "Make sure the papers are properly distributed."

"I will, my Lord," the Steward answered heavily. He took up the sheaf and left.

"Let's go out on the balcony," Zorachus said. This time the Kragehul followed promptly.

"That's a fine byrny, Halfdan," the Sharajnaghi said as they came out into the sunlight.

Halfdan looked down proudly at the silver-glinting links. "It's from Serkland---that is, your precious Kadjafi lands."

"I recognized the workmanship."

"I've got a shield too, but I left it in my room..." Halfdan paused, staring at Zorachus's clothes again. "Did you have any say about---?"

"Why the medallion?" Zorachus asked, pointing to it.

"You said I could armor myself exactly as I chose...silver wards off evil. That's why I wanted a silvered byrny as well. There are a lot of wizards in this city, and they're even worse than the other Khymirians."

"So I've heard," Zorachus said. "But..."

"But what?"

"Silver's only useful in rare situations...it affects only a few kinds of demons."

"I'll be protected from them, then."

"Yes."

"You should get a medallion too," Halfdan said. "A great *big* one, bigger than mine, to go with that tunic..."

"Enough."

"With a lot of fruit engraved on it..."

"You've made your point."

"You look like something I saw in a fever once."

Zorachus laughed. "It's just for tonight."

"What would happen if you wore something else---?"

"Can I have a garden, Master?" Asa broke in, looking hopefully at Zorachus.

Halfdan frowned. "Don't interrupt. And remember, he's not your Master anymore."

"You can both call me Zorachus," the Sharajnaghi said. "And yes, Asa, you can certainly have a garden."

She smiled. "I'll talk to the mason about it. He can wall a space on on our balcony and I'll have it filled with dirt."

"Hush," Halfdan said. "What makes you think Zorachus wants to hear your womanish prattle?"

"Haven't you ever wanted to hear womanish prattle?" Zorachus asked.

"Now and then. But there's a time and a place for everything. And when two men are talking, that's not the time."

Zorachus sighed. "I'm sorry, but I just spent a long voyage surrounded by men with nothing on their minds except torture and buggering each other, and it's good to hear a woman talking about gardens."

Halfdan mumbled something.

"I'll plant herbs and tomatoes," Asa said.

"What are tomatoes?" Zorachus asked.

"A kind of berry, I think. Not sweet, but delicious anyway. I bought some seeds in the market while Halfdan was being outfitted."

"Well, my blessing's upon them, for what it's worth. I'm already looking forward to the harvest."

There was a pause.

"You're a strange one," Halfdan said presently. "But I think we've got you figured out."

"Think so?"

"It was that business with the wheat that put us on to you," Halfdan continued. "Wheat's very expensive in Khymir. We decided you didn't come here for the money."

"Why then?"

"To take over the city," Asa said, "You're using food to buy support from the mob. But you'd better watch out."

"Why?"

"Remember those wizards I spoke of?" Halfdan asked. "You'll run up against them sooner or later."

"I'll deal with them," Zorachus said.

"With the Priests of Tchemobog?" Halfdan asked sarcastically.

Zorachus nodded. "I'm a Seventh-Level Sharajnaghi Adept. And we Sharajnaghim are the strongest wizards in Thorgon Karrelssa."

"I don't know," Halfdan said, eyeing him critically. "You don't look like much of a wizard to me."

"What should wizards look like?"

"The *powerful* ones are a lot older than you."

"What do you mean by powerful?"

Halfdan thought a bit and lifted his hands. "Powerful, you know."

"Like being able to transform things?"

"Like being able to lift them."

"Lift them?"

"That's the kind of power I'd like. Save me a lot of work."

"I see," Zorachus said. He knew of a binding-spell he could use without forceletting; the Influences were Right. Assuming a Griffin Stance, he uttered a formula, and before Halfdan knew it, he was floating three feet off the pave.

"Put him down!" Asa shouted, stamping her foot.

109

"Would you like to take a little whirl out over the treetops?" Zorachus asked Halfdan, who was gaping like a fish.

"No!" Halfdan cried.

Zorachus shrugged and lowered him. "How was that?"

"I'm convinced," Halfdan answered quickly.

Zorachus dropped stance and smiled.

Halfdan folded his arms on his chest. "Now."

Zorachus folded his arms too. "Now?"

"If you *do* take over..."

"Yes?"

"How will you treat my people?"

"I won't make war on them."

"That's good. You might be lying, of course. But you seem to be a just man, and seeming's all you can know about anyone, isn't it?"

Zorachus thought otherwise, but decided not to take issue.

Halfdan went on: "If you can keep my people from being attacked, I'll be honored to serve you."

"I'll promise you this," Zorachus said. "If my work here succeeds, the Kragehul will escape a great evil."

Halfdan grunted. "Good enough," he declared.

Not long afterward, word came that a palanquin and escort had arrived from Banipal Khezach.

"Well, Halfdan," Zorachus said, "We're off."

"And what am I supposed to do in the meantime?" Asa demanded.

"Surely you don't want to come with us," Zorachus said. "It's going to be vile."

"I don't want to be alone."

"Stay in our room and keep the door locked," Halfdan said.

"We won't stay any longer than we have to," Zorachus assured her. He turned to Halfdan. "Go down to the stables and get yourself a horse. Meet me around front."

They left the room, Zorachus going down to the front gate. A palanquin awaited him, attended by six muscular slaves and an armored overseer on horseback; a troop of redclads lounged against the wall.

"I'm Mancdaman Zorachus," the Sharajnaghi announced. The redclads snapped to attention.

"His Anointed Steward sends his greetings," one said, bowing.

The overseer motioned towards the palanquin. "For you, my Lord." He took out his whip, eyeing the slaves' broad backs.

"Wait a moment," Zorachus said. "I've a man coming."

The overseer nodded and rested the whip across his mailed thighs.

Zorachus stooped and lay down in the palanquin. It was heavily padded, voluptuously comfortable, the struts intricately carved; he looked up at the canopy. Beautifully painted in all-but-luminous colors, a naked fleshy woman and a greenish lamia arched over him, locked fiercely in each others' arms, bosom to bosom, the lamia biting the woman's neck, small trickles of blood crawling over the white flesh; Zorachus could not see much of the lamia's face, but the woman's was ecstatic, and she seemed to be looking at him sidelong…refusing to be engaged, he shifted his gaze, only to be captivated by the merging breasts. There was no clear line between them, just a soft dexterous blur, color into color, green flesh shading into pink…Zorachus felt a surge of heat in his loins. It was the first time anything Khymirian had aroused him; even on the street of brothels, amid those frenzied displays of carnality, had managed to keep the obscenity of it all uppermost in mind. But in this painting, obscenity seemed almost purified, *sanctified,* by the skill with which it was rendered; it was a wrench to tear his gaze away. He stared down at his hands. His palms glistened with sweat, much more than Khymir's heat could normally milk from them.

After what seemed an eternity, he heard hooves and leaned out of the palanquin. Halfdan rode near.

"All set, my lord," he called.

Zorachus gave a silent nod and signaled the overseer, whose whip hissed and cracked as the Sharajnaghi settled back.

111

"Hola, dogs!" the man cried. "Grab those poles!"

The slaves rushed to obey. The company started down the avenue of pillars towards Banipal Khezach.

Zorachus watched the columns slipping past for a while, but soon felt the urge to look back up at the canopy. It was all he could do to resist it, and he almost succumbed before something caught his attention on a strut beside him---an oval, carven face, leering knowingly at him with lecherous slitted eyes. The mouth hung open, twin tongues issuing from it, more heavily varnished than the rest of the face, seeming to glisten with yellowish saliva. One extended sideways, and a little globule of varnish hung from the tip. The other lolled down over the lower lip. Its tip curled, just a bit, and in the curl two tiny figures entwined. Despite his disgust, Zorachus looked closer. Intricately carved, a woman and a lamia embraced there, bosom to bosom, the lamia biting the woman's neck.

He looked away, and then, almost unconsciously, upwards; instantly he noticed (and wondered how he could not have noticed before) that the woman in the painting also had two tongues, one extending into the shadows on the far side of her face, the other hanging over her lower lip. And where the second curled, there was a small, oval, twin-tongued face leering down at him.

Feeling as though he were under some kind of direct spiritual assault, almost as if he was in the presence of the very degenerate who had invented these diseased images, he snapped his eyes shut and did not open them again until the palanquin came to a halt some time later. He got out as soon as it was set down.

Above him loomed the southern wall of Banipal Khezach, so tall that he could not see the central tower soaring beyond; the barrier almost seemed to be leaning over him, massive blocks rusty-hued in the late afternoon sun. Huge doors stood open; limned against a greyish glow, a line of redclads warded the threshold.

Halfdan dismounted, entrusted the horse to the overseer, and went with Zorachus to the threshold, the escort troops remaining behind.

As the pair neared the redclads at the entrance, a bizarre figure appeared behind the swordsmen and stumbled through: Tchernaar. He held a half-drained chalcedony wine cup, and was clad only in a studded leather harness that let his genitals dangle in plain sight--- he was plainly afflicted with some scrofulous venereal disease.

"Lord Mancdaman!" he cried, coming up close and tying to embrace him; Zorachus stepped back in disgust. Tchernaar followed, plucking at him, and Halfdan struck the envoy in the mouth. Tchernaar staggered and fell on his knees, blood dribbling over his chin.

Eager to be rid of him, Zorachus forgot momentarily that Tchernaar was probably intended as a guide, and he and Halfdan strode forward. The redclads letting them pass, they found themselves in a cavernous hallway, where they halted after a few moments, not knowing where to go, looking at their surroundings. Giving off a disastrous grey glow, the walls were carved into swirling bas-reliefs of life-size coupling bodies, every curve and depression of flesh brilliantly delineated. But for all their realism and wonderfully rendered action, the figures looked strangely lifeless. Zorachus guessed it was a trick of the light; everything seemed carved out of dead ash.

Suddenly he realized that his skin, for the first time since he passed inside the thunder-barrier, was no longer filmed with sweat; his mouth had gone dry. It was like moving from a steambath into a oven. Even so, he had an eerie impression that there was no real heat inside Banipal Khezach, that what he felt was coldness masquerading as its opposite....

Uncertain footsteps came from behind. He looked over his shoulder and there was Tchernaar, swaying and grinning, pointing to a small frosted-glass bottle hanging around his neck; it seemed to be full of some kind of squirming life.

"Worms," he giggled, drooling blood.

Zorachus turned again, but Tchernaar plucked at his arm, said, "Follow me, my Lord," and staggered down the hall. They followed a good distance along the corridor, then into a broad side passage, its black walls bare save for torches, and came to a redclad-flanked steel door. Tchernaar tripped a lever and the barrier slid back; they went through, the door closing noiselessly behind them.

It was dark inside, the only light coming from a few reddish gems glowing on the ceiling. Zorachus could barely make out the sides of a small, squat chamber.

"What now?" He asked. But before Tchernaar could reply, there was a lurch of upward motion.

"My master's lift," Tchernaar mumbled. "Only way up to his chambers. Makes it hard on the assassins. You have to think the right name..." He belched. "There's a demon beneath us, you see. Part of one, anyway. The rest of the body's in another dimension. The arm pushes up through the shaft, pumping up and down...."

The elevator halted and the door opened; they stepped into a narrow corridor and passed between two more redclads at its end, entering a large chamber whose floor and ceiling belled to form a concave lens. Zorachus knew the purpose of this architectural peculiarity; the room was designed to stifle sorcerous energies. He could feel that his powers were sealed inside him---there was a subtle but unmistakable pressure. Standing motionless, hands on hilts, ten Cohort Ravener swordsmen guarded the far door, five on either side of it.

Beyond stretched the banquet room of Kletus's quarters; lit by white orbs on pedestals, the hall was vast and windowless, walls, pillars and vaulted ceiling tricked out in gold-trimmed jade veneer.

The room was full of gaudily-dressed men and women, soldiers in various liveries, and black-robed figures Zorachus guessed were Priests of Tchernobog. Everyone seemed to be speaking or laughing at the top of their lungs. Ring-clotted fingers picked dainties from slave-borne trays, and electrum goblets gleamed against rouged lips. Some people lounged on the couches and pillows that had been arranged in a great circle in the middle of the room; others walked about. Mouths met hungrily and bodies rubbed against bodies. Hands palped and searched beneath sumptuous garments. Zorachus's first impulse was to turn on his heel, but he repressed it.

Nothing to be done, he thought.

Forehead deeply branded with the black hand, a bald man with an ebony staff appeared; he smiled broadly when he learned who had arrived, then turned and pounded the floor with his staff, the room resounding with the strokes.

"Lord Mancdaman Zorachus!" he announced.

The banqueters converged swiftly, and out of the throng came a huge man, a full head taller than Zorachus, clad all in black. He looked about fifty years old, with close-cropped grey hair and keen, vigorous blue eyes. His jaw was slablike, his brow massive and willful; his face radiated such dignity and confidence that Zorachus doubted he could be Khymirian. It was the countenance of an awesomely self-contained man, the near-perfect expression of inner density----courageous, ruthless, sheerly despotic.

"His Anointed Steward, Ghorchalanchor Kletus," the staffbearer said. "High Priest of Tchernobog, the Black Lord."

Kletus scrutinized the Sharajnaghi. "Welcome to the house of my god," he said.

Zorachus had the uncanny feeling that the High Priest did miss a jewel on his mantle or thread of embroidery on his tunic.

"My tailors did a fine job," Kletus declared.

"I don't know how to thank you," Zorachus replied.

Kletus smiled and pointed to Halfdan. "Who's that?"

Zorachus said: "My bodyguard, Halfdan."

"Expecting trouble?"

Zorachus shook his head. "I prefer to be on the safe side. Have I offended you? If so, I apologize."

"Think nothing of it. Some of my other guests brought men too. But I hope all this precaution proves unnecessary. It would be such a shame if anything marred your evening." He took Zorachus's arm; it was immediately apparent that the High Priest was tremendously strong. "But before the banquet begins in earnest, I'll introduce you to the others."

Followed by Halfdan, they waded into the crowd; Kletus singled out a tall thin woman.

"Lady Mournir Clethusancta," he said.

She was extremely beautiful, cheekbones high, nose and chin finely chiselled. Her eyes were an unearthly violet-blue, and her hair, black and lustrous, flowed down over her shoulders in thick perfumed curls. She was clad in a green silk dress that bared her flat belly and lifted her small naked breasts. Next to her was a voluptuous, identically dressed blonde, and Clethusancta had her hand inside the other's garment, stroking her loins, arm moving with sinuous serpentine grace; it seemed to have no joints. Both women were completely expressionless.

Zorachus found himself staring at Clethusancta's hand beneath the silk; he was hard before he knew it. He tried not to look, but his eyes kept wandering back. He hardly listened as Kletus went on with an anecdote about a poet who had killed himself over Clethusancta; it was only when the High Priest mentioned that she was a member of the Merchants' Guild that Zorachus began to pay attention---here was a prospective ally, although the Sharajnaghi did not like the thought of dealing with her.

Even if she was doing nothing provocative at all, she would surely evoke unwanted memories; it was a relief when Kletus, after introducing him to her unimportant companion, moved on.

"Kourgon Zarathonzar," the High Priest said, indicating a broad-shouldered, dark-haired priest who looked barely out of his twenties. "He's one of my lieutenants, a member of our High Council. A very powerful mage, for one so young."

"One so young?" Zarathonzar said.

Kletus laughed, and told Zorachus: "He'd be a powerful wizard at any age." He nudged the Sharajnaghi. "Tchernaar says you're quite a wizard yourself. Something about sinking a Kragehul ship?"

Zorachus nodded, then looking back at Halfdan to find the Kragehul's face considerably soured.

"It was self defense," the Sharajnaghi explained.

Halfdan's expression did not change, but he shrugged. Zorachus turned.

"Why apologize to him?" Zarathonzar asked.

"I prefer to keep his goodwill," Zorachus replied.

"He's a Kragehul then?" Zarathonzar sniffed the air. "I should've known. The stench is unmistakable."

Halfdan rumbled to himself.

"Does his belly hurt?" Zarathonzar asked.

Zorachus made no answer.

"How did you sink the ship?" Kletus asked him quickly. "I'm amazed you could do such damage at sea. You wouldn't have the Mancdaman Rings, would you?"

Zorachus nodded; there was no point in trying to deceive him.

"So they weren't lost after all," Kletus said.

Zarathonzar sneered at Zorachus. "The Mancdaman Rings, eh?" He spat a laugh. "So the demons did all the work. From what Tchernaar said, we all thought you must be quite a power. You're something of a disappointment."

"No need to get ugly," Kletus said. "Lord Mancdaman's our guest. And besides, a weakling couldn't do much with the rings---or so I've heard."

"I'm sure," Zarathonzar answered.

Zorachus eyed him. Zarathonzar's face was a study in will and arrogance; he looked very like a younger version of Kletus. But where the High Priest's countenance was clifflike, without a hint of weakness, Zarathonzar's suggested a high-strung, possibly hysterical personality--- in Zorachus's experience, such men were dangerous in a short, sharp fray, but at a terrible disadvantage in a longer fight.

Kletus, clearly displeased with his acolyte, turned from him to introduce Zorachus to several other people. Two were members of the Merchant's Guild, Clethusancta's close allies, apparently. One was named Marmaros Maranchthus, the other, Klissandrian Porchos; both were fat, middle-aged men of average height, richly dressed, with many jeweled rings sparkling on their fingers. They were polite to Zorachus, asking him about political conditions in the southlands, and his voyage. But with Kletus they were frigid, barely smiling when he attempted to joke, avoiding eye contact with him. Zorachus was pleased to note their obvious animosity towards the High Priest.

Presently, Kletus moved on to a huge black man in Cohort Ravener livery, who stood with his horned helm tucked under one arm. His features were heavy and immobile, a blue-grey sheen playing over them; they seemed cast in steel. Dead black, his eyes were like holes bored into a tomb.

"Cetewayo Thulusu," Kletus said. "Captain of the Cohort Ravener, and the greatest swordsman in Khymir. Armor's like paper to him."

"I'm honored to meet you, Lord Mancdaman," the black said slowly, bowing, his voice so extremely resonant that Zorachus could only wonder if the man had any internal organs.

"I saw some of your men in action yesterday," the Sharajnaghi said. "A very impressive display."

Thulusu's face remained expressionless. "As it's intended to be, my Lord. I'll relay your compliments to my troops."

At that moment, a midget in Priestly robes came up beside the Captain, the contrast in size comical and amazing. Kletus introduced the newcomer as Oulchar Lysthragon, adding:

"Another High Council member."

Looking at no one in particular and playing with a small silken purse at his hip, Lysthragon asked:

"Do you know what they say about me, Lord Mancdaman?"

"What?"

"Can't you guess?"

"No."

"You're sure?"

"Quite."

"Should I give you a clue?"

Annoyed and uncomfortable, anxious to get the conversation over with, Zorachus said: "Certainly."

Lysthragon whispered: "They say it behind my back."

Zorachus pondered this. "They say that you like to tell strangers what's said about you behind your back."

Lysthragon shook his head. "They say i'm *short,*" he answered, and grinned at the Sharajnaghi. Till then, his face had been soft and babyish, but as he showed his teeth, which were yellow and pointed, wrinkles spread shockingly, great furrowed nets of them, out from the corners of his mouth and from under his eyes, and he took on the look of a ancient monkey; Zorachus could only guess how old he was.

"Forty-five," the midget said, throwing his head back and laughing. His eyes, however, remained fixed on Zorachus; sliding his index fingers up his nostrils, he moved them in slow circles, as though he were very much enjoying what he was feeling.

"Do you know how pig vomit tastes?" he asked. "I do."

Kletus hustled Zorachus away, launching into a new round of introductions. Midway through, he finally let go of Zorachus's arm, produced a large wallet of meat, and began popping the chunks into his mouth, talking all the while. The sinister dignity of his appearance dropped away; even though the introductions somehow continued to flow, his mouth bulged grotesquely and he made loud gulping sounds. Finishing the wallet in an astonishingly short time, he tucked it away, produced another---much larger than the first--- and resumed eating. Emptying that, he took out a third, then a fourth, and by the time he was done with the fifth, he had introduced most of the guests.

Zorachus managed to forget nearly all of their names, but was roused to attention at the end; before him stood a stunning, red-haired woman, six feet tall and black-robed. Her face was pale, her eyes large and heavy-lidded; to his mind, she looked very near perfection.

"Lady Tchersachor Sathaswentha," Kletus announced.

The woman smiled invitingly at the Sharajnaghi and bowed her head. Zorachus smiled back in spite of himself and bowed, then turned to Kletus.

"I can't help but notice---" Zorachus said.

"Yes?" Kletus asked.

"She wears the robes of your order. Do you admit women?"

"Certainly not," Kletus answered.

"All appearances to the contrary?"

Kletus went on: "If they're *only* women."

Zorachus looked back at Sathaswentha.

A black-robed man stood in her place, red-bearded, pale-skinned.

"Lord Tchersachor Sathaswen*thar*," Kletus said.

Zorachus studied Sathaswenthar's face. The full lips were much less red, the eyelashes shorter, the ruddy hair cropped, and, of course, there was the beard. But the features were the same.

"Very convincing illusion," Zorachus said. Caught off balance, he did not suspect it was anything more. "Which one is the real you?"

'This one," Sathaswenthar said, tapping his chest. "But it wasn't an illusion. The breasts were real. My hips were round and wide. You're a man who appreciates female flesh. I could tell by the way you looked at me. Perhaps---"

"Not yet," Kletus broke in. "There'll be time for that later," he signaled the Steward and cried to the guests: "Dinner will be served shortly. Take your places."

He led Zorachus over to a couch which, appeared to be unpadded iron, its legs very stout. But mystifyingly, when the Sharajnaghi and his host sat down, it groaned beneath them---Zorachus could not imagine how their weight could make the metal give voice, but before he could ask Kletus about it, the High Priest said:

"You really should take Sathaswenthar up on his offer. *His* knowledge of male needs makes *her* a very good mount."

"I don't doubt it," Zorachus said.

The words had barely left his mouth when Sathaswenthar sat on the couch next to theirs and, before his eyes, turned voluptuously female. Sathaswentha's tongue, moist and pointed, snaked out and glossed her upper lip. Wondering how much of this he was going to be subjected to, Zorachus smiled, but fortunately, slaves came by with appetizers and goblets of wine, giving him an excuse to ignore the creature.

The shrimp, bread, and cheese were all very good, and the wine was splendid. Once he drained his cup, Kletus tried to press another on him, but Zorachus was not about to let the High Priest get him drunk. Kletus had already downed several goblets, but they didn't seem to have affected him. He remained aloof from the food until the viands were brought, though he started in then with a vengeance--- Zorachus began on the meat at the same time, but Kletus rapidly outstripped him, even though the Sharajnaghi had a strong appetite; the High Priest ate with both hands, shoveling huge fistfuls of flesh down his gullet. Occasionally, he paused to breathe or drink, but soon resumed his attack on the meat. He ate until his sweat, defying the dryness of the air, poured down his face, and the veins of his forehead stood out like cords; his nose ran in torrents, his jaws champed and champed, and his teeth grew fouler and fouler with hanging threads and tissues, spiderwebs of sinew through which new handfuls were greedily stuffed. Bits of meat escaping his teeth ran over his lower lip in thick streams of saliva. He finished nine-tenths of a yard-wide, high-piled platter, magnanimously granted Zorachus the rest (even though Zorachus's appetite had deserted him) and called for another; quickly devouring its contents, he called for a third, eating ever more quickly, ever more grimly. Again and again his beslimed blood-caked hands dived into the piled flesh. He ignored all other courses, the pastries and pies and heaped bowls of delicacies; his hunger remained fixed on the meat.

For an hour at least he continued his incredible singleminded gluttony. Then, skin purple and blotched, eyes rolling back in their sockets, he sagged and smiled, working at his clotted teeth with a fine gold pick, wiping the foulness from his face with a silk napkin. His robes were completely soaked with perspiration and clung to his body; guessing that Kletus had eaten well over a hundred pounds of meat, Zorachus was astounded to see that the High Priest's stomach was not the least bit swollen.

The other feasters had long since glutted themselves; conversing wearily with each other, they lounged lazily, fondling each others' buttocks, breasts and genitals.

Kletus clapped his hands. Sweat flew from his sodden sleeves, dousing Zorachus.

Two huge nude men, powerfully muscled and heavily scarred, marched into the center of the ring formed by the pillows and couches, hands behind their backs. One was bald, while the other had long yellow hair. They looked to Kletus.

He nodded.

They crossed their arms on their chests, hands cased in steel gauntlets with half-inch spikes jutting from the knuckles.

Bowing to Kletus, they squared off. Their ponderous movements roused the feasters; fondling hands moved more swiftly.

The two men closed and the onlookers screamed wildly as the gauntlets flashed, spikes hammering into flesh, both punches connecting. Blood streamed down yellowhair's cheek, poured from holes in the bald man's chest.

The boxers backpedalled, closed again. The bald one blocked a punch and smashed a ferocious blow into yellowhair's right shoulder. Shrieking, the blond man retreated. Arms windmilling, his foe followed eagerly.

Yellowhair planted his feet, absorbed two horrific blows to the arms, and began to land strokes of his own. The boxers traded punch after punch, gauntlets slapping and thudding against quivering flesh.

The floor was soon splattered with blood.

Struggling against an ever-more desperate desire to intervene, Zorachus watched helplessly as the fighters bludgeoned and ripped each other. He could not even safely look away---he dared not reveal how this sport sickened him. Any hint of squeamishness might brand him a weakling, an undesirable ally, to a man like Kletus. Out of the corner of his eye he could see the High Priest glancing at him every few seconds.

The combat seemed to go on forever. The boxers each lost an eye, reduced each other's faces to pulped meat; teeth tumbled from writhing mouths, and a patch of skull showed through a rent in the bald man's scalp. Shoulders and pectoral muscles hung in tatters.

And still the terrible gauntlets swung.

Please god, Zorachus thought. *Put an end to it ...*

The bald man slipped on a patch of blood-greased stone; totally blind after the last exchange, unaware that his foe had fallen, yellowhair lashed out in desperation, spinning completely around. His antagonist raised himself on one arm and rammed a fist into yellowhair's stomach, and the blond man fell with a scream. The bald one crawled forward and struck him in the stomach again. His victim jerked up into a sitting position--- and caught a brace of steelshod knuckles square in the forehead. Bone gave, and he flopped backwards, dead.

His conqueror stood up wobbling. To the sound of rabid applause, he extended a gauntlet towards Kletus, smiling hideously with what was left of his mouth.

Kletus gave a laugh like stones rattling down a scree, and signaled Oulchar Lysthragon.

"Pay him," he cried.

The midget grinned, face wrinkling hideously as he rose and took the purse from his belt. The boxer turned to him.

Lysthragon hurled the purse. As it flew, its drawstring came somehow undone and the purse's mouth yawned open, a swiftly widening black cavity---in seconds the flying hole was yards wide.

Dumbstruck, the boxer retreated clumsily, tripping over the blond man's corpse. He thrust his hands up and screamed, voice echoing hollowly inside the descending maw. Then the hole dropped over him, cutting off his cry, and the only sound was the hiss of fabric against floor as silk shrank and bunched. Soon there was only a small purse where he and his victim had sprawled.

The applause had stopped while the purse did its work; delicious awe had silenced the audience. Now the clapping resumed, this time for Lysthragon. He bowed and sat back down, sending a slave to retrieve the purse.

As the applause slacked off, Zorachus asked Kletus: "Do you always deal with the winners that way?"

Kletus shook his head. "We prepared that little surprise in your honor. Of course, once the news gets round, we'll have a hard time hiring boxers. I hope you realize the sacrifice we made for you."

Out in the middle of the ring, slaves with mops and buckets were cleansing the blood from the floor. When they finished, Kletus motioned to his Steward. Shortly, a small, brown-skinned woman, raven-tressed and exquisitely formed, strode out into the circle, clad only in gold breastplates and a jeweled kirtle. Lithe and muscular, she posed seductively, oiled skin glistening.

"Beautiful, isn't she?" Kletus asked. "One of you will have her tonight."

Over on the right, Clethusancta shoved her blonde companion from her lap. "Your terms?" she cried, rising.

Kletus did not answer. "Anyone else interested?"

Several noblemen shouted the affirmative.

"*How* interested?"

They shouted extravagant bids of gold and jewels, striving to outdo each other, and Clethusancta, who had quickly joined in. But Kletus shook his head.

"I don't want your riches," he said . "I want a show... of *skill*."

At his words, two redclads marched up to the girl, deposited their swords on either side of her and marched off.

"How many of you would be willing to foot the dance of steel for her?" Kletus asked.

"I'm game!" Clethusancta replied.

Her former plaything rose from the floor, grabbing desperately at the merchant queen.

"Please, my Lady," she implored. "Take pity on me..."

Clethusancta had long nails, thickly lacquered with a metallic polish that made them steel-hard; eyes fixed on the swarthy slavegirl, she raked the blonde's face. Pawing at her torn flesh, the blonde tottered back, shrieking.

Clethusancta looked at her at last, smiling coldly. The blonde snarled, whipping a dagger from her belt.

Instantly, Clethusancta sprang like a great hunting cat, knocked the blade from the blonde's grasp, and ripped her throat out. The blonde crumpled, to scattered applause.

Picking up a napkin, Clethusancta daintily wiped her fingers, having somehow avoided most of the jetting blood. She returned her gaze to the slave girl, who smiled in appreciation.

"You'll have your chance, Clethusancta," Kletus cried, and turned back to the noblemen. "But what of you? Will any of you meet her, blade for blade?"

Only one accepted the challenge, a man named Balorg Tchaldusaar. He stepped out into the ring and, with a quick movement, threw off his robes to reveal a lean, sinewy body. Naked but for loincloth and sandals, he advanced to the swords and picked one up.

Across from him, Clethusancta slipped out of her dress and shoes; nude and barefoot, she went to the other sword with long graceful strides, muscles shimmering under her skin. She picked the blade up, then kissed the swarthy girl full on the lips and slid a hand into her kirtle.

At the sight of her taking such liberties with the prize, Tchaldusaar cursed and swept the slave aside. His blade flashed at Clethusancta, who parried the stroke and launched one of her own, flicking a shallow slash across his chest. He screamed, retreating a step; Clethusancta laughed at him. Again he closed in a whirl of steel. Three times their blades met, ringing. But in the lull that followed, Kletus stood up towering from his iron couch, arms outspread, voice filling the hall like a thunderclap:

"Enough! Whoever looses the next stroke, dies that instant!"

A shadow fell on Tchaldusaar and Clethusancta, and the swarthy girl cried out and ran from the circle. Above the combatants a mass of dark cloud had appeared, dim red light pulsing inside it. Clutching what might have been an alien arbalest, a vaguely human shape, with eyes like live coals, was silhouetted against the glow.

"The umpire," Kletus said. "And a strict one."

Tchaldusaar and Clethusancta lowered their swords.

"That's better," Kletus said mockingly. "We don't want mere butchery, you know. The boxers were quite enough. It's time for something... *aesthetic*. Assume your stances."

They raised their weapons again, bodies arching and tightening, sinews standing out like wires.

Kletus clapped his hands. Invisible musicians began to play; with unearthly pipes, strings, and drums, they performed an orgiastic melody.

Clethusancta and Tchaldusaar whirled in time, gyring gracefully, swords whistling. Their blades met in a shower of sparks and sprang back, the screech of stricken metal one more clash of percussion in the demonic music.

"They *must* keep the rhythm," Kletus told Zorachus. "The first to miss a step, or strike out of time, will be killed by the umpire. That usually happens before a fatal wound's dealt.---" He cried out suddenly as Tchaldusaar gashed Clethusancta's right thigh. "For a second there I thought I'd spoken too soon ... "

Zorachus asked: "How often do you have these matches?"

"All too rarely, I'm sorry to say. There was a time when everyone who was anyone knew the dance, or made some pretense of learning it...but the young don't want to be bothered anymore. They care so little for grace... " Kletus cried out again; Tchaldusaar had scored a glancing blow on Clethusancta's shoulder. "Those two out there are among the few who still know it.... I guessed they wouldn't be able to resist the girl---or the chance to kill each other legally. There's an old grudge between them."

Zorachus found this contest less horrible to watch than the first, since it demanded such speed and agility; it even held a certain fascination for him. Clethusancta, who was beginning to assert herself, was a marvel to behold; even the blood streaking her skin could not detract from her beauty. Indeed, the trickles and droplets only seemed to enhance the muscles they touched, the limbs they rilled from, glittering ruby-red....

Stop it, he told himself, appalled that such an idea could enter his head. Struggling to free his mind from the dance's spell, he forced himself to concentrate on the thought of steel tearing flesh, of human bodies, God's own images, being shredded into so much bloody refuse...

The dance itself began to aid him. The participants still moved swiftly, but they were less graceful now, clearly straining to maintain their paces, pain evident in every step. Wounds swelled or sagged open hideously, revealing the ripped tissues within. The dance was showing its true face.

Clethusancta had gained the upper hand. She had been slashed several times, but none of the wounds was serious. Tchaldusaar had taken a deep slice across the ribs that was pouring out blood at a tremendous rate. Finally, after an exchange in which Clethusancta split his nose, he fumbled his paces, and the demon umpire loosed its bolt. The missile penetrated Tchaldusaar's chest and came out his lower back, spending itself as it struck the floor, skidding lazily to a halt. Wobbling, he continued upright, but let his guard drop; Clethusancta stabbed him in the throat and he toppled backwards. To wild applause, she straddled his still-jerking legs and started to strip off his loincloth. But Kletus leaped to his feet and, banishing the umpire and the invisible musicians with a violent gesture, called her to a halt.

"You won't mutilate him in my hall!" he cried.

"Why not?" Clethusancta demanded, sword still poised.

"The girl's your prize."

"I'll have his *meat*!" Clethusancta shrieked.

"I'll kill you on the spot," Kletus replied.

That was too much for Clethusancta's fellow Merchants.

"This is getting out of hand!" Klissandrian Porchos cried.

"Tell *her*," Kletus replied.

"Clethusancta..."Porchos began.

She stamped and shrieked.

"Let her take it," Porchos told Kletus.

"I don't find her as intimidating as you do," the High Priest answered.

"Tchaldusaar has no more use for it," said Marmaros Maranchthus.

"*I* rule here!" Kletus roared.

"No one's disputing---"

"Then we are in agreement," Kletus broke in. "And that slut---that *perfect* whore--- will *not* use this occasion to glut her hatred of my sex."

Clethusancta trembled with rage. "I won't be denied!"

"Won't you?"

"You can't afford to---"

Kletus boomed a scornful laugh. "I'm High Priest of the Black Lord, *sow*. Defy me, and I'll brush you from existence. In the temple of my god, your gold counts for nothing."

"Kill me," Clethusancta answered, "and you'll have to kill the whole guild. The city will explode in your face. *We* grant the dole. *We* make life possible--- you take it away. You prey on the poor, drag their sons and daughters off to be sacrificed. Your throne's not secure, High Priest."

126

Kletus laughed again. "So?"

"Let me have my trophy."

He stared at her venomously; his left hand rose, and Zorachus was sure he was going to enter a stance. Flinching back, Clethusancta and the other Merchants apparently thought so too.

Then a change came over the High Priest, and he shrugged and let his hand fall. "Perhaps we can compromise," he said. "What will you give me for my permission?"

Victorious, Clethusancta smiled. Even with her face splashed with blood, she was still ravishingly beautiful; she thought a moment and beckoned to the slave girl, who ran over eagerly.

"We'll make love here," the Merchant Queen announced. "For everyone to see."

"Do you guarantee a memorable performance?" Kletus asked.

"Your banquet will be the talk of Khymir."

"Very well," he replied.

Immediately, she started to cut into Tchaldusaar. But once again Kletus stopped her.

"Afterwards," he said.

Clethusancta nodded. "This *is* your hall." She laid the sword down; kneeling, she stripped the slave girl and stretched languorously back beside Tchaldusaar. The girl settled atop her and began to lick the blood from her skin.

Watching them, Zorachus felt that terrible heat in his loins again, but was soon distracted---Kletus leaned forward and looked past the Sharajnaghi, made several quick hand gestures, then settled back.

Zorachus guessed the signals had been to Sathaswentha; she had arranged herself in what was known, for lack of a better term, as a "sitting stance," small shields, almost invisible, dissipating and reforming about her hands.

Noticing Zorachus's attention, she smiled as if they were sharing a little joke, then began to whisper…

Out on the floor, the girl was sucking one of Clethusancta's small breasts, her hand working between the erchant's Queen's legs; she lifted her face just long enough for her to brush glistening fingers on

Clethusancta's erect nipple, then lowered her mouth once more. Clethusancta heaved luxuriously beneath her, stroking her back, caressing her legs with naked feet.

Sathaswentha completed her spell.

The slave-girl's head lifted again. Clethusancta tried in vain to force it back down. Puzzlement twisted her face---then terror.

Scales of chitin were sprouting on the girl's forehead and cheeks.

Her eyes bulged, migrating to the sides of her face, dividing into glittering facets; twitching antennae thrust out between them. The corners of her mouth drew inwards, pressing the opening into a vertical slit; mandibles sprang out on either side of it, clashing. Clethusancta screamed and struggled, but the girl held her fast, pinning her arms to the floor. The wasp-face descended, jaws pinching and chewing into Clethusancta's left breast. Blood fountained; pulpy sounds gave way to crunching as the mandibles reached Clethusancta's ribs...

Once the Merchant Queen went still, Sathaswentha, chuckling, undid the spell on the girl. The slave's face jerked up out of the hole in Clethusancta's ribcage and she tried to scream, but all that came out was a torrent of glistening scarlet vomit.

Sathaswentha rose and assumed what looked like a Dragon Stance, crying an incantation. Twin purplish beams shot from her hands, striking the girl and Clethusancta, who shrank and withered, puckering like leaves cast onto a fire. When Sathaswentha halted the bolts, not even ash remained. She sat down to widespread clapping.

But some in the audience were not so pleased. Faces livid, Clethusancta's allies were on their feet, glaring at Kletus and Sathaswentha.

"Murderers!" Porchos cried, voice quivering with rage and amazement.

"What do you care if one of my slaves dies?" Kletus asked.

Startled by the joke, Porchos hesitated, then shouted with renewed fury: "Are you mad? Jesting at a time like this?"

Kletus shrugged. "Clethusancta defied me in my own house. I had every right to have her killed---and you know it."

Maranchthus said: "You should've spared her all the same. It would've been better all around."

Kletus smiled freezingly. "Are you threatening me?"

"Merely stating facts."

"State another such *fact*, and you'll go home in pieces."

Porchos and Maranchthus whispered to each other and, bowing curtly to the High Priest, started for the door together with their followers, the other Guildsmen and their relatives not far behind. Kletus detailed a priest to command the lift-demon for them.

"They're such fools," he told Zorachus. "Also inconsiderate, behaving so rudely at your feast.. I don't think they respect you."

"I can live without their respect," Zorachus replied. "I am, however, a bit amazed by their disrespect for you."

Kletus studied his face. "As I said, they're fools."

"Their threats carry no weight?"

"I didn't say that," Kletus replied, watching the slaves dragging Tchaldusaar's corpse away. "The mob prefers them to us. They have thousands of troops and hundreds of wizards. But the Priesthood's stronger. We control the Cohort Ravener, the Navy, the Marines. And we're the most powerful mages in Khymir, blades in the hands of Tchernobog."

"Then---"

"Why don't we just crush the Guild?"

Zorachus nodded.

Kletus said: "They have their uses. We prefer not to sully ourselves with trade. Besides importing the grain and the spices that keep everyone happy, they sell our gold for us....if truth be told, most buyers would rather deal with them."

"I see."

"You're skeptical?"

Zorachus shrugged.

Kletus asked: "Why *do* you think we spare them?"

"I don't know---because Tchernobog isn't powerful enough, perhaps?"

Kletus's reaction was unexpected. Zorachus anticipated anger, but the High Priest merely smiled, and said:

"You only show your ignorance."

"Truly?" Zorachus prodded.

"He is the *summit*. Unexcelled."

"But---"

"Yes?"

"I've heard that another created him."

Kletus laughed. "You mean that...*flatulence* your Sharajnaghi mentors pretend to worship? How could something like *that* be the maker of my Lord? Tchernobog is what he's willed himself to be, self-existent, the eternal principle of pure spirit. At most, the Sharajnaghi God is only one of his avatars--- the aspect which best reveals his humor, I think. Which would explain why Sharajnaghim are such masters of farce."

"They're effective enough," Zorachus said.

"That *is* the prevailing opinion," Kletus replied. "Though I can't imagine how they function in my universe."

Zorachus stifled the obvious answer: *They're in the real one, they don't need to....*

He thought of Qanar-Sharaj, and sweet memories stabbed him to the marrow, his first meeting with Raschid, Ghaznavi congratulating him on the clock he had invented, the ordination....

Tchernaar came up beside Kletus. He seemed to have sobered a bit; he was less wobbly, though he shivered with excitement. His lip was badly swollen where Halfdan had struck him.

"My Lord," he said, "I'm ready." He tapped the bottle hanging from his neck.

Kletus smiled. "You've been a faithful servant. I won't keep you any longer. This is as good a time as any."

Tchernaar slipped the bottle off and proffered it to Kletus. "Will you pour them over me?"

Kletus shook his head. "There's no need. When you're out in the ring, lay the bottle on its side and uncork it. I'll tell you what to do after that."

Tchernaar nodded gratefully, kissed Kletus's hand, and entered the circle. Kletus took up a napkin and wiped the spot where Tchernaar had pressed his lips.

Reaching the center, Tchernaar turned round and round to make sure he had everyone's attention; satisfied, he stopped and cried:

"My friends, these are my last moments among you. The time has come for me to die---and die well." He held up the bottle. "I have some little friends in here...worms, brought from another plane by His Anointed Steward, just for me....Overcome with gratitude, as you might imagine, determind to appreciate them, I have resolved to give myself..."

"Give yourself?" Zarathonzar cried. "What, are they going to fuck you?"

"Devour me," Tchernaar said.

"The wormies in that little bottle? That'll take a while."

"Don't worry---"

"We won't."

"I'll feel no pain----"

Zarathonzar looked slyly at Kletus. "Of course you won't."

"Zarathonzar," Kletus said, "this is a solemn occasion."

His lieutenant laughed, but said nothing else. The High Priest motioned Tchernaar to continue.

"I seem to have lost the thread," the envoy said.

"You were about to tell everyone how the worms' saliva---"

Tchernaar nodded. "Is a powerful drug. One which brings incredible ecstasy...." Tittering, he began to fondle himself; he was already erect.

"Say good-bye," Kletus said.

Tchernaar barely managed it, then threw off his harness, laid the bottle on its side, and uncorked it, retreating.

It started to grow. Soon it was a foot long, then a yard, its frosted sides becoming transparent. A squirming knot of huge worms could be seen inside, also growing, maggot-shaped but black as oil.

Tchernaar sank to his knees, staring raptly at them. "Thank you, Lord Kletus," he said repeatedly, rocking to and fro in anticipation.

And all the while Kletus, having assumed a sitting stance, was force-letting just as Sathaswentha had done.

Presently, bottle and worms stopped growing.

"Crawl in," Kletus told Tchernaar.

Tchernaar looked at him and gave a pathetic, swollen-lipped parody of a smile.

"Go on," the High Priest urged.

Tchernaar looked back at the bottle. Out of its mouth came the liquid slithering sounds of the worms oozing ceaselessly over each other. As yet, the clotted mass had not moved from the back of the vessel.

"You'll *love* it," Kletus said.

Tchernaar hesitated a few more seconds. Then, like a pale shaven dog, he scrambled into the opening. The worms crawled forward, and he dived among them, embracing the pulpy bodies.

Kletus rose. Assuming a stance unfamiliar to Zorachus, he raced through a formula; with invisible strands of will, he lifted the cork, which had also grown, and impelled it tightly into the bottle's mouth, muffling Tchernaar's first cries.

They were not cries of ecstasy.

The envoy was struggling violently with the battening worms, which obscured half his body. The bottle rolled back and forth, and from time to time there was a glimpse of his shrieking face.

"I lied about the worms," Kletus cried, laughing.

The audience roared with delight.

"I don't know if they even *have* saliva," he went on. "I'm afraid it would take an even bigger idiot than him to enjoy their company....There must be one somewhere, I'm sure, but *his* antics wouldn't be so amusing---in short, we couldn't do better."

He saluted the bottle and sat back down; the couch groaned loudly, as if under the weight of several tons.

"What did he do to deserve that?" Zorachus asked.

"He asked me to suggest a good way to die," Kletus answered.

"But he was your man. You said he was your faithful servant. . . ."

"I'd be willing to say it again. The fact is, I want him to *keep* serving me--- right up until his soul oozes its contemptible little way from his mouth. He pleases me best by dying in abject agony. It's as simple as that."

"Simple as that," Zorachus said.

Kletus studied the Sharajnaghi's face. "Do I worry you? Really, I shouldn't. You can defend yourself, can't you? You have those wonderful rings...Moreover, we're partners. I don't kill anyone I need. I'm not a frivolous man."

At those last words, Zorachus nearly burst out laughing, but as his eyes wandered back to the bottle, his grim amusement died. Tchernaar, still bucking under the vermiform blanket, had turned around and was trying to push the cork from the bottle. The audience shouted and stamped, offering mock encouragement; they jeered in disappointment as he dropped back from the stopper, apparently exhausted. But as the worms chewed deeper, he seemed to get his second wind and launched himself forward with a terrific effort; the cork fell from the bottle-mouth and he poked his head through. His eyes widened as they found Kletus.

"I'll kill you!" he cried. Somehow, agony had dredged a spark of manhood from within him; groaning, wheezing, he began to pull himself from the hole. The audience cried out in cruel approval. Half his body slid out onto the floor. He crawled still farther, trailing worms. He was nearly clear of the bottle mouth...

Then he stopped.

Zorachus thought he was dead. Several worms were embedded deep in the envoy's chest, and the Sharajnaghi guessed one had found his heart.

But he was wrong.

Tchernaar's expression changed. It went blank, then became a mask of delirious pleasure. Little ragged giggles came out of him. He twisted slowly, languidly, like a man atop an invisible succubus. He lifted himself once more on his hands and knees. Gradually he backed into the bottle, rejecting the world outside, withdrawing into his self-contained universe of abominable rapture. Like a man losing himself in a vast, comfortable bed, he lay down, placidly accepting the worms' gnawing services.

Kletus roared an oath; the unbelievable had happened. Leaping up, he resumed his stance and flipped the bottle upright. Tchernaar and the worms slid down into the bottom. Rumbling an incantation, Kletus revoked the spell by which bottle and worms had grown, and they shrank to their previous size; the crimson liquid that had been Tchemaar gushed out through the bottle's mouth, geysering up and up, almost splashing the ceiling before collapsing upon itself.

133

With a gesture Kletus vaporized all but a few drops. A dozen small dark shapes also remained, tumbling amid the red beads; striking the floor, the worms crawled back towards the bottle, leaving small trails of blood.

Kletus sat back down; again the couch gave voice. He turned to Zorachus. Already he seemed to have regained most of his composure.

"Have you taken a fancy to anyone here?" he asked. "Besides your bodyguard, that is?"

Halfdan growled something in Kragehul.

"Be still," Zorachus said.

Halfdan obeyed.

"He has a ugly temper," Kletus said.

"You insulted him," Zorachus replied. "He's a Kragehul, remember? I don't sleep with him. He's merely a bodyguard."

"I was just making a little joke…. Tchernaar told me you don't like manflesh." Kletus looked at Halfdan. "However, it would be wise for this strawhead to remember he's already given me sufficient cause to grind my heel on him." He returned his gaze to Zorachus. "Now then. Did you see anyone you liked? It's going to be an hour till the next round of entertainment. You'll have to pass the time somehow."

"I really have my pick?"

"Absolutely. You're the guest of honor and may not be refused."

"Very good. Is there someplace we can talk?"

"There will be plenty of time for talk later. In the meanwhile there's Sathaswentha, or. . ."

Zorachus shook his head. "I'm the guest of honor. Don't refuse me."

Kletus laughed. "Very well. We can go to my garden."

"A blood-fruit garden?"

Kletus laughed again. "Nothing so prosaic. Come with me."

Chapter 9

THE HIGH PRIEST led the way to a small iron door.

"Wait here," Zorachus told Halfdan.

Kletus unlocked the door and opened it.

"After you," he told Zorachus, and the Sharajnaghi went in.

Kletus followed, closing the door behind him.

"Did you say something?" he asked.

"No," Zorachus answered, but he lied; he had uttered the beginning of a Kadjafi curse, softly, almost unconsciously, the instant he saw what the room contained. Even after the banquet, he could still be shocked.

Most of the dirt floor before him was carpeted with what appeared to be nude men bathed in a sourceless white light, completely motionless, intertwined in a bewildering variety of sexual position, sucking and buggering.

All were exact duplicates of Ghorchalanchor Kletus.

Mirrors covered the chamber's walls and ceiling, multiplying the High Priest's images a thousandfold. Vistas composed entirely of his reflections stretched into infinity like demonic theophanies.

"The bodies are grown from a kind of fungus I bred specially to my purposes," Kletus said. "They have the exact feel and warmth of human flesh, but they're much tougher. A boulder couldn't crush them." He strode over to one, which lay on its belly. "See that cord? There, at the base of its spine? That's the connection between the body and the main growth, down in the soil. It's long enough to allow considerable freedom of movement." At his words, the duplicate rose up on all fours, crawled about, and stopped still. "All of them are completely subject to my will. I can make them assume any position I want."

Straining to keep his voice free of the horror he felt, Zorachus asked: "Why do they all look like you?"

Kletus laughed. "You might say I needed a place where I could be alone with myself----an erotic necessity until my need for the erotic vanishes altogether. You see, I learned quite a while ago that nothing in the external world could satisfy my basic desires---except where the external provided an extension of myself, or became an extension of my will. It seems to be the same for everyone; hence, that inevitable progression from heterosexual to homosexual partners, and in some cases, masturbation in a room full of mirrors."

"No one can love another?' Zorachus asked.

Kletus nodded matter-of-factly. "Even when someone develops an attachment, he desires only those qualities that he himself shares. Thus, when he makes love to his partner, he loves only himself."

To blot out his surroundings, Zorachus decided to focus on the argument, saying: "Let me see if I'm understanding you correctly. Let's suppose a man and woman are engaged in furious sexual intercourse---"

"It happens," Kletus said.

"You'd say he takes no pleasure in the fact that she has female genitals, correct?"

"Yes."

"If that's true, what is he enjoying?"

Kletus replied: "The fact that she's pressed beneath him, conforming to his will. He may think that he's enjoying her body, but actually he takes pleasure only in those aspects of her that have become extensions of himself."

Zorachus smiled thinly. "What about a man who prefers the woman on top?"

"That's a more complex situation, of course," Kletus answered, very seriously. "But his pleasure stems from the basic human need to inflict humiliation. In order to most fully appreciate our success in inflicting humiliation, we must humiliate ourselves. When the woman's on top, it is a sign of dominance, but not dominance she exercises. It's the man who's actually holding himself in subjection, humiliator and victim both."

Wondering how long the High Priest could maintain this line, Zorachus asked: "Is that what you feel? When the woman's on top?"

"I don't have sex with women anymore," Kletus answered haughtily, apparently annoyed by the mere suggestion. "Female flesh doesn't arouse me." He waved a hand over the motionless replicas. "Are they female?"

"Please don't take offense," Zorachus answered. "I was merely trying to find out how much first-hand experience you've had. Of such feelings, that is."

Kletus said: "When I still found women attractive, I didn't analyze my desires. But now I'm able to put things in their proper perspective."

"Did you decide----consciously decide----that you disliked women because they were different from you?"

Kletus shook his head. "It was gradual. More evolution than decision. I simply found myself spending more and more time with men. But now I know why that preference won out. Females are reminders of ambiguities that I don't appreciate. These days, the only pleasure I take from them is watching them being tortured, or killed. I did feel some excitement when Clethusancta killed the blonde. And I very much enjoyed watching her and that slave die."

"And the boxers? Did you enjoy watching them pound each other to rags? That was male flesh."

Kletus nodded. "Something I've also discarded my taste for---my *sexual* taste. Most male flesh, that is. I will of course step in when some bitch is going to inflict some insult upon it---I couldn't let Clethusancta carve Tchaldusaar up, for example. But for the most part I remain preoccupied with myself. I don't even roger these facsimiles anymore. Not that looking at them no longer arouses me; but I use them only for inspiration. I prefer to think of them as pictures in my mind, anyway. Watching them couple is almost literally a dream. After all, they embody my fantasies the instant I imagine them…destroying them in various ways is even more gratifying. Their very toughness--- a reflection of my own power--- makes it quite a challenge. I exult in my own creations even as I annihilate them…." He paused, chuckling. "It's so easy to think of myself as one of them, almost to incarnate myself, as it were, to imagine my own feelings as I sacrifice myself to myself… I tell you, when i'm in this room, I'm so *sufficient. . . .* "

"I'm surprised you ever come out at all," Zorachus said drily, concealing his awe at the sheer depth of Kletus's self-absorption.

"That would be too…unambitious," the High Priest answered. "I cannot--will not---forget that there's an outside world. I feel the insult very deeply. But when the world's my own sweet portrait…"

"Just where will I fit into this 'portrait' of yours?" Zorachus asked.

Kletus laughed soothingly. "You'll be well provided for."

"In return for what? Becoming an extension of your will?"

"In effect, yes. Except that you're already mine. I sent for you; here you are. You respond to my will, a finger on my hand."

The High Priest's brazenness was so astounding that Zorachus simply had to smile.

Kletus smiled too. "You find my arrogance amusing?"

"It's just that I've never met anyone quite so *straightforward.*"

"I can afford to be straightforward. I'm the center of my universe, and my universe will eventually be all center. I can see no point in allowing you illusions about our relationship."

"I hope you don't think I'll become more docile," Zorachus said.

"I think you'll become more *pragmatic,*" Kletus said with a fatherly smile. "After all, you do want to take full advantage of your situation. If you'll remember, I said we were partners a while ago..."

Zorachus nodded. "That's why I wanted to speak to you. But all this talk about being a finger on your hand....that doesn't sound like partnership. It sounds like slavery."

"You're wrong to draw the distinction," Kletus answered. "I never said it was an *equal* partnership. Everyone's my slave, even if they don't realize it. I know you must find that galling; all men hate those who command them, and that's as it should be. But you should take everything into consideration. My fingers are pampered. There's a place for you in the Priesthood. A high one."

Zorachus was silent a few moments. "I'm not sure I want to join your order."

Kletus smiled with good-natured dubiousness. "Come now! What else could you want? To stay in your palace and glut your senses? I don't think you're that sort. Not many men would want to talk business when they had a chance to lie with Sathaswentha. Believe me, I find that tremendously admirable. To be so young and have such restraint! I still haven't overcome my need for the erotic. I was raised in typical Khymirian fashion... we've never laid enough emphasis on will, or on *self,* for that matter. I was taught to see desire for pleasure as desire for external things; wallowing in flesh only increased my confusion. I'm only now transcending it. But I will say I'm transcending it with a vengeance."

"What about all that meat?" Zorachus asked, remembering the High Priest clearing platter after platter.

"What of it?"

"It's flesh. It's not yours. And you don't seem to be transcending your appetite."

"I've no appetite for meat," Kletus replied. "I've an appetite for *eating* meat. As for it not being mine, I correct that... *it* turns into *me*. Very satisfying. Either it becomes me---submits---or becomes shit. Not that it was ever much more than shit to begin with."

"That's an article of faith in your order, isn't it?" Zorachus asked. "That flesh is vile?"

Kletus laughed. "We have no articles of faith. You don't even have to believe in Tchernobog, just so long as you observe certain formalities. Take your father, for example. He became a complete atheist. Very reform-minded. That's why he was so popular. He only got into trouble when he tried to turn the Priesthood into a mere secular government.

"Now, as for flesh, it's worshipped as well as damned. The grossest sensuality and the struggle for purification go on side by side. The former's merely more visible. Practically all the lower-level adepts are sensualists. But if they want to advance, a belief in the ultimate importance of spirit is very useful. Most full initiates have recognized flesh for what it is. Lysthragon and Sathaswenthar both share my views, for example."

Zorachus was puzzled. "Sathaswenthar? Then why does he transform himself and try to seduce men?"

"To mock the sexual act, especially the *heterosexual* act: it begets flesh. But it's also a kind of spiritual exercise. All that slime makes it so very easy to keep the body's true nature in mind. And by enjoying men the way women do, he reminds himself what pigs women are."

"What about Zarathonzar? Isn't he a full initiate?"

"No. He has much to learn, but we're very close, and I'm teaching him everything. Already he despises women, and has begun to butcher the young boys he presently favors. More promising still, he's taken to spending more and more time alone with his mirrors. Soon he'll be a perfect servant of the Black God."

"The Black God," Zorachus mused. "Your Lord and Master."

Kletus looked at him sidelong.

"I'm just wondering where he fits into your universe," Zorachus said. "I should think yours would merely be part of his."

Kletus seemed unperturbed by the question. "His goals and mine are, to all intents and purposes, the same. I think of him the way I think of myself."

"It sounds very cozy," Zorachus said, admiring the High Priest's rationalization in spite of himself. "But what exactly are these common goals of yours?"

"To expand our influence, of course. Even now we're planning a great enterprise, one in which you'll play a very important part..." Kletus smiled conspiratorially.

"And what is this enterprise?" Zorachus asked, wanting desperately to learn that Ghaznavi had been wrong, that the mission to Khymir had been unnecessary all along, that the nightmare was over instead of just beginning....

"The conquest of Muspellheim," Kletus said, each word falling like a hammer blow against the fragile glass of Zorachus's hopes. "Tchernobog wants victims. I want meat. The Kragehul will satisfy us both."

Appalled yet not surprised, Zorachus asked: "You eat *human* meat?"

"Certainly. What could be better than turning *people* into myself?"

Suddenly Zorachus remembered what he had eaten at the banquet. He felt a surge of nausea but maintained his composure, asking quietly: "Is that what you served me?"

"It was beef---on the platters," Kletus answered. "I wouldn't serve manflesh to someone without asking. It *is* an acquired taste. And why waste it?"

Zorachus was relieved, though much of his queasiness remained. "Why attack Muspellheim?" he asked. "Can't you make do with the slaves you already have?"

"I could, for a while. But my needs, like Tchernobog's, are growing. Soon, quite literally, they'll know no bounds."

Zorachus was dumbstruck. He knew the High Priest was talking about thousands of bodies, hundreds of thousands. He did not doubt Kletus's intention to devour them all, and he knew Kletus had acquired some means of doing precisely that...the merest hint of the cannibal's voracity had been revealed at the banquet.

140

"And you need my aid?" Zorachus asked.

Kletus nodded. "You'll be invaluable."

"What do you expect me to do?"

"Throw my Khymirian opponents off balance. As you know, the city's divided into two camps. The first's made up of the Priesthood and most of the nobles, the second of the Merchant Guildsmen and their followers. The Guildsmen will oppose the invasion. They get everything they need through trade, and they dislike foreign adventuring----they've been burned at it. But they'll also be unwilling to leave such an undertaking solely in Priestly hands. We'll have to levy much more than our present tithes to hire the necessary numbers of southron mercenaries, and since Khymir will serve for quite some time as a staging area, the mercenaries themselves will tilt the balance of power overwhelmingly in our favor. To prevent that, the Guildsmen will fight ferociously.

"But you'll undercut them. Your arrival was eagerly anticipated---the Mancdaman name is *illustrious*. It raises hopes, evokes memories of better times; you've already demonstrated your desire to help the poor. I heard how you made a great many friends this morning. When you support the invasion, people will listen to you. They'll be reassured when you tell them that the Priesthood isn't going to use its new regiments inside the city. After all, wasn't your father the famous reformer Mancdaman Zancharthus? And didn't he try to make the Priesthood less oppressive? The mob usually backs the Merchants, but they won't this time."

"You're certain of that?" Zorachus asked.

"Perfectly," Kletus replied. "A little voice told me." He laughed.

"When do you want me to join your order?"

"As soon as possible, naturally. If I could make an announcement tonight---"

Zorachus raised a hand. "As I said, I'm not sure...."

"And, I suppose, you're not sure about backing the invasion, either."

Zorachus nodded. "I need some time to think. Will you give me a day?"

"I'd prefer not," Kletus said smiling, but with a hint of menace in his voice.

Zorachus was unfazed. "Don't pressure me."

The smile vanished,. Kletus's eyes bore down upon the Sharajnaghi.

"What are you worried about?" Zorachus asked. "Aren't you certain I'll join you? Would you have told me your plan otherwise?"

"No," the High Priest admitted.

"Very well then. Do you mind if I don't rejoin the banquet? As I said..."

"You need to think." Kletus acquiesced with a nod.

"I'll return to my palace, then. Will you see me out?"

Kletus shook his head. "Have my Steward help you with the lift." Behind him, the replicas began to writhe; his left hand wandered under his robes, and returned with a meat wallet.

"You'll have my decision tomorrow," Zorachus said. "Farewell."

Leaving the chamber, he was overjoyed by the sight of Halfdan's bluff, ruddy face.

Water in the desert, the Sharajnaghi thought.

"What's this?" Halfdan asked. "Did you think I was going to wander off?"

"Not at all," Zorachus said. "It's just---"

He checked himself; how *could* he explain, to a man who had not been through that door? Even the city outside would seem like a place of primal innocence compared to the High Priest's Garden.

Passing through the banquet chamber, they found the Steward, and shortly they were back at the great south gate. Seeing the palanquin again, remembering the painting on the canopy and the twin-tongued face, Zorachus decided he would rather walk; feeling safe enough, and wanting to speak with Halfdan, he also dismissed the guards.

"Did you feel the air in there?" Zorachus asked the Kragehul once they were some distance from the tower.

Leading his horse, Halfdan nodded. "Like Death Himself had sucked all the life from it. I never thought I'd find this Khymirian damp so pleasant...what did you and Kletus talk about?"

Zorachus told him. Halfdan swore when he heard of the invasion, but was delighted with Zorachus's plan to throw in with the Guild.

"You're a slippery one, aren't you?" he said. "A real shape-changer."

142

Chapter 10

THE NEXT MORNING, Zorachus asked Louchan where Klissandrian Porchos lived.

"Lord Kletus asked me to meet with him," he explained. "There was some trouble at the banquet, and he thought I might be able to smooth things over..."

He got directions and set out with Halfdan through the steaming streets, hiding his face with a hood to avoid being mobbed. Porchos's palace was on the southeast side of Khymir; the trip took well over an hour. The Guildsman seemed delighted by the visit.

"We're not disturbing you?" Zorachus asked.

"Certainly not," Porchos replied. "You came at just the right time. I'm sufficiently recuperated---" he chuckled.

"From?"

"Some love-play."

"I see."

"Broke in a little Tarchan girl. Tiny wisp of a thing, five years old..." Porchos smiled and seemed lost in reverie.

Zorachus's eyes wandered, taking in the details of his sumptuous surroundings. His attention was swiftly drawn to a rampant gold dragon, set in a niche--- the statue was a perfect example of motion captured in an inanimate object. He read aloud the name engraved on the base: "Lazarak---"

That roused Porchos; he turned to look.

"Lazarak of the Golden Mail," he said. "A name revered in Khymirian history. He was a great general."

"A dragon?" Zorachus asked.

Porchos shook his head. "He became one. After his burial."

"I've never heard of such a thing," Zorachus said. "Is it just a legend?"

"Nothing of the sort, although no one knows for certain why it happened. Some say the Black Lord transformed him for some reason. Others say Lazarak was enchanted by a power from the very stones. That seems more likely to me. Our catacombs are full of prodigies. Strange forces well up

143

from the center of the earth. The lowest levels merge into tunnels infested by the Shreeth---"

"Shreeth?"

"Dwarfs, goblins, whatever you please...captured ones turn up in the arenas, from time to time. They're incredibly strong and ferocious. Amazing mouths...."

Zorachus was still staring at the statue of Lazarak. "Is he still alive?"

Porchos nodded. "And completely mad. He's trapped---the tunnels are too narrow for him to escape. Now and again he tries to smash his way out, hurling himself against the walls of his prison, widening his chamber, breaking into other vaults. But mostly he sleeps. And dreams of revenge."

"On whom?"

"The Black Priests. He grew too powerful, you see, and they had him murdered---which is why I don't think their god was responsible for his transformation. Obviously, Tchernobog had no use for him to begin with.... In any case, one of their assassins drove a spear through the gilded scale-mail Lazarak always wore. The hole can still be seen; his mail became his new skin when he changed, and there's a fiery wound in his chest.

"But so much for Khymirian lore. Come on: I've a place where we can talk more privately."

He led Zorachus and Halfdan to a large room in the center of the house.

"It's perfectly soundproofed," the merchant said, sitting in a large padded chair. "I had one of my wizards do the work. It was all very expensive, but a man must have a place where he can speak without being overheard. Sit down, sit down."

Zorachus settled across from him and Halfdan planted himself behind the Sharajnaghi's chair. Zorachus had thought it unwise to leave the Kragehul outside; they were, after all, in enemy territory. There was always the chance that Porchos might seize a chance to eliminate Kletus's prized new ally. But the Merchant did not seem to mind Halfdan's presence.

"Formidable-looking guard you've got there," he observed.

"I like to think so," Zorachus said. "I'm surprised you don't travel with any...those men last night were all Maranchthus's, weren't they?"

"How did you guess?"

"Little things. They didn't seem to care about you."

Porchos laughed. "His little army. He's always telling me I should have one. He doesn't put as much faith in my mages as I do." He plucked at his multicolored robe. "This is my bodyguard."

"Armor?"

"Hardly. Have your man try to slash me."

"Are you quite sure ...

"It'll be all right."

Zorachus shrugged. "Go ahead, Halfdan."

"You must be joking," Halfdan replied.

Porchos said: "If you're worried, use the flat."

Halfdan grunted, drew his sword, and advanced, swinging half-heartedly.

One of Porchos's sleeves lengthened with a whoosh, whipping round the blade and wrenching it from Halfdan's hand. As the Kragehul cried out in amazement, Porchos's other sleeve shot out, wrapped around Halfdan's neck, and snapped back again. Halfdan cursed and retreated. Both sleeves shortened to their previous lengths.

"The robe's a living creature," Porchos explained. "From another dimension, of course. I've many such garments. At the slightest hint of danger, the robe disarms the attacker and extrudes needles full of poison. If I'd willed it, that second blow would have been fatal."

Rubbing his throat, Halfdan picked his sword back up and resumed his post.

"Maranchthus is skeptical?" Zorachus asked. "Haven't you ever given him a demonstration?"

"He was inexplicably unimpresse," Porchos answered. "After we left the banquet, he lectured me for half an hour. Said I'd wind up like Clethusancta. She never travelled with a guard of any sort. "

"Would it have made any difference if she had?"

"Maranchthus likes to hear himself talk. She could've had a whole squad of suicide troops, and Kletus wouldn't have been fazed."

"Then why didn't you try to persuade her---"

"To back down? She wouldn't have. But I thought Kletus might, to avoid marring your evening....I should have known. He's so *aware* of his power..."

"Pity he has so much," Zorachus said.

Porchos eyed him silently.

Zorachus went on: "I'd like him so much better if he had none at all."

"Harsh words," Porchos said.

Zorachus shrugged.

"I thought you were partners," Porchos said.

"He thinks so too. Told me I'm a finger on his hand. But he's going to find out otherwise."

"You didn't, by any chance---"

"What?"

"Make some sort of discovery---"

"About?"

"Him and your father?"

Zorachus shook his head. "Is there something I need to know?"

"There are rumors---"

"To what effect?"

"That Kletus planned the murder, did all the work---"

"Even though Ordog became High Priest?"

"Yes."

Zorachus wondered if there was anything to it, although he wasn't sure it mattered. He had never known his father, couldn't *begin* to comprehend the man's sacrifice, and couldn't imagine how he could possibly detest Kletus any more.

"There *are* other schools of thought, however," Porchos continued. "One holds that a redclad officer acted on his own, because he hated your father's friend Jagutai..."

"What do you think?"

"That whatever happened, your independent spirit is admirable."

Zorachus laughed.

"Does Kletus know about it?" Porchos asked.

"He will, as of this afternoon. I'm going to denounce him. And his Priesthood. And his plan to invade Muspellheim."

Porchos's skin paled. "To do *what?*"

Zorachus told him Kletus's scheme.

"But why bring this information to me?" Porchos asked.

"Surely it's obvious. I *must* ally myself with the Guild."

Porchos smiled and thought a bit. "Your name would be very useful to us, now more than ever.... We suspected Kletus had some plot in mind, but we never guessed it could be so grandiose... did he say when he was going to put it into effect?"

"No. But he was very anxious to get my decision. I expect my denunciation will set him back very badly."

Porchos nodded. "Undo his plan altogether, perhaps."

"Will the guild support me, then?"

"*I'd* like to support you," Porchos said. "But I can't speak for my colleagues."

"I should think---"

"I should think so too. But people are unpredictable. They seem perfectly solid on the surface, but underneath? Great shifting quagmires, no more real than anything else. Which is to say, not real at all."

"Nothing is real?"

"I don't think so. Not this moment, at any rate. Riding those little girls often seems real enough. But the rest..." Porchos laughed. "Ah well, I don't suppose I'd have it any different. Wouldn't it be dreadful if things *were* real? What a thought. Gives one the shivers."

"It doesn't bother me," Zorachus answered. *Thank God,* he thought.

Porchos's face twisted with incredulity. "No?"

Zorachus shook his head.

"Surely it's just a passing thing."

"No."

"Odd," Porchos said.

"When will you contact the other Guildsmen?" Zorachus asked.

Porchos rose. "I'll send for them straightaway." He rubbed his hands. "If only I could see Kletus's face when he finds out what you've done."

Banipal Khezach's main altar-room was located at the top of the central spire, but there were many chapels throughout the temple; in one of these, a dark barrel-vaulted chamber on the first floor,   Sathaswenthar and Kletus were administering one of their order's charities.

The room was packed with clamoring beggars, waving hunks of meat and plucked chickens in their scab-crusted hands. Their smell contended pungently with the sickly sweet incense burning on the altar of the black hand.

Kletus pointed to two of the mendicants. One had a withered arm and the other, leaning on a crutch, a paralyzed leg; their toothless maws gaped as they shrieked their delight. Buffeted and cursed by their fellows, they came forward, proffering their gifts of meat. Kletus took up the flesh and turned to the blazing oblation dish, lowering the offerings slowly into the devouring flames. As he did so, Sathaswenthar silenced the crowd and intoned a prayer to Tchernobog, his words echoing hollowly through the hall:

"Black Father,
Spirit of spirits,
Power is thy name.
Your will endures,
Your black grip holds,
Your reign will last forever.
See these unclean things destroyed,
And grant us your favor,
So that we might deal with others
As they would deal with us.
Lead us not into discomfort,
And deliver us from disease;
For yours is the cleansing force,
Almighty against all things seen and touched,
That can succor us from our flesh."

As the prayer closed, Kletus turned, strode to the chosen beggars, and laid his hands upon their matted heads.

"Fight well, my sons," he said. "Tchernobog's blessing--- and a sack of gold--- to the victor."

The beggars stepped back from the dais, the other mendicants screaming encouragement, oddsmakers among them taking bets. The contest promised to be fairly even; the man with the withered arm was more mobile, but the cripple, who could balance on his right leg, had his crutch for a weapon.

They squared off, eyeing each other grimly. Some time passed. Neither made a move. For the spectators, suspense became boredom.

"Come on, my sons," Kletus prodded.

The cripple hopped forward, swinging his crutch at his opponent. The latter laughed and leaped out of range----only to lose his footing and fall backward, knocking his wind out against the hard stone floor. Three more hops, and the cripple had him; stunned, the fallen man sprawled helpless as the crutch rose again and again, cracking his ribs and finally his skull. The other mendicants roared, some with glee, some, having bet on the wrong man, with dismay.

Panting, the victor turned to Kletus. Once he received his reward, there would be more beggars chosen, more offerings, more fights.

But before the cripple could hobble up to the altar, Kourgon Zarathonzar, dragging a struggling man, thrust his way out of the crowd and hurled the beggar from his path. The crowd rumbled to see their peer treated so, but, undaunted by their displeasure, still clutching his captive, Zarathonzar turned, assumed a one-handed stance, and launched several keening greenish bolts into the crowd. A dozen beggars fell with broken bones, but even they picked themselves up and joined the mad dash for the door, the victor of the contest stumping along furiously at the rear.

"That was impolitic," Kletus told Zarathonzar calmly as the din faded.

"Politics be hanged!" Zarathonzar shouted, hauling his captive to his feet. The man wore a messenger's blue tunic, and had been badly beaten about the face. "This fool was spreading them!"

"Spreading what?"

Zarathonzar plucked a sheet of crumpled vellum from his belt. Kletus took it, his eyes widening in angry amazement as he realized his plans had been revealed; seeing Zorachus's signature, he loosed a thunderous cry, then handed the vellum to Sathaswenthar.

Jerking the messenger by the tunic, Zarathonzar pointed vehemently at the man's bloodied face, saying: "He was in Kralorg Square. He'd posted several of the damn bills, was reading another to the rabble."

"Lords, please," the messenger wailed. "I was only doing my job. Porchos hired me, but .... "

"*Porchos!*" Zarathonzar screeched, as if no more hateful name could be uttered. "*Porchos!*" An earsplitting torrent of unintelligible syllables poured from his mouth; clutching the messenger's throat with his left hand, he lifted him up off the floor at arm's length, shaking him as a child might shake a rattle. Suddenly, his right hand flew upward in a blur, catching the messenger hard under the nose, jamming his nasal bones into his brain and killing him instantly. Zarathonzar tossed the corpse away as if it were so much refuse.

Kletus, meanwhile, had gotten a grip on himself.

"If I were you," he said, "I'd try not to lose my mind whenever something angered me."

"Yes, you're the very model of restraint," Zarathonzar jeered. "What was that bellow just now?"

"I didn't break into gibberish."

"Spare me," Zarathonzar snarled.

Making a mental note to repay this insubordination, Kletus nodded, conceding: "There are more important matters. Killing Mancdaman Zorachus, for example."

Chapter 11

ZORACHUS and HALFDAN returned to the Mancdaman Palace even as the denunciation, copied hundreds of times by means of a spell, was being disseminated. With them came a large company of Guild troops in browned mail, bearing kite-shaped shields. The palace guard, having been told to obey Zorachus in everything, stood idly by as the new retainers took over.

Some time later, Louchan appeared. He had been off on an errand, but was not surprised to see the Guild soldiers, or his underlings packing---he had read the denunciation. Meeting Zorachus, he grinned wickedly.

"Good luck, Lord Mancdarnan," he said, clearly hoping Zorachus would get nothing of the sort.

"And good luck to you, Louchan," Zorachus said, trying to mean it. "Perhaps your new master will be easier on you."

Louchan bowed. "Thank you, my Lord," he said, and made off.

Eventually, the old household gathered near the main stairway, and Zorachus gave everyone a year's pay. Then the Guild troops herded them all out.

As night approached, another contingent of Guild soldiers arrived, accompanied by a group of servants drawn from the vast labor force the Guild commanded. To safeguard Zorachus's meals, food-tasters were included, along with "kitchen-hawks" to monitor preparation. There was also a mason, to build Asa her garden---Zorachus had made sure that no mere change of staff would delay her tomatoes.

The newcomers were led by Louchan's replacement, a flabby little Tarchan named Alandax Sharthas, whose main qualification was that he had been Assistant Steward of the palace when it belonged to Kordus Kragon, one of Thagranichus Ordog's lieutenants. Besides that, he had an extremely commanding personality, surprisingly so, in light of his appearance; servants and soldiers jumped when he spoke. He also despised Khymirian attitudes; it was evident even in small snatches of his conversation, and generally he ended orders with phrases like "Get to it, you degenerate!" During one brief lull in the evening's activity (there was much moving in and rearranging to be done), Zorachus, wondering why the Tarchan had remained in Khymir after being freed, asked jokingly if he liked the city.

"Oh no, my lord," Sharthas said, shaking his head head like a sad old hound. His commanding mien had vanished---he was speaking to the master of the house. "Did I say something that led you to believe---"

"Not at all. As you might have noticed, I've been finding your contempt for things Khymirian quite amusing. Downright congenial, if it comes to that."

"That was my impression," Sharthas said.

"So. Why do you stay?"

Sharthas gave a watery smile and wiped sweat from his neck. "I won't burden you with the details."

"I don't mind," Zorachus said.

The Steward's face reddened; he seemed to be thinking of some excuse not to continue the conversation. Noticing several guards moving weapons into the wrong room, he roared directions at them and they stopped by the threshold, looking confused.

"Really, my Lord," Sharthas said, "I should attend to---"

"Of course," Zorachus replied. "But once things are squared away, you should come up to my room for a bit. Halfdan and Asa will be there. We can all have some wine."

Sharthas smiled uncomfortably. "That's very kind of you. But to be frank, I really don't want to share your bed. I know that sounds insubordinate, but I wasn't brought up in Khymir and I have different ... How do you say it ... Preferences..."

Zorachus laughed. "I wasn't brought up in Khymir, either. All we want to do is talk. Get acquainted. There won't be any groping, my word on it."

Sharthas was hesitant. "Well.... I suppose I could get enough work done.... But I'm sure it wouldn't be till midnight, at least."

"We'll see you then," Zorachus answered. Sharthas hurried off to deal with the guards, his meekness dropping away.

The night bustled on. Echoes frequently made it sound as if Sharthas were shouting in several places at once; there were few matters that did not receive his loud, competent attention. But after a time the activity began to slacken. Zorachus went with Halfdan and Asa to relax on his balcony, with a bottle of some lesser Tarchan vintage.

The Khymirian night oppressed them at first. Closer, denser than usual, the humid air hung heavy in their lungs. Gloom swarmed about the small circle of light from their lamp.

They passed the wine around. It took a while to hearten them, but gradually their spirits rose. The darkness seemed to recede a bit; the night seemed less thick.

Asa told of the problems she had had with the new mason. He was a foreigner of some sort who did not understand Khymirian very well, and her efforts to explain her plans to him seemed quite hilarious in retrospect, although she had been very frustrated at the time. He apparently thought the word *tomato* meant *wax tadpole*, and had spent a lot of time trying to demonstrate to her that she would not be able to raise such creatures (or mold them) in the structure he had outlined. Almost until the end, her every attempt to enlighten the fellow had gone horribly wrong, and by the time she finished telling Halfdan and Zorachus about her struggle, they were stretched out on the polished stones, sides near splitting.

Recovering, Zorachus said: "Reminds me of this merchant I met in Thangura once...." and went on to describe how the fellow had been part of a trade mission to an eastern land; woefully ignorant of the language, he had many misadventures, finally accepting some malicious advice on what to say to the monarch at an audience. When the time came and he stood before the throne, he said proudly: "Your majesty, I hope your wife becomes a big whore in my country." The hall filled with gasps, but the king only smiled and said: "That will be fine, but she'll have to send the money back here.'"

Halfdan came up with one of his own, a long and somewhat melancholy tale about a Tarchan man whose name sounded very much like "Pig, spit on me," in Kragehul. Visiting Muspellheim, he was doused in spittle whenever he introduced himself, and surrounded by furious Kragehul, blundering into four swordfights before he finally found out what was happening. But by then it was too late; one arm hacked off at the shoulder, he said to his opponent as he sagged down, dying, "Hell, it isn't even my real name..."

Zorachus laughed. "What's funny about that?"

Halfdan explained, very seriously: "He got killed because he was going about using this stupid name that...oh come on."

"Come on yourself."

"You laughed. I heard you."

"That was a sad tale. Tell me something *funny*."

"You do it," Halfdan told Asa, who launched into a story about her cousin Gerd, who was so ugly her parents made her sit at the door to scare off evil spirits.

"That was more poignant than funny," Zorachus said.

"Poignant?" Asa asked.

"Hard to explain."

"You laughed at some of it."

"Not at the more poignant parts."

"Whatever that means," Asa said, and nudged Halfdan. "Tell him about uncle Ingmar."

Halfdan gave a lengthy and colorful description of the man's character.

"That was funny," Zorachus declared.

Asa nudged Halfdan. "Don't stop..."

"Hmm?"

"The prawn story..."

"Right," said Halfdan, and related how Ingmar, having just rogered Gerda the Goosegirl, had explained to aunt Aud that he *couldn't* have done what she suspected because he'd been turned into a prawn by a sorcerer...maintaining he had witnesses, Ingmar had roused one in the middle of the night and been beaten bloody by him...Zorachus laughed right up until the end, when Aud chopped the fingers on Ingmar's left hand off with a hatchet.

"I thought it was quite funny till then," the Sharajnaghi said..

"That was the best part," Halfdan replied.

"Perhaps I should tell you a story about a man who was *actually* turned into a prawn."

"Let's have it," Halfdan said.

"This story is attested to---"

"Begin," said Asa.

Zorachus gave them the terrible tale of Nurheddin al-Nazrawi.

"Eee-yew," Asa laughed. "Eaten by his own true love?"

"What did I just say?" Zorachus asked.

Asa kept laughing. "That is definitely *not* funny."

Halfdan was laughing too. "Yes it is. Especially if it's true."

"I swear," said Zorachus.

"Actually," Asa said, "the part about how he was still wearing his pants..."

"Prawn-sized pants," Zorachus said.

"And she had to take them off to eat him..."

Halfdan joined in: "And he still had little cheeks..."

Soon all three of them were roaring. It was some time before they settled down, and a long lull followed. Tired of laughing, they did not mind the hush at first. A wonderful hour had passed. They lay quietly on the balcony, contented.

But contentment could not sustain itself. The dark seemed to creep inward once more. Little by little, feeding on their silence, the night's oppression came on them again.

Zorachus remembered how hot it was, became aware of how much he was sweating; his hair clung to his head, his clothes to his skin. But he resolved to ignore the heat and the lung-smothering humidity, refused to be pinioned by the steaming stillness. He drove himself to speak, even though the words themselves had no great urgency---any would do to push aside the damp, warm pillow stifling them.

"I invited Sharthas up," he said. "I'm surprised he isn't here yet."

"That fleshy little loudmouth?" Halfdan demanded, sitting up, roused by his own contempt.

"Did he shout at you?" Zorachus asked.

"No. But I don't like him."

"He was nice to me," Asa said.

"He knows we're high in Zorachus's favor," Halfdan announced. "If Zorachus wasn't the master..." He glanced at the Sharajnaghi. "Why *did* you ask him up?"

"For some talk," the Sharajnaghi replied. "He isn't a Khymirian, you know."

155

Halfdan jeered. "Tarchans aren't much better."

"Don't be silly," Asa said. "That Tarchan hostage your father held wasn't a bad sort. You said so."

"He hit my father pretty damn hard when he tried to escape," Halfdan shot back.

Asa frowned. "What would you expect? He didn't want his wife to pay all that ransom. That's really very reasonable. Besides, he taught you how to play chess." She told Zorachus: "Halfdan's a very good chess player, you know."

"I am that," Halfdan said sullenly.

"And you owe it all to that Tarchan," Asa answered.

"This Sharthas never did me any favors," Halfdan grumbled.

"He helped me find the mason."

"He's ugly. And he's probably a Guild spy."

"The house must be full of them now," Zorachus said. "But better Guild spies than Kletus's. We don't have to be quite so shy about showing how un-Khymirian we are...."

"Asa and I have never been shy about that," Halfdan broke in.

"Well, *I* had to be careful. If Kletus had thought I was mad, he might never have revealed his scheme... but the Guild's committed now. They can't withdraw their support. Of course, I don't want them to know my *real* plans..."

There was a knock at the door.

"That must be him," Zorachus said, and went in to answer it. Returning with Sharthas, he sat, motioning the Steward to do likewise. Sharthas complied hesitantly.

"You look a bit taut," Zorachus said. "Have some wine. It'll loosen you up."

Sharthas plucked at the sagging flesh under his chin. "Actually, my Lord, I could do with a bit less slack," he answered. "But as you're the master here...." Taking the bottle, he downed several gulps.

"Save some for us!" Halfdan cried.

"There's plenty left," Sharthas answered apologetically. Halfdan took the bottle away from him, hefting its contents.

"The wine reminds me of home," Sharthas said wistfully. "blessed Tarchan. All that sweet ignorance..."

"How did you wind up in Khymir?" Asa asked.

"I lived in a little village at the mouth of the Arkflight," Sharthas began. "Kragehul swept in one day and carried me and my brothers off--- "

"And you still haven't forgiven us for it, have you?" Halfdan broke in.

"I was quite upset at the time," Sharthas said. "But I don't think much about it now. As a matter of fact, I suppose I was treated rather well. From what I could gather, we were the best booty they could find. It had been a dismal raid and they wanted to save what little they had. They were going to sell us as thralls. But they never got the chance.

"Halfway up the muspel coast, they ran into the Khymirian fleet. They fought fiercely but were heavily outnumbered. The ship I was on caught fire and my brothers were killed, as were most of the crew. The Khymirians took me off, but tossed me in the brig---decided they'd sell me themselves, along with the surviving pirates. It was then that I started to see just how easy I'd had it with the Kragehul. The Khymirians acted like....well, Khymirians; at the time I found it hard to believe their cruelty. It frequently slipped their minds that they wanted us alive----they tortured several of the Kragehul to death, and I got my share, too. But as you can see, I managed to survive, and was sold as scullery help into the household of Kordus Kragon. Eventually, I worked my way up to Assistant Steward."

"How did you gain your freedom?" Zorachus asked.

"In a dice game. Kragon was a great one for gambling. He'd gamble with anyone for anything. One night, when he was alone and drunk, he invited me into his room and brought out his dice. 'Come on, Sharthas, you hangdog," he said. 'I'll play for your clothes, and you can play for your freedom.' He won time after time. Never seemed bothered that he was winning things that were already his. Finally I was down to my left shoe---and then he lost. Next afternoon, in the throes of a terrible headache, he signed my manumission. Somehow he remembered our deal. It surprised me greatly. He'd been so drunk."

"I'm surprised he paid up," Zorachus said. "I wouldn't have expected a Khymirian to be so conscientious."

"It was the way he was," Sharthas said. "He could sit down and eat live babies, but he never cheated at gambling and always paid his debts. I'll never understand Khymirians. Most of us.... rather, most of them, are wicked or insane, and the rest are both."

"Yet you stay among them," Halfdan said suspiciously.

The Tarchan nodded.

Halfdan barked a laugh. "Gorm's hammer! If I had my freedom, I'd be out of this city before you could blink."

"You *are* free," Zorachus said.

Halfdan harrumphed and pointed to Sharthas. "If I were *him*, and I had my freedom, I'd leave."

"Why do you stay, Sharthas?" Asa asked.

Sharthas looked pained. "I'd really rather not talk about it."

"Do you have a woman here?"

Sharthas remained silent.

"If it *was* a woman, he'd tell us,"Halfdan jeered. "It's probably a boy---if it's human at all."

"It's a woman," Sharthas replied.

"Couldn't you take her with you?" Asa asked.

"She's not mine."

"Is she married?"

Sharthas downcast his eyes. "She's a slave. In a brothel."

"Khymirian?"

"She's from Numalia."

"Ugh," Halfdan said. "Black."

Asa asked Sharthas. "Can't you buy her?"

He shook his head. "Even if I had the money, her master wouldn't sell. She's much too popular. God, she's beautiful." Pausing, he smiled slightly. "And expensive. My poor purse. I try to visit her every week or so."

Halfdan asked: "Don't you have any backbone, man? Forget her and leave this sty. She's just a woman."

"Just a woman!" Asa cried. "And what am I?"

"Nothing more."

"Do you know anything you'd like better?"

"A woman with a bit more respect."

Asa laughed harshly. "The kind who'd like you better for insulting her?"

"I didn't say that. And I didn't insult you. I insulted *women*. As a race. I don't see why you should take it personally---"

"I don't see why you should talk that way at all---"

"Asa---"

"Belittling me and my mother---"

Halfdan's jaw dropped. "I never said anything about your---"

"And as for poor Sharthas..." Tears welled up in Asa's eyes and she laid a comforting hand on the Tarchan's knee. "I understand how he feels. It must be terrible."

"What's your woman's name?" Zorachus asked Sharthas.

"Chatonha," Sharthas replied.

"Barbaric," Halfdan sulked.

"I like it," Asa said stoutly.

"I bet she has a ring in her nose," Halfdan went on.

"She wouldn't have any such thing," Asa returned.

"Actually, she does," Sharthas said.

Asa's face clouded.

"It's really rather fetching," Sharthas said.

"Do you fetch her with it?" Halfdan asked.

Very disturbed, Asa withdrew her hand.

Guessing how she felt, Sharthas opened his mouth to make a further defense of the bauble---then closed it again, wearily resting his chin on his palm, eyes full of embarrassment.

Halfdan folded his hands behind his head and smiled smugly at Asa. She ignored him.

Delighted with the absurd note on which the conversation had faltered, Zorachus studied the three of them with great amusement, unable to empathize much with Sharthas's discomfort; Halfdan and Asa were obviously right about noserings.

Suddenly warm stinging sweat trickled into his eyes. He rubbed them, but the salty irritation remained. It was some time before his sight cleared.

He looked at the others again. Their expressions had changed, become apprehensive. He told himself it was the silence; their voices had held back the night's oppression, but now it had settled once more, black pressure squeezing perspiration-slick flesh.

Yet he quickly realized it was not just the silence and the turgid air. Something was about to happen. His mind hummed with sensation, as it had when he had passed beneath the thunder-barrier, a feeling that the atmosphere had taken on some kind of charge. But where the energy he had felt under the clouds was clean, righteous despite its rage, the force he felt now was utterly foul, redolent of a spiritual corruption that had suppurated for ages.

And he had sensed it before, he was sure of it, in the palanquin, looking at the images of that twin-tongued face.

But had they been mere images even then?

A titanic hissing came from the west, and bloody light swept across the city, bathing the balcony. He and his companions leaped to their feet. Asa clutched at Halfdan, but he pushed her away and drew his sword, red light flashing on the steel. Sharthas prayed. Zorachus stood tensely, silently, arms at his sides.

A half-mile distant, a vast, leering, crimson-glowing face hovered over Khymir; double-tongued, it was the face from the palanquin.

"Mancdaman Zorachus!" the apparition thundered, forming the syllables even though its tongues continued to loll and crawl outside the mouth. What might have been a giant woman and a lamia sheltered in the curl of the lower tongue. "I am Morkulg the Mask, herald and messenger of his Anointed Steward Ghorchalanchor Kletus, High Priest of Tchernobog and Lord of Khymir. You are challenged, as all Khymir is witness, to meet his servant, Kourgon Zarathonzar, in a wizards' duel in Kralorg Square, tomorrow at the fourth hour. And there will you surely die."

Morkulg's leering eyes creased shut and his jaws began to grind, fangs driving into the tongues; black blood spurted as the tongues hitched gruesomely back into the mouth, and there was a shriek as the points stabbed through the shapes that the lower one held; then the tongues disappeared behind the fangs. Chewing steadily, drooling dark streams, Morkulg shot backward through the night sky. In seconds he was nothing more than a dwindling red star on the horizon, a point of light that flared and vanished. But his words still echoed from the mountainsides and over the rooftops, and as the reverberations faded, an outcry of human voices rose from all parts of the city.

"Sharthas," Zorachus said, "I must speak with my councilors."

"Of course, my Lord," the Steward replied in a trembling voice, withdrawing.

"Tell the guards we're not to be disturbed----unless there's a message from the Guild."

"Certainly," Sharthas called over his shoulder.

"Are you going to accept?" Asa asked Zorachus once Sharthas had disappeared. "If they can control demons like that ......"

"It was only a phantasm," he replied. "Not much more than an illusion...I could conjure one as frightening."

"But it looked so real. And I could *feel* it...."

Zorachus nodded. "It was the image of a real demon. And they gave us a taste of his presence, to add to the horror. But he wasn't fully invoked."

"Can you take Zarathonzar?' Halfdan asked.

"I expect," Zorachus replied.

"There's sure to be some sort of treachery."

"I wouldn't be surprised. But I can't back down. Kletus wants me dead, or humiliated. Either way, he wins."

"Well," Halfdan said, "if you beat Zarathonzar, the guards and I'll do our best to protect you afterward. We'll have to leave enough troops to hold the palace---"

"The Guild will send us more," Zorachus said.

"Will you let me go with you?" Asa asked.

"To the *duel*!" Halfdan demanded.

"Yes."

"Out of the question."

161

"Much too dangerous," Zorachus agreed. "However it goes, there'll probably be a riot...Halfdan and I might be killed."

Asa said resolutely: "Sharing your fate would be the only honorable thing."

"Oh?"

"Halfdan's my husband---"

"I've heard."

"---and you're my friend."

"I'm deeply flattered," Zorachus said. "You'd still be better off alive."

"I'm coming with you," Asa insisted.

"I'll lock you in your room," Halfdan snapped.

"You wouldn't dare!"

"Try me."

Asa folded her arms on her chest. "All right then. But I'll make your life hell if you do come back. And if you don't, I'll kill myself. So there's no point in *not* taking me."

"Would she kill herself, Halfdan?" Zorachus asked.

"She can be awfully contrary," Halfdan said.

Zorachus's first thought, pure philosopher's reflex, was that he should try to demonstrate the immorality of suicide. But Asa had the look of someone whose mind was set, and furthermore, he did not know how to begin arguing about that particular subject with a Kragehul barbarian.

And even if you talk her out of killing herself, there's her other threat...

"Would she really make your life hell?" he asked Halfdan.

"As I said, she can be awfully..."

"Contrary," Asa broke in.

Halfdan shrugged and tried to look as if he had never opposed her accompanying them in the first place. "You can come--- If Zorachus agrees."

Zorachus nodded his assent. "She is *your* wife." He felt a twinge of jealousy; for an instant he doubted his wisdom in choosing celibacy. Could he have inspired such devotion in a woman?

162

Halfdan kissed Asa, gave her a hug that brought a gasp to her lips. "Yes," he growled affectionately, "for good or ill, she's mine."

Chapter 12

KRALORG SQUARE LAY southeast of Banipal Khezach. Once it had been a kind of religious bazaar, where cults had competed for worshippers, but over the years the sects had withered, and their temples had fallen into scabrous disrepair. Defaced and weathered idols stared down mournfully from facades covered with moss and mold. Usually the square was almost empty, with a few diseased whores, plying their trade in alleys and alcoves, drawing the meager traffic it still saw.

But today "Dead God Place" (as the area was sometimes called) was thronged; public wizards' duels were extravagant entertainments that came along once in a lifetime. Spectators fought and elbowed each other for places. Some were mounted on crates, wagons, or stools; others had slaves to stand on, or had hired men for that purpose. Many people had gone up onto the roofs or balconies of the temples. The most reckless (or death-hungry) stood on the rim of the dueling circle, or even inside. Oddsmakers threaded their way through the crowd, and pickpockets did splendid business. Vendors hawked food and drink, as well as a drug said to make violence more arousing to jaded onlookers. Troops of beggars extorted money from helpless victims. Small groups of redclads were scattered throughout the crowd; tall black hand standards stood, as if in benediction, over several of the units. A single large contingent of Guild soldiers waited on the eastern side of the square.

Zorachus and Zarathonzar arrived with their followers at roughly the same time, shortly before the Fourth Hour. Eager for the duel to begin, the crowd parted to let them pass, though the Priest and his men drew a storm of curses and catcalls.

Stepping up to the edge of the dueling circle, Zorachus scanned the enemy retinue. Zarathonzar was the only Priest evident. Apparently his colleagues thought it prudent to keep out of the danger zone. He was well-protected nonetheless; with him stood at least twenty Cohort Ravener swordsmen, one a towering black---Thulusu.

A lock of damp hair fell before Zorachus's eyes, trailing sweat across his forehead. He brushed it back up, cursing the heat, his stomach knotted with apprehension, for Halfdan and Asa as well as himself...

Please God, he prayed, *protect me and my friends, and grant me victory.....don't let my mission end in this place, I beg you...*

The last few minutes passed sluggishly, but finally a sundial on one of the temple facades indicated the Fourth Hour; Zarathonzar swaggered into the dueling circle, and the crowd hushed.

"Mancdaman Zorachus!" he cried. "Come forth, dog!"

Zorachus turned and shook hands with Halfdan.

"Good luck," the Kragehul said and stepped back.

Zorachus reached for his ring pouch, but as he did so, Asa leaped up, hugged him tightly, and kissed him on the cheek. For an aching moment he returned her embrace; he had never held a woman before.

"Win," she said. "You must win."

"Come forth, dog!" Zarathonzar shouted, the sound of his voice incredibly hateful in Zorachus's ears. Stifling the anger that spurted up in him, Zorachus let Asa go, smiling at her. Then, still feeling the warmth of her lips on his cheek, he turned and went out into the circle, moving off to the right to reduce the chance of a stray bolt striking his followers.

Thirty feet from Zarathonzar, he halted, entering a two-shielded Dragon Stance. Zarathonzar assumed something like a Basilisk Stance, one shield up. The two faced each other like iron statues, garments hanging motionless in the stagnant air.

Suddenly, Zorachus realized he had forgotten to put the demon-rings on.

She distracted you...

He dared not open the pouch; if he dropped stance, he'd leave himself wide open.

Oh you horrible fool...

Blood pounding in his throat, he squinted through the bright afternoon haze towards his foe, telling himself to forget the mistake.

What's done is done...

Zarathonzar's free hand whipped forward in a crimson glare.

A reddish spiral bolt, flinging off green sparks, struck Zorachus's shields in a dazzling blast, caromed skyward and dissipated. The impact jolted the Sharajnaghi, but not badly---it would have taken several such bolts to harm him even if his shields had been down.

Zarathonzar launched another and another, probing. Zorachus let his defenses look weaker than they were, and at the fourth impact, dropped

165

his forward shield. Seeing that, Zarathonzar immediately discarded his protection, raising his hands for a swift double strike.

But as the Priest's shield vanished, Zorachus launched a strike of his own, a staccato line of glittering blue crescents that hammered into Zarathonzar's stomach. The Priest's robes exploded in black tatters and he hurtled back several feet. Yet to Zorachus's amazement, he did not fall; indeed, Zarathonzar retained enough control to raise two shields. Half his muscular body laid bare, he drew himself erect, eyes burning.

Zorachus lashed out with cataract strikes. Zarathonzar withstood them with ease, watching the Sharajnaghi warily, obviously expecting another ruse.

Zorachus maintained his strikes for several more seconds, then shifted into a binding stance and shouted a summoning spell. He knew it would not work---he had not done enough forceletting---but Zarathonzar shifted stance too and began a counterspell. Zorachus had not expected him to finish forceletting so early in the duel, but it did not matter; the Sharajnaghi's feint had done its work.

Dropping his remaining shield, Zorachus launched two powerful greenish beams straight down into the ground. Bits of crushed cobblestones peppered his trouser legs as he shot into the Air.

Too late, Zarathonzar grasped what was happening. Freeing one hand, he unleashed a savage sun-bright bolt which passed between Zorachus's legs and slammed devastatingly into the crowd behind.

High above the smoking pavement, Zorachus thrust his arms up and sent two maximum crescent strikes over the top of Zarathonzar's remaining shield. Stunned, the Priest catapulted backward to the cobbles, shield dissipated, hair burned down to the scalp, tattered robes blasted from his body. Thunderous cheers rose from the crowd.

Landing, Zorachus eyed Zarathonzar's prostrate form. He supposed he would have no more trouble with him---for the time being, at least.

If only I could finish him, he thought. *Put him out of the war once and for all...*

But that was out of the question. Sharajnaghim were forbidden to kill helpless enemies. He was disgusted with himself for having thought of it at all. And yet---

Zarathonzar was a Priest of Tchernobog, a mass murderer, monstrously evil. He deserved to die.

166

They all deserved it....

"Enough," Zorachus told himself, shaking his head. Turning, he headed back towards his retinue.

Halfdan was standing with his arms crossed, his whole demeanor very smug, as though he had expected the outcome. Asa was waving and jumping up and down, most of the crowd doing likewise. The uproar hadn't diminished at all.

But Zorachus had only gone a few paces when it simply stopped, broken by what sounded like a single vast intake of breath, the momentary pause before an explosion of screams and warnings. People were pointing to something behind him---Asa looked absolutely frantic. He spun, hurling up both shields.

Incredibly, Zarathonzar was on his feet again, swaying as he entered a stance; two yard-long spears of furious energy, white and crackling, shot from his palms. Zorachus's bucklers held, but the bolts did not deflect or dissipate; hanging in midair, they grew sharper, brighter, thinner. Finally, no more than bitter glaring threads, they pierced the shields. Zorachus had shifted an instant before and they missed his body, but one halted over his right arm, the other beneath it; both pressing into his flesh, they expanded once more, somehow keeping their focus, tangible as oaken dowels. Before he could think of a counterspell, they lifted from horizontal to vertical, dislocating his arm. Flesh split. Pain tore his mind in white-hot bursts. His shields deserted him and a long shriek came ripping from his throat. The adamantine spears tilted back and back....

Then they were gone. Through agony-bleared eyes, he saw Zarathonzar teetering, pawing dizzily at his head. Zorachus's crescent strikes had taken their toll, the Priest's astounding recovery notwithstanding.

Forcing his mind to function, Zorachus sized up his position. His right arm was useless for strikes, though he could still emanate a shield from the palm. Grabbing his dangling right hand, he tucked the fingers inside his belt, palm outwards. With a supreme effort he forced energy down through his shrieking tissues; a weak shield took shape.

Across from him, Zarathonzar managed to restore one of his shields, but it was no stronger than the Sharajnaghi's. Zorachus launched a yellow left-hand strike, the most powerful at his command, and Zarathonzar's buckler shattered. Zorachus gave him another, full in the chest. Zarathonzar's skin purpled with a massive hemorrhage.

167

Even so his strength did not give out; his repelling forces had been disrupted, but his binding forces were another matter. Clumsily, he assumed a one-handed binding stance, and without even a spell, ripped up the pavement before him, forming a barrier of cobblestones.

Zorachus launched a bolt at the wall. It struck with a vicious crack and powdered stone spat from the cobbles. But the barrier still stood and, even as the sound of impact echoed from the surrounding temples, the wall rose and hurtled at Zorachus with tremendous speed.

He blasted it again, widening the gouge he had made. Still in one piece, the wall swept near.

He dodged. Momentum carried it into the spectators. There was a sickening crunch and a chorus of screams and shouts.

Zorachus hit Zarathonzar with two more bolts, stabbing with cruel precision into the Priest's hemorrhaged flesh. Zarathonzar went down on one knee---

And was up again in an instant.

Incredible, Zorachus thought, appalled by the Priest's endurance. *So much for first impressions...*

Cries from the crowd told him the wall was moving again; he wheeled to see the careening mass almost upon him. Dodging it, he remembered the rings, but found he could not undo the pouch one-handed.

The wall started back at him, picking up speed. He struck it with a bolt which might as well have been aimed at the sky, then opted for the first spell that leaped to mind, muttering a four-word formula, hoping he had exhausted enough of his repelling energies, sensing he was just on the borderline....

Most of the wall vanished---he had opened a dimensional portal, a doorway to another plane, in its path.

But a chunk was sheared off; trailing a streak of pulverized stone, it kept coming, crashing into his feeble right-hand shield. Mere stone would have penetrated; the shield was proof only against magic. But magic held the remnant together and the missile could not strike home. Even so, his stricken shoulder was badly twisted by the impact and he rocked to the pavement, screaming with pain, shield gone.

The chunk shot forward, halted over his face, then descended like the maul of an invisible giant. He rolled. Striking the pavement where his head had been a split instant before, it shattered.

He lifted himself on one elbow. Zarathonzar stood across from him, unsteady but still in his binding stance. The gigantic bruise had darkened to black; elsewhere his skin was pale white. Zorachus guessed he was dying. But he also knew the Priest might yet be able to drag him down.

The Sharajnaghi conjured another portal; it opened under Zarathonzar just as the Priest bound one of the cobbles from the wall-fragment and sent it glancing off Zorachus's chin. The Sharajnaghi was not badly hurt but his mind was jarred, his spell broken; as Zarathonzar plunged into the portal it snapped shut about his waist, slicing him in half.

The Priest looked downwards in agony and amazement, gesturing helplessly. Then his arms fell at his sides and his head sagged; chin on chest, he died, a nude torso resting upright on the pavement like a broken statue.

Zorachus got to his feet. His right hand slipped from his belt, and his dislocated arm hung limp at his side, sleeve soaked with blood. Warm sticky moisture plastered his tunic to the side of his chest. He stared stupidly at the red drops falling from his right thumb.

It occurred to him that the crowd was strangely silent. Looking up, he noticed redclads spreading out on the western side of the circle, hemming the throng; two ranks deep, the cordon lengthened steadily.

Turning, he stumbled toward his followers, who had formed a shieldburg. Halfdan and several retainers rushed out to join him.

"Where did all those redclads come from?" the Sharajnaghi asked as they hurried him along.

"They hid their numbers," Halfdan said. "Stayed in small groups till the duel began and everyone was distracted. Then they gathered around those standards---"

They got Zorachus inside.

"We're fucked!" someone shouted.

A great lane had opened in the crowd; people were throwing cobblestones at a large body of redclads who were jogging along in their armor as though nothing were happening.

169

"Where are the Guild troops?" Zorachus asked Halfdan, wincing at a throb from his shoulder.

The Kragehul pointed. Many of the soldiers were still mounted on the wagons and stools they had climbed upon to watch the duel.

"Bastards haven't stirred an inch," Halfdan said.

"Might've been bought," Zorachus said.

"Might just be cowards," Halfdan replied.

As the redclads neared the shieldburg, a whistle sounded, and they drew themselves up, stamping. It shrieked again; some distance back, alternating ranks moved left and right, then raced forward along the outsides of the column, sealing the burg off north and south. The side facing the dueling circle was still open, but not for long; led by Thulusu, the men from Zarathonzar's retinue, much reinforced, were coming, mail-scales rattling, booted feet striking the pave with a steady sharp crunching noise.

Halfdan looked at the blood blackening Zorachus's grey tunic. "Will you be able to help us? We'll need some magic to get us out of this..."

"I don't know," Zorachus replied.

"WII then, get into the middle of the square."

Supported by Asa, Zorachus complied weakly.

Halfdan looked round at the retainers. Those nearby had turned anxiously towards him, faces grey---they knew what the redclads were capable of.

"Yes, you're in it now," he cried. "But fear won't save you."

One of them said: "We can't just stay here..."

"No we can't," Halfdan answered. "Since our friends in the main body don't want to join us, we should join them---put our backs to those wagons! Look, it's not that far!" He went to the eastern side of the burg. "Keep your shields up! Let's go! Nice and steady!"

They started forward. For an instant the redclads held firm, but they seemed more startled than resolute, as though they had been expecting, simply, to cow their foes into submission. But then they began to back up, the crowd behind them opening once more, throwing stones, shouting for them to let Zorachus pass.

The shieldburg pressed on. Zorachus wondered how long the redclads would allow their humilition to continue. Then Thulusu's voice boomed out and the scarlet ranks stiffened; huge two-handed swords flashed free. Zorachus's men drew their brands in reply.

Halfdan returned to the eastern side of the wedge. Thulusu's men had filled the gap left by the shieldburg's brief advance.

"What's the meaning of this?" Halfdan cried, taking a place in the line and brandishing his sword at thulusu. "Lord Mancdaman defeated Zarathonzar in fair combat!"

"Indeed," Thulusu replied. "It's only fitting that he should receive Lord Kletus's congratulations---face to face. My men'll gladly serve as an honor guard."

"And what if he refuses?" Halfdan demanded.

Thulusu grinned down at him, teeth gleaming white. "Then you'll all die," he said with high good humor.

Halfdan squinted at him for a few moments, then said over his shoulder: "What do you think, Lord Mancdaman?"

It was some time before Zorachus answered. "I'm afraid I don't care a fig about Lord Kletus's congratulations," he called in a loud but trembling voice.

Halfdan turned back to Thulusu. "You heard him," he said apologetically---

And slashed at the giant black's face.

Jumping backward, Thulusu barely saved himself; even so, the bridge of his nose was shorn through.

"Kill them!" he cried to his men. As they crashed in on all sides, blades beating upon the retainers' bucklers, he charged at Halfdan, roaring, hewing. In moments the top of Halfdan's shield was reduced to splinters; the Kragehul had not managed to launch a single stroke when the grip was smashed from his hand. With a powerful descending sweep, Thulusu battered the Kragehul's sword down, and a second blow ripped Halfdan's byrny, plucking padding from his gambeson.

Clapping both hands to his hilt, Halfdan tried to go on the offensive, but his first two strokes were effortlessly parried, and then Thulusu's steel came whistling in repayment. Halfdan ducked; the blade caught the top of his helmet and shaved it away. The helm was strapped on tightly, and he felt for an instant as though his head had been torn halfway off his neck; cursing, grimacing, he saw Thulusu raising his sword for the final blow, and struck upwards as the redclad's blade descended. There was a spatter of blood as his edge sheared off Thulusu's right hand at the wrist. Thulusu howled, his stump geysering scarlet as he retreated, the whole redclad center buckling backwards with him, men scrambling to bear him up or shield him....Halfdan laughed fiercely, shaking his head, things popping in his neck.

For the moment he had no one to fight.

But redclads were flowing back in at the sides now...he chopped one, but his blade bounced from armor and the man moved farther to the right. Another rushed up; Halfdan hacked him in the shoulder. Scales jumped into the air. Then Halfdan felt a shock on the head, he blinked, and the man had been replaced by a different redclad. Halfdan deflected one slash, leaped over the next, and hacked into the man's chest. So much blood boiled forth that Halfdan thought for a moment the red scale-mail was melting, but the man barely flinched, and bashed a great dent in Halfdan's helm, tearing the scalp beneath. Blood streaming down his brow, dripping past one eye, Halfdan grunted and lunged, driving his sword deep through the hole in the redclad's armor. The man shrieked and hurled himself back off the point, falling in a heap.

All at once Halfdan realized there were redclads on either side of him; the front line of the wedge had been broken. He slipped back through the second shieldwall, panting.

A dead retainer fell beside him. Halfdan took the shield from the corpse's arm and leaped back into the fight. He wounded two redclads and killed another, but the retainers flanking him were hewn down and he had to retreat once more.

The shieldburg shrank steadily. The terrible Cohort Ravener swords rose and fell, and the air was filled with the boom and crunch of them pounding the buckler-walls; bits of rim and wood flew from the battered shields. If the redclads had not been too eager, hampering themselves with their own numbers, the fight would have ended quickly.

Even so, it promised to end soon enough. The retainers were far overmatched, and the Guild troops showed no sign of coming to their aid. The spectators hurled more and more stones at the redclads, but kept their distance.

Sick and weary, Zorachus leaned on Asa's shoulder, watching the carnage close in. Near them a redclad broke into the shieldburg, sword wheeling. Two retainers set on him, but he killed them both with a single stroke, then rushed at Zorachus and Asa.

Asa hurled a dagger. It struck the redclad's left eye pommel-first, and he yowled and dropped his sword. Leaving Zorachus tottering, Asa stooped, snatched up her weapon, and jabbed it hilt-deep in the redclad's throat. Mouth working soundlessly, he grabbed her wrist with both hands. She punched his injured eye with her free fist, and he let go and stumbled off, the knife still in his neck. Three retainers struck him down in a flurry of steel.

Arms raised in triumph, red-gold hair streaming, Asa gave a ringing yell, then rushed back to Zorachus, lending him her shoulder once more.

"Showed the bastard, didn't I?" she cried. "Did you see?"

Laughing, she called to Halfdan in their tongue, but if he heard, he gave no sign, hacking ceaselessly at the redclads, felling one after another, a tower of strength in a crumbling fortress.

Zorachus was seized with admiration for him and his mate. They were bloodthirsty and barbaric, but greathearted, unafraid, even joyous in the face of certain death; simply knowing that such souls existed sent a wave of sheer exhilaration coursing through him, driving back the weakness in his veins. His mind freed itself from pain and dizziness. Was there any way he could save his friends?

The rings.

He could wield one, for a while at least...pointing to the pouch, he told Asa:

"Open it. Hurry!"

Once the drawstring was undone, he took out a ring and slid it up his finger with his teeth.

A retainer's severed head bumped against his foot. Two redclads bounded in over the decapitated body, one behind the other.

Zorachus discharged the ring into the first. The bolt went clear through him, ripping into the next man---both flew backward out of the wedge.

Zorachus raised his good hand, fist clenched, and sent four bolts crackling over his retainers' heads into the surrounding enemy. Hornhelmed heads and armored chests shattered in billows of pink steam; melted mail-scales streaked like meteors.

The redclads faltered, pulled back from the shieldburg. The retainers laughed and jeered at them, waving their notched swords and blade-chewed shields.

But it was not over yet. The redclad commanders rallied their men and again the long curving brands thundered into the battered shieldwall.

Zorachus answered with a fresh series of blasts. Scalemailed bodies spun and crumpled. Mouths belched smoke and blood. The redclads retreated once more.

At that, the Guild Captain finally ordered his men into the fight. Ripping their swords free, they leaped down from their stools and wagons, the crowd letting them through, egging them on.

At the first shock, some redclads went down, but after the firebolts, Guild troops were almost a relief; the redclads began to take a deadly toll, the sound of their swords like the chopping of cleavers in a butcher shop. The Guild soldiers wavered, their losses frightful, mounting almost every time a curving brand fell.

In the meantime, though, Asa had cooled Zorachus's ring with water from a bag, wrenched it from his seared flesh, and switched it to an unburned finger; now he dealt out more firebolts, killing six redclads outright, blowing arms or legs off five others.

That was too much for the rest. Keeping good order, giving the Sharajnaghi's men a wide berth, they withdrew towards the dueling circle, which was still cordoned off by their comrades. The Guild troops made no attempt to follow, though they killed the redclad wounded with relish.

The redclads pushed out across the circle. When they reached the far side, one of their officers sounded a horn-blast and the cordon-troops backed towards their comrades.

Rumbling and jeering, the mob followed cautiously. As the last cordon-troops rejoined their fellows, the redclads were pelted with stones and soon engulfed by the crowd. Closing ranks, they continued westward from the square, hacking apart any who stayed in their path.

As the redclads withdrew, the Guild troops came to join Zorachus's men. But the retainers cursed them for not coming sooner into the fight, and another battle would have broken out then and there if Halfdan and the Guild Captain had not prevented it. Once things settled down, the Captain, smiling broadly, came forward to meet Zorachus.

"Glad to see you're alive, Lord Mancdaman," he said.

"If he is, it's no thanks to you," Asa snapped, shifting under Zorachus's arm.

"Shh," Zorachus said. "He ordered his men in---eventually. I'm wondering, though, what his masters will say when they learn what happened."

"I waited till I saw a real opening," the Captain explained. He leaned close to Zorachus, and in a low voice said: "Those fools of mine would've been slaughtered if you hadn't panicked the redclads. A crowd of bumbling cowards, that's all I've got to work with. Maranchthus is too much of a miser to hire real swordsmen, and... ."

"So you think your men are bumblers and cowards?" Asa demanded, shouting with all the lungpower at her disposal, which was considerable. The captain's jaw sagged. Curses went up from his troops.

"Cowards?" cried one brown-mailed soldier, clutching a bleeding arm. "*We're* cowards? Who told us to hold back?"

"Asa, not another word," Zorachus said. In spite of everything, he did not want to see the Captain murdered on the spot. But his weakness had returned, and he delivered the command with little authority.

"He said Maranchthus is too cheap to hire decent troops," Asa crowed.

"Bitch," the Captain snarled, and wheeled to face his men, minded to make some denial. But the sight of their faces shattered that hope, and he darted off to the side. A half-dozen soldiers rushed after him, swearing, more soon joining the chase.

"Was that necessary?" Zorachus asked Asa numbly.

A shriek erupted in the near distance, then was brutally cut off.

"I couldn't let him get away with it," she replied, wincing as more and more of Zorachus's weight fell on her.

"I'm sure the Guildsmen would've...." His voice trailed off. Somehow, he could not bring himself to feel any pity for the man. He was too exhausted.

"Think you can make it back to the palace?" Halfdan asked. "You've lost a lot of blood."

175

Before Zorachus could answer, a wave of dizziness swept him. His legs seemed to go boneless, and in spite of Asa's support, he fell on his knees. "Healing spell..." he mumbled, and collapsed. The world upended in oblivion.

Wounds bandaged, Thulusu lay brooding on a cot in his austere quarters, waiting for Kletus. Finally the High Priest arrived with Lysthragon and Sathaswenthar. Thulusu started to sit up, but Kletus waved him back down.

"I grieve to have failed you, my Lord," the black said. It was completely heartfelt; he was capable of deep devotion to a man he freely chose to acknowledge as his master, and Kletus was that man, embodying the only human qualities Thulusu valued----strength, ruthlessness, and will---to an almost superhuman degree. Thulusu had been shamed in the service of his iron-hard ideal, and though his voice was calm and his face impassive, his anguish was intense.

"Don't fret over it," Kletus answered, very businesslike. He had already read several reports of the events in Kralorg Square. "The fault was mine. Who'd have thought he'd still be able to cause trouble after a bout with Zarathonzar?"

"I should've stayed," Thulusu said.

"Your men wouldn't hear of it. And really, it's a good thing."

"I let that Kragehul bastard take my hand off..."

Kletus smiled soothingly. "You're not made of steel. A fighter can't always be in top form."

"I let him enrage me."

Kletus lifted his hands. "All in the past. You're one of my best servants, and we'll have you back in action soon enough. I'll speak to old Morthus, downstairs..."

"That codger that tries to suck on everyone's hands?"

"Hands are his speciality," Kletus said. "He's forged some good ones, too..."

"How do you feel?" Sathaswenthar asked Thulusu.

The black raised his bandaged stump. "Like gutting the man who did this to me."

"That's better," Kletus said. "Rage against *him*. Not yourself. The self is sacred. I've willed it so." He paused. "However, the man you want---the bodyguard---will probably be dead before you get a chance at him. We'll be avenging Zarathonzar and your great black paw very soon."

"What happened to Zarathonzar's body?" Thulusu asked. "It was still sitting in the square when I was borne off."

"The main force didn't have time for it," Kletus said ruefully. "Pity. The crowd tore it apart. The available half, that is. Carried his head about on a pole."

"He deserved better," Thulusu said. "He fought well."

"As well as he could, no doubt."

"It seemed an even enough contest to me."

"It wasn't."

"I know Zorachus felled him quickly, but he came back---"

"Zorachus spared him."

"Spared him?"Thulusu asked.

"Why, I don't know."

"Maybe he thought Zarathonzar was dead."

Kletus shook his head.

"For a moment there, I thought Zarathonzar had exploded," Thulusu said.

"Stun-bolts produce all sorts of startling effects," Kletus said. "They'll Blow your clothes off, among other things. But they simply don't kill."

"But what makes you think Zorachus is so powerful? He could hardly stand when the duel was over. Zarathonzar almost had him."

"Zarathonzar took him by surprise. Zorachus thought he was out cold--- and with very good reason. Yet even with the advantage of surprise, Zarathonzar still lost."

"But .... "

A twinge of impatience entered Kletus's expression. "According to my observers, Zorachus opened two dimensional portals all by himself. Quite a trick---especially after Zarathonzar had already torn one of his arms half off. We *mustn't* underestimate him. If the reports are correct--- and I have no reason to think they're not--- Zarathonzar fought the most powerful mage who's ever lived."

Thulusu was silent for a few moments, digesting this. "Then why didn't Zorachus kill him right off?"

"I don't know," Kletus answered, but the look in his eyes plainly showed that he had already given the matter some hard thought.

"It's almost as if. . . ." Lysthragon ended in a senile titter.

"As if what?" Kletus asked.

Lysthragon grinned his mindless monkey's grin. "He took all that Sharajnaghi nonsense seriously."

Kletus snorted at the very idea, knowing Lysthragon was simply indulging his taste for absurdity. But Thulusu asked:

"What nonsense is that?"

"Zorachus was once a Sharajnaghi," Sathaswenthar explained, "a member of a wizard's order called the *Comahi Irakhoum*. Publicly, Sharajnaghim always maintain that killing should be avoided unless it's absolutely necessary---that helpless foes should be spared, for example."

"What could be more necessary than killing one's enemies? What difference does it make if they're helpless?"

"None, of course," Kletus replied. "As I'm sure Zorachus himself realizes. I can't imagine him, or anyone, sparing a foe because of the Sharajnaghi Code."

"Then why *did* he do it?" Thulusu pressed.

"Who can say? Perhaps he doesn't *like* killing, or thinks he doesn't. There *are* people who seem to be repulsed by bloodshed."

"The entertainment at the banquet seemed to make him most uncomfortable," Sathaswenthar put in.

"Still," Kletus continued, "He can't be too squeamish. He wouldn't have chosen to set himself against us."

A slight smile touched Sathaswenthar's lips. "True enough."

"He's badly wounded," Kletus said. "If we conjure a sending, we might finish him tonight."

"What about the Guildsmen?"

"We'll deal with them soon enough. But he must be eliminated first. They're spiders. He's a serpent."

"You're frightened of him," Thulusu said, disturbed to detect apprehension in his idol.

Kletus nodded. "He's thirty-three years old and already wields a power greater than mine," he said with disarming candor. "In a very real sense, he's one of my nightmares come true. Why shouldn't I fear him?"

Thulusu pondered the High Priest's reply. It occurred to him that the man Kletus feared might be a more worthy master; but then he thought about Zorachus sparing Zarathonzar, and his lack of enthusiasm at the banquet...it *was* possible that Zorachus had no taste for blood, that he was a weakling at heart despite his prowess....

Thulusu decided to put the matter aside for further consideration. In the meantime, Kletus was still the closest thing to perfection that he had certain knowledge of, and he watched with admiration as his Lord brought out one of his meat-wallets and took a huge mouthful of human flesh.

Chapter 13

ZORACHUS WOKE. DULL pain gnawed deep in his shoulder, and his burned fingers ached, but it seemed to him that some measure of his strength had returned.

He heard a gentle whirring noise beside him. Asa was sitting next to the bed, playing raptly with a lever-operated wheel-toy.

They were not in his room; this one was much bigger, almost cavernous, and there were no windows. The ceiling writhed with swirling ornaments, and the walls were knobbed and irregular. Larger-than-life statues of copulating bodies thrust up from the floor, obscene marble lumps, bright blood-red, as was almost everything else in the room. The chamber looked like the inside of a candlelit internal organ. The only details breaking the effect, even slightly, were several silver candlesticks on a grotesquely carved cabinet.

He looked back at Asa. She was still playing with the toy, but noticed presently that he was awake.

"He's come round," she called to Halfdan, who stood outside talking with two guards. He came in, silver medallion gleaming on his chest.

Zorachus sat up, asking: "Why did you put me in this room? It may be the ugliest place I've ever seen."

Before Halfdan could reply, Asa cut in: "We wanted to surprise you."

"Thanks," Zorachus said.

"It's safer than yours," Halfdan said. "No balconies or windows."

Zorachus nodded. His left hand, fingers swathed in linen strips, wandered over to his wounded shoulder. "Who tended me?"

"Porchos sent a surgeon," Asa said. "The best in Khymir, from what I gathered. Kadjafi named Aliphar. He did the strangest things to you."

"Such as?"

"To start with, he took a bit of your blood and made passes over it. Then he picked one of the slaves he'd brought, stuck a little tube into his arm, and ran the other end into yours...that little bandage is where the tube went in. The slave made fists and his blood started pumping into your veins. Aliphar stitched you up, and before he finished, switched slaves, since the first one was looking a bit pale..."

"It the damnedest thing," Halfdan said.

"Sounds like it," Zorachus replied.

"Said he came up with the idea, all by himself. Asa and I were pretty leery about letting him use it on you, but...seems it worked."

Asa said: "We thought it would be days before you woke up---"

"If you woke up at all," Halfdan said. "Your shoulder clotted before we got halfway to the palace, but your clothes were already sodden."

Zorachus eyed a shaved and threaded strip on Halfdan's scalp. "Aliphar sew you up too?"

The Kragehul shook his head. "Sharthas. He's good with a needle, I'll give him that."

Zorachus was silent a few moments. "Any word from Porchos?"

"Congratulations."

"Was that all?"

"He said you should stay put here."

"Did he send any reinforcements, by any chance?"

"A hundred and fifty troops."

"Any wizards?"

"Four, from his own household."

"Four," Zorachus said, almost to himself, pleasantly surprised. When he had asked the Guildsmen to supply him with a new household, they had turned down his request for mages, saying they feared to weaken their own defenses; but he had guessed they did not trust him enough to lend him such help.

"They'll stay until you've recovered," Halfdan said. "they're downstairs. Do you want to talk to them?"

Zorachus shook his head. "How's Sharthas managing? He must have his hands full with all those new troops."

"He's doing just fine. Seems to thrive on it."

"What's been happening in the city?"

Halfdan answered joyfully: "All hell's broken loose. Riots, looting, fires, all sorts of fighting..."

"How's the guild faring?"

"Well in the south, badly in the north. Pretty much as you'd expect."

"There was a wizard's battle a half a mile from here," Asa said excitedly. "Some Priests were trying to get back to the tower and Guild magicians attacked them. When it was over, a whole palace was lying in ruins and both groups had killed each other to a man."

"You've touched off a real blaze, Zorachus," Halfdan said, "Fate's working mightily through you."

Asa said: "Let's just hope---"

"What?" Zorachus asked.

"It doesn't make you undo yourself."

"Cheerful thought."

"That's why I stopped."

"Listen," Zorachus said. "If I'm undone, it'll be by my own choices. I put myself into this situation."

"Fate makes your choices," Asa countered. "You do what you're destined to do."

"No," Zorachus answered.

"No?"

"I think human beings have something called free will."

"And what's that?" Halfdan asked.

"The power to make their own choices. Decide their own destinies. Partially, at least."

"That's foolish," Halfdan answered. "Decide our own destinies? No man lives till nightfall whom Fate dooms at dawning."

"Perhaps not. If Fate's preparing to drop a rock on my head, I'm in deep trouble, certainly. But the mere fact that Fate's planning such a thing doesn't *cause* me to walk underneath. The choice isn't thrust on me from outside."

"Why would you think something like that?" Asa asked. Plainly the idea of such freedom was quite foreign to her.

"Because that's my experience."

"When you walk under falling rocks?" Halfdan asked, in all seriousness.

"When I make choices," Zorachus said. "As far as I can tell, I make them freely."

"That's just how it seems," Asa said.

"Well yes. But why ignore the feeling? It's telling you something."

"That's what you say."

"And I'm just getting started. There are all *sorts* of problems with saying people aren't free."

"That's what *you* say," Asa laughed.

Zorachus shrugged. "Consider evil people."

"I'm considering."

"If you say they do bad things because Fate makes them, you're also saying they're no worse than good people."

"Am I?" Asa asked.

"Yes. Because good people are driven--- by Fate--- to do good deeds. No one's responsible for their actions."

"That's true, but . . . " Asa's voice trailed off.

"If Fate controls everything," Zorachus went on, "then you and Halfdan are no better than Khymirians."

"Where do you get that from?" Halfdan broke in. "How can you say we're as bad as they are?"

"Oh, I don't think you are," Zorachus replied.

"But if we say there's no free will," Asa said slowly, working it through, "then we have to admit we are, right?"

"Right," Zorachus said. "And if you insist on saying you're better than they are ..."

"Then we have to say that there's free will."

Zorachus nodded. "Pretty good, eh?"

Asa smiled; she had never encountered philosophical argument before, even of such a rudimentary sort. But then she looked very stern and jabbed a forefinger at him. "Mind you, I'm not convinced. I'll have to think about this."

"By all means."

"No better than Khymirians, the very idea," Halfdan muttered.

Zorachus said, "I told you---"

"And as for that business about Fate and the rock---"

"What of it?"

"If Fate knows exactly when to drop it, how can you say she didn't destine you to be under it? After all, she's Fate. That's what she does."

"Suppose I drop a rock on you," Zorachus answered. "Just because I know when you'll be under it, does that mean I put you there?"

"No."

"Well, maybe Fate just watches. And drops the rocks at the right time. The same way I would."

"But why---"

"Would I want to drop a rock on you?"

"Yes."

"Same reason as Fate."

"Oh."

"You know," Zorachus said, "I'm awfully hungry. Would one of you go collar a servant, and---"

A shout from outside cut him short.

Sword drawn, a guard rushed in.

"We saw a face!" he cried, speeding towards the bed.

"What kind of face?" Halfdan demanded.

"Like the one in the sky last night, only small," the doorward said. "Two tongues."

Zorachus's stomach tightened; sure enough, he began to feel Morkulg's presence. He grabbed for his ring-sack, only to find it was not around his neck.

"Where's the pouch?" he cried, swinging his legs over the side of the bed.

"We didn't take it off," Halfdan answered, unsheathing his blade.

Asa said: "The last time I saw it, I was putting your ring back after the fighting."

"You had it when we brought you here," Halfdan assured the Sharajnaghi. He bit his lip. "Wait a second... Aliphar's slaves were all over you---"

"Thieving bastards," Asa spat.

The guard shifted his sword from hand to hand, asking, "Orders, Lord Mancdaman?"

Remembering that Porchos's mages were downstairs, Zorachus said: "Fetch the Guild wizards. Hurry!"

The man turned and sprinted for the door. Zorachus watched him for a moment, looked away--- and swept his eyes back, shouting with terror and surprise.

Diffused through the man's surcoat, like a wide reddish stain, was a leering image of Morkulg the Mask.

Hearing Zorachus, the soldier stopped and spun, trembling. "What's wrong?" he screamed.

"The face," Zorachus answered, rising. "It's on your back!"

The doorward turned round and round, looking over his shoulder, trying frantically, impossibly to see it. Each time he revolved, the image grew fainter.

"It's gone!" Zorachus called at last, but the words left his mouth in a white plume; all at once the room had gone arctic, marrow-biting. He could no longer feel any trace of Morkulg's presence--- but what other threat did the cold portend?

Hearing the cries, the second guard had entered and stood not far from the threshold. Without warning, the door slammed thunderously shut behind him. Whirling, he tried to open it.

"It's jammed" he shrieked over his shoulder. "We're trapped in here! Help me!"

Halfdan and the first guard bolted over. They pushed and struggled, but the barrier did not yield.

"Don't waste your strength!" Zorachus shouted. "Get out of the way! Maybe I can blast it down!"

They moved aside. He entered a stance and loosed a fusillade of strikes. The door held.

"Come back over---"

Before the Sharajnaghi could finish, the candles faltered and winked out. The room went totally black.

"Stay where you are!" he cried. "I'll conjure a demon to smash the door!"

He uttered a spell, but felt no diminution of power; something was interfering. He tried another spell. Still nothing.

"Magic's not working!" he shouted.

"Is there anything you can do?" Asa asked frantically, invisible in the darkness at his side.

"I don't know...." He stopped, hearing a soft slithering in front of him.

"What's that?" Asa wailed.

"Maybe nothing."

"It sounds like a snake! A *big* one!"

"Might just be a trick. To frighten us."

"Can't you make some light?"

"Not in *this*---"

The slithering grew louder, and there was a series of short, venomous hisses, followed by abrupt, utter silence.

"Zorachus!" Halfdan bellowed. "Should we come across now?"

"No!" cried a fleshless voice. "Not yet!"

Wild laughter filled the room, followed by sounds like a gigantic axe thumping into flesh.

"Halfdan!" Asa screamed. Zorachus heard her start forward. Blindly he snagged her dress and yanked her back.

"Is there something out there or not?" she cried.

Before the Sharajnaghi could answer that there was no point risking it, Halfdan cried:

"I'm all right!"

The laughter and the chopping sounds were already fading. Silence fell once more---

Only to be broken by one last horrific thud, directly in front of Zorachus and Asa. Warm thick fluid splashed over them.

"Blood!" Asa cried, flailing about. Zorachus's hand met hers and clasped it.

"Ignore it," he told her, certain now that the real threat had not yet appeared. "You faced the redclads---"

"This is different. I can't see---"

"There's nothing out there. We're just being toyed with, mocked---for now."

"For now---?"

Zorachus's voice rose to a roar: "Halfdan! Try it!"

Footsteps clattered through the darkness.

"Over here!" the Sharajnaghi called. "Follow the sound of my voice!"

That proved unnecessary. Light was provided.

Of a sort.

It spread from one corner of the room, a disastrous grey glow that leeched flesh as colorless as ash and blackened red marble, making the chamber seem one huge cavern of rotting tissue; dead and frigid, it was the only kind of light that could have appeared in that darkness, no threat to the nothingness of shadow.

Its source was an oval sac seven feet long. Inside, a huddled figure, indistinct through the translucent membrane, was immerged in some kind of fluid. The sac rocked gently back and forth, quivering.

"Toying's over," Zorachus told Asa.

The guards reached the bed, Halfdan some distance behind them; he had stopped the instant the glow appeared, staring at the sac.

"Halfdan, get over here!" Zorachus yelled.

"Whatever that thing inside is," the Kragehul growled. "I'll stab it before it crawls out!"

"No!" Zorachus commanded.

But Halfdan ran heedlessly over to the sac and thrust at it several times.

The membrane would not give.

"Get away from it!" Zorachus cried.

Halfdan kept stabbing.

There came a low bubbling cry, and the shape within moved; membrane bulged and ripped, and waxen embryonic fingers, armed with curving talons, thrust through, stinking amniotic fluid gushing about them, lit by their effulgence. The hand retreated for a moment, then tore the sac wide open. Colder than ice, a noisome wave drove Halfdan back.

The sending struggled and kicked in the swiftly draining sac, batting about savagely with its taloned hands, pantherish snarls erupting from its throat. The membrane was already partially shredded when Halfdan rose and splashed forward, hacking at a clawed foot. The blade sprang back notched, and the foot lashed out, dealing him a blow that sent him somersaulting fifteen feet backwards.

The thing sat up, sac slipping down over its shoulders. Shaped like a sexless human fetus, the glowing body rose dripping, nine feet tall, the great discs of its eyes, still partially sheathed in their translucent lids, a delicate robin's egg blue.

Slowly it stepped out of the sac and made for Halfdan.

The Kragehul got to his feet and half-staggered, half-ran to the bed.

"Remind me to do everything you tell me from now on," he told Zorachus.

"I might be able to open a portal!" Zorachus cried. "When I give the word, follow me!"

As the fetus approached, he ran swiftly through the spell, but once again, felt no loss of power. He guessed the demon had been interfering with his binding magic from the first, even before its eidolon had taken on matter.

"Scatter!" he cried.

They split up.

Reaching the bed moments later, the fetus ripped the massive headboard off and hurled it at Halfdan and Asa.

They dodged.

The wooden missile struck a wall and shattered in a burst of splinters.

The two Kragehul ran past the first guard, and for some reason the fetus turned its attention to him; dragging the mangled bed, rubbing an eye sleepily with its free hand, it wandered in his direction. He tried to dash away; it hurled the bed. Trailing a long whirl of silken sheets, the great

188

mass whooshed through the air. A jagged spar caught the guard's leg, snapping bone. He flopped down screaming.

The demon thudded forward and flipped the bed aside. Across the room, Zorachus tried to distract it with bolts, but it seemed not to feel them---snatching up the guard by the heel, it spun him twice around its head, and smashed his skull against the ceiling. Then, dragging the corpse, it shambled off toward other prey---Halfdan and Asa again.

They were raising a din by the door, knocking and shouting, answering thumps and muffled cries from the hallway, breath smoking in the cold. But as the fetus drew near, Halfdan heard it and looked back just in time to see it lash out with the dead guard. He ducked, yanking Asa down with him; colliding ferociously with the door's reinforced oak, the body burst inside its mail, its whole surcoat going instantly black with blood, steam gusting from the cloth as hot gore met frigid air. Halfdan and Asa darted to the side.

The demon cast the corpse down, then scrutinized the door for a few seconds, as if wondering at the sounds coming from the other side. Then it turned.

Suddenly a long leathery whip wrapped around its neck, jerking it forward on its hands and knees. Zorachus had found a spell that worked; draining his half-restored strength to the dregs, he had summoned a knobbed monstrosity that looked like a sea anemone with legs. Standing back from the fetus, thin tentacles switching viciously through the air, it landed strokes that would have shredded steel, even as it tightened its grip on its opponent's neck.

Never flinching, the fetus rose effortlessly under the rain of lash-blows; growling, it tore through the whip binding it as though it had been a piece of grass, seized two more of the flailing appendages, and yanked them from their sockets. Zorachus's demon fell back with a ululating cry.

Snatching up a sculpture, the fetus stamped forward and smashed it down on its foe. The whip-demon crumpled and vanished. After hanging in mid-air for a moment, the sculpture struck the floor and split in two.

The fetus looked about, spied the second guard cowering in a corner. Grabbing another sculpture, it rolled it over the floor at him.

The guard started from the corner, then retreated before the rumbling marble juggernaut. With a mighty impact, the statue wedged itself in front of him, between the walls. He tried to scramble over it; the demon closed in and plucked him out. Holding him suspended, oblivious to his curses and the jabs of his dagger, it yanked the sculpture free, lifted one end, shoved his head and shoulders under---and dropped three tons of marble on him. There was a loud crunch; the guard's heels drummed the floor and went still.

The fetus turned.

Dazed by his sorcerous exertions, on his knees by the ruined bed, Zorachus was an easy target.

The demon thudded over to him and its huge glowing hands reached out.

"God, God...." the Sharajnaghi mumbled, watching numbly as the taloned fingers opened to seize and mangle---

Then jerked back.

The monster straightened, a titanic gasp blasting spittle from its mouth.

The Kragehul had fallen on it from behind, Halfdan with his sword, Asa with dagger and silver candlestick. Neither blade had any effect, but the candlestick burned and tore; Asa dealt two horrendous lacerations before realizing it.

"Silver!" she cried. "Silver wounds it!"

Bellowing, the demon pivoted, and they fell back. Halfdan sheathed his sword, grabbed two candlesticks off a cabinet, and slung the medallion from around his neck.

Swaying, the demon remained where it was, reaching to feel the gashes smoking on its back and thigh. It loosed roar after roar, but made no attempt to follow the Kragehul.

They watched it for a few moments, panting, lungs smarting with the cold.

"Come on!" Halfdan shouted at last, and they rushed forward. He flung a candlestick as he charged; it struck the demon's brow in a spatter of vapor, and the fetus reeled and clapped a hand to the wound.

"Want some more?" Halfdan cried. Swinging his medallion at the end of its heavy chain, he bashed one of its knees. The monster tried to grab him, but Asa's candlestick came down with a crack across the clutching hand. The demon howled; Halfdan's medallion took a chunk from its flank. The demon staggered sideways.

Retrieving the candlestick he had thrown, Halfdan hurled it again. The fetus's left knee cracked and the demon toppled. Floundering desperately, it tried to rise, knocking a statue over in the process.

Halfdan and Asa swept in to right and left. The chamber echoed with the thump of their weapons bludgeoning home. Silver gleamed as it rose and fell.

After breaking the demon's arms, the Kragehul moved in at its head. Wide blue eyes rolling in their sockets, lids twitching, the demon twisted and shuddered as its skull was battered in. Finally, with a long hiss, it went still, glow blinking out. The room filled with darkness once more.

But the gloom was short-lived; candlelight flared anew and warmth banished cold. Halfdan and Asa stared down at the spot where the sending had sprawled. No trace of it remained.

The crash of a battering ram started up behind the door, which quivered with each stroke.

Ignoring the sounds, the Kragehul went to Zorachus. Lying on his back, he smiled up at them, face pale.

"Demon's dead, I take it," he said. "Something about silver?"

"Candlesticks," Asa answered.

"And my medallion," Halfdan added smugly. "Came in handy after all. How do you feel?"

"Exhausted," Zorachus said.

At that moment, the door burst off its hinges in a shower of shattered jamb, and several green-robed men dashed in and assumed sorcerous stances, looking very fierce.

"Porchos's wizards," Halfdan told Zorachus.

"Awe-inspiring," the Sharajnaghi said.

Seeing the danger was over, the wizards dropped stance; guards poured in. Sharthas pushed his way to the front of the brown-mailed throng.

"What happened, my Lord?" he asked as he came up.

"We were playing midwife," Zorachus said.

Chapter 14

THE SHARAJNAGHI ASKED to be taken to his own room, having decided it was safe as any other. On the way, he told Sharthas about the theft of the rings; the Steward hurried off to dispatch a messenger to Porchos.

As the group entered the chamber, Zorachus saw the sullen redness of the sky outside.

The whole western quarter must be burning, he thought anxiously. It was imperative to get back in fighting kemper...

He had some food brought and it refreshed him somewhat, though he was still deathly tired. For several hours he kept himself awake by sheer force of will, long enough for a fraction of his power to return, sufficient for a healing spell. Then he made everyone leave except Halfdan and Asa, who promised to keep very quiet. Tightening his concentration, he lowered himself into a trance. Luckily it did not need to last very long; his wounds had been well tended, and there was no trace of infection.

Midway through the following morning he reassumed consciousness. He sent Porchos's wizards off with the news that he had recovered; he also ordered more food. The Kragehul ate with him, but afterwards he sent them out and changed.

The chamber's thick stuffiness quickly drove him out to the balcony, though it was little better there. For a moment he viewed the smoke-columns rising in the west; then he passed through the wrought-iron gate to the adjoining balcony and got his first look at Asa's tomato garden, which the mason had built the afternoon before.

"A passable job," Asa said.

"Will you be able to grow wax tadpoles in it?" Zorachus asked.

She laughed.

It was a small enclosure in the middle of the balcony, ringed by knee-high walls of mortared stone, brown loam coming up almost to the rim. Several rows of long sticks stood in the soil.

"When are you going to plant the seeds?" Zorachus asked.

"Right now," Asa replied. "Want to watch?"

"Of course."

She went over by Halfdan, who was sitting on the rim, his face the very picture of boredom, a trowel and watering-can beside him. Asa picked them up, giving him a nudge with her elbow. He grumbled, and crossed his arms over his chest. Coming back to the Sharajnaghi, she produced a small sack of seeds and started to work.

"Zorachus," Halfdan said, "why pretend you're interested in this piddling little garden?"

"I like plants," Zorachus returned, watching Asa. "I very much approve of gardening."

"Do you like those plants in the park out there? All those flowers that look like they're made of human skin?"

Zorachus shook his head. "I can't stand them," he said. "But the reason I can't is that they're perversions of the real thing. Do you follow me?"

Halfdan thought a bit. "No."

"All right," Zorachus said. "Back in Qanar-Sharaj, the home of my order, there's a great dome. To be sure, it's nowhere near as big as some of the domes in Khymir. But we hold our most solemn rites there; it's a very holy place. And one of the holiest things about it is a sea of plants that covers the inside walls."

"You worship these plants?"

"No, but we see their Maker's hand in them. They're living images of his thought, words which He's spoken. And inasmuch as anything is His word, it's holy."

"Words which He's spoken," Asa said. "I like that."

"Do you know what it means?" Halfdan asked.

"I like it anyway."

"Pah!" Halfdan said. "Who is this Maker? Which God is He?"

"The one who made all the others," Zorachus answered. "If they exist."

Halfdan boomed a laugh. "He made Gorm, and Ygg the All-Father?"

"He's the origin of everything. What does it say in your own tales about the gods?"

"All sorts of things."

"But did they make themselves? Or were they made by something else?" Zorachus was guessing here, but he knew what pagan cosmologies were like in general.

"They were born when the ice was licked away by the Mother of Cows," Halfdan answered stoutly.

"But they didn't make themselves?"

Halfdan's brow clouded. "No."

"Do you really want to say that your gods---the beings you worship---came from ice and cow spittle?"

"You're not looking at it the right way," Halfdan snapped.

"No?"

"When you put it like that, it sounds disgusting."

"All right. Maybe the spittle had nothing to do with it. Maybe it was because the cow's *tongue* was touching the ice. Even so, this bespeaks a pretty humble beginning for the gods---"

"Damn it all---"

"Don't lose your temper," Zorachus said.

"There was magic at work!"

"Must've been," the Sharajnaghi said. "But where did it come from?"

"The cow and the ice."

"Where did they come from?"

"The mist."

"And where---"

" The Great Void."

"And the magic must also have come from the Void?"

Halfdan pondered the question. "Yes."

"But can something come from nothing?"

"It was a *magic* Void," Halfdan said.

"That doesn't solve your problem," Zorachus replied.

"Why not?"

194

"You're admitting you need something more than a void."

"You just argue with everything I say---"

"No, I'm taking most of what you say for granted. Magic, mist--- fine. But a *void* couldn't produce them-- or anything. If they came out of nothing, something must have *brought* them out."

"And this something is the god you worship?" Asa asked.

"Yes."

"But why say this something's a god at all? Why couldn't it just be ... well, a source?"

"Consider what it's the source of," Zorachus said. "Gods, men, everything about them, including…" He tapped his head. "Reason."

"So?"

"It simply won't do to say that reason comes from something which has none itself. But once we admit that reason must be *begotten* by reason, then we must also admit that this source must be a person, a thinking being---in this case, a god."

"Ah," said Asa.

Halfdan broke in: "But anyway---"

"Yes?" Zorachus asked.

"What does all this have to do with hating those trees out there, or thinking it's so wonderful to watch a woman planting tomatoes?"

"Everything," Zorachus replied. "If my god is the source of all reason and life, then anyone who rejects him rejects those things as well. Turns towards nothingness, becomes perverted. That's the whole Khymirian way, as nearly as I can tell. And that garden is a reflection of it. But Asa's reflects something else---"

"She doesn't believe in your god," Halfdan said.

"She doesn't have to. Growing tomatoes is part of His plan."

"You've never ever had tomatoes."

"I trust your wife. Is she right to want tomatoes?"

"Yes…"

"So much for your objection."

195

"Wait---"

"Wholesome desires come from My God, Halfdan," Zorachus said. "They are an aspect of reason. Asa's trying to give reason a foothold in Khymir. It's a marvelous thing."

Halfdan was silent. He had gone back to thinking about what Zorachus had said about the gods.

"You're not angry with me, are you?" Zorachus asked him.

"You're a blasphemer, that's what you are," the Kragehul said. "Making fun of the Mother of Cows, trying to make Ygg and Gorm seem unimportant. . . . "

"I wasn't trying to make them seem unimportant. I was trying to point out their relationship to my god---if indeed they exist."

But Halfdan was not satisfied. "You were saying they're not as *important* as him. And that's blasphemy."

"Well, perhaps I'm wrong," Zorachus replied. "But...I believe I'm right. And, inasmuch as we think we see the truth, the truth must be preferred."

Halfdan mulled the words. "I suppose."

"And, you must admit, if the god I'm talking about really exists, I'm doing you a favor in pointing Him out. You can't fault a man for goodwill."

Halfdan softened at that, "I wasn't faulting you for your goodwill," he said, almost apologetically. "I was faulting you for your blasphemy."

"I understand," Zorachus said. "No offense taken."

"All right."

"You're a deep fellow, Zorachus," Asa said.

Halfdan laughed. "Good thing he's got more going for him than depth."

Zorachus laughed too. "I don't know what I'd do without you two..." he paused. "Actually, yes i do."

"And what's that, deep fellow?" Halfdan asked, with a smirk at Asa. Digging, she didn't notice it.

"I'd go out of my mind," Zorachus replied.

"What are you talking about?" Halfdan asked.

"The reason I decided to make friends with you."

"You didn't want a bodyguard?"

"I didn't say that. But I needed---I still need---more than that."

Asa looked up from her work. Suspicion glinted in her eyes and Halfdan's.

"People I could *talk* to," Zorachus said quickly. "Who weren't Khymirians. Or infected by Khymir."

"So you could trust them?" Asa asked.

"So I could *like* them. So they could distract me---from this *place*. This stinking quagmire could drag me right under."

"Asa and I have been here three years," Halfdan said. "We've resisted it."

"You had each other," Zorachus said.

"You think the Khymirians would seduce you if you were by yourself?" Asa asked.

"No," he answered. "But they might succeed in enraging me. Prodding me into a bloodbath."

"And what would be wrong with that?" Halfdan demanded. "How else do you expect to take over and change things?"

"They're human beings."

"They're pigs in human form," Halfdan shot back. "Pigs should be butchered."

Zorachus shook his head. "They're badly hurt....they've mangled themselves terribly. But they're still human."

"I'll be damned," Halfdan laughed.

"So would I," Zorachus said.

"That's crazy. You couldn't kill enough of them to suit me."

"I know how you feel," Zorachus said. "But God's my judge, not you. And killing human beings is a grievous thing. Even if they're Khymirians."

A slow grin crept over Halfdan's face. "You're having me on. If you were so worried about killing them, you wouldn't have come here at all. You've probably slaughtered several thousand already---all this fighting's your work after all."

"It could be worse."

"For one of those poor dead Khymirians?"

"I came to save lives."

"Whose?"

"Your people's."

"What are you saying?" Halfdan asked.

"I was sent to stop Kletus's invasion."

"You don't want to take over the city?"

"No."

Halfdan was stopped dead by the reply. Every bit as surprised, Asa stopped working and took up the interrogation:

"You're not doing this for yourself?"

"I came to thwart the Black Priests," Zorachus answered. "I've no intention of setting myself up in their place."

This took a while to sink in.

"The better I know you," Asa said, "The stranger you seem."

"But should we believe him about this?" Halfdan asked.

She sighed resignedly. "Might as well."

He grunted in agreement, then chuckled. "Such high purposes you have, Zorachus."

The Sharajnaghi made no reply.

"I'd think, though," Halfdan went on, "That they'd make you a lot less queasy about killing Khymirians. After all, it has to be done."

"That doesn't mean I have to like it," Zorachus said.

"When a man likes his job, he does it better. Hate's a powerful weapon---"

"One which God condemns."

Halfdan snorted. "Him again. One very strange god, by the sound of it. But that's just the kind you'd be worshipping, isn't it?"

"He is the only one of His kind."

"Wouldn't you like him better if he was a little more reasonable?"

"No point thinking about it. He is what He is. And a man who claims to worship Him *cannot* let himself be enraged."

"Well, I suppose it makes sense," Halfdan said. "*If* your god's truly so finicky."

"*If* he exists," Asa added.

"And certainly," Zorachus continued, "the idea that I'd snap---"

"Give the pigs what they deserve?" Halfdan asked.

"---- shouldn't be too hard for you to understand."

Asa wiped her brow and got back to work. "Not at all," she said. "One of my favorite stories---"

"Ugh," Halfdan said.

"--- is about two men driven *mad* by Khymirians. They kill *hundreds* of them."

Halfdan spat. "I'll never know why you like that tale."

"Even though *hundreds* of Khymirians get killed?" Zorachus asked.

"It's *rotten*."

"It's nothing of the sort," Asa assured Zorachus. "And the end is beautiful."

"The end's all wrong," Halfdan rumbled. "I would've killed the bitch."

By this time, Zorachus's curiosity was whetted. "I'm going to have to hear this story."

Asa looked up. "Now?"

"If you wouldn't mind. Would it keep you from your work?"

"No."

Halfdan muttered a curse. "If you're going to tell it, I'm going inside."

"Zorachus wants to hear it," Asa replied, as if that were the only justification necessary.

"Well, keep your voice down."

Halfdan strode off. She began:

"In a Kragehul village, not far from Khymir, lived a man named Rane and a woman named Astrid. They were tall ,handsome, and so much in love that they were the laughing-stock of the whole village and didn't care at all.

"But their happiness was shattered on their wedding-day. Khymirians attacked the town, seized the young and strong, killed the rest. Rane fought fiercely, but was knocked senseless; Astrid was captured too.

"They were taken to Khymir and sold into the household of a Kadjafi merchant, a very unhappy man named Haroul. He was terribly homesick and hated everything Khymirian, but his dealings with the Guild weren't going well, and he couldn't leave.

"Astrid caught his eye, but he was an honorable man, and wouldn't take a woman from her mate, even if he owned her. He never told her how he felt, but to get closer to her, he made Rane his personal guard, and the three of them were always together after that, great friends.

"Haroul's dealings dragged on and on. The Guild grew angry with him. Finally, a war broke out.

"Haroul got the worst of it at first, but then the Priesthood began to help him secretly, sending him a powerful wizard. The war became a standoff---so the Guildsmen took a new tack.

"They knew all about Rane and Astrid, and Haroul's hatred of Khymirian ways...hoping to break him, they slipped two people into his house, a beautiful man and woman, to seduce his friends and show him they were no better than Khymirians themselves.

"Setting to work on Rane, the man caught a dagger in the ribs before getting too far. But the woman, after several weeks, managed to worm her way into Astrid's bed.

"Rane discovered them and cut off the woman's head. Terrified, Astrid wrapped a sheet about her and fled from the house. But Guild soldiers caught her.

"Rane told Haroul what he'd found. At first, Haroul was stunned. But then he was filled with wrath.

"A message came from Banipal Khezach. Too late, it warned of the Guild plot. Red-hot as they were already, Haroul and Rane grew hotter still. Haroul called out his retainers, fifty fierce-eyed Kadjafim, and they all marched to the Guild headquarters with the Priestly wizard.

"They wiped out a troop of Guild soldiers at the gate, but as they were crossing the courtyard, Guild wizards came out on the balcony with Astrid, shouting they'd kill her if Haroul and his men didn't lay down their arms.

"But the Priest set a demon on the man holding Astrid, and freed her; lifting her with magic, he brought her down from the balcony. Rane knocked her out; then the Priest blasted the door open, and Rane and Haroul led the way into the house.

"There was a great slaughter. The blood of Guild wizards and soldiers ran like mountain streams down the stairways. Haroul was stabbed, and Rane was slashed across the chest.

"Even so, they broke into the chamber where the Chief Guildsmen had fled and glutted their hatred. The room looked like a butcher's shambles when they left.

"Slowly they made their way down to the courtyard, followed by the few retainers that remained and the limping Priest. Astrid was waiting, sick with remorse. She wailed and begged Rane's forgiveness. He looked at her with a face like a stone mask and drew his sword.

"Haroul let out a scream. He tried to kill her himself, but Rane cut off his swordarm. Haroul looked at him, then fell to the pavement, dead.

"Weeping, Astrid reached out to her husband. He raised his blade. She bowed her head, waiting for the blow. His sword whistled down---and stopped an inch from her neck. He could not kill her. He loved her too much. Dropping the blade to the cobbles, he knelt beside her, forgiving her with all his heart. Her tears became tears of joy as he clutched her to him. And the next morning, they left Khymir, never to return."

Asa rose, stretched gracefully to get the kinks out of her back, and sat down on the garden wall. "I got the tale from old Gudrun, who lived outside our village in a tumbledown shack. I think I must have been her only friend. Everyone else stayed away from her, said she was a witch who told bad fortunes and then made them come true. They used to call her Gudrun Death Horse. She was always kind to me, though. Told me dozens of stories, but none of them stuck in my mind like that one. I was so shocked when I learned the Guild hadn't been wiped out."

"Why do you like the story so much?" Zorachus asked.

"The ending. It's wonderful. To think he'd forgive her like that..." She smiled.

"You know, listening to you and Halfdan, I wouldn't think your hearts had much place for forgiveness."

"Oh, Halfdan says he'd have killed her, if he'd been in Rane's place. But I'm not so hard-minded. I could've forgiven her. After all, women are so...."

"What?"

"Beautiful."

He understood her far too well. How could someone be so insensible, such a stone, that women would leave them unmoved? It was so *natural* that they should awaken desire--especially in someone who had never tasted their love. Their beauty promised so much; *Asa's* promised so much.Gazing at her face, he felt a keen pang of longing.

If only you hadn't taken the vows, he told himself, *Halfdan would have quite a battle on his hands.*

He caught himself.

But you have taken the vows. And Asa is Halfdan's. They're one flesh.

"Zorachus?" Asa asked. "Is something the matter?"

He looked away from her.

You love her, don't you, fool?

"Zorachus?" she pressed.

You've fallen in love with another man's wife. You, a Sharajnaghi Master...

"I'm going back to my room," he said. "I'm still feeling a bit dizzy."

"Should I get Halfdan?" she asked.

Zorachus shook his head, and returned to his chamber.

As he lay down on the bed, he noticed his reflection in a mirror close by. His face was red and sweaty. His cheeks and forehead looked like raw meat.

"Pig," he grunted, but did not turn away. Staring steadily at himself, he sat up; a morbid impulse pushed him over to the glass. His face was even more repulsive close up. Distended pores oozed perspiration; one of his nostrils had begun to run. He wiped his nose, saw another stream trail down. For the first time in his life, he felt a surge of disgust at the very idea of flesh. He was a soul encased in muck, and the muck was smothering him...

"Sharajnaghi Master," he jeered. But all he could see in the mirror was a Khymirian.

After all, you were spawned here, by a Priest of Tchernobog and a temple prostitute…they sent you away, but Khymir drew you back… is this pit your destiny? Is overreaction the chief danger? Or seduction?

The longer he stared, the more his reflection seemed to be gloating at him, eyes filled with wicked amusement.

Like it has a life of its own, he thought.

Smiling, it nodded.

What in---

As he stood paralyzed, its hand shot toward its belt, snatching the hilt of a dagger he was not wearing; licking through the surface of the mirror, the blade flashed at the Sharajnaghi.

Reflexes took over; he dodged, knocking down the mirror with a kick. Glass splintered, and there was a scream.

Around each mirror-shard widened a pool of blood..

The door banged open and the guards charged through, brandishing swords and silver candlesticks. Asa rushed in from the balcony, followed shortly by Halfdan.

"My reflection just tried to stab me," Zorachus said, twitching a nervous grin. He had never heard of such a thing before, but he had no doubt that the attack had been conjured in Banipal Khezach. Turning to one of the guards, he said:

"Find Sharthas….I want every mirror in this palace removed. I don't want to see my face in this house again."

Chapter 15

NEAR SUNSET, A dispatch arrived from Porchos.

"My rings have been recovered," Zorachus told Halfdan and Asa. "And there's a Guild war-council tonight."

"When do we leave?" Asa asked.

"*We?*" Halfdan demanded. "That fight in the square wasn't enough for you?"

"No.

"You're not coming this time, Asa," Zorachus said. "Kletus might send another demon. You'll be safer here."

"But I'm not going to stay---"

"Oh yes you are."

"Well then," Asa said, "Shall I take it out on Halfdan when you get back?"

"Halfdan has nothing to do with this."

"That's right," Halfdan smirked.

"And don't tell me how you'll kill yourself if we don't come back," Zorachus went on. "If we're killed out there, you'll probably die too. But *you* might die in an attack even if *we* didn't."

"That's telling her," Halfdan said.

"You're going to be very sorry, Halfdan," Asa said.

"He'd be sorrier watching you ripped to pieces," Zorachus answered.

"But---"

"You're not coming, and that's final."

She stamped, and crossed her arms on her chest. "I saved your life last night. And if I hadn't hit that redclad in the eye with----"

"Think of this as me returning the favor."

"What's changed? If you're so worried, why didn't you leave me behind the other day?"

Zorachus wanted to answer: *I didn't know I loved you then.* But what he said was: "We let you bully us."

"*I* bullied the two of you?"

"Give it up, Asa," Halfdan said.

She turned her back on them, simmering.

An hour later, Zorachus and Halfdan rode from the palace escorted by thirty retainers on foot, many bearing torches. The darkening streets were nearly deserted; Zorachus did not see an unshuttered window. The air smelled of smoke and rotting flesh. Bodies of Priestly sympathizers hung heels up from balconies and walls. Ravens cawed and flapped in the stinking dusk; horn blasts and hoofbeats sounded in the distance, and muffled thunder growled.

Coming up on Porchos's house, Zorachus saw a line of severed heads impaled on the spikes along the top of the outer wall. They glistened in the torchlight, already cooked slimy by the heat, even though he knew they must be relatively fresh.

The company passed through the heavily-guarded gate into the courtyard. Screams echoed dimly from inside the house; it occurred to Zorachus that he might be listening to the man who had stolen his rings.

Swiftly taken to Porchos's soundproofed sanctum, the Sharajnaghi saw that all the Chief Guildsmen were there. Terse greetings were exchanged and Porchos handed Zorachus's ring-sack to him.

"Doctor Aliphar apologizes for his slave," the Merchant said. "the culprit's being punished, even as we speak..."

Zorachus looked into the pouch. The rings flamed. He pulled the drawstring and hung the sack around his neck.

"I suppose we'd better get down to business," Porchos said. "If you'll all come to the table please..."

On it was spread a great parchment map of Khymir. A red line divided the city roughly in half. Wooden blocks of various sizes marked key positions.

"The black blocks are enemy strongholds," Maranchthus explained. "Green is for Guild. We control most of the south; the Priesthood owns the north." He pointed to a green block just south of the red line. "That's your house, Lord Mancdaman." He indicated a black mass directly across the line, by far the largest block on the map. "That's Banipal Khezach."

205

"We've been considering whether you should stay in your palace," Porchos told Zorachus. "It is, after all, so close to the tower. You might take up with me. Your house would be well-garrisoned, of course."

"You'd have all the sorcerous protection you could want," Maranchthus added.

Zorachus guessed their concern for his safety was genuine enough, but undoubtedly they also planned to move against him once the Priesthood was finished, and hoped to deprive him of his troops and stronghold ahead of time. He intended to flee as soon as his work was done, but he had no way of knowing how quickly that could be accomplished--- or how swiftly the Guild would act

"Well?" Porchos asked.

"I'd better stay," Zorachus announced.

"And why do you think that?"

"It would look like cowardice if I moved out."

"Your safety's more important than show," Maranchthus said.

"It's not just a matter of show," Zorachus replied. "It would be wise to keep a mage of my rank at the palace simply for combat purposes. You don't have any other mages of my rank, do you?" He assumed that they had had observers at the duel.

"No," Porchos said, then looked at Zorachus sidelong. "Why didn't you kill Zarathonzar when he was stunned?"

The question caught the Sharajnaghi off guard. Knowing the truth would simply not be believed, he scrambled for an answer that would ease their suspicion of treachery.

"It's rather hard to explain," he began.

"Try anyway," Porchos answered.

"You've heard of the Influences?"

Porchos and the others nodded.

Zorachus said: "It's...*imprudent* for me to kill---that is, kill with magic--- on certain days."

"Imprudent."

"Very good chance that a lethal spell will... redound."

"Redound?"

"Yes."

"What do the Influences care?"

"As nearly as I can tell, they don't. But death affects magic. And in my particular case..."

"What about all those redclads you blasted?" Maranchthus broke in.

"*I* didn't blast them," Zorachus returned.

"Who did?"

"The demons in my rings. When I'm endangered, they intervene---even to the point of manipulating my body so they can take proper aim."

"Remarkable," Porchos said dubiously.

"But Zarathonzar wasn't endangering me," Zorachus said.

"He wasn't?" Maranchthus asked.

"Not once I'd stunned him."

"What about when you cut him in half?"

"It was an accident. I was only trying to transport him...he broke my concentration, caused the opening to snap shut prematurely."

Maranchthus said no more, apparently convinced. But Porchos was not.

"Why didn't you kill him?" he asked.

He's no fool, Zorachus told himself. He shrugged and smiled. "For mercy's sake," he said. After all, the Guildsmen had to stick with him.

"You expect us to believe that?" Porchos demanded.

"It's the truth."

The Guildsman snapped: "Then we don't want the truth."

"I didn't think you would. Let's just say I didn't because of---a quirk."

"That *quirk* nearly buried us all," an obese Guildsman grated, sweat running from his chin like drool. "What if he'd won?"

"He didn't," Zorachus said. "That's all that matters."

Porchos seethed. "Why didn't you kill him? I insist on the truth!"

"I don't have to answer to you," Zorachus answered.

"What kind of game are you playing?" Porchos cried, face livid.

Zorachus smiled. "I don't play games. The real world's much more interesting. Do you gentlemen have anything more to say?"

There was a long silence. Then Maranchthus answered thickly:

"We want you to draft another denunciation. A very vicious one. It doesn't have to make any sense. We just want to get people's blood up."

"Very well," Zorachus said.

"We have some other work for you, too."

"What is it?"

"As you can see from the map, there are still some enemy strongholds left in our territory. But only one of them," he pointed to a large black block, "Is a real threat: Bone-in-the-Throat, the Southside Armory. It's vital that we take it soon."

"Very soon," Porchos said.

"Why?" Zorachus asked.

"We control the city gate and we've got the harbor ramp blocked up," Porchos replied. "But the enemy has the harbor itself, and we think there are over a thousand troops down there---marines, raiders, sailors. They can only enter the city one way---through the lift in the armory. If they reached Bone-in-the-Throat and broke out, they could overrun a large part of the Foreign Quarter."

"Now, we have agents inside the armory, and one of them's a wizard; he's been sending messages through his familiars. He and his comrades have been stirring up quite a hornet's nest, lighting fires, damaging the lift, sabotaging efforts to repair it. But, the Priests also have wizards inside, so it won't be long before they discover our men and get the lift working.

"By tomorrow morning, we'll be able to muster three hundred troops for an attack on the armory. But we also need a wizard---a very powerful one--- to breach the doors."

"I see," Zorachus said. "Will you give quarter?"

"We'll offer it, of course."

"But will you *give* it?"

"Please. Anyone who's stupid enough to surrender *deserves* to become an object lesson---"

"You couldn't sell the prisoners as slaves?" Zorachus asked. "Exchange them for men held by the Priests?"

"We don't need slaves. And if any of our men have been caught by the Priests, there probably isn't enough left to exchange. But that's beside the point. Will you help us?"

"On one condition. Any enemy troops who surrender will be turned over to me."

For a moment the Merchants looked stunned; then their eyes blazed. He had expected their anger; plainly they thought he was trying to gain recruits. But he could not allow the prisoners to be used as "object lessons." Not if he had a direct hand in their capture.

"What will you do with them?" Porchos burst out.

"Probably sell them," Zorachus answered. Actually, since Sharajnaghim were prohibited from owning slaves, let alone trading them, he did not know what he would do.

"You don't need the money," Maranchthus snarled.

Porchos asked: "What's this strange aversion to spilling blood?"

"Do you accept my terms?" Zorachus asked, wondering if a suitable prison for the captives could be bought.

Porchos and Maranchthus stepped back from the table, and the other merchants clustered round them. Whispering, the group moved into a corner, hissing like a knot of vipers. But after several minutes they came back again, looking flustered.

"We accept," Porchos said.

"Now," Zorachus said, "about that denunciation...."

It took several hours to grind out the first draft. He tried to give them pure vitriol, but in the end, the vituperation was very closely reasoned--- whether that would add or subtract from its effect, he could only guess.

He wrote a second draft and signed it, learned when and where tomorrow's attack would be mustered, and took his leave. Gathering his escort, he started back to his palace. Torches flaring, the column wound northward through the nighted streets.

Riding beside the Sharajnahgi, Halfdan said: "What did you think of Asa's story?"

209

"I liked it well enough," Zorachus answered. "It reminded me of the three of us...."

"What do you mean by that?" Halfdan asked sharply

"The good part. The three of them against Khymir."

"That's all right," Halfdan said, relaxing. "I suppose we are alike that way. But that only makes it more horrible."

"Rane forgives her. I don't think that's horrible at all."

Halfdan spat. "She should've been killed."

"Isn't someone entitled to a moment of weakness?"

"It all depends."

"On----?"

"What they *do*. Some sins rot people away. Damage them beyond cure....would *you* have forgiven her?"

"I think so."

"Would you forgive yourself if you made love to a man?"

Zorachus hesitated. "I'd like to think so ..."

Halfdan pounced: "But you wouldn't, would you? You'd always smell the rot."

"Yes."

"Why be harder on yourself---"

"Than on someone else?" Zorachus asked. "I wouldn't know why they did it. I *couldn't* know how much they were damaged...It would be different with one of my own sins. Tell me, Halfdan: would you kill Asa if she betrayed you that way?"

Halfdan's face went grim as a stone mask. "In *any* way," he said.

Zorachus felt a sick pang.

"If she betrayed me with a woman," Halfdan went on, "I'd do a lot worse than just kill her."

"Don't you love her?"

"Why do you think I'd get so angry?" Suddenly the stone mask broke; Halfdan laughed. "Luckily though, she's not going to do anything, and I won't have to either." He goaded his mount with his heels. "Ygg blast this grade!"

The street slanted steeply, the winding bed of a ravine of leaning facades. Blackwall hill, up which it climbed, was a long ridge running east to west. One of the few rises in Khymir, it was well-known as an endurance test, but, if one was bound from Porchos's house to the Mancdaman Palace, there was no quick way round it. The retainers staggered and puffed, dragging their mailed bodies up the slope as shadowy stone faces grinned down at their efforts from walls on either side. Black moths, drawn by the torches fluttered about the troops like spots before the eyes of a drunken man.

The column reached a short level stretch, where Zorachus ordered a brief respite; then the climb resumed. They skirted a sluggish tide of black sludge flowing from the door of a house with the words *Priests Pigs* splattered over it in white paint, and entered a stinking tunnel formed by overarching roofs; gloom thickened about their bobbing torches. Utterly undisturbed by the presence of so many humans, a battalion of black rats marched unhurriedly from one garbage-floored alley to another, each bearing a bit of sharpened bone in its jaws. Zorachus and his men eyed them respectfully, and there were more than a few murmurs of relief when the rodents were left behind...the column moved deeper and deeper into the tunnel.

Suddenly, a shutter banged open on the right, the sound reverberating like thunder between the crazily tilting facades; retainers swore, drawing steel and silver, and Zorachus snatched for his ring-sack.

An old crone stood at the window, silhouetted by a green glow, face lit by the retainers' torches, gnarled hands gripping the sill like bird's claws.

"What do you want?" Zorachus cried, reining his mount around.

She said nothing, but a hooded figure appeared behind her and bellowed: "Go to *sleep!*"

At first, Zorachus did not know if the command was for him or her. Then a cord went round her neck, and she jerked backwards. Both figures vanished, but presently a hand rose behind the wall, grabbed the shutter and closed it.

"Come on!" Zorachus cried to his men. The ascent continued. Yard by yard, the air, already foul, worsened drastically; a stench strong enough to be tasted filled the upper reaches of the tunnel. Its source proved to be a dead redclad, hanging head-down from the arch at the tunnel's end.

Wasn't there when we came south, Zorachus thought.

Hands over their noses, the lead retainers trudged past, coughing. Then came Halfdan and Zorachus…and the chain holding the body broke. With a sound like a melon smashed by a hammer, the redclad struck the pavement head-first beside zorachus's horse. The beast shied and the retainers downhill halted, shrinking back from the corpse. Zorachus watched the body, half expecting it to get up. But the only hint of movement was the squirm of maggots that had burst from the broken skull.

"He won't hurt us," the Sharajnaghi cried.

The men below hesitated and whispered to each other---but finally started forward.

"So many omens," Halfdan said quietly as he and the Sharajnaghi goaded their horses up the grade.

Zorachus did not answer.

Ahead, the way ran straight; the hilltop could be seen, not far now, the walls of the street-canyon standing out dimly against the sky, which was seared now and again by far-off lightning. Eager to finish the climb, the company moved more quickly. Mailed tramping and the clop of hooves echoed hollowly.

Glancing along one side of the street, Zorachus noticed another strung-up corpse, a naked man. Attached by one heel to a balcony hanging far out over the cobbles, the body was strangely contorted, spine curved, limbs bowed jointlessly, one leg tied literally in a knot. *Broken on the wheel,* Zorachus thought.

A feeble breeze swept down from the crown of the hill, the first wind of any sort he had felt in Khymir. The corpse swayed back and forth, much more than the Sharajnaghi would have expected---his gaze followed the dead face as it swung. The mouth was flung open in a silent howl, dark insects flying in and out. Glazed, bugging from their sockets, the eyes stared sightlessly---

Then slitted in a knowing leer.

Two tongues erupted from the gaping mouth.

Morkulg's aura struck Zorachus like a blow.

"God save us," the Sharajnaghi breathed.

212

Still hanging rigidly upside down, the corpse detached itself from the balcony, rose, and vanished in the gloom. Some of the men saw it shoot skyward; oaths rang out.

"What's wrong?" Halfdan demanded.

Before Zorachus could answer, red light flooded over them; house-huge, tongues twitching, Morkulg rose over the hillcrest like a bloodstained moon.

"An illusion?" Halfdan cried.

Zorachus's rings glittered as he slipped them on. "No, but it's not real either. Not yet---"

Their mounts snorted and kicked; Halfdan's reared, spilling him. Wind knocked out by the fall, he floundered on the cobbles. Moments later, Zorachus also went down. Both horses clattered off frantically, and so did the retainers. Zorachus and Halfdan were nearly trampled.

"Stand your ground!" the Sharajnaghi roared, leaping to his feet, thigh and forearm smarting where he had taken the ground. The retainers ignored him.

He rushed over to Halfdan. "Can you get up?"

Halfdan only gasped. Zorachus thought of carrying him, but looked crestward first.

Morkulg's lower tongue was lengthening, tip uncurling; a glowing greenish-yellow bundle rolled out, hurtling down the slant, nothing illusory about it.

Zorachus planted himself in front of Halfdan, blue lightning snaking from his rings and slamming the bundle to a smoking standstill.

The phosphorescent mass remained motionless for a moment. Then it snapped upright, standing on end; a cyclonic blur, it unwound.

Zorachus launched two more bolts. They passed between the now- parted halves of the bundle---a nude woman and a lamia, long dead, skin hanging in tatters from their bones, charred holes showing where the first bolts had struck them. Shrieking like fugitives from a madhouse in hell, they swept downwards, hands reaching out talonlike.

The demon-rings flamed.

The woman kept coming till she dropped in two pieces.

It took three blasts to hammer the lamia apart.

213

But neither monstrosity was finished. The pieces shuddered, crawled and flopped down the slant. Shrieks poured from the decayed throats.

Zorachus turned to Halfdan. The Kragehul was trying to rise. Zorachus moved to get a shoulder under him but heard the fragments scrabbling close. He spun, demon thunderbolts flaring from his fists, blowing the pieces into even smaller bits. Barely slowing the charnel onslaught, he succeeded mainly in multiplying the fragments squirming to the attack. Patches of moldy skin humped toward him over the cobbles. Sinews wound side to side like snakes. Severed below the wrist, flung skyward by the shock from a crackling strike, the lamia's left hand flipped through the air, scuttling up Zorachus's trousers like a giant spider. He grabbed it, wrenched it loose, and hurled it away. Another dead hand locked onto his boot; the top of the woman's body, now only a head, shoulder, and arm, reeled itself forward, grinning jaws clacking. Zorachus blew the worm-eaten face to steaming bits, but the hand still held, skeletal fingers knifing through his boot leather. Unable to yank it free, he sent a demon-bolt ripping across its back and it exploded. Somehow, a finger spun up into his beard, wriggling. He plucked it away before it could pierce him. A tiny chunk of decay wormed into his mouth; he spat it out and staggered back retching, suddenly aware of Halfdan at his side.

"Can you run?" the Sharajnaghi croaked.

Halfdan gulped air, bringing his heel down on a strip of corruption that squirmed too close to him. Ragged claw marks showed on his hands.

"I'll try," he said. "But look! The carrion's stopped moving!"

It was true; yet Morkulg the Mask still hung above the hillcrest, his light washing the street in blood, and Zorachus saw he had fully materialized---the real attack would begin now. The time for games was over.

The Mask's sideward tongue lashed out and down, vanishing behind the houses on the left. The other lunged down the street, a sinuous, gleaming tentacle--- Zorachus blew on his rings, then burned several holes in it. It flinched back, wavered, came on again. He and Halfdan turned and fled.

Before they had gone too far, the first tongue gushed out of an alley ahead and came questing up the hill at them. No escape that way.

People were shouting from balconies on either side of them; doors opened and curious red-limned faces looked out. Zorachus hurtled through the nearest entrance, dodging a teenage girl; Halfdan bowled her over, pounding after the Sharajnaghi along a taperlit corridor.

Behind them, a tongue swept in over the threshold, crushing the girl, flooding the hallway, a tide of dark glistening muscle. Zorachus could feel the floor vibrating beneath him; displaced air pushed against his back.

He and Halfdan dodged into a side passage. The Kragehul kept running, but Zorachus stopped and turned, assuming a stance. He loosed as many cataract strikes as he could...then, as the rumbling from the hall set his teeth chattering, he mouthed a spell. The Influences were with him; a portal opened in the main hallway. It was not big enough for the whole tongue to slide inside, but even so the careening mass was neatly cored, the hollowed sleeve shooting past the junction. Outside, Morkulg loosed a cry that shook the foundations of Khymir.

Zorachus snapped the portal shut. The sleeve retreated, its thunder fading swiftly.

He heard a crash above him, more rumbling, and footbeats thudding in back of him. He spun to see Halfdan racing towards him. Beyond the Kragehul, the second tongue rolled down a flight of stairs like a cascade of oil. Smashing two fleeing children, it roared towards Halfdan, rapidly outstripping him. The Kragehul hurled himself out of its path, launching his huge body at an adjoining door and knocking it down, scrambling through as a chorus of shrieks sounded within. The tongue slid swiftly towards Zorachus.

Practically at his feet, he opened another, larger portal; the tongue passed inside, yard after yard vanishing into thin air. He retreated into the main hallway and closed the portal, severing the tongue. Like a giant wounded worm, the stump shot backward along the hall. Morkulg roared; the floor and walls shook, and dust rained from the ceiling.

Halfdan burst from his refuge with a nude dwarf clutching his neck, kissing his face. He reached back and flipped the creature into the opposite wall with bone-breaking force, then ran up to Zorachus.

"What did you do?" he asked breathlessly.

"Shut a portal on the tongue."

"Can you open one for us?"

"We'd be killed. The Influences aren't right..."

"You and your magic," Halfdan growled. "Let's try and find a back way out of here."

They ran down the main corridor, paying no attention to the fearful people peering out at them from half-open doorways. Halfdan panted: "What do you think he'll try next---"

There came a beating as of many small wings, and a dense darkness came billowing down a flight of stairs up ahead. At first it looked almost like a cloud of flying leaves, but Zorachus discerned red-eyed faces and pinions just before the swarm engulfed him. Tiny fangs and claws raked him. Bubbling with blood, piping voices chittered obscenities in his lacerated ears. Trying to keep his face and throat covered, he was driven swiftly back.

Not far from the front door, he fell.

Where's Halfdan? he thought, just before the Kragehul tripped over him, shrieking. Battling to ignore pain and distraction, the Sharajnaghi rose and assumed a stance, started a spell, lost the thread after a white-hot spurt of agony, started again. Talons peeled skin back from his wounds, scraped bone-deep through his flesh; his whole body quivered in torment. But somehow he finished.

A loud buzzing swept the hall. The demons stopped ripping at him. Lowering his bleeding hands, he looked up---and laughed.

Scores of hornets, each bigger than a man's thumb and haloed with a golden aura, swarmed among the swirling pinions, diving in and out, planting sting after sting. Soon the floor was littered with the batlike demons. The tiny bodies swelled amazingly as the venom did its work; then they popped in puffs of purple vapor, and vanished. The surviving demons swirled out through the door, hornets humming in pursuit.

Zorachus crawled to the threshold, chanced a look outside. The black wings sped towards Morkulg, silhouetted by his blood-red light. The Mask's eyes were wide open like black tunnel mouths. The foremost demons reached shelter inside, but the rest were cut off as the huge lids closed, and the hornets made short work of them before starting in on Morkulg himself. His mutilated tongues lashed vainly to fend them away; great domes, aggregates of a hundred stings or more, bulged from his stricken flesh.

He roared, eyes opening once more to reveal pools of eddying yellow light. Hurling himself to his feet, Zorachus rushed back from the threshold.

Outside, two flaming beams flared from Morkulg's eyes, converging on the house. The doorway erupted in a blast of blue and crimson fire. Incandescent stone crumbled, flew in molten showers.

Scorched and deafened, Zorachus and Halfdan raced once more down the main hallway. Behind them, the front of the house collapsed under fresh salvos.

Choking on clouds of dust, bumping into panicked people, they pelted along the quaking corridor. At last they emerged, with several others, in a blind, high-walled courtyard.

Almost at once, red light bathed the enclosure and black fluid splattered out of the sky. They looked up.

Morkulg hovered above them, parallel to the ground, wounded tongues dangling. The hornets still swarmed about him and had taken a horrendous toll; his features were wildly bloated, the mushrooming welts beginning to burst, puffing dark vapor. His eyes were swollen shut, but one twitched open, a mere slit. Yellow fire seethed between the bulging lids, ready to strike downward.

The welt-vapor ignited with a heavy *whoom*.

Morkulg rocked as flame exploded across his face; his eyelids vanished, blasted away, baring blazing sockets. Howling, he shot skyward, twin tongues whipping like burning snakes; up he sped till he was tiny with distance, shattering at last in a saffron fireball that disappeared almost as soon as it blossomed.

"You're a marvel," Halfdan panted beside Zorachus.

"I'm *lucky*," the Sharajnaghi gasped. "I didn't know the welts would burst and burn that way...Distracting Morkulg was the best I hoped for. And anyway, the hornets did the real work."

Halfdan and the other people drew back as the insects buzzed near Zorachus, circling around him, waiting to be returned to their plane--- warned by some alien foreknowledge, they had barely escaped incineration when Morkulg caught fire. Zorachus thanked them mentally and dismissed them.

"Come on, Halfdan," he said. "Let's see if we can find our men."

Chapter 16

AS IT TURNED out, the retainers were also looking for Zorachus, and he and Halfdan met them shortly after emerging from the half-ruined house. From down near the tunnel mouth, the soldiers had seen Morkulg's destruction and were anxious to get back into Zorachus's good graces. Luckily for them, he was not particularly angry, since they would have been of very little use.

The column returned to the Mancdaman Palace. Sharthas tended Halfdan's wounds; Zorachus went to his room and lowered himself into a healing trance.

He woke well before dawn, and sent a guard to knock next door and wake Halfdan up. The Kragehul still looked very sleepy when Zorachus met him and Asa out in the hall. Halfdan had an arm around her nightrobed waist; Zorachus felt a twinge of jealousy but stifled it.

Halfdan gave her a kiss, and she dragged herself back to bed without the slightest protest that she had not been allowed to join them.

The two men went downstairs, mustered forty troops, and set out through the still-dark streets. Eventually, they came to the bonfire-lit barracks yard where Porchos and Maranchthus waited with three hundred brown-mailed soldiers and six Guild wizards. Both Guildsmen were mounted and armored.

"I see you're not wearing a bodyguard," Zorachus said to Porchos.

"They're no help against arrows," Porchos replied.

"Or anything else, I'll wager," Maranchthus muttered.

The company departed.

Night was already fading. Even though the city was still steeped in the shadow of the eastern mountains, the sky was pale blue by the time the armory came in view.

"That's it, up ahead," said Porchos. "In the plaza." Zorachus could not see much of it, just a section of black wall---the end of the street was barricaded, and the houses on either side shut off most of the view. But once the Guild force went into one of those, he got a better look through an iron-grilled window.

Round-walled, squat and black, Bone-in-the-Throat sat hublike in the center of the plaza. All the streets leading to the circle---those he could see, at least--- were barricaded with cobbles, Guild troops manning the rude walls, sharpening swords and spear points on stones, adjusting straps on helmets and shields. Figures stirred in the windows of the houses fronting the plaza---Guild archers.

Eyeing the armory's loophole-flanked main entrance, Zorachus asked: "Are there warding spells on those doors?"

Porchos nodded. "Our mages will counter them."

Zorachus had been hearing them; they were in some other room, letting off bolts. "I presume you told your troops about our agreement?"

"Yes."

"Very good," Zorachus took the demon-rings out.

Porchos sent word to his wizards, telling them to proceed with the counterspells.

Zorachus watched the doors. He guessed they were locked by a great central bolt, or perhaps several, and decided his best strategy would be to loose strikes all along the crack between the valves. Halfdan stood behind him with a water bag, ready to douse the rings.

Off in their room, the wizards droned the counterspells. Blue light flashed from the armory gates and bits of stone cracked off the lintel; cobbles leaped up from the street in spurts of dust.

Zorachus raised his hands, positioning the rings before openings in the window grille, readying himself to strike....

A postern creaked open in one of the armory doors and a white flag spattered with dark spots pushed through the crevice.

"What kind of trick---" Porchos began.

"It might not be a trick at all," Zorachus replied. "Remember your promise. Let's hear what they have to say."

Porchos hesitated, then took up the trumpet he wore on his baldric and sounded the Guild cease-fire. An armored figure staggered through the postern, waving the flag and pushing back his helmet.

"That's one of our agents," Porchos said as the man drew nearer. The fellow stumbled, landed on his hands and knees, picked himself up and kept coming. A long rent could be seen in the mail on his chest. He passed out of sight beyond the corner of the window.

Shortly a Guild officer entered the room with the wounded man clinging to his shoulder; laying him on a cot, the officer stepped back, and Porchos and Maranchthus hurried over, followed by Zorachus.

"Armory's yours," the agent whispered, blood trickling from his mouth. "They're all dead---"

His eyes rolled up and he stiffened.

Porchos turned to Maranchthus, beaming.

Marancthus grinned back at him, saying: "All dead."

"Lieutenant," Porchos said to the officer, "send someone over to check."

The officer nodded and left.

"What do you think happened over there?" Zorachus asked Porchos.

Porchos laughed. "Can't you guess?"

Zorachus said nothing, though a sickening possibility had occurred to him.

Soon a soldier, making slowly for the armory, came into view outside, looking back over his shoulder from time to time with a face pale as whey. The closer he got to the postern, the more tremulous his steps grew; whimpering, he stopped before reaching it.

"Go on, dog!" a harsh voice cried, "or we'll shoot you ourselves!"

The scout started forward again. He paused momentarily at the threshold, then vanished inside. Several minutes passed before he reemerged and beckoned.

Porchos turned to Zorachus. "I think you should come with us," he said. "It might cure you of some delusions."

Despite his apprehension, Zorachus nodded. He and Halfdan followed the Chief Guildsmen out into the street. Soldiers crowded along behind, Zorachus's retainers mingled with the rest.

The scout still stood near the postern. Trembling but smiling, he saluted Porchos and Maranchthus as they came up.

"Coward," Maranchthus snapped and spat on him. As he started past, almost as an afterthought, the Guildsman whipped a poniard from his belt and buried it in the scout's beard. Remaining upright only long enough for Maranchthus to pluck the blade free, the scout fell forward. Zorachus and Halfdan had to step over him to enter the postern.

Before them stretched a broad corridor echoing with Porchos's and Maranchthus's laughter, puddled with blood and strewn with the bodies of the armory's defenders. Many still clutched the blades they had slaughtered themselves---or their comrades---with.

The Sharajnaghi and Kragehul paused, but Porchos beckoned, grinning smugly, and they slowly strode forward over the bodies. Dead men stared at them, some blankly, some grimacing; others, still smiling with the terrible pleasure they had taken with them into the next world, had been masturbating or having sex with each other even as they died. Many had gone far beyond mere suicide; one man had literally smashed his brains out against a wall, while another, a severed thumb clenched in his teeth, had bitten off the fingers of one hand.

"No prisoners here, Lord Mancdaman," Maranchthus called back gloatingly.

Zorachus ignored him, marching like an automaton. "We would've spared you," he whispered to the dead, horrified to the core of his being.

They came out in the central hall. There, the bodies were less thick. Porchos and Maranchthus halted by the elevator shaft. Above it was a hole in the ceiling where the pulley had been anchored; the lift itself had fallen down the shaft.

A corpse lay by the rim of the pit. Porchos turned it over with his foot.

"Another of our men," he said as Zorachus and Halfdan came up. "The wizard. He must have ripped out the pulley."

"And died soon after," Maranchthus said. "I'm surprised our other man lasted as long as he did."

"They must've thought he was dead. That was quite a slash…and besides, they had other things on their minds. Suicide requires some concentration, I expect. Even when you're enjoying it."

"I would've fought," Halfdan said, eyeing a tangle of corpses nearby.

"Yes, you Kragehul always prate about fighting to the end," Porchos said. "Last stands and heroics and all sorts of tedious shit…but what do you know about anything? *They're* the ones who've accepted death. You're all posturing and posing, but *they* sent themselves away…didn't know we had such a soft touch among us." He jeered at Zorachus. "Of course, if they had, it would've been even *more* foolish to go down fighting...but given what they believed, they acted most judiciously. They were trapped, mice under the cat's paw; as far as they knew, they were about to wake from this senseless dream in any case. And so they chose to die by their own hands. Some thought it would be less painful...some made it as painful as they could, and came like sleepers in heat."

"I would've fought," Halfdan repeated.

"You," Porchos replied in a voice thick with contempt, "are a stinking barbarian dolt."

Halfdan regarded him silently.

"Stop staring at me, dog," Porchos spat.

The Kragehul's expression had grown almost thoughtful.

"Halfdan," Zorachus began---

Just as Porchos slapped the Kragehul across the face.

Roaring, Halfdan grabbed the Merchant by the throat, holding him out at arm's length over the shaft. The Guildsman's eyes bulged out and he gripped Halfdan's wrist with both hands. Soldiers rushed towards them, shouting; Maranchthus leaped in back of Halfdan, poniard in hand.

"Drop him and you're dead," he snarled. "Set him on the rim."

Knowing Halfdan would be killed the instant Porchos was safe, Zorachus extended his hands, rings gleaming.

"Maranchthus," he said, "Get back."

The Merchant's eyes darted sidewards. "Are you out of your mind?"

"Get...back," Zorachus said. "Slowly. And tell your men to withdraw."

Maranchthus did as he was told. Zorachus's troops remained as the others retreated.

The Sharajnaghi said: "Halfdan, set Porchos down."

Halfdan snarled something unintelligible.

"Halfdan!" Zorachus barked.

The Kragehul obeyed. Coughing and sputtering, Porchos collapsed on the floor. Zorachus knelt by his side, keeping his eyes on Maranchthus and the troops.

"I apologize for my bodyguard," he said.

"Too late!" Porchos cried.

"And for threatening Maranchthus just---"

Porchos shrieked: "I want...the Kragehul's...*head!*"

Ears stung, Zorachus looked sidelong at him.

The Guildsman's face was blotched with red spots and his bloodshot eyes glistened and twitched; quivering, his spittle-flecked lips were peeled back, and his teeth grinned whitely, clenched tightly together. The sight was enough to make the Sharajnaghi want to leap up and smash Porchos's twisted, bloated hideousness with both feet, to print his heels deep in the Merchant's features, feel bone snap and make blood spurt....

Struggling with himself, arrow-scar flaming red on his cheek, he looked back at Maranchthus and the soldiers. They were all wearing the same mask as Porchos. How easy, how splendid it would be to unleash a spate of demon-bolts, tear their heads apart, send eyes and teeth and bits of skull flying....

He cast his gaze floorward.

"I'll punish my servant myself," he said.

"The pig's *HEAD!*" Porchos shrieked, jerking upwards, spit spraying from his lips, spattering Zorachus's chin. The Sharajnaghi wiped the drops away with a trembling hand.

"Do you want my support?" he asked.

"You need us as much as we need you! Kill him!"

"Don't be ridiculous," Zorachus answered, rising. His hands clenched and unclenched at his sides, and light pulsed behind the knife-sharp facets of his rings; aroused by his anger and torment, the demons ached to kill. "We'll be off now. Come on, Halfdan."

As they started for the door, Zorachus waited for the Guildsmen to shout something to their troops, but they remained silent, and the Guild soldiers all slid well over to the right as though the floor had moved beneath them...he and Halfdan went out into the corpse-strewn corridor beyond.

Soon he heard footsteps and looked back. His retainers were following; even if they had been hired by Porchos and Maranchthus, they knew who the real power was.

As the Sharajnaghi and the Kragehul reached the street, Zorachus said:

"Don't you ever---*ever*, damn you---slip like that again."

223

Halfdan looked shamefaced and made no reply, which was just as well in any number of ways; feeling grotesquely hypocritical, Zorachus wished he could bite the words back. He had almost snapped himself; his mind still roiled with thwarted slaughterlust.

God, God, he thought. *How I want to kill them all....*

Returning to the house across the plaza, they went out the back and mounted up. The retainers formed a column and the company set off.

Zorachus and Halfdan were silent all the way back to the palace. Going directly to his room, the Sharajnaghi lay down.

Sleep proved impossible. If he was not torturing himself for coming so close to the brink, he was remembering the heaps of suicides...he was under seige, hemmed in by loathesome foes and allies hardly less detestable. Afflicted by the urge to usurp God's place, wreak a judgment day all his own, he was also unable to do good, powerless to mitigate the savagery in which he found himself, trapped in a city where cruelty was taken so much for granted that his enemies would slay themselves before they could even be offered mercy...He shook his head, digging his fingers into his scalp, almost wishing that he could rip his skull open and let his pent-up frustrations come exploding forth...He needed to pace, or better still, take a long solitary walk, calm himself down, drain off the pressure building inside him, pray.

Pray most of all.

He stood, considering the garden: it was too dangerous, and being surrounded by those waxen, fulsome leaves would only intensify his mood.

He went out into the hall, telling the guards not to follow. Finding a narrow staircase, he ascended, coming out at the top in a vaulted corridor that had plainly gone unused for some time. A thick layer of dust covered the floor, matted the tapestries on the walls; sunlight seeped through slit casements on the right. Praying silently, he started down the passageway.

Rounding a corner, then another, he came to a stretch where the dust had recently been disturbed. Footprints showed, shiny and black, baring the marble floor, leading from a stairwell to an open door. Despite the turmoil inside him, his curiosity was picqued, and he went to the door and looked inside.

Seated at a small table in a small windowless room, a bottle, goblet, and burning candle before him, Sharthas was cutting groove after groove in the tabletop with a little knife...there was something extremely disquieting about the scene, as though he were a ghost condemned to repeat some meaningless action...

Suddenly he looked up, saw Zorachus, and shot to his feet, mouth sagging. Zorachus was astonished by his reaction; the Steward looked like a man who had just committed a murder.

"Why aren't you working?" Zorachus demanded, partly for lack of anything better to say, partly because Sharthas's behavior was so suspicious.

"Actually, sir ... Lord Mancdaman. . . .

Zorachus went to the table. It was old and splintery, top scarred with carved initials and dozens of Sharthas's grooves, each of which ended in a deft, tightly cut curve.

Sharthas saw Zorachus looking at them and said, "It's a habit of mine, a little twitch. The table was so old, I assumed no one would mind. . ."

"Why aren't you working?" Zorachus asked again.

"I finished my morning rounds," Sharthas said and gulped. "Most of them, anyway .... Things are well in hand ... I just thought I'd have a nip." He nodded toward the bottle.

"Why did you sneak all the way up here? Feeling guilty?"

Sharthas nodded. "I feel guilty about everything."

"I see," Zorachus said, picking up the bottle. He sniffed the mouth and winced. "Couldn't you do better than this?"

"I'd never take any of your *good* wine, and---"

"Smells like pretty strong stuff."

"It is."

"Good enough," Zorachus said, pulled up a chair, and sat. He motioned Sharthas back down. "I can use a jolt." He took a long pull.

"If I might be so bold," Sharthas said, "is there something the matter?"

Zorachus nodded. "How long have you been up here?"

"Not very.... decided I needed a dose of fortitude after Halfdan shouted at me. He was in such an evil mood, standing at the bottom of the main stair and cursing. Did you quarrel?"

225

"I was pretty sharp with him. Porchos slapped him. Halfdan laid hands on him....We could have both been killed. And I almost..."

"What, my Lord?"

"Never mind. Did you hear what happened to the garrison?"

Sharthas nodded. "One of the guards told me."

Zorachus took another pull. "I saw a man who'd chewed the fingers from one of his hands. He still had a thumb hanging from his mouth. There was another who'd smashed his brains out against a wall. You'd think he would've died long before his skull opened. He must have been a very determined man..." He looked at Sharthas. "There are children, insane children who mutilate themselves any way they can. You can't talk to them or reach them. They've shut themselves off from the whole universe. They're like mad animals, or worse, and all they ever seem to think about is smashing their heads against walls and gouging out their own eyes and chewing off their fingers."

After a pause, Sharthas said: "Maybe they know something you don't."

"About?"

"Themselves. Maybe they're born with a sense of justice the rest of us lack."

"I don't believe it," Zorachus answered.

"Then why do they do it?"

"I don't know."

Sharthas continued, "Of course, maybe they don't have a reason at all. Maybe they're just like the rest of us." He laughed. "People are such wretched things."

Zorachus studied the Steward's seamed, weary face. "You've been in Khymir too long."

"Long enough," Sharthas agreed. "But I can't help thinking we're all Khymirians inside."

"You think I'm like that?" Zorachus asked---and immediately, almost gloatingly, reminded himself of his own bloodlust, and his yearning for another man's wife....

"You might be an exception," Sharthas said. "You seem to be a decent sort. But at the risk of being insubordinate..."

"Go on."

"You're only human, my Lord. And you must have come to Khymir for something. Considering what this city is like---"

"I hate Khymir," Zorachus said.

"So do I," Sharthas answered. "But we both stay, don't we? We could go if we really wanted to."

Zorachus leaned forward. "*You* can go. I'll give you gold, all you can take. Leave and never look back."

Sharthas gave a watery smile. "Very generous of you. But what about my lovely black whore?"

"Leave her," Zorachus said.

"You make it sound very easy. But I want her more than anything else in the world. I have to stay to get what I want."

"You can change that," Zorachus pressed. "Force yourself to see what she's doing to you."

"I don't have to force myself. The fact that I'm her willing slave is always before me. It only deepens my conviction that I should be enslaved."

"Drivel," Zorachus snapped

"Yes," Sharthas said meekly. "It *is* drivel. If I had an ounce of brains or nerve I'd stop participating in the farce. I'd kill myself. But since I can't do that, I must soothe my conscience the best I can."

"By debasing yourself further?"

"By destroying myself. Just by inches, admittedly, but that's the only way open to a coward like myself."

"Why not try to be cured?" Zorachus asked. "Leave Khymir. Go to Thangura, to Qanar-Sharaj. The order that raised me has many wise and holy men. They'd try to help you..."

"I don't deserve help."

"What did you do to deserve annihilation?"

"The same as everyone else. I was born."

"You really think we're all damned from birth?"

"I suppose."

227

"That we have no free will?"

"We have it," Sharthas said, "but it just makes things worse. We know exactly what we're doing, what our choices are. And in the end, we fall. Nothing makes us fall. But we do."

"How do you know?" Zorachus asked.

"How, my Lord? I've lived in Khymir these past twenty years. Can you tell me that such a sty could exist if human beings weren't rotten at the core?"

"Then why isn't every city like Khymir?"

"How do you know they're not? Do you really know what other people are like behind closed doors? Snot-eaters and scab-pickers, rubbing themselves on beds and reaching into their pants and thinking vile thoughts?" He paused. "Have you ever thought of stabbing your best friend? Just found that thought in your mind?"

"I don't know what you're talking about," Zorachus said. Even for a man in Khymir, he was sweating profusely.

"Maybe you don't, my Lord," Sharthas conceded. "Maybe you're made of steel."

"Would it make you happier to know I had such thoughts?"

"Nothing would make me happier," Sharthas replied. "Knowing you were like me would only convince me further that the world's as I see it. Knowing that you're not would only make me see how much more wretched I was."

Zorachus felt cornered. "You're talking nonsense."

"Of course. Everything is nonsense."

The Sharajnaghi realized the futility of argument. Still, the instinctive reply rose to his lips: "Even saying that everything is nonsense?"

Sharthas stood up. "There's a fly on your sleeve," he said, pointing.

Zorachus looked at his sleeve. There was no fly.

And Sharthas was gone.

228

Chapter 17

IN THE WEEKS that followed, Zorachus was attacked eight times by sendings. He destroyed them all with small cost to himself or his followers, but took scant comfort. He knew the Priesthood would not relent no matter how many of their demons he conquered, and there was always a gnawing dread at the back of his mind.

Three Chief Guildsmen were killed during the same period. The first was silently flayed by a demon in his bed, the next torn to pieces by a being that materialized beside him in his armored palanquin. Shortly after the second's death, the Priesthood slipped men into Guild territory to post promises of more assassinations and offers of rewards for deeds done in the Priestly cause. The Guild countered with threats and offers of its own, and held a public demonstration of the deadlier sorcerous arts, in which three Guild wizards executed several dozen "traitors" in various hideous ways. Marmaros Maranchthus presided over the affair, extolling the Guild's might and ferocity.

Next morning, he was found in his bath chamber, squashed like a wad of clay into a corner of the ceiling.

The Guild, meanwhile, had had little success with its own sendings, one reason being that Zorachus took no part in them, even though he was asked repeatedly; Sharajnaghim were not permitted to use conjured beings for any purposes other than training, immediate self-defense, or immediate protection of others. The Order's Divine Dispensation was strictly limited in regard to demons, and non-demonic entities were not to be endangered except in the direst need. But Zorachus never explained any of that to the Guildsmen, inventing excuses about the influences instead. He knew the Merchants knew he was lying, but they would have thought the same if he told them the truth, and taken insult as well. They were not fools. After a time they simply stopped requesting such help from him. And the failures of their wizards continued to mount.

Yet in matters other than sendings, the Guild had much success, and Zorachus, to a large degree, was responsible. He was the linchpin in several spectacular victories, actions that cut off and smashed large raiding-parties from the north. And most important of all, with his speeches, public appearances, and tracts, he kept the Guild cause popular. Finding it necessary to go beyond simply attacking the Priesthood (his audience already knew what the Priests were like, and were easily bored) he managed, without ever explicitly describing anything of the sort, to conjure up images of a new golden age, a time of unending orgies and bloody games that would spring into existence the instant the priesthood fell. Never once did he actually lie; the Khymirians, so adept at self-deception, supplied themselves with all the falsehoods necessary. Still he hated the charade. He was, after all, the instigator, if not the author, of so much untruth. And he had to spend so much time trying to think like a Khymirian, trying to guess what turns of phrase would best deceive a degenerate.... Whenever he finished writing a speech or pamphlet, he felt covered in slime.

But sometimes it seemed as though everything he did gave him that feeling. Meeting with the Guildsmen was like crawling down a sewer, but returning home was, in its own way, even worse---he could hardly walk from the front gate to his room without seeing one obscenity after another. Most of the household were Khymirians or foreigners sunk in Khymirian ways; he tried, through Sharthas, to rein them in, but when it came to their pleasures they would not be restrained. The coupling bodies seemed like fixtures in the halls and parlors, and the air grew stale with the odor of lubricants, genitals, and sweat. Whenever he was not out on Guild errands, he kept more and more to his own chamber, with the Kragehul his only company.

They were the strongest anchor his mind possessed, but even so, he knew his friendship with them was growing ever more tainted, spoiling in the throbbing Khymirian heat. The closer he drew to them, the more he wanted Asa; faced with an opportunity to crumble further, he took it. More than once, when Halfdan turned in early, Zorachus stayed up late into the night with Asa, listening to Kragehul myths and telling her about his faith...his eyes would linger on her face and he would feel a strangely heady mixture of exaltation and guilt. But the exaltation always deserted him when she left; often too anguished to sleep, he told himself that his feelings were corrupt, that he should never allow himself to be alone with her, that he must do without his most cherished drug.

But whenever he saw her, he could not control himself; if she offered to stay, he could not refuse. And though he prayed desperately for the strength to stifle his love for her, he slipped farther and farther into the web...

Eyes blank, jaw sagging, the young novice lay panting atop Sathaswentha, bearing her long muscular legs on his shoulders. Sathaswentha gazed up at him, feasting on the drained idiocy of his face. With one last deep thrust, he finished.

Smiling contemptuously, she said: "Get off."

He obeyed, and she sat on the edge of the bed. He stroked her back weakly, all his youthful strength drained for the moment. Laughing, she stood, went to a basin and washed herself. Her robes were slung over a chair nearby; rapidly she slipped them on, stepped into her shoes, and changed sex.

"Must you leave?" the acolyte asked.

"I've duties in the main chapel," Sathaswenthar replied. "Get dressed and go."

"Did you enjoy yourself?"

"After a fashion."

Puzzlement crossed the acolyte's face. "What do you mean?"

"That we weren't enjoying the same things."

"Ah, of course," the novice said, completely misunderstanding him. He began to rub himself slowly against the sheet, clenching and unclenching his sweat-glistening buttocks. "Would you like me to be the woman?"

"I'm *done* with you," Sathaswenthar said, voice keen with menace.

The novice gulped. Rising, he dressed and left hurriedly. Sathaswenthar followed him into the hallway; watching him flee, he remembered what it was like to lie with the young fool. It had been a particularly edifying session; the novice had a passion for clumsy positions, and his body was a gushing wellspring of sweat and slime.

They had been a most ludicrous sight in the mirror, twined knots of blood-purpled flesh, wallowing and squatting...It would be very useful to summon up images of their lovemaking during meditations on the baseness of flesh.

Of course, Sathaswenthar would not recall the delicious sensations, or remember sinking several times to the novice's brutish level, losing all control...he would take only what was useful from the experience, refuse to admit to himself that he had felt any sensual pleasure, stifle all suspicion that his frenzied couplings had not moved him any closer to true spirituality. Who was he to question the method? Tchernobog had set his seal upon the Way of Sensuality. To know the organic was to hate it...

A different novice hurried up.

"What is it?" Sathaswenthar asked.

"My Lord," the man said, "His Anointed Steward wishes to see you in his quarters."

Sathaswenthar nodded.

The underling swept off.

Sathaswenthar went swiftly to Kletus's chambers. Lysthragon was with the High Priest.

"There you are," Kletus said as Sathaswenthar arrived. "Good news."

"About what?"

"We have someone in the Mancdaman Palace."

Sathaswenthar clapped his hands together. "Splendid."

"Indeed," Kletus said.

"What's the plan, then? Poison?"

Kletus shook his head.

"Too many food-tasters?" Sathaswenthar asked.

"A small army."

"What about stabbing? Is our someone suicidal?"

"Merely a spy," Kletus said. "Zorachus must eliminate himself."

"And how can we get him to do that?" Sathaswenthar asked.

"Our fly on the wall's been watching Zorachus very closely...says he's infatuated with his bodyguard's wife. Zorachus won't sleep with her, but he's passionately attached nonetheless."

"Why won't he sleep with her?"

"*Because* she's his bodyguard's wife. Apparently he thinks there's some kind of sacred bond between married people."

"What?" Sathaswenthar asked.

"Zorachus is insane," Lysthragon said, distorting his face with his fingers; turning his back to Sathaswenthar, he jerked his head round, looking over his shoulder like a demented owl. "In-*sane.*"

"Incredible as it might seem," Kletus said, "He really does believe some of those cracked Sharajnaghi teachings."

Sathaswenthar laughed. "*I* know," he said. "We should try to persuade him that he's been misbehaving here. Maybe he'd leave."

"Don't talk nonsense," Kletus said.

"Just a suggestion. We still haven't heard what you have in mind."

"We take the wife," Kletus said.

"And demand---what? Do you really think he'd exchange himself for her?"

"I doubt that he's *that* crazy," Kletus answered. "But we might let him think he could save her *and* escape in the bargain..."

"I'm listening."

"Suppose her abductors left some kind of trail."

"Which would lead---?"

"Into the lowest levels of the catacombs. The Shreeth would be able to deal with him, don't you think?"

"Undoubtedly," Sathaswenthar said. "But why go to so much effort? If he follows the trail, we could simply ambush him."

Kletus shook his head. "He's too powerful."

"Sink a quarrel into a man's spine, and it doesn't matter how powerful he is. We could lead him between two houses full of crossbowmen..."

"I've already made up my mind," Kletus answered.

But Sathaswenthar was unwilling to let it rest. "Why is it necessary to use the Shreeth?"

Kletus made no answer.

"Lysthragon," Sathaswenthar said, "what do you think of all this?"

Lysthragon giggled and turned once more. He was chewing something; when he gulped it down and showed his teeth in a monkeylike grin, they were stained green.

"If Lord Kletus has made his mind up," he said, "What can we do?"

"Nothing," Kletus said.

Sathaswenthar scrutinized the High Priest. "What is it that you're not telling us?"

"Nothing," Kletus replied, "Save that I've been---how shall I say it---*inspired.* And no matter how much you try to dissuade me, I'll remain

233

convinced of my inspiration. Don't you remember when we turned on Ordog? All the times I ignored your well-thought-out plans and relied solely on my own genius? When the Voice speaks to me, I listen."

"That's all very well," Sathaswenthar said. "But surely our goal is to see Zorachus killed. And surely we'd increase our chances if we posted men to shoot him."

"It's not necessary," Kletus answered.

"You know," Sathaswenthar said thickly, "Your 'Voice' advised us to bring Zorachus back to Khymir."

"That's true."

"But somehow it neglected to tell you that he'd betray us."

Unfazed, Kletus answered: "If his bretrayal results, as I believe it will, in the final annihilation of the Guild, he'll have served my purpose well enough. My Providence is mysterious in its workings. But have faith. All will be well."

But Sathaswenthar could summon no faith. He sensed that something was badly awry, and as sometimes happened when he was anxious, he began to change rapidly from sex to sex.

Knowing full well what the transformations signified, Kletus said: "Get out of my sight."

Thinking a crossbowman or two might be stationed anyway, Sathaswentha-Sathaswenthar took his leave.

The sunset was red as a live coal, silhouetting the western thunderclouds; threatening shadow-shapes of men and monsters reared against the last light. Slowly, the crimson glow died

And the sky purpled, deepening to black, shrouding Khymir in night.

Zorachus was in Halfdan's room. Dead to the world, Asa lay on the bed; she had had a great deal of wine at dinner. Zorachus had helped Halfdan carry her upstairs.

"Can't say I blame her," Zorachus said, weary and slightly sick.

He also had drunk too much, and felt as though he were sweating inside a soggy blanket. The touch of Asa's flesh had only added to the heat.

"I know what you mean," Halfdan said. "Lately all I want to do is sleep."

Zorachus smiled in grim sympathy. "Blot the whole world out?"

"Just this damn city," Halfdan said. "Did you see those girls in the hallway?"

Zorachus shook his head.

"They were in one of the niches. Looked like a snake eating its own tail."

"We could have our meals up here," Zorachus suggested. "Keep to ourselves. Shut it all out... as much as possible, at least---"

It occurred to him that he sounded like Kletus, but he thrust the thought aside.

Halfdan asked: "Wouldn't that mean we'd have those food-tasters crowding about in here?"

"Hadn't thought of that," Zorachus said. "That would indeed defeat my purpose."

"Those people give me the shivers."

"They're necessary," Zorachus said.

"Even so..."

"Why them in particular?"

"Haven't you ever watched them? They enjoy their work. They stand around waiting to die of poison, and they *enjoy* it. That look they get on their faces....Gorm's Hammer, I'm glad they don't go near my food or Asa's..."

Zorachus shrugged. "I suppose I'm not as sensitive about it...I spend my time wondering when one of them is going to drop."

"That damned ritual," Halfdan went on. "First one tries the dainties. Then another tries the wine, and a third tries the meat. . . . "

"Enough," Zorachus broke in. "I'd rather not think of them at all."

"What would you rather think about?" There was the hint of an edge in Halfdan's voice; Zorachus wondered if he were finally feeling the strain of their perpetual company.

"Asa's garden." the Sharajnaghi replied. "I think I'll go out and see how it's doing."

Halfdan snorted. "You and those plants."

Zorachus headed for the balcony, picking up a lamp. "Care to join me?"

Halfdan said nothing.

Zorachus went out by the garden. Lamplight fell on rows of green climbing vines, the only wholesome plants he had ever seen in Khymir. He thought of the dome at Qanar-Sharaj, the sea of leaves, the fresh green smell...

He stood beside the garden for some time, lost in his memories. Then a loud knocking and Sharthas's muffled voice brought him back to Khymir. Off in the distance, thunder rolled.

Leaving the lamp on the garden rim, he went back into the room. Halfdan opened the door.

Sharthas looked terrified.

"Lord Mancdaman!" he cried.

"What's the matter?" Zorachus demanded.

"There's a giant beetle."

"Where?"

"In the kitchen!" the Steward squawked. "It bit one of the cooks!"

Zorachus and Halfdan followed him downstairs, trailed by the doorwardens.

Four feet long, the beetle was horned and studded, standing motionless on its jointed legs, chitin shining, antennae poised. Guards clustered by the entrances, watching it. The kitchen help had cleared out.

Zorachus slipped the rings on, crying: "Get back from the doors!"

As if startled by his voice, the insect flinched, and began to emit a piercing whine. Then it spread its wings and whirred through the air, straight at him.

Demon-bolts crackled, and the beetle exploded. Bits of chitin and yellow blood spattered the floor and tables nearby---and vanished.

"So much for that," Zorachus said, wondering why his foes had dispatched such a lame sending.

As he started back for the stairs, several breathless retainers rushed up; a small demon had appeared in one of the armories. He went with them and killed it, but it was not long before yet another minor sending was reported.

"I think I'd better go up and stay with Asa," Halfdan told the Sharajnaghi. "Something might appear in our room."

"Go on," Zorachus said, and went to deal with the third demon. For the better part of an hour, he blasted man-sized toads, crabs, and bats all over the first floor of the palace. Guessing they were only a prelude, he fully expected something more dangerous to appear any moment, but it never did.

Finally the materializations stopped. Returning the rings to their pouch, he went back up to the Kragehuls' room with the doorwardens---

And discovered Halfdan sprawled on the floor.

Zorachus rushed to his side. Halfdan's eyes were closed, but he was breathing.

The bed was empty---Asa was nowhere to be seen.

"Try to bring Halfdan round," Zorachus told the doorwards and went over to the bed.

A trail of red drops led from it out onto the balcony, which was still faintly lit by the lamp he had left on the garden's rim. He followed the trail to the railing, which was liberally splashed; two grappling hooks clutched the marble and thin silken ropes dangled over the side. Torchlight from a window bathed the flags below. Even from the second story, red spots were visible.

Turning, he noticed for the first time that most of Asa's plants had been rooted up, ripped apart. He hardly knew whether to laugh or shriek.

He went back into the room. Halfdan was up on his knees, shaking his head groggily.

"Did you find Asa?" he asked Zorachus.

"They took her," Zorachus said. "What happened to you?"

"There was a man in here," Halfdan answered. "He had some of Asa's jewelry, the necklaces I bought her the other day. Must've stayed behind to do some thieving.... When I saw him I went for my sword, but he was too fast. Caught me with a kick, right in the side of the face..."

The Kragehul got to his feet, wobbling.

"Can you walk?" Zorachus asked.

"Oh, I'm ready to split some skulls," Halfdan said. "They took my wife."

And my love, Zorachus thought, burning with the same rage. Indeed, splitting the bastards' skulls would hardly satisfy him; for a moment he saw himself wrenching his sword out of a shattered brow and licking the blood off the edge.

Enough, fool, his conscience cried.

"Come with me," he said. Halfdan and the retainers followed him over to the droplet trail. "See those red spots?"

Halfdan said: "If they've hurt her---"

"It's not blood. Color's wrong. It's a deliberately laid trail."

"And we have to follow it," Halfdan said.

"Of course."

Halfdan nodded. "They must have an ambush set up…"

"I expect," Zorachus said. "Asa must've been drugged at dinner. It would be hard to get to my food, but hers…"

Halfdan rubbed his bruised cheek. "Who could've done it?"

"No use worrying about it at the moment," Zorachus looked at the doorwardens. "Tell Sharthas that Halfdan and I are going to get Asa back." He took his rings back out.

"Just the two of you, my lord?" one of the guards asked.

Zorachus put the rings on. "We'll move faster that way. And quieter."

"Come on," Halfdan said. "She might not have long to live. "

If she's still alive at all, Zorachus thought.

They went out on the balcony, climbed over the side. As they lighted on the flags, Zorachus muttered a spell that sent a shaft of white light stabbing from his left palm, and they raced off down the stone path leading into the park, following the droplets under the trees. Reaching the park's western exit, they found the gate flung wide, and paused.

"I wonder what happened to the guards here?" Halfdan asked.

"They're probably in the bushes somewhere," Zorachus answered, "Grinning ear to ear."

He leaned out, looked right, then left along the street. It was narrow and empty, brooding with the wartime hush. Torches guttered in wallset sockets, and the red drops were plainly visible on the cobbles, leading south.

"What if they split up here?" Halfdan asked.

"And the ones leaving the trail don't have Asa at all?"

"Yes."

"We'll just have to trust them."

Halfdan laughed. Zorachus hid his glowing hand under his tunic, and they slipped through the gate. For a short stretch they had the garden wall on their left, but after that it grew more nerve-wracking, with houses on either side of the street.

What are we blundering into? Zorachus thought. *When are they going to spring the trap?*

A dark shape lurched out of an archway; the Sharajnaghi nearly blasted it before he realized it was only an old man. Zorachus barked a nervous laugh, almost wishing that it *had* been an attacker, that the suspense was over and the killing could begin....

Blinking stupidly, the old man sat down, crooning to himself.

They dashed on. Doors and alleys flashed by...where would the attack come from?

Up ahead, across from each other, two second-storey windows gaped, the first Zorachus had seen unshuttered. Pulling his hand from his shirt, he beamed light into the opening on the right.

A crossbowman stood there, weapon raised. Dazzled by the glare, he loosed his bolt prematurely, and it sang by Zorachus's ear; Zorachus ducked reflexively and a second bolt, from the other house, barely missed his head.

As the arbalesters tried to reload, he stopped, flinging his arms out. Demon lightning flared. Bodies rocked back from the windows and smoke billowed out into the night.

"Let's hope that was the ambush," Zorachus said as Halfdan came up beside him.

"Let's hope the whole Priesthood will just drop down dead," Halfdan answered.

They started forward once more.

After a time the street wound to the west and narrowed, becoming a mere crevice between scabrous, dank facades. It brought them to a small square, where a slender stone booth, keystone carved into a skull, reared up from the cobbles, black doorway yawning like the mouth of a giant serpent. The droplets led into the darkness.

Zorachus went to the entrance. A strong charnel smell rose in his nostrils, borne by a warm, damp wind. He sent a beam of light down into the murk. A long stairway was revealed, plunging steeply, endlessly, its walls covered with grey mold and trickling with greenish rivulets. The steps were worn and slippery looking, clearly marked with red spots.

"I wish I'd worn my armor," Halfdan said.

"Do you have any idea where these steps lead?" Zorachus asked.

"Down to the catacombs," Halfdan said. "Porchos told you about them, remember? When you asked about Lazarak?"

"Lazarak," Zorachus said, almost under his breath, remembering the tale of a murdered general transformed into a dragon in his tomb. A chill swept the Sharajnaghi despite the heat.

"What in hell do those bastards have in mind?" Halfdan asked.

"Who knows? In we go."

Chapter 18

SLOWLY THEY HEADED down the steps. Footing was treacherous and they almost fell several times. Large spiders and spiny insects scuttled out of their way. Glowing worms dropped on them from above, squealing like tiny babies if trod upon. Scaly tails jerked into holes as the men approached. At one point, Zorachus spotted a small rag doll, stained and tattered, lying on the steps below, and got close enough to see that there were several nails driven into the head; then a rat stuck its snout from a crack, snatched the doll's leg in its mouth, and yanked the toy from sight.

The stairs plunged down and down, the air growing heavier with the smell of decay. Nodules appeared on the walls, fistsized fungus-domes, looking uncannily like small, repulsive imp faces. When brushed, they burst, green muck vomiting from their "mouths," its sour stench contesting the sweet death odor.

"Tell me, Zorachus," Halfdan said while wiping a spattered hand on his trews, "did your God create these filthy quats?"

"Yes," Zorachus replied.

"Then why---"

"Tchernobog must've made some changes somewhere along."

"You've got an answer for everything, haven't you?"

"No. You just always ask the right questions."

Uncomfortable with his own glibness, Zorachus continued in his mind: *Why don't you ask who made Tchernobog? Or why God gave him the power to act contrary to His will!*

They reached the bottom, coming out in a chamber so low they could barely stand upright. There were many rounded arches in the walls, entrances to tunnels and stairwells, and rotting rope ladders hung from mouths in the ceiling. A steady stream of the glowing worms was pouring from one of the ceiling-holes; a teeming mound of them had collected on the floor.

Feeling the demon-ring beginning to eat into his flesh, the Sharajnaghi changed ring-fingers as he and Halfdan, breaking into a jog, followed the trail into a passage on the right. The tunnel was lined with niches, and tiers of moldering bodies rose to the ceiling. The linen swathing the corpses was darkly stained---even with embalming, bodies did not keep well in the heat and damp. Here and there a slime-covered skull, phosphorescent vapors drifting from its eyesockets, grinned out at Zorachus and Halfdan as they passed; pools of black ooze gleamed on the charnel shelves. The smell was horrific, as most of the corpses were fairly new---there was apparently a swift turnover among occupants of the niches. Bones, skulls, and linen wrappings littered the floor.

The droplet trail led straight ahead for several hundred yards, then veered to the left, going down another flight of steps into a great serpentine hall. Here the dead were better preserved, in niches faced with glass so thick that Zorachus guessed it must be nigh unbreakable. The bodies often seemed quite pristine, neatly bandaged bundles with hardly a spot of fluid. The stone around some of the niches was intricately carven and there were nameplates of engraved iron. Individual sarcophagi began to appear, finely worked adamantine cases; the coffins became more and more fabulous, their transparent sides supported by slender metal dragons and floral work.

As the richness of the tombs increased, so did the skill of the embalmers. Presently there were no cerements to be seen; naked corpses, their flesh as pink as life, met the eye. In some instances there were even two or three bodies in a single coffin, placed in natural looking coital positions, mouths sagging with soundless moans, glass eyes rolling in simulated passion. There were also pets among the dead---monkeys, snakes, and cats, lamias and other hybrids, bizarre creatures with bits of human anatomy, usually sexual, set among parts wholly alien; often these too were coitally entwined with human corpses. In one coffin was a nude woman, perfectly preserved, legs wrapped around a human-headed crocodile.

Zorachus and Halfdan paused to rest, but soon continued on their way, goaded as much by the horror of their surroundings as eagerness to find asa. They descended more levels; Zorachus, hands burning, changed ring fingers several times. Finally, in spite of the risk, he put the rings back in their sack.

They passed through a huge echoing chamber half-a-mile long, its cyclopean tombs warded by stone demons thirty feet high, then stumbled through the rubble of a partially ruined chapel dedicated to a grisly maggot-god---a gigantic figure of the worm deity arched over the crumbling altar, blind face gnawing a stone infant. Smaller maggots had been carved all along the length of the statue, tunneling in and out. Halfdan stopped, cursing at the idol.

"Are you just going to stand there swearing?" Zorachus asked.

Halfdan picked up a chunk of stone and hurled it.

"You hit the baby," Zorachus said.

"I was putting him out of his misery," Halfdan replied.

Shortly they reached the brink of a vertical shaft five feet wide. A series of rungs, splotched with red and set close together, led down the side of the shaft. Zorachus stabbed a beam of light into the gloom below. There were tunnel mouths at odd intervals beside the rungs, but he could not see the bottom of the shaft.

They started down. Small and hard to grasp, the holds made for a perilous descent---they did not seem designed for human hands.

After hundreds of yards, Zorachus and Halfdan alighted in a tunnel to rest, flexing their fingers---then took to the rungs once more.

Soon they came to a hole wider than the others; the red drops led over its threshold. This tunnel was thickly coated with mold, and yard-long curtains of nitrate hung from its ceiling; the occupants of its niches had rotted away completely. Heaps of broken stone marked numerous cave-ins, and there were many cracks in the floor and walls, some tiny, some a foot wide. The size of the cracks increased farther in, and the rubble piles grew larger, one finally blocking the passage; there the trail turned to the left, down an adjoining passage.

That tunnel appeared to be obstructed too, some distance along, but a closer look showed that the trail led up over the rubble, toward the hole in the ceiling left by the collapse. Climbing up and over the scree, they followed the droplets to an open doorway, through which came a slowly pulsating, yellow light, and an intermittent roar.

"What do you think's making that sound?" Halfdan asked.

"Sounds like a sleeping. . ." Zorachus stopped dead, realizing what he was about to say.

Halfdan gave an uneasy laugh. "Doesn't it, now?"

They reached the doorway and there they halted, filled with dread.

The floor before them sagged in a vast depression, a crater walled with cinders and crushed rock. At the bottom slept a titanic, golden-scaled dragon, neck curled to one side. Curving horns flanked its head, and wrinkled leathery pinions were folded across its back. Roaring yellow flame jetted from its nose as it breathed, and there were many small fires about it, bubbling fumaroles of molten rock.

"Lazarak of the Golden Mail," Halfdan said in hushed tones.

Zorachus nodded, awestruck.

Halfdan asked: "Didn't Porchos say that he tries to smash his way out?"

"When he wakes," Zorachus said. "That must be where all this rubble came from...I see why all those surrounding tunnels collapsed."

"Let's try not to wake him, then."

Zorachus eyed the trail, which led out onto the sloping debris. He started to put his luminous hand into his shirt, realized he would probably need it for balance, and revoked the light-spell. He and Halfdan went out onto the rubble, following the droplets around the rim of the depression. They moved slowly, planting their feet with extreme caution, trying to disturb the stones and cinders as little as possible.

Lazarak slept on.

The trail drew them towards a half-crumbled doorway. Halfdan pulled ahead, reaching the opening first; Zorachus sped up unconsciously, recklessness creeping into his movements.

Stones shifted; the scree gave way beneath him. In a rattling shower of rock fragments and pulverized slag, he rolled down the slope at breakneck speed, dust billowing about him.

Bruised and bleeding, he came to a half-buried halt barely five feet from one of Lazarak's outstretched front claws. The Sharajnaghi lay completely motionless, wondering if those excruciating aches were from broken bones, his dizzy gaze riveted on Lazarak's face.

To his horror, the horned head began to turn; a great red eye cracked open.

But just then a fresh slide of small stones came rattling down over Zorachus's head and shoulders, burying him completely.

He did not breathe, not even knowing if he could. He held his breath until his mind reeled---then exhaled slowly. The stones were loose, and there was air, tasting of soot and slate.

He remained under the debris for several minutes, then gradually lifted his head. The stones falling off seemed to make all the noise in the world, but Lazarak took no notice. He had only stirred in his sleep; it took more than a minor slide to rouse him.

Zorachus raised himself on one elbow and felt for the ring pouch. It was still around his neck. He looked back up the slant. Halfdan was near the doorway, peering down at him.

Working his way out of the stones, the Sharajnaghi limped back by Lazarak's tail, as far away from the dragon's hooded eye as possible, before starting up the side.

The loose tumulus all but denied him purchase; gaining even a few yards was exhausting labor, and it sometimes seemed he slid back two for every three he climbed. But, clawing at the slope with numb persistence, he gained the top at last and stood there awhile, working his bruised arms.

Halfdan beckoned impatiently. Zorachus started circling back toward him.

Slowly his movements grew clumsier and clumsier. His battered muscles were cramping, and he almost slipped twice. Stride by agonizing stride, he dragged himself along the rim of the crater, collapsing at last on the door's threshold. Halfdan pulled him in.

"How badly are you hurt?" Halfdan said.

"Nothing serious, I think," Zorachus said. "I've got to rest a bit..." Setting his back against the tunnel wall, he closed his eyes.

Instantly, Halfdan was on him, shaking him violently.

"Stay awake," the Kragehul snarled. "We've got to find Asa."

Zorachus nodded dazedly. Halfdan yanked him to his feet.

"Can you walk?" the Kragehul demanded.

Zorachus nodded again.

"Light your hand back up and we'll be off."

Zorachus complied, and they started down the tunnel, jumping over cracks, climbing piles of rubble. Summoning hidden reserves of strength, Zorachus pushed his body mercilessly.

Have to find Asa, he told himself, again and again. Eventually, the aches went numb and the cramps worked themselves out. Impatient, Halfdan began to trot; Zorachus kept pace.

The trail took many twists and turns, descending steadily into regions where niches had never been carved into the stone, leading at last to the bank of a slow, dark river. A final splotch of red had been placed on the left side of the passage-mouth, the downstream side.

Zorachus leaned out over the water, searching the tunnel's walls with his hand-beam. There were no ledges to follow. Pulling out his sword, he knelt, thrusting it down into the warm water. His arm went in to the elbow before the blade-point connected with a hard bottom.

"It's not too deep," he said pulling the sword out. Looking back at Halfdan, he wiped it on his trousers and resheathed it. "Not by the edge at least. They probably carried her."

"I don't think so," Halfdan replied, pointing to an eyebolt in the wall set back several feet from the bank. "They had a boat tied up here."

"But we'll have to wade," Zorachus said and climbed over the side, Halfdan following. They headed downstream, the warm current a balm to Zorachus's battered legs.

He and Halfdan slogged forward for what might have been an hour, eventually reaching a large, runneled grotto. Several mouths opened on it; the nearest, a crawlspace, was just above the waterline, a spit of greyish rock extending from it. A small boat was drawn up on the stony projection.

But the craft proved empty.

And no trail led away.

"Maybe they ran out of dye," Zorachus said.

"Maybe they didn't come down in the boat at all…" Suddenly Halfdan cocked his head to one side. "Did you hear anything?"

"No," Zorachus answered, beaming light over the entrance of the crawlspace.

"Something like splashing?"

Zorachus shook his head, face dimly grey-lit by the reflection from the stone. "If they didn't come down in the boat," he said slowly, "if they let it drift down with the current, and left by another route, then who pulled the boat out of the wa---"

"Shhh!" Halfdan hissed. "Listen!"

Zorachus listened. This time he heard it, faint but distinct, coming from one of the tunnel mouths. He took the rings out again and put them on.

"Shreeth," Halfdan said. "Porchos told you about them, remember?"

"The creatures that live under the catacombs," Zorachus said. "Now I understand."

"Kletus wants *them* to take care of you."

Zorachus nodded. "And they have Asa."

The splashing came steadily closer, accompanied by clicks and strange whistling sounds.

"In we go," Zorachus said, dropping to his belly and entering the crawlspace.

"What if they come in after us?" Halfdan demanded.

"Depends on how big they are." Zorachus replied, scrabbling along the stony floor. "Are they man-sized?"

"Smaller, I think."

"Then they'll catch up to us pretty quickly---if they follow. They might not know we're here."

They managed to get a good way into the tunnel as the splashing grew steadily louder behind them.

They're making straight for this passage, Zorachus thought. *Any second now they'll be inside---*

The splashing stopped; there was an exchange of snarls and clicks that sounded like some sort of conversation. Then the scuttling and scratching began.

"Here they come!" Halfdan cried.

"Lie flat!" Zorachus answered. "Flat as you can!"

Halfdan pressed himself against the floor. Zorachus backed up and twisted his head round, stabbing the light-shaft through the narrow space between Halfdan's back and the ceiling. Milky eyes gleamed and blinked in the beam, and gnarled blue-green hands shot up, warding half-glimpsed faces; but the Shreeth still scuttled forward.

Zorachus loosed a carefully aimed demon-bolt. There were shrieks like the wrenching of rusty gates, and thick yellow smoke, stinking like scorched pork, billowed over Halfdan.

"You burned my back!" Halfdan cried, starting up, coughing.

"Keep down!" Zorachus snapped, wishing he'd had the foresight to let Halfdan go first.

Halfdan obeyed and Zorachus loosed another bolt, but there were no more shrieks, no noises of any kind; the smoke blocked his vision.

247

Are they all dead! he wondered.

"Come on," he said, eyes watering at the reek.

They hauled themselves forward. There was no sound of pursuit.

As they rounded a bend, a red-lit opening appeared in the distance. But the passage began to narrow, and soon they felt the squeeze. Only by the most violent exertions could they progress, and Halfdan's burned back was badly scraped.

"I can't say how much I hate this," the Kragehul gasped.

"I think it's a bit wider up here," Zorachus said. "Yes…easier…feel it?"

"No," Halfdan said.

"Come farther---"

They made better progress for a time. But as they neared the exit the passage tightened again. Writhing and struggling, they inched forward.

"I'm losing all my skin," Halfdan said. "This is a bad dream---"

"I'm almost there," Zorachus said.

"Don't say it if it's not true."

""I… *swear…*"

Worming through the opening, Zorachus found himself on a narrow stone bridge. He looked over the side, a hot powerful draft sweeping his face. Five hundred feet below snaked a river of molten lava, glowing fiercely, shimmering under heat convections. The far wall of the chasm was limned in lurid red.

Still in the tunnel, Halfdan said: "I hear something. I think they're dragging the bodies back. . . ."

Zorachus turned. The Kragehul's head and arms emerged, but he came no further, chest and back pressed tightly against the stone.

"Stuck," he said.

Zorachus grabbed his wrist. They strained and struggled for several vain minutes, then stopped to rest.

Behind Halfdan, the dragging noises continued, growing steadily more distant.

"All right," he said. "Again."

They resumed their efforts but accomplished nothing. When they paused once more, Zorachus realized he could no longer hear the dragging.

Maybe they'll just leave us alone. Maybe they never met anything like the demon-bolts, and they'll just go---

Faint scuttlings revealed this for the wishful thinking it was.

He and Halfdan got to it once more, struggling feverishly against the stone vise. Halfdan scraped forward an inch, then two. He began to scream at the pain from his burns. Zorachus's fingers dug powerfully into his flesh.

The Shreeth came closer and closer. Halfdan squeezed forward another inch, stuck fast again. He pushed with his feet, squirmed and fought.

"Can you use the rings?" he gritted, tears of pain and exertion rolling from his eyes, face drenched with sweat. "They're right behind me."

"There's not enough space!" Zorachus answered, pulling with all his might. "Come on! Push!"

Halfdan kicked and strained. Zorachus's nails bit through his skin, drawing blood. The Sharajnaghi's teeth shone white. The slitherings and scrapings were loud now, so loud....

Halfdan slipped free. Zorachus dragged him forward.

A three-fingered claw shot through the opening, grabbing Halfdan's left ankle with tremendous power. He set his right foot against the wall, bracing himself.

Letting one of Halfdan's arms go, Zorachus sent a demon-bolt crackling over the Kragehul's legs, into the passage. The claw opened. The Sharajnaghi let Halfdan scramble past him, loosed more bolts. Screams from the crawlspace, then silence.

Rising, he blew on the rings, switched them to different fingers, and started across the bridge with Halfdan.

A shadowy tunnel mouth opened on the far side, about four feet high. As they entered, Zorachus called a halt, looking back at the crawlspace.

Several smoking bundles, the dead Shreeth, came rolling out through the opening and tumbled over the sides of the bridge.

"There's so little room in that tunnel," Zorachus said. "There could have only been one of them pushing those bodies, maybe two ... Those things must be *strong.*"

"They're strong all right," Halfdan agreed. "Felt like my leg was being pulled from its socket---"

Stunted figures crawled onto the span, rose, and pelted forward, brandishing what appeared to be clubs. Since they were coming single file, Zorachus could not see how many there were.... Stepping back out, he assumed a Dragon Stance.

Cataract strikes knocked the Shreeth off the span in twos and threes. More rusty-gate shrieks; black against the molten glare, dwarfish bodies hurtled down, catching fire as the heat increased, striking the lava in orange spatters.

Once the bridge was cleared, Zorachus watched the far side for a few more minutes. No more Shreeth appeared. Hunching over, he went back into the tunnel.

The floor sloped downward steadily, and the passage curved to the right, like a descending corkscrew. The spiral tightened; small steps appeared. The heat intensified, and the air grew stifling, developing a bitter tang. Patches of sulphurous phosphorescence appeared on the walls. Zorachus extinguished his hand-beam.

At the bottom of the stairs, three crawlspaces waited him and halfdan.

"What do you think?" Halfdan asked.

"Have to pick one," Zorachus answered.

"How?"

Zorachus got down on all fours and looked into each, listening. Then he rose to a crouch and said:

"No way to choose."

"So?"

"You guess."

"Why?"

"She's your wife---"

Halfdan snapped his fingers, said: "That one," and they wriggled into the left-hand hole. The squeeze was not too tight and they squirmed right along, coming out in a circular chamber big enough for them to sit upright. There they rested, eyeing the way out---a wormhole piercing the ceiling at a slant.

"Do you think we'll find her?" Halfdan asked.

"I don't have the slightest idea," Zorachus answered. "And even if we do, that's no guarantee we'll get out of this. It'll be a long climb back. And Kletus must've been pretty sure the Shreeth would finish us."

They sat a while in silence.

"What if she's dead?" Halfdan asked.

"No point even thinking about it."

"Oh no? What if *she's* dead, but *we* get out of here alive? What then?"

"What are you talking about?"

"With your magic, we could break into Banipal Khezach---"

Zorachus shook his head.

"Why not?" Halfdan asked.

"A Sharajnaghi can't kill for revenge."

"Who gives a damn about your crazy scruples!"

"Halfdan---"

"I won't let her sleep unavenged."

"Listen," Zorachus said. "I'd like to tear Kletus's eyes out with my own nails, just for what he's done to us already. But...."

He paused, imagining the High Priest with his sockets emptied, head jerking back and forth, blood rushing down his cheeks...The Sharajnaghi twitched a smile before choking off the sheer pleasure of the thought.

"But what?" Halfdan demanded.

"For all we know, she's still alive," Zorachus said wearily.

"Does that mean you'll help me if she's dead?"

"I didn't say that," Zorachus answered.

But what will my answer be when I find out!

Another silence. He felt the cramps returning.

"Let's go," he said. "I'm stiffening up."

He looked up into the hole.

Blinking back at him was a flat, scaly face with round white eyes, its fanged grin six inches wide, impossibly manic, backswept lips lined with deep wrinkles.

Amazing mouths, Porchos had said; Zorachus thought he knew what the merchant had meant now, but he had just begun to learn...Falling like a moist sack over his head, the lips tightened under his chin, yanking his whole body up off the floor, drawing his face toward the glowing teeth. A stinking crevice opened between the jaws, wider and wider, yawning to accommodate him from brow to chin...

Then the fissure snapped shut, the slimy teeth sliding harmlessly down his nose.

The lips went slack. He tumbled back to the floor, gasping for breath.

A silver dagger hilt jutting from its temple, the Shreeth's head nodded limply through the hole.

"Thanks," Zorachus told Halfdan, shuddering violently, the smell of the thing's breath still in his nostrils.

The Kragehul grunted something, reached up and pulled the dagger out. Green in the yellow light, blood streamed forth, and the lolling head swung horribly to and fro, distended lipsack swaying.

"Just to make sure," Zorachus said, and stuck his hand up over the corpse to fire a demon-bolt along the tunnel.

Instantly, a scaly grip locked on his wrist, jerking him up into the hole. Lacking the space to pull him past its dead cohort, the creature began to twist his arm, apparently trying to wring it off.

He loosed a bolt. Flying stone and flame stung his hand as the Shreeth let him go. Turning his fist dead-on into the tunnel, he launched a second bolt. Shrieks mingled with the echoes of the ring-blast and a broad runnel of green blood sought a path beside the first Shreeth's body. Cooling the ring in the rilling fluid, Zorachus switched it to another finger, shouting: "Back to the stairs!"

They crawled from the chamber. Coming out in the stairwell, they stood panting, pondering their next move.

Stone rasped on stone. "There!" Halfdan cried, pointing.

Two doors, which had been perfectly concealed in the stairwell's irregular walls, were grinding open above.

Zorachus's first thought was that he and Halfdan should retreat into one of the wormholes behind them, but the passages were too narrow for quick escape.

"Up the steps!" he cried, drawing his sword; their only chance was to get above the Shreeth, gain the advantage of position...

"What if there's a whole hive up there?" Halfdan demanded.

"Come on!" Zorachus answered.

But it was already too late; the Shreeth were pouring from the openings. Raising their clubs, they came down the steps like a flood.

Zorachus blasted the first five to steaming rags and others tripped over the mangled dead, but the cascade of tumbling bodies forced him and Halfdan back from the steps; retreating towards the wormholes, the pair set their backs to the wall. Parrying with his sword, killing with his lefthand ring, Zorachus saw that the Shreeth were not carrying clubs at all---one hand was drastically elongated, fingers fused into clawed knobs, some of which were embedded with iron studs or spikes. Each of his parries connected with a loud *chock!*, and the impacts left his swordhand tingling.

On his right, sweeping his blade two-handed, Halfdan batted strokes aside and sliced through shoulders and elbows, sent heads flying....for a brief span the two held out.

But the odds against them were too great. A club-hand glanced off Halfdan's skull, and he fell. Zorachus jumped astride him, fighting furiously, but moments later the sword was knocked from his hand. He cleared a space before him with demon-bolts, blowing bodies backward. Then a Shreeth rushed up from the side and struck him down. Head ringing, the Sharajnaghi tried to rise, but they swarmed over him, hit him twice more, and bound his limbs. He was dimly conscious of them removing his sword belt, and bursts of dull pain penetrated his hazebound mind as the creatures pulled the rings from his scorched fingers; some kind of fetid covering went over his head, and he was lifted up and borne off, belly-down, head nodding and swinging.

Chapter 19

THE JOURNEY LASTED some time. His mind cleared, but the Shreeth had him at the shoulders and knees, and his body rapidly became one great bow of pain.

At last the creatures halted in an intensely hot place, even more stifling than the stairwell. Some kind of assembly was in progress; snarls, whistles and clicks went back and forth. Underlying all was a steady rumble, intermixed with hollow bubblings and rushings.

The parley went on for what seemed an hour, at least, during which Zorachus's captors continued holding him rock still. It seemed they were incapable of fatigue.

If only they'd put me down, he thought. There were "stances" a bound mage could adopt, but the configuration the Shreeth had him in was, perhaps, even more useless than it was excrutiating, and the Influences precluded any spells he could use without forceletting.

Eventually, the Shreeth fell silent, and those holding him started forward again. He heard their feet clanging, as if on metal; once across the resonant surface, they went a short distance and turned, set him down---

At last!---

and retreated.

A second group clanged out, deposited something behind him---Halfdan, he guessed by the grunt---and withdrew; a third group laid something else in front of him. Some kind of complex activity followed, accompanied by rhythmic clicking; Zorachus was certain it was a ritual. When it ended, there was a sound like something sliding from a sack, and a thudding impact.

"Bastards!" came Asa's voice.

His heart leaped.

The covering was yanked from his head; she lay before him, bound head to foot. Her face was bruised, her upper lip swollen, her hair filthy and lank, but the mere sight of her seemed to justify all the fear and agony he had endured since setting out...even if he died in the next few minutes, he had reached her side. She smiled ruefully at him.

The Shreeth withdrew---more clanging, then a ringing grate of metal on rock.

Asa raised herself, looking over him. "Halfdan too," she said, and sank back down. "You're a pair of idiots, but I'm glad to see you."

"A pair of idiots," Halfdan said groggily behind the Sharajnaghi. "That's a fine thing to say."

"You followed the trail, didn't you? They said they were leaving a trail..."

"When did you wake up?" Zorachus asked.

"Before we went underground..." Asa laughed. "You know, they ran into a Guild patrol, but they managed to lie their way out of it. Said I was a spy, that they were bringing me to Porchos. If only I hadn't been gagged..."

"Why did they take it off?"

"They didn't. Those little monsters did. I was beginning to choke on it. Asked them to take off the ropes too, but---"

"How did they drag you through that narrow passage?"

"The really tight one?"

"I would've thought you'd be scraped to pieces."

"They put me in a hide bag," Asa said. "The outside was waxed, I think. They spilled me out of it just before they took the hoods off you and Half- -"

"A pair of idiots," her husband broke in, nudging Zorachus. "After all we've been through, the first thing she does is call us a pair of idiots."

She snapped something at him in Kragehul and a vicious argument ensued, the two of them snarling back and forth over Zorachus.

Ignoring them, he sat up slowly, looking about.

They were on a small circular island of rock. To the right, separated from the island by a twenty-foot gulf, was a huge, yellow-glowing cave hollowed from the side of a redlit cliff face. A metallic gangway lay by the edge of the cliff, obviously what the Shreeth had used going to and from the island. Some fifty feet beyond the gangway was a great crowd of prostrate Shreeth, growling and clicking in unison, brows pressed against the rock.

To the left stretched a vast lake of molten lava; Zorachus guessed it was at least a hundred yards below the surface on which he sat. The lava seethed in spots, sending up incandescent geysers, but was covered with a shiny black crust elsewhere. Sheer precipices hemmed the lake, and islands of black stone reared up from the liquid rock. One of these, directly

255

in the middle, was carved into an angular stone face with heavy hooded eyes.

Zorachus lay back down, wormed his way around the rim of the island. It proved to be the crown of a smooth-sided pillar of rock. Crimson and saffron fires swirled three hundred feet below.

He rested. Next to him lay his sword, sheathed; the demon-rings had been placed on the scabbard. Halfdan's sword and dagger, also sheathed, were nearby. A ritual circle of metallic powder had been drawn about the weapons.

Zorachus looked back at the Shreeth. They were still prostrate.

"Why did they put us out here?" Halfdan asked. He and Asa had settled their differences and were sitting up now; tears in her eyes, she was gazing wistfully at him. Stung by a pang of jealousy, Zorachus looked away from them, saying:

"We're sacrifices. That's why they took us alive. The idol in the lava must be their god. They laid us and our weapons here as an offering."

"But what are they going to do with us?" Halfdan asked. "Just let us starve, or die from the heat?"

"It's getting hard for me to breathe," Asa said.

"Think you can last a bit longer?" Zorachus asked.

"What do you have in mind?"

"Getting us untied, at least."

"How?"

"*Radere Supircidas.*"

"Rad-what?"

"Excellent Squirrels. Now shhh."

Zorachus arranged himself, generated two shields from his palms and dissolved them, repeated the process until he drained off enough force to conjure, then changed position and muttered a formula; two dark squirrel-like creatures with pale human hands materialized beside him, wearing jeweled necklaces and gold belts. Sniffing the air, they eyed him attentively.

"Hot," one said, in white Quarossian, fanning itself.

"I know," Zorachus replied in the same tongue. "Free me and my friends."

256

They started in on his bonds with hands and teeth. Thongs popped and slackened, and the creatures turned to Halfdan, then Asa.

And all the while Zorachus watched the Shreeth, wondering when they would look up.

The Squirrels completed their work. He thanked them and returned them to their own dimension.

"What now?" Halfdan asked.

"Pretend you're still tied," Zorachus answered. "If our luck holds, I'll---"

One of the Shreeth, larger than the rest and wearing a spiny bone headdress, had risen; going to a great gong hanging from a frame, it struck three crashing blows with its club-hand. The notes rang out across the burning lake, and the stone walls gave them hollowly, ominously, back again. Then the Shreeth resumed its place among the others.

"Didn't like the sound of that," Halfdan said. "Almost as if it was summoning something."

"We'd best be off," Zorachus said.

"How?"

The Sharajnaghi did not answer, but rose to his feet and assumed a Griffin Stance. Binding the gangway, he lifted it gently, turned it around, and set it down over the gap between pillar and cliff edge. Halfdan and Asa started to get up, but he motioned them back down and uttered a spell.

Suddenly he was awash in yellow light; a squadron of golden hornets had appeared above him.

"Oh!" Asa cried, clapping. "Oh!"

He dispatched them across the gap. A shining storm, they descended on the shreeth, furiously planting sting after sting.

But the Shreeth made no effort to flee or resist. Barely flinching, keeping their faces pressed against the stone, they continued to growl their prayers---Zorachus was astonished to see such devotion.

But he guessed the hornets' venom would work even on the pious

Going to the weapons, he slipped his rings on unburnt fingers, took up his sword belt and girt it on. Halfdan got his brand and Asa snatched up the dagger.

"Let's go," Zorachus said, and they started out onto the bridge.

A thunderous cry struck them from behind---hair lifting, Zorachus felt a literal jolt, and the pillar shook beneath him. He looked back through streamers of rock-dust dislodged from the ceiling.

Two patches of bubbles had broken the black crust before the idol, and from them rose a pair of immense stone hands, lava sloughing from the blunt fingers. The idol's vast slumberous eyes opened, revealing slits of cobalt-blue fire.

It had taken a long time to wake.

Dashing over the gangway, its intended victims could hear the colossus slogging forward through the lake; ahead, the Shreeth were finally rising, wobbling, sting-swollen, batting vainly at the darting hornets. Welts spurting dark vapor, the creatures stumbled toward the fugitives.

Making for a luminous mouth in the right side of the cave, Zorachus blasted several of the foremost Shreeth, who burst into flame as they catapulted back against their vapor-streaming fellows. Body after body flared, fire running hungrily from limb to limb.

Zorachus banished the hornets. Threading a gauntlet of blazing figures, he and his companions pelted into the tunnel.

Outside, the stone giant roared again, and sent a smoking hand crashing into the temple-cave, crushing dying Shreeth; a huge forefinger jabbed into the tunnel, just short of the fleeing humans. Then, with a boneshaking rumble, it withdrew.

The trio raced on. The phosphorescent tunnel narrowed and forked; from the lefthand passage came shrill cries and footbeats, distant, but coming closer. A trail of green blood led from the other. Halfdan grinned at Zorachus.

"We wounded a lot of them at the stairwell," he said.

"Not nearly enough---" Zorachus stopped, amazed by the malice he felt towards the creatures. After all, they weren't human...

Clearly startled to hear such a sentiment from the Sharajnaghi, Halfdan said:

"That's the spirit."

God, Zorachus thought, *what is happening to me?*

He dashed into the tunnel, leading the way through a labyrinth of yellow-lit corridors.

Coming upon four Shreeth at a junction, they went right through them, hacking. Only one managed to raise a cry.

But others answered, and others answered them; soon there was an unceasing clamor of pursuit.

"How far back do you think they are?" Asa panted to Zorachus.

"Hard to tell with the echoes," he answered. "But they must be close."

"And gaining," Halfdan said.

"I can go harder," Zorachus said.

"So can we," Halfdan answered.

Zorachus took him at his word. They seemed to lengthen their lead. But Asa could not keep that pace for long, and the Sharajnaghi called a halt.

Halfdan said: "We could find a better place for a stand---"

Zorachus cut his protest short. "This'll do. Stay back." His words were barely audible with the approaching din; when he resummoned the hornets, the spell was completely drowned out.

A crowd of Shreeth surged into view around a bend, and the hornets streaked to meet them. Stings drove through scaly hides, but with suicidal zeal the Shreeth continued their headlong rush, screaming in pain, slapping at the elusive attackers.

Zorachus retreated. The Shreeth began to stagger, bandy legs giving out. One after another they toppled, yet still they wriggled and scrabbled along the floor.

Banishing the hornets, Zorachus sent a single demon-bolt into the crawlers. They burned like a river of oil.

The fugitives pressed on, the passage shrinking about them; after a time they had to walk hunched over.

"We'll be on our bellies in a minute or two," Halfdan said.

"I don't think so," Zorachus said. "They carried us the whole distance." As if to prove his point, the tunnel came shortly to a flat dead end.

"The blood trail leads right up to the stone," he said, running his hands around the edge of the barrier. "I think this is one of the doors that opens on the stairwell---"

A small patch of stone gave beneath his touch, rocking up on one end with a click; the barrier grated outward. Going through, he found himself on the steps. Halfdan and Asa came out beside him. He returned the rings to the pouch, then stood listening, flexing his fingers.

"I don't hear anything," Halfdan said.

"Neither do I," Zorachus replied. "We might make it yet."

"Don't jinx us."

They rested a while longer.

"Up we go," Zorachus said at last.

They ascended. As they passed the point where the yellow phosphorescence faded, Zorachus kindled the glow in his hand once more. They climbed steadily until stair became ramp; legs aching, lungs burning, they rested again. But their breath was only half- caught when a low drumming, as of pounding feet, started below.

"They want some more hornets," Halfdan said.

"I've used up my privilege."

"What?"

"My order has a covenant---"

"With wasps?"

"A Sharajnaghi can call them three times."

"You only used them twice."

"You're forgetting Morkulg. But I don't think I'd have the power in any case...I'm just too tired. Let's get to the bridge. I might be able to blast it away behind us."

They resumed the ascent. Reaching the span, they crossed over. Asa slipped into the wormhole first; Halfdan struggled after, but had less difficulty going in than he had coming out.

Zorachus yearned to follow. He thought there was some chance the whole bridge might collapse under the demon-bolts. But launching the strikes meant facing the bridge, and he couldn't back into the tunnel.

Sheathing his sword, he took out his rings again and slipped them on, fingers quivering with pain at their touch. He hurled bolt after bolt at the center of the bridge. They kicked up great sprays of sparks and sent a few stone-chips flying, but did little else.

260

Nostrils filled with the odor of his own seared flesh, he eyed the far doorway, listening to the echoing footbeats. Crouching, he turned, shouting into the crawlspace:

"It didn't work! I'll hold them as long as I can!"

"We'll wait by the water!" came Halfdan's reply.

Zorachus switched ring fingers gingerly, rose, and turned. The Shreeth were screaming now; by the sound of it, there were thousands of them.

Assuming a Dragon Stance, he stood and waited, fully expecting to die. His most telling magic was denied him, and while he might still loose bolts, or whip his body into a frenzy of sword-work, he knew it would not be enough. He prayed.

The din grew. One by one, the Shreeth rushed out across the bridge.

"Good-bye, Asa," he said, and started in with cataract-bolts. Struck off-center, the first Shreeth spun round, its club-hand swinging wide, knocking the second Shreeth off the bridge; Zorachus was just about to give it another blast when it stumbled after its unlucky comrade.

A third took the next discharge straight in the face, but it had been bent so far forward that the strikes merely straightened it; the next in line smashed into it, and they both fell forward. Another jumped over them, but Zorachus pummelled it back into them as they were scrambling up, and all three whirled into the void.

He kept hammering the front of the line. None of the creatures got farther than the middle of the bridge---until his cataract-strikes were exhausted. The Shreeth gained a few yards before he switched stances and lashed out with yellow stun beams. Struck, the monsters simply dropped, and began to pile up. Finally one rushed up and began flinging the inert forms off the bridge. Zorachus debated whether to blast the creature and let the barrier stand, or allow the thing to dispose of its brethren. The Sharajnaghi chose the latter course, waited till the Shreeth finished---

Then stunned it.

But that was the end of the yellow bolts.

Dropping stance altogether, he extended his fists, rings gleaming.

The stunned Shreeth had fallen on one knee, head hanging limp; Zorachus let the next in line brush it off the bridge, then loosed. Demon-bolts splashed the chasm walls with blue light. Shreeth twisted, jerked, exploded; heads tumbled forward as bodies were ripped out from under them. It was butchery pure and simple, and to Zorachus's relief he took no pleasure in it, hoping against hope that the creatures would learn the lesson, turn, and run. But they kept pouring across the span, a shrieking file of inhuman suicides.

The heat from the rings grew too great. Zorachus spat and blew on the righthand one, reached for his sword. With a terrific effort he forced his seared fingers to lock around the hilt and swept the blade free.

A Shreeth charged in. He lopped its club-arm off at the elbow and kicked the screeching horror in the chest. Rocking backward, it was hurled out of the way by the creature behind, which then caught Zorachus's point square in the eye; lips going slack, mouth sagging over its chin as though its face were melting, it quivered hideously on the end of his blade, then slumped in a heap as he ripped the sword free. A third Shreeth leaped over the crumpled form; parrying a club stroke, Zorachus grabbed the creature in midair by the wattled neck and cast it sideways into the void. A fourth came flying at him and he ducked under its blow, slashing it across the belly and sending it spinning over the edge.

There was a lull in the onslaught after that, and he stood panting, watching another file speed, wondering if he should use the rings again....

Suddenly, the one he had stabbed in the eye jumped up in front of him, club-hand raised. Zorachus's hands came up and two demon-bolts took it just below the neck in a tremendous flash of light; when the flare faded, he saw the Shreeth's corpse still on its feet, a huge gouge blasted out between the shoulders, the head and much of the chest gone. Kicking the body from the bridge, he turned the rings on the approaching line. But it was only moments before the heat forced him to relent, and it was cut and thrust once more.

His sword sang home again and again. His victims whirled head over heels toward the lava, catching fire like moths above a flame, splashing in the molten stone. Pushing himself to the limit and beyond, he fought numbly, mechanically, reflexes totally in control; hardly realizing what he was doing, he began to advance. One after another, the Shreeth raced to meet him---and were slaughtered.

He reached the center of the bridge, steel tearing through a scaly throat. Blood spraying from the wound, the Shreeth dropped from sight. Zorachus moved to meet the next---

And halted. Ahead, the bridge was empty, clear all the way to the door.

And the door was silent.

He thought of raising thanks to God---but for some reason he could not bring himself to *say* anything.

Just tired, he told himself.

His head whirled. Whatever had sustained him during the fight was gone now, and he felt for the first time the full pain of his burns.

He turned and took several steps, swaying, almost falling over the side. Gulping, he sank to his knees. Without wiping his sword, he resheathed it, and put the rings back in their pouch. Slowly, he crawled back to the wormhole. He stopped and sat with his back to the opening, feeling he could go no further, trying to watch the far doorway. His eyelids felt leaden. He allowed them to close---

And woke with a start some time later. Halfdan's voice echoed down the tunnel behind him:

"Zorachus!"

The Sharajnaghi turned around, too weary to be angry with himself for dozing off.

"I'm here," he cried. "I killed them all ... I think."

"Are you wounded?"

"My hands are burned."

"Can you make it?"

Zorachus nodded.

"Can you make it?" Halfdan repeated, more urgently.

"Yes!" Zorachus shouted irritably. Crawling into the hole, he managed to get several yards before falling asleep again...

The next thing he knew, someone was tugging at his wrists. He opened his eyes. His palm was still glowing, and in its light he saw Asa staring at him, face written with consternation.

"Are you all right?" she asked.

"You're lovely," he said. "It was all worth it."

"Are you all right?"

"I will be when I've gotten some more sleep---" he closed his eyes again.

She tugged at him once more.

"Mind the fingers!" he yelped. "Where's Halfdan?"

"Back by the water... sent me because I'm smaller. Let's go."

Zorachus squirmed sluggishly forward. He did not know how he could possibly make it back through the wormhole, but found that the sight of Asa's face sustained him---he had never dared to look her straight in the eyes for such a long while, and now he had unimpeachable cause. It was almost like a drug; instead of being frightful, the crawl began to seem like some sort of dream...he was almost sorry when they came out.

But his mouth was parched in a way he had never experienced before; he dragged like a lizard down to the water and gulped his fill. Crawling back from the edge, he turned over and looked up at Halfdan, who was sitting on the gunwale of the boat.

"Have you seen any of them?" Zorachus asked.

Halfdan shook his head. "Haven't heard anything, either. What happened back there?"

"I must have killed a hundred...most of it was sword work. Not that I didn't use my rings. They almost ruined my hands-especially my sword hand...Look."

"Ugh," Halfdan said. "Smells good too."

"We'll have to find a place where I can enter a healing trance, or I won't be able to climb those handholds in the shaft."

"Couldn't you float yourself up?" Asa asked. "With magic?"

"My powers will be nearly nonexistent for a while. The influences are about to shift against me, and I'm drained enough as it is. I'll be lucky if I can manage the trance."

"Do you think you can wade upstream?" Halfdan asked.

"I expect so," Zorachus said. "But I'll fall apart afterwards. "

"That'll be all right. Kletus's men felt the landing was safe. I suppose the Shreeth don't come much farther than this backwater..."

"I hope you're right," Zorachus said, rising. Once again, warm water soothed aching muscles; even against the current, he got on fairly well. But toward the end he grew dizzy again, and the Kragehul had to support him. Reaching the landing, they climbed up and went a few hundred yards into the tunnel before halting. Zorachus lay down and extinguished the handbeam. He was a long time lowering himself into his trance.

264

Chapter 20

AFTER TWO HOURS the Sharajnaghi reassumed perception. Restoring the light, he wiped his ooze-covered fingers on his already filthy clothes. The burns were gone.

Halfdan eyed Zorachus's fingers. "That healing magic of yours never fails to amaze me. You'll have to teach it to me someday."

"It took me four years to learn it," Zorachus replied.

"Ah, well," Halfdan said sadly. "I don't suppose we'll still know each other in four years." He paused. "It's a shame. You're a splendid fellow---in your own strange way."

"I don't know what to say," Zorachus replied. "But who knows when we'll part company?" He laughed. "The war might drag on forever. "

"Never," Halfdan said. "If things go on as they are, everyone in Khymir'll be dead in a year."

"I was only joking."

Halfdan blinked.

Asa asked Zorachus: "Will you go back south when the war's done?"

He nodded. "To Qanar-Sharaj…"

"You don't sound too happy about it."

"I am, believe me," he answered. He knew he had been happy there, once; but he no longer knew *how* he had been happy. He tried to remember Raschid's face, Ghaznavi's, the great dome and the leaves…nothing. There was only Khymir now…and Asa. The incontestable fact that his love was poisoned seemed oddly unimportant to him. He was desperate to tell her how much he dreaded leaving her. He had endured so much for her sake....

"Where will you and Halfdan go?" he asked.

"To Siglafstad."

"Siglafstad?"

"My uncle Siglaf's holding," Asa said.

"Quite a place," Halfdan said. "Perhaps you could visit it after you leave Khymir. You could probably take one of Siglaf's ships south. He's always sending them to the Kadjafi countries on trade ventures."

Zorachus got to his feet. "I'll consider it. But in the meantime---"

He found himself staring at Asa. She gave him a puzzled smile.

"Let's get going," he continued.

They set off along the droplet-trail.

"At first I thought the dye was your blood," Halfdan told Asa.

"That's what they wanted you to think," she said. "They had huge skin bottles of the stuff. There was a big black man who did nothing but carry it. There were two other blacks, even bigger than him, carrying me. They took turns."

"Did you make it hard on them?" Zorachus asked.

"I tried. But I was trussed up tight and they were very strong."

Climbing ramps and stairs, they came to corridors where the stone was cracked and rubble littered the floors; it was not long before they found themselves on the threshold of Lazarak's chamber.

"One last hurdle," Zorachus said, nodding toward the slumbering monster, revoking the light spell as they headed out slowly onto the dragon-lit debris.

"Watch yourself," Halfdan whispered to Asa. "the rubble is loose, so plant your feet carefully. One misstep and down you go to His Lordship there."

They crept forward yard by yard, and for the time being at least, the tumulus held firm beneath them. Small stones and cinders bounced down the slope, but mercifully, nothing larger. Lazarak slept on.

Whenever possible, Zorachus stole glances at the monster, half out of suspense, half from wonder; in his own way, Lazarak was beautiful, a marvel of shining golden scales, his saurian face perfectly serene, almost regal. It was hard to imagine that the dragon was capable of rampages that had hollowed a cavern hundreds of yards wide and unguessably high. Zorachus marveled to think of Lazarak's vengeance-lust...

And suddenly found himself sympathizing with it. He understood completely how one might go to fantastic lengths to strike back at Khymir---under the right circumstances, nothing might seem too extreme. The dragon's plight was so similar to his own; like Lazarak, he had been terribly provoked, and he also was trapped, prevented from consummating the vengeance he desired, not by stone walls, but by conscience. He was pinioned by the law, the curse God had written in his heart; his deepest impulses were being repressed, his freedom smothered, his nature violated.

It was only human to want to return evil for evil, pay it back ten, twenty, a hundredfold---especially when exacting such retribution was well within his power. He had the capacity to inflict horrors on his enemies that even they could scarcely imagine. What would he not be capable of if he unleashed his full fury? He smiled, relishing the possibilities. How glorious it would be to show Kletus what it truly meant to trifle with Mancdaman Zorachus, to visit all the torments of hell on the High Priest, to fall on him like the Wrath of God....

A large flat stone tilted beneath him, and he nearly lost his footing. Breathing hard, he stopped for a few moments. He had not been paying attention. His mind had been rambling, filling itself with demonic nonsense, gnawed one moment by resentment against Heaven, titillated the next by fantasies of becoming Heaven's scourge... that close call had been a warning sign, he was sure of it.

"Thank you, My Lord," he said under his breath. "Forgive me. And give me strength, I beg you." Bending his mind to the task at hand, he continued on.

But suddenly, despite his newfound concentration, a brief image of the leaves in the great dome flashed to mind...

Gradually, they worked their way around the curve. More than once the slope shifted slightly beneath them, seeming to foreshadow some greater treachery, and they paused, hearts in their throats; but always the rubble settled back into fragile stability. Lazarak's dreams went undisturbed, his scales rasping monotonously against the debris as he breathed: flames gushed from his snout, receded and gushed again, reflected fire gleaming sun-bright on his burnished horns.

The trio slowly moved ahead. The doorway was still tiny with distance, but they were closing the gap, if only at a slug's pace. Two hundred yards and they would be safe---

"Think I'm on a bad patch," Halfdan said.

And started to slide.

Digging toes and hands into the cinders and rock fragments, he caught himself almost instantly, but the damage was already done. Bits of debris bounced and rolled, dislodging bigger pieces, and the slope soon collapsed below him. Churning towards Lazarak, a rattling wave of stone and powdered slag swept over several of the molten pools, the dragon's foreclaw, and much of his snout.

Zorachus and the Kragehul remained rooted in place, eyes rivetted on the monster. Dragon fire quickly melted through the stones blocking his nostrils; bit by bit the slide slackened. He did not move.

Halfdan stood up cautiously. Once the slide ended, the trio started forward once more.

"Thought I'd really done it for a moment there," Halfdan whispered.

Another close one, Zorachus thought. *How much more of this can I---*

Something red flared on the fringe of sight; he looked down at Lazarak. The dragon's great right eye was open now, bright glowing crimson, slit-pupilled like a cat's. He had had his fill of sleep.

"Oh my God," Zorachus breathed.

Lazarak lifted his head, stones and dust raining from his snout. The monster's teeth grinned wickedly, and he turned his head this way and that, eyes radiating a malice more scorching than any sane mind could engender...raising himself on his forelegs, spiked maw opening wide, he emitted a geyserlike hiss, then a tremendous raw combination of bellow and shriek. Stone shattered at the cry; deafened, Zorachus and the Kragehul rushed forward over the rubble, casting all caution aside. Behind them, boulders cracked off from the cave wall rolled down into the depression, each starting its own stoneslide.

Lazarak did not see the humans; his terrible eyes were blind. But even if he could have seen, he would have taken no notice. For now, he had only one purpose, the one which had consumed him for a hundred years and more: to resume his war against the prisoning stone.

Bellowing once more, muscles playing and knotting beneath his shimmering armor, he rose on his immense hindlegs, spreading his wings. Surging with fiery maggots, a huge rent smoked in his chest, unhealed, unhealable, a wellspring of endless pain, a perpetual reminder of how he had been betrayed. Wings beating with a force that scattered rocks like dust motes, he craned his head round, his wrath erupting in a hurricane of flame, melting a vast stretch of wall. Then, pinions thudding, tail whipping, he leaped aloft, hurtling up and up, smashing at last against the ceiling; flame billowed and blossomed across the scarred vault, and he shot downward in an incandescent shower of sparks and molten rock. Checking his descent, he swept upward once more, this time at a slant, thundering into a wall, ripping and goring and pummelling the stone, blasting out his cry of fury, raging at the barriers that defied him.

Zorachus and the Kragehul raced for the exit, the debris beneath them quivering like a living thing, settling and shifting, a fog of dust puffing up between the stones.

Asa fell. Halfdan grabbed her arm as he passed, dragging her forward over the rubble.

An instant later, a fifty-foot swath of the tumulus they had just crossed gave way. Halfdan paused and Asa rose, robe torn, stained with blood.

Not realizing she had fallen, Zorachus had pulled far ahead of them, but suddenly the scree shifted under him and he rolled with it fifteen yards. Somehow he managed to get to his feet, wobbling. A second slide poured down toward him and he dashed out of its way, then scrambled up a patch of rocky grade stable enough to give him purchase and rejoined the Kragehul near the door.

Splashes of molten stone had fallen by the exit, partially blocking it with jagged, still smoking detritus. Zorachus and Asa dived through; looking up for a split second, Halfdan saw a cloud of splintered rock hurtling down. He was not close enough to lunge through the door, so he pivoted, sprinting to the right as the cascade crashed down before the door, burying it beneath a mound ten feet high.

He looked up once more. The dragon circled overhead, battering the walls and striking the ceiling. Stone fell all around the Kragehul as the slopes slithered downward; the tumulus before the doorway began to collapse. He went toward it, saw the lintel come into view. Soon a gap two feet wide had opened between lintel and rubble. He got down on all fours and tried to crawl through, but a plummetting rock gashed his arm and he halted; the rubble gave way with greater speed, and he slid backward five feet. The shifting slowed; scrabbling up, he slipped through the opening. Moments later it was buried again, and a gust of flame, dust and stone fragments followed him over the debris on the far side.

Zorachus helped him to his feet. The Sharajnaghi's hand was glowing once more, and when the light showed Halfdan's arm, Asa cried out; ears still numb from the dragon's roars, Halfdan did not hear. But neither did Asa---for an appalling moment she thought she was dumb as well as deaf.

Hurriedly they descended the scree into the tunnel beneath, the entrance of which had been widened by Lazarak's ongoing earthquake; pelted by stones falling from the ceiling, showered by dust, they leaped over cracks and plunged past crumbling walls, section after section of the tunnel sagging and collapsing behind them.

They sped on. The droplet trail was dust-covered much of the way, but where the patina was less deep, the red soaked through, just enough for them to find their way.

After a time they reached places where the tremors were muffled, and the tunnels showed no signs of collapse; panting, they stopped to rest. All had gotten blows on the head and shoulders, and their blood flowed freely. But the worst wound was Halfdan's gash. Tearing a strip from her robe, Asa bandaged the wound as well as she could, and after a time the blood stopped.

They pushed on to the shaft and began the climb. Every few levels, Halfdan's bandage worked loose, the blood starting afresh each time; again and again they slipped into the nearest tunnel mouth to retighten the rag.

Coming to the top of the shaft, they continued upward through the catacombs, plodding finally to the foot of the last staircase. Far above shone a tiny rectangle of sunlight; after a long pause, gathering up their strength, they began the daunting trudge toward it. The climb proved one of the greatest torments they had yet endured, for Halfdan was by that time very weak and had to be supported and pulled, even dragged. But eventually the charnel smell lessened and the light from above grew and they emerged at last, blinking and stumbling, barely able to hear their own blissful cries.

Chapter 21

FOR OULCHAR LYSTHRAGON, cruelty was best savored in combination with puerility. Nothing pleased him better than dealing out little doses of idiot malice.

This is not to say he did not appreciate viciousness on a grander scale. But the lack of intimacy and the risks that were sometimes involved rendered such cruelty unsuitable to him as pure entertainment. He much preferred inserting himself like a poisoned sliver into situations that held no hint of danger, irritating those who suffered him with perfect imbecilities, and remaining immune (so he thought) simply because of the silliness of his manner. Indeed, most people, including himself, never realized how destructive he could be. His victims often ignored him for a mere clown---even as the hidden current of his nonsequiturs contaminated their minds. When he encountered a susceptible individual, he could, in the course of a brief conversation, awaken every insanity lying dormant inside them; meeting him was the start of a profound and irreversible process, which he himself was undergoing, for he was just such a person, withering in the stench of his own decomposition.

Today he sat in his little chamber at a little table. On his right was a pail half-filled with dead toads, on his left a covered pail containing live ones. Before him was a small circle, carved into the tabletop, and a foot beyond that was a yard-square bed of nails.

He took a live toad out, covered its eyes with a tape of his own devising---he loved sticky things---and set it down in the circle. Grinning his wide, wizened grin, he waited a few seconds, then tapped the toad's hindquarters, triggering a leap forward onto the nails. But the amphibian did not die outright; Lysthragon pressed down on it with two fingers, twisted it about, pried it up and dropped it back down several times until it stopped moving. Then he lifted it off the impaling points and dropped it in the pail on the right.

There was a knock at the door and he went to answer it; a novice told him he was wanted in Kletus's garden, where the High Priest and Sathaswentha awaited him.

"I see," Lysthragon said, and pointed back to the pails. "My toads are in those. I want you to keep an eye on them. Especially..."

"Yes, my Lord?"

"The dead ones."

The novice, a new recruit, knew little of Lysthragon, and cracked a smile. "I must be off, my Lord," he said.

Instantly Lysthragon snatched one of his hands and bit his thumb, teeth shearing to the bone. The novice tried to wrench his hand away, but Lysthragon held it fast, and the shrieking nonentity only tore his flesh further.

"Please, my Lord!" the novice cried. "Let me--'"

Lysthragon drove a small fist twice into the fellow's groin before releasing the maimed digit, and the novice fell on his knees, grimacing with pain.

"Do as I say," Lysthragon hissed, shoving his bloodpainted mouth next to the novice's ear, "or I'll eat your face."

The novice nodded.

Paying him no further heed, Lysthragon went to Kletus's garden. Inside, he found the High Priest's fungoid replicas filled with wallowing life, a pumping, clasping, pale-pink sea, stretching to infinity in the mirrors. Kletus himself seemed to be paying no attention to them, but stood talking to Sathaswentha and Thulusu. Of the three, only Thulusu looked unruffled, his huge body completely at ease, helmet under one arm, steel hand resting on his belt. Sathaswentha trembled as if with ague, and darkish blotches of stubble flared and disappeared on her cheeks. Kletus was sweating profusely, eating chunk after chunk of meat, voice half-strangled.

Lysthragon pointed to the replicas as he came up. "Pink worms," he said.

"Some people bite their nails," Kletus replied. "Animating those bodies is my little nervous habit. At least it's original."

"Zorachus is alive," Sathaswentha said.

Lysthragon grinned at Kletus, infantile face creasing into a mass of wrinkles. "What happened to your precious Shreeth?"

Emptying his meat wallet, Kletus took out another. "I don't know," he answered. "Our spy said he went down into their tunnels…"

"And fought his way back out," Sathaswentha said. "I hope he never decides to pay us a visit."

Kletus answered, "Strong as he is, he could never take us headon."

"Strong as he is, the Shreeth should have killed him," Sathaswentha shot back. "Your voice played you false. Admit it."

"Why don't *you* admit you'd like to take my place?" Kletus snarled, bits of meat dropping from his mouth.

"I'd be satisfied if you'd simply listen to advice."

Kletus said nothing, simmering. Lysthragon moved closer to him.

"You can ask for our opinions anytime," the midget said, pushing Kletus's sleeve up. "Our tongues are always at your disposal."

He licked the High Priest's arm.

Kletus growled, hurled his meat wallet down, grabbed him by the hair and lifted him squealing off the ground; turning, he hurled him in among the churning replicas.

After being buffeted for a few moments, Lysthragon rose, and keeping his eyes full on Kletus, spat on the replicas before him.

Kletus roared and assumed a stance; knowing he was no match for the High Priest, Lysthragon screeched. But before kletus could launch his bolts, Thulusu came between him and his prey.

"I hear the Merchants laughing already," the black said.

Kletus's arms dropped to his sides.

"Very prudent," Sathaswentha said.

Kletus gave her a basilisk-like stare. "Keep this in mind," he said. "I'm your best protection. If it weren't for me---"

"The situation would be very different," Sathaswentha said.

"Zorachus would do exactly as he pleased with you."

"He wouldn't even be an issue."

"My Voice---"

"Dispenses the most absurd counsel imaginable."

"Things are proceeding---"

"Badly."

"Nothing can defy my will," Kletus said.

"Then we've nothing to worry about," Sathaswentha replied, mock-cheerfully. "The Shreeth killed Zorachus."

By now, Lysthragon had threaded a path through the replicas. He was no longer grinning. The soft child's face had returned, puffed and petulant.

He had not expected Kletus to react so strongly, even to the spitting; although he did not realize it, he had already passed the point where he could gauge the danger in a given situation. He had seen Kletus's agitation. He had known his actions would badly aggravate him; indeed, that was the point. But it had not occurred to him that Kletus would lash out. Details were becoming independent in Lysthragon's mind; his ability to recognize contexts was decaying. The idiocies he had fostered for use on others had not only crept into the center of his being; they were hastening his dissolution even now, and he had neither the will nor the inclination to oppose them.

"Lord Kletus rules everything," he said. "He willed me to lick his arm. Simply *had* to have my spittle." He giggled. "Spittle is everything. Spittle and piss."

Kletus battled to control himself. "I'll tolerate this," he said.

"How very forbearing," Sathaswentha said.

"I could kill you both, but I'll let it go---for now."

"And then what?" Sathaswentha asked. "Will your Voice tell you the proper time to settle with us? Will you trust it then? It might not be telling you the truth. It's lied before."

"Spittle and piss," Lysthragon said, circling Kletus, plucking at his robes. "We should all be High Priest."

"You need us," Sathaswentha told Kletus. "Agreed, you might be able to kill us. And you could probably survive the loss of two wizards of our class. But what if our men turned on you, as I assure you they would? They don't love you, my lord. They love you less than they love us, which is saying something. No, I'd think you'd want to preserve their loyalty. Especially now that your Voice isn't working anymore."

"Blasphemy," Kletus growled.

Sathaswentha smirked. "What blasphemy is there in simply telling the truth? I recognized your plan as a fool's dream the minute I heard it."

"Spittle and piss," Lysthragon said, plucking at Kletus again. "We should all be High Priest."

Kletus looked at the mirrored ceiling.

"You should listen to me," Lysthragon said. "You should think hard about every little thing I say."

"I'm Grand Master of this order," Kletus rumbled. "*I* will lead. I *alone*. My Voice is infallible. "

"Then why is Zorachus still alive?" Sathaswentha asked.

Seeming to come from everywhere at once, a chorus of voices whispered: "Because I willed it so."

The temperature plummeted; the Priests looked wildly about. In the mirrors, the reflections of Kletus's replicas were rising slowly to their feet, eyes rolled back, even as the replicas themselves remained writhing on the floor.

"I am Kletus's voice," the reflections said, plumes of chill vapor puffing from their mouths, smoking forth from the glass. "*I* am his inspiration, his genius. *I* am *Tchernobog*. "

Despite his terror, Kletus smiled. His vindication had come.

Tchernobog continued: "*I* chose Kletus, made him High Priest. *I* told him to bring Zorachus back. Before the Guild is broken, Zorachus must fall...by luring him into the tunnels, Kletus brought him almost to the edge. One more push, and he will be destroyed."

Stuttering with cold and fear, Kletus asked: "Wha-what m-must we do, my Lord?"

And Tchernobog answered.

Kletus's smile became a nervous grin. "M-my Lord and My God," he said. "As easily as that...."

"Have faith," Tchernobog replied. "All will be well."

The reflections of the replicas sank down once more, and dry heat filled the room. Kletus regained his composure almost immediately; triumph glittering in his eyes, he looked at Lysthragon and Sathaswentha. They had moved closer to one another, trembling.

"Shall we all be High Priest?" he asked.

Sathaswentha was silent. Lysthragon loosed a jittery giggle.

"Lysthragon," Kletus began, "You said before that I willed you to lick my arm. Well, now I'm willing you to lick my foot."

Lysthragon's mind was not so badly decayed that he would disobey the chosen of Tchernobog. He even took a certain pleasure in complying. After all, it was insane to enjoy it.

The gash in Halfdan's arm festered and he grew feverish. Sharthas seemed helpless, so Doctor Aliphar was brought in again. A day later, the fever broke, but Halfdan had lost much blood, and kept to his bed, sleeping for long stretches.

During that time, Zorachus tried to find out who had drugged Asa. Porchos sent a special interrogator, adept at throwing people off balance, and servants were brought to Zorachus's room and questioned. Some apparent headway was made; one of the foodtasters, a young girl, got very agitated, even though she confessed to nothing. Zorachus and the interrogator decided to give her a second session, and Sharthas was sent to fetch her.

Grimacing, hand slashed, the Steward returned a short time later, saying she had attacked him after hearing the summons, then stabbed herself. Zorachus wanted to feel some sorrow at her suicide, but found he could not force it. He was too relieved that the culprit was out of the way.

Her replacement arrived two days later---a tall, handsome black woman with a voluptuous figure and straightened hair. Her name was Leahkalah, and she rapidly established herself as one of the palace's best-traveled bodies, with a marked preference for women. Zorachus found her practically unavoidable; she was present at all his meals, of course, and at times he seemed unable to leave his chamber without seeing her and her latest female paramour embracing in some niche or parlor. Even when she was not present, she kept tongues wagging; whenever he overheard the guards or servants talking among themselves, it was always about her.

One night, as he and Asa dined alone (Halfdan was asleep upstairs), Leahkalah and another female food-taster, a young blonde, having completed their duties, retired to a nearby couch and started in on each other. Zorachus was taken completely aback by the sheer brazenness of it, and wondered at first if she had been told that such behavior was forbidden around him. But then he realized his own responsibility; he had already been much more lenient with her than with the rest of the household. It was much harder to clamp down on performances that aroused him. More than once he had come upon her making love, and had lingered just long enough to guarantee the lubricity of his dreams.

It was much the same now; they were both naked and feasting hungrily on each other before he finally ordered them from the room. Gathering up her garments, Leahkalah smiled mockingly at him, then left with the blonde.

He tried to finish his meal, but found he could down nothing but wine. There was no conversation. Every time he looked Asa's way, she avoided eye-contact with him.

After a time they went back upstairs. She left him at his threshold and he watched her go, eyes held by the sway of her hips.

Suddenly she stopped, staring at a niche on the right. He went to see what the matter was.

Leahkalah, nude and sweating, mouth sagging in a silent gasp, stood against the back of the niche. Also nude, the blonde knelt before her, a chain about her waist, bare feet crossed, rings on her toes; something gold was just visible between her buttocks. Her head was bobbing slightly, Leahkalah's palms cupped behind it; one of Leahkalah's long, muscular black legs was draped over the blonde's shoulder. Zorachus could hear a soft wet lapping sound.

Leahkalah's eyes rolled and fluttered; noticing Zorachus and Asa, she extended her pink tongue, glossing the red thickness of her upper lip.

Zorachus looked at Asa. Her cheeks were brightly flushed.

"Go on," he told her. "Halfdan's probably awake by now."

What might have been a flicker of guilt crossed her face; she went slowly to her room.

Zorachus looked back at Leahkalah. Her hard black eyes swept him up and down in lewd inspection. She lifted her left hand, grasped her own nipple between thumb and forefinger.

"That's enough," Zorachus said.

"No," she answered. "Keep watching."

He breathed out through his nostrils, eyeing her nipple as she began to roll it. Candlelight glistened on the round puckered tip.

"I said---" he faltered as a long moan broke from her lips; her whole body shuddered, and all at once she pulled the blonde's face back from between her legs, slid down the wall, and wrapped her arms around her, kissing her repeatedly.

Body screaming for release, Zorachus turned and entered his room. Closing the door, he leaned up against it, his penis stone-hard along his thigh.

You should just cut it off, he thought. *Either that, or tell those whores to come inside...*

For some moments he swung back and forth between those extremes as though they were the only thoughts he could have.

Pushing them out of his head at last, he succeeded only in remembering that final glimpse of Asa's face, that flicker of guilt.... What had she felt, staring at the lovers in the niche? Had she too been aroused? One wicked corner of his soul was thrilled by the idea, and a new image, deliciously poisonous, entered his mind: Asa kneeling before Leahkalah, thrusting her face greedily forward, glutting herself on the black woman's flesh.

God, he thought, *to have them both....*

"Stop it," he said, pressing his hands against the sides of his head; for an instant he seemed to feel his temples expanding, as if his skull were about to burst. Sharthas's words came back to him: *we're all Khymirians inside...* Zorachus would not argue now. He knew he could not trust himself. And the shame in Asa's expression proved beyond all doubt that she was every bit as much a pig.

Proved? came reason's voice. *Beyond all doubt?*

But the protest was so thin, so tinny, like a hateful insect buzzing in his ear...He was sliding deep into the trough and mere logic would not check the descent. Asa was such a part of him now; how could she not be infected, when he was so diseased?

"Stop it," he said again, this time in a feeble whisper, rocking his head from side to side, pulse hammering, stomach filled with nervous heat. He sensed he was going mad, but that only increased his self-contempt. He could control his mind no better than he controlled his lust. He was a Sharajnaghi, a *Master,* but his blood was winning out over all his training. The veneer of the *Comahi Irakhoum* was being stripped away from him, and layer after layer of hidden perversity was being revealed. It was no longer enough for him to covet another man's wife---now he wanted her with another woman, grew inflamed at the very thought of them embracing, kissing, suckling on each other... His imagination raced. The squirming possibilities seemed endless; there were so many ways to savor the poison, to smother himself in honeyed damnation, to go giggling and smiling like Tchernaar into the putrescent dark, the endless death of the spirit he so richly deserved....

The heat in his stomach surged. It was only with a ferocious effort of will that he choked back the vomit; tendons stood out like cables on his neck, and the veins of his temples bulged. His bones seemed to vibrate inside his flesh.

He staggered out into the middle of the floor, thought of the mirror that had been removed, looked over at the spot where it had stood. If only the glass had still been there---he wanted desperately to smash some image of himself, purge the rage and frustration he felt. But he realized that even that would not have satisfied him; he was seized by an urge to slam his face against something, flatten his features into pulp. Going to the wall before him, he stood quaking in front of it for a time, fighting the need to snap his face forward even as he summoned the will to do it, aching to feel the punishment. The spark came; "Pig," he grunted to himself, and butted his face into the stone, the impact exploding against his brow and nose. White-hot pain flared inside his skull and blood trickled from his nostrils.

"Pig," he said again, and smashed his face against the wall once more, then tottered back and fell to his knees, shaking his head.

Gradually, the pain subsided. The turmoil in his mind eased---somewhat.

He rose. Self-loathing still gripped him, but now that he had punished himself he could allow reason and his faith in Asa to reassert themselves---if only just barely. He forced himself to acknowledge that he had no right to impute his corruption to others. To fill his soul with venom against his love was monstrous.

You don't even have the right to judge a Khymirian...

Wiping the blood from his nose, he went out onto the balcony and tried to pray.

It proved impossible. The night was close and sticky, and he kept hearing snatches of obscene conversation---about Leahkalah---from below; ever since Asa's abduction, guards had been stationed beneath the balconies.

He decided it might be best to seek the less-frequented parts of the palace and walk himself out of his deadly state of mind.

He went back into the room and noticed that blood had dripped onto his grey Sharajnaghi tunic; not wanting to alarm his doorwards, he got a cloth, held it under his nose until the blood stopped flowing, then washed his face and hands at a basin and changed into a fresh garment. Going outside, he forbade the guards to follow him and set off along the corridor, heading resolutely away from the niche where he had seen Leahkalah and the blonde.

279

Watching her sleeping husband, Asa sat beside her bed, assailed by the close heat, acutely aware of the way her sweat-soaked clothes clung to her breasts and belly. She wished he were awake and well--- she wanted to talk to him, to feel his arms around her, to be distracted from herself. She would welcome his love.

But she would not wake him. He had not made love to her since the night before she was abducted, but she could manage. Smiling, she studied his face. She loved it dearly, and never more so than when he was asleep---it always reminded her of the first time she had laid eyes on him, one warm summer's day in her father's field where he had decided to take a nap; she had practically tripped over him. His face had been different then---no scars, no broken nose. But even then it hadn't been beautiful...she supposed he might be downright ugly now, in an endearing sort of way. Strange that she could love his face when there were other things far more beautiful, and beauty promised so much...

She thought about his body. She loved those hard muscles, and the way his hipbones and the bones at the tops of his shoulders jutted just a little bit...His strength was delightfully terrifying, and there was nothing she liked better than bearing his weight.

But there was nothing *beautiful* about his body. It was made for work, combat, and love, and fulfilled its tasks admirably. Yet there was nothing about it that existed for its own sake, worthy all by itself.

That was the difference between men and women, or so she told herself. Marvelous as they were, men needed women to give them beauty. She had never understood why so many of her female friends back in her village found male bodies so exciting; it was being sought after by men that had always aroused her, knowing and feeling she was beautiful, that she was the treasure, the thing worth having.

But it was not only men who yearned for beauty. Even before she was brought to khymir, she had thought of other women---Gudrun's story had awakened the desire when asa was twelve years old. And even though Asa accepted her people's prohibition on love between women, the longings remained. She was always on guard against them, but sometimes it was hard to shunt them aside, especially when she saw things, like Leahkalah and the blonde... Even now, her curiosity was up. Leahkalah's face and body were so handsome... Asa wondered if making love to her would be as splendid as she suspected.

Of course she entertained no real thought of putting those suspicions to the test. She was not a Khymirian. She had every intention of keeping faith with Halfdan, remaining true to her people's code. Still---

She was troubled. The sweat stains spread; she felt her nipples stiffening beneath the sodden fabric, and she had to keep her legs closed to keep the perspiration from running down between her thighs. She licked salty beads from her upper lip; her smooth flesh felt good beneath her tongue.

I wonder what Leahkalah's sweat tastes like? she thought---and banished the question from her mind.

Yet bit by bit, the heat seemed to increase, milking more and more sweat from her body; completely soaked now, her clothes were molded to her like a second skin.

You must be quite a sight, she told herself, almost wishing the mirror were still in the room. What did she need anyone for if she had a mirror?

Instantly she recoiled from the thought.

You should just lie down beside your husband and go to sleep.

But she was not tired enough. Perhaps she needed a walk, a good stretch of the legs in parts of the palace where there was little chance of passing coupling bodies.

Kissing Halfdan, she went outside, telling her newly appointed doorwards to remain behind. On an impulse, she looked at the niche; it was empty. Bare feet making no sound, she headed

Off; anticipating dark corridors, she pulled a taper from its

Socket, rounded a corner---

And stopped.

Several yards ahead, a life-size female nude, carved in ebony, stood beside the righthand wall; Leahkalah, fully clad now, was gazing raptly at it. Noticing Asa out of the corner of her eye, she turned her head. Silently they stood staring at each other. Then a slow smile spread across Leahkalah's full lips.

Hand glowing, Zorachus made his way about the upper stories, striding along the dusty passages, going up and down flights of stairs, praying on and off, growing steadily calmer. At length he decided to return to his chamber.

But as he approached the room where he had spoken with Sharthas----
he had passed it several times already---he saw that the door was now
open a crack, candlelight seeping out into the hall.

"Sharthas?" he called.

"Lord Mancdaman?" came the Steward's voice from within.

Zorachus entered.

Sharthas was sitting at the table, head down, the same wine bottle before
him, empty now. Zorachus sat next to him. The Steward did not look up.

"Finished for the night?" Zorachus asked.

"I think so, my lord," the Steward replied.

"You're not sure?"

Sharthas shrugged. "Maybe I simply wanted to be alone."

"You'd rather I left?"

"Certainly not, my Lord. But I'm surprised you're willing to talk to me
again, now that it's just the two of us. I thought I upset you the last time."

"Yes," Zorachus replied, and suddenly realized how strange it was that he
had put himself in the same situation. He did not really want to talk to
anyone, let alone Sharthas...what impulse had he acted upon? Was some
of his self-hatred still riding him? This would be punishment---of a sort.

"I'm such a bother when I get that way," Sharthas said. "No one should
have to put up with such talk. I'm terribly, terribly sorry."

Zorachus said nothing.

"That look in your eyes..." Sharthas's voice trailed off.

"What does it say to you?"

"That you despise me."

"I don't," Zorachus answered, truthfully enough. "I try not to despise
anyone." *Not even myself,* he thought.

"Yes," Sharthas said. "I think you try."

"Do you see that look in everyone's eyes?"

"When they look at me. Most people try not to...I don't blame
them...Would you like to talk about something else?"

"That new foodtaster---"

It was out before Zorachus realized it.

Sharthas nodded. "Everyone wants to talk about her."

That must be why I said it, Zorachus thought. He could not think of another reason--- dwelling on her was the last thing he needed.

Sharthas said: "None of the serving-women can refuse her."

"What's her name?"

Sharthas gave him a look---plainly he knew Zorachus knew the answer. "Leahkalah."

"Ah."

"Such a lovely black whore." A tear spilled from his eye. "Sound familiar?"

"I'm surprised she's a food-taster. With her looks, I would've thought she could do better."

Sharthas took out his knife, playing with it. "Food-tasters are a special sort. The professionals, at any rate. She doesn't care if she dies."

"She told you that?"

"Several times. But even if she hadn't, it's written all over her face." Sharthas started in with his blade, making grooves in the table, ending each stroke with that deft flip of the wrist. He had carved hundreds of little furrows since Zorachus's last visit.

"The knife reminds me," Zorachus said. "How's that cut of yours doing?"

"I just took the bandage off a few hours ago," Sharthas said. "I'm coming along nicely."

To prove his point he raised his hand.

Zorachus blinked.

Closed with stitches, the cut was shaped almost exactly like the grooves in the table, the flourish at the end unmistakable.

"My Lord?" Sharthas asked.

Zorachus stood and backed away, saying:

"You did it yourself."

"What?"

"You cut yourself. Those grooves gave you away."

Sharthas's eyes darted to the tabletop, then back to Zorachus; they widened in terror.

Zorachus went on: "*You* killed the girl, and cut yourself to make it look like---"

Sharthas hurled the knife.

Zorachus dodged, heard it rebound from the wall behind him. Clattering to the floor, it bounced against his boot.

Sharthas reached into his robes.

Zorachus scooped up the knife on the floor and threw it underhand; as Sharthas withdrew another blade, the missile caught him on the knuckle and bounced upwards, lodging beside his windpipe.

He gulped, dropped the second knife on the table, and pulled the first out. Blood squirted from the wound in long straight jets.

"Forgive me," he said, lowering his head, the blood striking his chin and splattering. He put a hand to the wound. Red streams pulsed through his fingers. His face had gone white.

Zorachus asked: "How long have you been working for Kletus?"

Sharthas said: "Ever since Chatonha found out I was your Steward. She's one of his agents. I couldn't resist her......." He lifted his head, chin dripping. "Beware, my lord---"

"Of what?"

"She's here. In this house. Snaked her way in with the Guild, took out her pretty nosering...*Leahkalah is Chatonha.*"

Zorachus thundered an oath.

Sharthas coughed. "They want her to seduce Asa...to throw you off balance..."

Zorachus bolted for the door.

"Wait," Sharthas cried.

Zorachus turned.

"Forgive me," the Steward begged.

Zorachus did not answer.

Sharthas's eyes closed. His hand slipped away from his neck; the blood had almost stopped. He slumped sideways from the chair.

Zorachus dashed into the hall and around to the stairs that came out by his room. That sick warmth had welled up in his stomach once again, and he launched into a desperate prayer as he hurtled down the steps, begging that his worst fears might not be realized. Coming to the Kragehul's room, he asked the doorwards if Asa was inside; one pointed off along the hall.

"She left a while ago, my Lord," the man explained. "Told us not to follow her.".

"Have you seen Leahkalah?"

"Went the same way, a bit earlier. What's wrong, my Lord?"

Giving no answer, Zorachus was off, charging down the corridor. He heard the guards coming after him but waved them back.

Rounding the corner, he slowed as the ebony statue came in view. The sight infuriated him; he wanted to hurl himself at it, topple it, smash it against the floor.

But before he could spring, he noticed a partially open doorway nearby and heard a moan; he went softly to the door, slipping inside. Going down a short corridor, he reached the threshold of a small room lit by a single taper. The glow bathed a large bed; Chatonha and Asa lay on the covers, nude and glistening with sweat, the black woman's face cradled between Asa's thighs. Asa moaned again, mouth slack, eyes closed, hips rocking gently. Lifting her face, Chatonha inserted two fingers into Asa's vagina, searched it for a few moments, licked them off, then lowered her face once more.

Horrified and aroused, Zorachus stepped into the room. Asa heard him and opened her eyes. They were glazed and empty---it was a moment or two before she saw him. Then they filled with shock and her body tightened.

Chatonha raised herself on one elbow; the sight of the Sharajnaghi seemed to amuse her. Sitting up, she beckoned with one hand, working Asa with the other.

Zorachus took another step, loins burning. He made slowly for the bed, noticing that Asa's hips were undulating again, even though her face was still frozen with dismay. He reached the bed, trembling. Chatona rose, grasped his shoulders softly. Her mouth sought his, tongue probing, saliva glutinous and salty.

He had never been with a woman--was that how their mouths tasted?

Or was that Asa?

Slime from the woman he loved?

His mind ripped free from the rutting fever, erupting with a lust far more potent. The arrow scar on his cheek flared red. He jerked his face back from Chatonha's kiss, and his hands swept up, sinking into her throat. She gasped, but there was no fear in her eyes; a self-satisfied smile spread across her face, contemptuous, even triumphant. Through the haze of madness he recalled what Sharthas had said: *she doesn't care if she dies.*

But that only fanned Zorachus's already white-hot fury, and as his face began to mirror the change within, twitching muscle by ridged muscle into a mask of mind-bending malevolence, her expression melted from smug superiority to pure terror, and he remembered *with relish* that the mere sight of devils was said to be one of the chief torments of the damned...

She started to fight, but her muscles were already drained by approaching death and there was little strength in her kicks and punches; when she tried to claw his face, it seemed like a mere caress. Her eyes bulged, and her tongue protruded, writhing slowly, wetly, like a transfixed slug; laughing, he let go of her throat, clapped a hand to the top of her head, and punched her beneath the chin. Her teeth snicked shut, severing her tongue, which trailed blood down her chin and dropped to the floor.

Her mouth sagged, and she started to draw a breath, the inhalation tugging on the threads of blood hanging from her upper teeth; but his hands went to her throat again, and there was brief expulsion of air that puffed the threads forward again.

"Enjoying yourself?" he grinned. "Is it good?"

He shook her and *squeezed,* as hard as he could. Cartilege gave, crunching beneath his hands, and all at once her throat seemed much smaller. Face darkened to purple, white eyes all but bursting from their sockets, she died.

He hurled the body aside, staring at Asa. She had not stirred, but now his murderous glare was more than enough to shatter her paralysis; leaping from the bed, she dashed past him from the room.

He made no attempt to follow but turned to Chatonha's corpse; yanking it up by the hair, he slammed it against the nearest wall. Then, drilling his blows home with a devastating combination of ferocity and perfect technique, he rained punches on the black flesh, and the room was filled with the explosions of his breath and the snap of broken bones. Her cheekbones caved and her brows were crushed. Teeth and fragments of teeth tumbled from her mouth. Blood spattered his face again and again, and his throat was worn raw with shrieks.

Finally he let her slide to the floor and turned. The doorwards stood clustered in the corridor, swords drawn.

"Get out!" he roared.

They did not move. He took several steps towards them, hands and face running with blood, eyes burning like live coals.

"Get out!" he roared again.

They retreated through the door. Paying them no more heed, he turned once more; going to the bed, he flipped it over onto Chatonha's corpse and shattered the frame with kicks. Then he took out the rings and slipped them on, and as his shrieks and roars turned into gusting mad laughter, he began launching bolts, blasting the mattress, setting it aflame, knocking chunks out of the window casement, loosing demon-lightning through the ceiling. Broken stone rained around him, striking his head and shoulders. His scalp was torn, his ring fingers scorched, but he felt no pain, his rage absolute, the raving dictator of his mind.

Asa, meanwhile, had sped back towards her room, bumping into the doorwards who were rushing even then to see what the shrieking was all about; she told them Zorachus had gone insane and had torn her clothes off trying to rape her. They raced past, and she ran to her door, hurling it open. Snatching up a robe, she put it on and dashed to the bed, shaking Halfdan violently.

"I'm awake," he mumbled at last.

She tugged on his arm as hard as she could. "Come on," she cried. "He'll kill us both!"

"Who?"

"Zorachus! He tried to..." She stopped short, realizing her husband would certainly attack him if he thought Zorachus had attempted to rape her.

"Tried to what?"

She tugged on his arm. "Come on!"

"Is that him screaming?"

She nodded.

"Did he hurt you?"

"No."

"Then what happened?"

"I don't know!"

Halfdan stood up, dressed himself, and girt on his sword. Asa grabbed his arm again, pulling him frantically toward the door.

"Let go," he said, and yanked free, pushing ahead of her into the corridor. He heard Zorachus's rings crackling now, and booming laughter...He staggered down the hall, Asa at his heels, grabbing at him repeatedly. Finally, he turned and slapped her across the face. She sank down whimpering.

He turned a corner. The laughter and crackling were coming from a red-lit doorway ahead of him. Intermittently, to the sound of the demon strikes, brilliant blue-white flashes blotted out the fire-glow. The guards clustered by the threshold, looking in.

The laughter and flashing stopped; the guards retreated, backing past Halfdan. Face twisted with wrath and webbed with blood, Zorachus emerged from the doorway, the rings flaming viciously on his smoking fingers.

"What's wrong?" Halfdan cried.

Zorachus shrieked at him hoarsely. Halfdan tried to stand his ground, but the pressure from the Sharajnaghi's mad-dragon eyes was too much...the Kragehul was back around the corner before he screwed up his will and managed to halt himself. Face wet with tears, Asa was still on her knees where he had left her.

"While there's still time, Halfdan...." she began.

"We stay here," he answered, drawing his sword.

Zorachus came into view, stopping several feet from them. His eyes were riveted on Asa and he raised his hands; Halfdan put himself between her and the rings.

"What happened, Zorachus?" he demanded, battling to keep his nerve.

Zorachus lowered his hands. "Leave this house," he said. "Take as much gold from the storeroom as you please, but go."

"Not till you tell me what happened."

A freezing smile bared Zorachus's teeth. "Go, or I swear to God I'll kill you both."

Halfdan's resolve snapped. Without another word, he hauled Asa up and led her away.

Zorachus watched them; just before they reached the stair Asa gave him a last, tormented, backward glance. In answer he loosed a ringing howl, then dropped on all fours, huge frame racked with sobs.

He was laid waste, a ruin. She had betrayed him, Halfdan, everything. She too was a Khymirian inside, lusting after her own image, embracing sterility for a twitch in the genitals. The loving wife and gardener were mere fronts for her worm-eaten passions.

Poor Halfdan! Poor stupid, trusting Halfdan. He had no idea what he had joined his flesh to, and Asa was not going to tell him. The irony was perfect and hideous, Halfdan Skarp-Hedinsson, hating all things Khymirian, unknowingly married to one....

A darker thought occurred to Zorachus, a more perfect irony. Was Halfdan like Asa? Like Porchos, like Lysthragon and Kletus, the whole filthy brood? The Sharajnaghi hardly knew what crawled inside the Kragehul's mind. Was the Halfdan he knew only a facade? With a shock he found himself unable to think otherwise. With that willful clarity that always characterized his best insights, he saw that he would never again be able to trust a human soul.

Least of all his own.

He had been aroused as never before by that scene on the bed. He had ached to join those naked bodies, and had given in, if only for a moment. He had kissed Chatonha, savored the taste of Asa on her tongue. And where it would have been bad enough to go further with that, his ultimate reaction had been far worse. For the first time, the blood-lusting demon that he had feared for so long had been released. He had enjoyed strangling Chatonha, severing her tongue with her own teeth, pounding her dead face into pulp. He knew that if she were alive again, he could slowly tear her limb from limb and exult in every second of it. His intellect and moral sense were appalled, but his bloodlust was not dimmed---killing Chatonha had not purged, but increased it. It wanted more blood, and he would not deny it. He would take vengeance on those who were forcing him to take vengeance, even if he were damned for it. He was perfectly aware that his only sane alternative was to leave Khymir. But he would not go until Banipal Khezach was a shambles of slaughter, and Kletus and his accomplices were dead.

Slowly he stood, unfolding his massive deadly limbs.

Chapter 22

THUNDER BOOMED ACROSS the rooftops of Mother Khymir. There was nothing strange in that, but even so, each new hammer-stroke set her inhabitants further on edge. The air itself seemed to bristle. Lovers drew more tightly together, hoping that somehow the mere pressure of flesh upon flesh would avert the danger...Prisoners huddled in the corners of their cells, the sane ones silently, the insane shrieking at the top of their lungs. Gooseflesh rose on addicts and drunkards even as they sprawled in their stupors, and they pissed themselves unconsciously...Somewhere, in a cold black realm where goodness and the laws of logic themselves were denied to the point of annihilation, the Great Tyrant reveled in the knowledge that the master stroke he had so long prepared was set in motion at last...

In full armor, Mancdaman Zorachus strode down the pillar-lined avenue towards Banipal Khezach, sword in hand. With all his heart and will he impelled himself forward, perfectly in control, without illusions about the task at hand.

He was full of power. He could feel it. Hate and rage had spurred a ferocious generation of energy, and the Influences were with him to a degree he could scarcely believe. So many spells were open to him, some without force-letting...He had already used one such formula back at the palace, summoning a demon of the Twenty-Seventh Plane. Trafficking with such an entity was strictly forbidden to Sharajnaghim, but he had needed information and had gotten it the only way he could....

A squad of marines rode in through the pillars ahead, carrying torches. They reined up in the middle of the road, talking, apparently unaware of his approach. They started laughing; there was a strange hysterical note to it all that made Zorachus think they were terribly nervous, perhaps without knowing why. He wondered what they had been laughing about, guessed the joke must be vile, and was seized by an active malice towards them---till then, he had thought of them as inconveniences to be brushed aside. But now he decided to do much worse than he had first intended.

As he drew nearer, one of them noticed him, crying:

"What's this?"

The rest looked.

"Nervy," one declared.

"Isn't that---" another began.

"Halt!" shouted a third.

Zorachus paid no heed.

Lowering their spears, they started towards him at a trot.

He stopped, raised the sword, uttered a spell. His blade glowed sickly yellow-green and a beam shot from its tip, splitting into several tangents. Screams rang out; wrapped in pulsing bilious light, the marines who had been struck dropped their spears and torches, rocking in the saddle. The first thing to go were their eyes, which ran out over their lower lids and down their cheeks; then the flesh sloughed from their skulls and tumbled down the front of their scale-mail, and muck sluiced from their sleeves. Their mounts went wild, bolting, and the other marines spurred and fled--- Zorachus thought of killing them too, but decided it was a waste of power. Hooves clattered away through the night.

He continued forward, lowering his blade. It occurred to him that he should already be begging God's forgiveness for using that spell. Sharajnaghim learned it only to devise countermeasures; it was banned even as a last resort. But that was nothing to him now.

Shouts up ahead---the redclads at the tower's entrance had seen the green flares, and were calling to the riders, who were swiftly putting distance between themselves and the tower. As Zorachus came into the glow from the wall-set torches, two guards were even then rushing to investigate, blades drawn. They swore when they saw him; he raised his sword once more, repeated the spell. The bolt licked out, forking, and they began to stagger; where their pant-legs were tucked into their boots, the fabric began to swell out, filling with liquefied flesh. Heads bowed, and helmets fell off, scalps sliding from skulls after them; the marines collapsed in fetid heaps.

Seeing that, their comrades retreated, rushing in through a postern in the lefthand valve, closing it behind them. Horns brayed from the windows on either side of the gate and crossbowmen appeared at the openings, silhouetted against the lights within, priming their weapons.

Sprinting for the great doors, Zorachus reached them before the arbalesters could loose and pressed his back against the knobbed steel, out of eye (and crossbow) shot from the window, safe for the moment.

Slinging sweat from his eyes, he cried a conjuring-spell. With a roaring noise, black smoke gushed up from the roadway, but only just so far; it mushroomed, then contracted upon itself, although the roaring continued, as though more smoke were shooting up into the interior of the cloud...A squat humanoid form took shape, faceless and heavily armored, four feet tall at most. Quarrels bounced off it, not making so much as a scratch.

Zorachus gave a mental command and the demon, feet clanging, rushed to the postern, pounding its maul-like fists against the steel. Within seconds the postern gave way and crossbow bolts hummed through the gap; striking the squat monstrosity dead-on, most of them simply bounced straight back.

The thing was now standing motionless, awaiting Zorachus's next order; receiving it, the demon charged through the entrance. A hellish cacophany erupted inside, thuds, shrieks, clangs, ripping and wrenching sounds. Splashes and misty bursts of blood flew through the postern, together with fragments of weapons, bits of armor, smashed helmets...the din intensified swiftly, accelerating until Zorachus could no longer make out individual sounds.

Then, suddenly, it stopped.

He entered the postern.

Inside, the air was rusty-tasting with vaporized blood; the ceiling was dripping, and the bas-reliefs were sprayed, their light tinted now, bathing a floor littered with dismembered bodies. Zorachus could not imagine that any of the guards had escaped; even the stairways leading to the windows were choked with mangled dead. Standing statue-like near Zorachus, the demon itself seemed to be made all of blood now.

Up ahead, some way off still, a crowd of acolytes and redclads was on the way, shouting; the mere fact that they were coming at all was proof that they had no idea of what had just happened, and were still too far to make sense of what they were seeing...not knowing how close they would come, Zorachus sent the demon to meet them, and soon another stretch of hallway had gone red.

As the demon started back, Zorachus dispatched it into the side passage where Kletus's lift was located; by the time he reached the lift-door, the thing had already dealt with the two guards there. But the demon vanished just as he arrived---the spell that had conjured it was shortlived and unrepeatable.

Zorachus entered the car, thinking the lift-demon's name, which he had learned from the being he had summoned back at the palace; the car rose. Cutting his thumb with his sword, he wrote the name on the wall in blood, and when the car halted, added the Black Malgronese word for "stay," to hold the lift in place and bar Kletus's quarters to all reinforcements for an hour at least.

He stepped out in the corridor that led to the sorcery-proof chamber. Two guards shouted at the far end, clapping hands to hilts.

He rushed forward, rings blasting. The redclads hurtled back against the walls on either side of the door, then slid to the floor, mail-scales rasping down the stone blocks. Broken bones crackled as the bodies settled.

He reached the threshold, looked in. Ten redclads rushed up onto the floor's low crown and halted, Thulusu among them, steel hand gleaming.

"Come in, Lord Mancdaman," the huge black called, voice echoing hollowly.

Zorachus seized a longsword from one of the corpses and entered the room slowly, holding the great brand high in his left hand, the shortsword low in his right.

"At last you've decided to pay us a visit," Thulusu continued cheerfully, deciding then and there that it was time to abandon Kletus, all his doubts about Zorachus dispelled....what havoc the man must have wrought downstairs!

"Why are you smiling?" Zorachus asked, walking up the slant.

"Admiration, believe it or---"

Zorachus had come close enough for Thulusu to see the implacable glint in his eyes; all thought of treason left the redclad Captain. He felt as though he had just been plunged into icewater.

"At him!" he cried, and they all swarmed down, drawing their swords, steel flashing bitterly.

Zorachus roared in answer; a deafening promise of annihilation, the sound alone almost pounded them to a standstill.

Charging up on the left, he avoided the bulk of them, but two still blocked his path; veering toward the outermost, he ducked a stroke whistling at his head and lunged with his shortsword, punching the point through scale-mail, driving six inches of steel into the man's chest.

The other redclad rushed in, but before his blow could fall Zorachus slashed his hands off with the longsword. The redclad's weapon clanged to the floor, hands still locked around the hilt. Blood spurting from his stumps, the man screamed and rolled down the slant.

Thulusu and another redclad sped to take his place. Zorachus's shortsword was still buried in the man he had stabbed; whirling the corpse around, he hurled it off the point, into their path, and all three tumbled down toward the door.

He ran crabwise to the top. A redclad pelted up at him, sword held high. Zorachus jerked back from the descending stroke, felt its wind on his cheek. His opponent lifted his brand once more; Zorachus shoved his longsword into the hollow of the redclad's throat and the man toppled backward like a falling tree.

A redclad charged up on the left and dealt Zorachus a glancing blow on the helmet. The Sharajnaghi answered by slamming his shortsword into the redclad's side, feeling savage satisfaction as his arm vibrated with the shock of hilt against scale-mail. He tugged; air hissed from the punctured lung, following the blade from the wound. Blood frothed in the hole, a crimson lather of it sliding down the redclad's body as he collapsed, face almost comical with amazement.

Footbeats clattered behind Zorachus; he sensed motion on the right. Looping the longsword so that it pointed backward, he dropped to one knee. Two brands hissed inches above his head; driving the longsword into the man behind, he twisted around and sent his other weapon chugging into the redclad on the right. Disengaging both blades, he leaped up, bounded over the stroke of a redclad before him and split the man's head.

He now stood alone on the bulge. A redclad waited off to the left, watching him tensely. Thulusu was over by the door with a third man, who suddenly tried to dash from the room.

Thulusu's steel whirled. Screeching through the neck guard of the man's helmet, it sheared off his head just above the jaw. The black pointed to his remaining man, bellowing:

"I'll give you the same if you run!"

Zorachus laughed. "You won't get the chance!" he cried. "you're both *mine!*"

"Come on!" Thulusu cried.

Both redclads hammered up the slant.

Zorachus went for the one on the left. The redclad proved much faster than he expected; Zorachus tried to parry with his longsword, but his singlehanded grip was no match for that two-handed sweep---the curving hilt was wrenched from his grasp and the blade bounced across the floor. He lunged with the shortsword; the redclad parried and the Sharajnaghi's weapon shattered, jagged shards flying.

He almost opted for his pommel-mace then and there, but heard Thulusu hard upon him and dashed to the right toward a fallen sword, both redclads following. He nearly reached the hilt, but slipped on a patch of blood-spattered floor, rolling down the slant five feet past the brand. Battling to his knees, he reversed his grip on the shortsword's hilt, springing the pommel catch. Thulusu's man was nearest him, closing in, sword gleaming. Zorachus hurled himself to the side of the descending blade and swung his arm; shooting out on its chain, the pommel wrapped around the redclad's leg just under the knee. Zorachus pulled and the man went down, sword flying from his grasp as he struck to the floor. Zorachus dropped the hilt shard and grabbed up the longsword with both hands, just as Thulusu launched a terrific stroke at his head. Zorachus managed to parry, even though the impact knocked him on his side. Thulusu recovered and slashed downward. Zorachus rolled away. The sword bit the floor in a puff of sparks and powdered stone.

The Sharajnaghi leaped to his feet. He and Thulusu traded a half-dozen clanging blows. Zorachus took a shallow cut across the chin, bashed a dent in Thulusu's helm. Thulusu flashed a white grimace, blood streaming down his face, red on ebony.

The other redclad, having freed his leg and snatched a fallen brand, stormed into the fight. Zorachus retreated, setting his back to the wall. Longsword whirling in a flashing triple-butterfly stroke, he defended himself flawlessly, watching for an opening.

Thulusu's man faltered, pausing in mid-return. Zorachus charged forward on the man's free side, slashing deep into his ribcage, cleaving heart and lungs. The man spun to the floor trailing a bright crimson spiral.

Thulusu leaped over the corpse. Zorachus turned to face him. Grunting as their blades connected, spittle bursting from their lips, they jolted back and forth, the chamber ringing like a stricken bell about them. Thulusu gashed Zorachus's arm; Zorachus replied with a stroke that reft the hem of Thulusu's scale-mail, ripping his left thigh. That was the deeper wound; soon Thulusu's trouser leg was shiny with blood, and his movements, still swift, grew clumsy, the sliced limb sagging beneath him. After one savage parry, he staggered and nearly fell, leaving his right shoulder wide open as he fought for balance....

Zorachus's sword sang down, shearing mail, severing the black's right arm. Still holding his blade with his remaining hand, Thulusu stumbled backwards, uttering a string of garbled curses, which Zorachus assumed were directed at him.

But Thulusu was cursing himself. He had had all the time in the world to switch allegiance, and now---.

Zorachus came in close.

Thulusu raised his brand for a last stroke, but he felt a terrible jolt, just like the one when his other arm had come off. For some reason, though, he could still feel both limbs; he was pondering this phenomenon when the next jolt struck his neck, and his head started tumbling...

Is he doing our drill he wondered, just before he struck the floor and found himself looking up at his own body, or rather, the part below his shortribs, which all at once collapsed because it had been hewn through both thighs...

Zorachus bent into view, picked him up by the helmet-horns.

Mouth working, Thulusu tried to apologize, but had no wind to speak with...Zorachus laughed and spat full into his eyes.

Thulusu blinked; suddenly he was in motion, spinning chin over crown through the air, growing swiftly colder...Zorachus had hurled him. A flash of wall was followed by a flash of floor, then wall, then ceiling, then wall again, this time much closer...

The very last thing was a short, sharp crunch.

It seemed to Zorachus that Thulusu's helmetted head flattened somewhat when it struck; hoping the black had still been conscious enough to see the wall rushing towards him, he went to the entrance of Kletus's chambers.

Before him, the vast banquet hall was empty. It occurred to him that he might have time to discard his armor---now that he was past the sorcery-proof chamber there was less need for it, and while it was useful against force-bolts, the presence of so much iron could interfere disastrously with the casting of higher-level spells. But the Influences were so strongly in his favor that he guessed he should risk leaving it on.

"Kletus!" he cried.

Echoes ran and faded.

"*Kletus!*"

He strode forward.

"*KLETUS!*"

At that, the High Priest emerged unhurriedly from a doorway on the far side, and came some distance out onto the floor.

"I'm here, fool!" he cried. "But not alone!"

He signalled.

Sathaswenthar and Lysthragon appeared and planted themselves on either side of him.

"You're in *my* universe, Zorachus!" Kletus roared. "You're one of my fancies, my whims. And I've grown tired of you."

Zorachus halted, flinging the sword away.

Each Priest assumed a different stance, one shield up. Entering a Dragon Stance with two shields, Zorachus started to pray---

Then caught himself.

Kletus shouted. Multihued fire burst from his free hand. Lysthragon and Sathaswenthar joined in instantly; pillars and ceiling flashed with reflected color. Strike after strike hurtled against Zorachus's defenses. Purple spirals and keening yellow rectangles exploded on his shields in puffs of flame. Venom-green snakelike bolts coiled on impact, shattered in emerald splinters.

He felt his foremost shield weakening; soon it winked out. The Priests doubled the intensity of their strikes. Knowing he must reduce the odds, he launched several bolts, just enough to drain his repellent forces, and uttered a spell.

The floor under Lysthragon revolved suddenly, but he reacted with astounding speed, trying to whirl back into position. Zorachus launched a demon-bolt; the Priest's shield deflected most of it. But a white-hot sliver burnt a trench across his shoulders, setting his hair and robes ablaze. Shrieking, he dived to the floor, rolling to extinguish his robes and slapping at his burning locks.

A fresh spate of strikes from the other Priests kept Zorachus from finishing him; reforming his first shield, he tried the revolving spell against Kletus. But the High Priest had second-guessed him and already started a counter spell; he spun halfway around before stopping, protecting himself with his shield. Even so, his bolts were momentarily cut off.

Zorachus turned his attention to Sathaswenthar, dropping both shields. One of the Priest's serpent-bolts struck him full in the chest, knocking him back several paces. But the brunt was absorbed by his mail and padding, and he snapped back into stance, lashing out with the most potent strikes at his command, twin twin bluish beams that shattered Sathaswenthar's shield as though it were the thinnest glass. The Priest catapulted to the floor; dazed and groaning, he began switching uncontrollably back and forth between his male and female forms.

By that time Kletus had recovered, but Zorachus had already recalled his left-hand shield, and so staved off the High Priest's onslaught, further confusing him by switching to a Griffin Stance. Dividing his concentration between defense and a binding spell, Zorachus stretched out his right hand, pointing at Sathaswentha-Sathaswenthar, lifting the protean body off the floor. He spread his middle and fourth fingers; a crimson fissure opened in the Priest's face, splitting it from crown to chin, and the black robes ripped below; entrails spilled to the variegated floor in a torrent of blood. Wrenched apart, Sathaswentha and Sathaswenthar, two dripping human flanks, hung quivering in midair. Zorachus hurled them both at Kletus, bowling him sideways.

There came a wild giggling from behind the High Priest; grey smoke curling from his shoulders, hair burnt away, Lysthragon rushed up and raised a single shield. Snatching at his purse, he lowered the buckler for an instant and hurled the pouch at Zorachus. Its mouth widened, an ever-expanding window into nothingness.

But Zorachus had been waiting for this; a spell sprang to his lips. The hole was still yards off when another maw, this one crimson, yawned above it; plunging, it engulfed the smaller hole and snapped shut, vanishing in the process.

Lysthragon screeched hideously and stamped the floor, looking for all the world like a scorched mad baby. Riddled by insanities of his own devising, pierced through with searing pain, dismayed by the loss of the purse, his mind snapped; as if Zorachus were a doting parent who might be cowed by a tantrum, the midget plunged forward, pouring out mispronounced obscenities.

The red mouth opened above him. Seeing its reflection on the floor, he tried to dodge, but it engulfed him shield and all. His screams echoed hollowly for an instant inside the invisible throat; then the jaws closed, and the cries were cut off...Zorachus wondered if the Priest was happy to be reunited with his purse.

The mouth blossomed once more, and Zorachus turned it on Kletus, who was even then struggling to his feet, one shield up, shaking his head, still untangling himself from the ruin of his androgynous lackey. The High Priest saw the crimson maw sweep in and conjured a yard-long scorpion; as the mouth descended, the scorpion shuttled up his body, crawling into the red-lit shaft, sting flicking. The mouth jerked upward, trailing a long agonized hiss. The jaws snapped shut for the final time.

Zorachus and Kletus reassumed their original stances, and the fight roared on. Bolt after bolt keened through the air, exploded on shields or rebounded wildly. Struck veneer cracked and shattered, spitting splinters of jade. Light globes vanished in flurries of glass shards. The floor quaked and dust poured from the ceiling. Shields buckled; new ones rose. Counterspell followed spell, and the wizards bellowed and shrieked, dodging violently, avoiding green and blue-lit portals that yawned to receive them. Demons appeared and joined furious battle; soon whole companies of them were brought into play, clashing phalanxes of talons, whips, and lances. Chitinous claws ripped armor and fragments of studded plate whirled and flew; slathering fangs tore rubbery flesh. Noisome vapors, yellow and purple and green, swirled above the struggling bodies. Zorachus's rings flamed, bolts converging on winged monsters and splitting them open in mushrooming blasts. The hall reverberated with shrieks and rattling cries, the sound of struck armor, and the hammer of scaled feet on stone. Demon swordsmen towered over the chaos, mailed in rime that was harder than steel, hacking at each other with adamantine blades, slashing off limbs in spatters of frigid steam. The wizards fought as none before, the Influences with them both, freeing unguessed depths of power; the more they battled, the more strength they seemed to have. Zorachus's fury spurred him on to greater and greater feats; Kletus met every challenge, counterattacking with impossible force and skill, knowing he was invincible, the chosen of Tchernobog, certain zorachus would be destroyed....

But it could not go on forever; Zorachus had no doubt that Kletus would break first, and finally the moment came---one of the High Priest's demons simply vanished. Another gap opened, then another, and Kletus's remaining demons began to falter. Zorachus's demons pressed the advantage quickly, ripping through their opponents in a storm of blood and riven armor, closing in on Kletus.

The High Priest moved back. His last demons went down. Even before they blinked back to their own planes, Zorachus's horrors trampled them underfoot, crunching shells and bone.

Kletus's universe was in its death throes. His mind reeled with fear and despair. He knew now that Tchernobog had lied to him; Zorachus could not possibly lose. But Kletus also knew that he was the only thing in the universe, and now even he was slipping away, victim to one of his own dreams. It was all quite insane...

Vain bolts crackled from his hands. There was still defiance amid his terror. A few of the onrushing monsters were pummeled back. A few more plummeted into the portals he opened. The rest crested over him, a seething, bounding wave....

Zorachus banished them with a gesture.

Kletus stood gaping for an instant, blinking stupidly, and before he could restore his shields Zorachus had the immense gratification of blasting him in the stomach with two demon-bolts. They would have ripped a normal man apart, but Kletus's belly only showed two small smoking holes. He staggered, but kept his feet.

Zorachus blasted him again. Kletus toppled backward, oily flames licking from the new wounds, sputtering out as he struck the floor.

Zorachus went up beside him. Pink spittle bursting on his lips, the High Priest tried to form the words of a spell, but his only sound was a thick gargling.

Zorachus started a formula. At the sound of it, Kletus shook his head in horrified disbelief.

Zorachus finished. "Wondering where I learned it?" he asked. "A demon told me. The same one who told you, as a matter of fact."

Kletus was still gargling, frantically now.

"Counterspell?" Zorachus asked. "Too late. Time to pay for all that gluttony."

To avoid showing the effects of his excesses, Kletus had magically compacted his fat into hard square knots, like muscle; the same spell had ennabled him to bear the horrific burden.

Zorachus had revoked it.

Kletus pressed his face with his hands, trying to hold his cheeks in place; defying his efforts, they bulged up through his fingers, pushing his palms back, swelling monstrously.

"Your universe is all mine now," Zorachus said hurriedly, while Kletus could still hear.

Then he stepped back.

Bones crackling under tons of fat, Kletus's whole body was billowing. His robes split; his arms were forced out almost at right angles to his torso. A thickening roll of lard thrust his chin up and back, and his cheeks sagged over his eyes. A puddle of distended close-cropped scalp widened behind his head. His skin grew steadily more translucent, revealing the pale curds within. It began to burst, snapping back in wrinkled folds which drew fine webs of blood across the fat....

The white mountain's growth continued unabated for a time, then slowed and stopped. Kletus had become a vast glistening mass splayed obscenely over the floor, without a trace of limbs or head, or any indication it had once been a human being.

At first, Zorachus had watched the metamorphosis with heady exultation. But as it progressed he felt the first stirrings of horror. It was more than mere disgust at the transformation, although that was part of it; there was time to think now. The orgy of slaughter was over, his enemies slain; the lust for vengeance that had spurred him on, flinging back his conscience, was sated. And conscience was reasserting itself. By the time the corpse had swelled to its hideous limit, Zorachus's revulsion had deepened into cold guilty nausea....The glistening abortion on the floor was his work. Once it had been a man. Now it was a diabolic jest at flesh.

He turned. His gaze fell on the halves of Sathaswenthar, male and female. Those bloody flanks had also been human. So had Lysthragon, and Thulusu, and Chatonha, all the guards and acolytes. He guessed he had butchered well over a hundred people. And while he did not doubt that they deserved death, and Hell even more, he also knew it was not his place to take their lives---not when his sole motive was revenge. He was a murderer, soaked in the blood of his fellow men.

You'd be damned now if you'd been killed, he told himself....Seeing the pit he had so narrowly skirted, he was seized by a kind of vertigo, which intensified horrendously as he realized he had not skirted the pit at all, that he had hurled himself in and not yet checked the plunge, not yet repented. Worse yet was the knowledge that repentance might not be possible---most souls were damned long before their bodies gave out, at the instant they were so mutilated by sin that willing not to sin became impossible. Death for them merely meant the removal of physical distractions, the entry into unalloyed spiritual torment. He knew he might already be in Hell, irrevocably.... Had he crossed the boundary? He remembered his terrible insight back at the palace, his realization that men were universally, totally corrupt. His whole personality was nothing more than a thin crust over a mire of total depravity. And if that were true, how could he repent?

He dropped to his knees, begging God to show him he was wrong. He prayed madly, ferociously, for succor. But a Voice whispered there was something inside him that would reject any aid he received. He tried to ignore the Voice, to remind himself that God could still touch him.

But only if He chose to do so, the Voice insisted. *And why would he reward murder with salvation?*

Despair choked off supplication. Without God's help, how could he renounce the trap he had created for himself? He had enjoyed killing Kletus and the others. He would never be able to feel remorse for that. He might be rocked to the core by fear and guilt---but not by remorse. The memory of his infernal rapture still thrilled him, singing in the marrow of his bones. Trying to disgust himself by imagining the gruesome details of his revenge, he succeeded only in increasing his relish. Nor was it any use telling himself that Kletus's death and transformation were the very stuff of Tchernobog's mirth; it only strengthened his certainty that Tchernobog was right about human flesh. Seizing on the heresy of that only made him hate Kletus more; Kletus had convinced him in the first place, exposed the maggots inside Asa, brought the Sharajnaghi's own evil to full fruition. Kletus deserved death. The very fact that he had goaded Zorachus to kill him proved it...

Zorachus rose trembling. He could not repent. With frightful, willful, insane clarity he knew he would never be able to. How could he forgive Kletus for damning him?

Shrieks scraped up through his throat, formed themselves into obscene blasphemies. He cursed God for causing it all, even as he told himself that God was not responsible; even though he believed in total depravity, he still could not reject his own guilt, his own responsibility. Knowing that blaming God was blasphemy, that he was only maiming his soul further by blaspheming, he screamed out more blasphemies at the being that allowed him such license...

Stripped raw, his throat began to spray blood into his mouth. He crumpled back to his knees. Through tear-blurred eyes he saw a dagger lying next to Sathaswenthar's female flank. For a moment all he could think of was killing himself; scrambling like a mad animal, he rushed to the dagger on all fours and drew the blade. With quaking hand he poised it before his heart---

Then let it drop.

Suicide was useless. It would only fling him sooner into the realm of pure torment.

Pure torment---his terror increased tenfold as he considered it. It was better to remain in the body, to deaden the soul with its own destruction, numb it completely before all distraction ceased....

That was it, then.

Spiritual suicide.

The self-immolation of the will.

He heard whispering and footsteps and looked up. A redclad and a Priest were coming towards him; the holding spell in the demon-lift had decayed some minutes before.

He stood. They halted, but after a few moments the redclad asked, in a trembling voice:

"Have you killed them all?"

Drying his tears on his sleeve, swallowing blood and phlegm, Zorachus said: "Yes."

They kneeled; the redclad laid his sword on the floor, hilt towards Zorachus.

Zorachus strode forward. Reaching the sword, he picked it up. A frigid calm had descended over his mind. He knew what he must do.

"Rise," he said.

They obeyed. Eyeing the Priest, he asked:

"What do you know of the High Priest's duties?"

"Little," the man said. "But there are books. Shall I fetch them?"

Zorachus nodded. "Be quick about it."

The Priest hurried off. Zorachus hefted the sword in his hand, looking at the man it belonged to. The redclad was staring at him with terror and something like adoration.

For no reason whatsoever, Zorachus split the man's head to the chin.

Here ends the first part of the history of the Fall of Mancdaman Zorachus.

The second part is called *The Nightmare of God,* and tells of the revelation of Tchernobog's true design, Zorachus's crimes as High Priest, and the perils and exploits of Halfdan, Asa, and Raschid Kestrel in the war which follows.

COMING SOON----KHYMIR: THE RPG, BY RICH STAATS AND MARK E. ROGERS

Born in 1952, author-illustrator Mark E. Rogers is best known for the Samurai Cat books: *The Adventures of Samurai Cat, More Adventures of Samurai Cat, Samurai Cat in the Real World, The Sword of Samurai Cat,* and *Samurai Cat Goes to the Movies.* The sixth and final installment in the series is *Samurai Cat Goes to Hell.*

His other books include the Zancharthus trilogy(*Blood + Pearls, Jagutai and Lilitu* and *Night of the Long Knives*), *The Dead, Zorachus, The Nightmare of God, The Expected One, The Devouring Void,* and *The Riddled Man.* One of his novellas, *The Runestone,* was made into a movie; and *The Dead* is presently under development as a feature film---with a screenplay by Mark---at KNB-EFX.

Mark's work has been adapted by Marvel comics, and has appeared on the cover of <u>Cricket Magazine</u>; he's published three art portfolios, and a collection of his pin-up paintings, *Nothing But A Smile,* is available from Xenophile Books. www.XXXenophile.com Some of Mark's illustrations may be found at www.merogers.com

Mark lives in Newark, Delaware, with his wife Kate---a philosophy professor at the U of D---and their four lovely kids, Sophie, Jeannie, Patrick, and Nick.